C000184916

JUST ANOTHER CENTURY

MARIA HARLAND

[The] past is not simply there in memory...
It must be articulated to become memory

– Andreas Huyssen

Typeset in Minion Pro

Typesetting and publishing by UK Book Publishing

www.ukbookpublishing.com

ISBN: 978-1-914195-67-9

Front cover photograph – Lewis and Dorothy's wedding December 29th 1937

Back cover photograph – Joan Dowds wedding to John Alan Creigh April 3rd 1959
Back row; Mr Rolston, Tony Craig, Joseph Grainger Creigh,Mary Hilda
Creigh, Father John Dowd, Peter Creigh, Nan Malloy,?,?

Middle row; Mrs Taylor, George Taylor, Groom and Bride,
Dorothy Dowd, Merle Rolston, Lewis Dowd.

Front row; Dolly Smyth nee Dowd, Anita Young nee Le Britton, Helen?,
Anthony Dowd, Pauline Dowd, Martin Smyth, Mary Smyth.

Dedicated to my grandchildren, Lily Rose, Thomas James, Iris Mary, Henry Alan and Frankie Mae. These five amazing children are the future, and this is, and has always been their story.

O'Dowd Family Tree

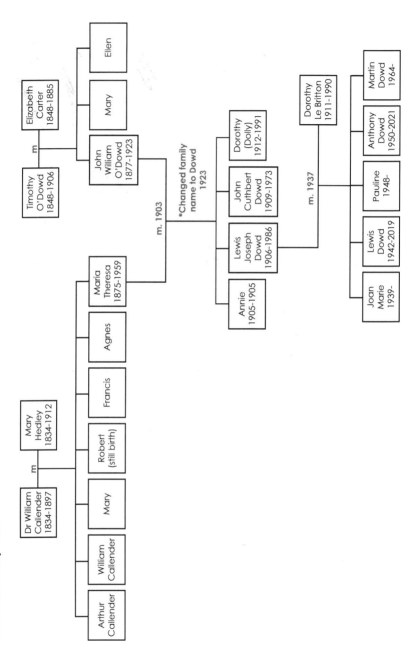

Dr William Callender 1834-1897 — m — Mary Hedley 1834-1912

Children:
- Arthur Callender
- William Callender
- Mary
- Robert (still birth)
- Francis
- Agnes
- Maria Theresa 1875-1959

Timothy O'Dowd 1848-1906 — m — Elizabeth Carter 1848-1885

Children:
- John William O'Dowd 1877-1923
- Mary
- Ellen

Maria Theresa 1875-1959 — m. 1903 — John William O'Dowd 1877-1923

*Changed family name to Dowd 1923

Children:
- Annie 1905-1905
- Lewis Joseph Dowd 1906-1986
- John Cuthbert Dowd 1909-1973
- Dorothy (Dolly) 1912-1991

Lewis Joseph Dowd 1906-1986 — m. 1937 — Dorothy Le Britton 1911-1990

Children:
- Joan Marie 1939-
- Lewis Dowd 1942-2019
- Pauline 1948-
- Anthony Dowd 1950-2021
- Martin Dowd 1964-

Le Britton Family Tree

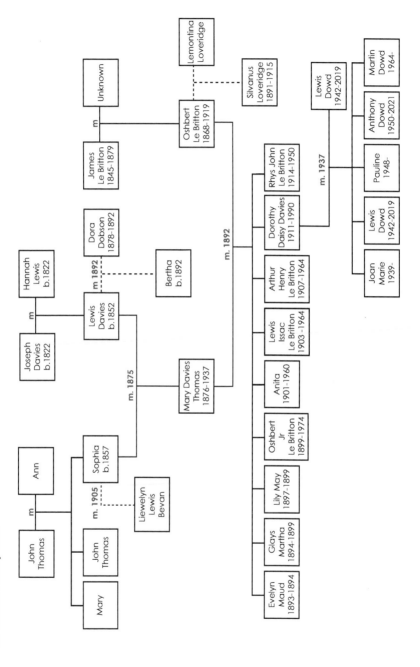

PROLOGUE

1875 THE HOUSE, ASHLEIGH GROVE, JESMOND

*T*he house sits perched at the end of a terrace of Tyneside flats. The house perceives himself rightly or wrongly to be superior to the rest of the street because the builder has spend more time overseeing his build and as a conclusion his windows, doors and internal furnishings are of far better quality than the foot soldier flats he adjoins. His wooden banister is more highly polished, his ceiling rose more detailed and his cornices more decorative. The house is especially proud of the elaborately carved barge board which is fitted to the gable end section of his pitched roof. The house feels this marks him out as special and worthy of his place guarding the entrance to the Grove. Once built the house stretches upwards on the very tips of his footings; he is that proud and that confident. His sister is a house of similar stature at the other end of the terrace and they joke together that they are the bookends of the Grove. "We are not ordinary houses," the house proclaims loudly in his rather bombastic voice then he swiftly follows on from his rather boastful declaration by adding, "to the contrary I would say that we are the most extraordinary houses. Is that not true sister?" His sister is not as bumptious nor as loud but even she is compelled to agree. "I concur with my brother; we are arguably the

2

most extraordinary houses on this entire street." But as they say, pride comes before a fall and the so-called unremarkable little flats will soon have reason to gloat at the house's misfortune. This is because their builder is a greedy man and as he witnesses the flurry of middle class migrating to the area he will take the bold decision to squeeze another house onto the end of the street. The architects objections will be noted and ignored and a lesser qualified architect hastily employed and instructed to 'make it work'. As a consequence the house will have his sculpted barge board unceremoniously removed and carelessly dropped to the ground where it will lay gathering dust and dirt until it is loaded up and disposed of in landfill. The new house will then be built into the party wall and take pride of place at the end of the street. It would be stretching the truth to say that the house feels pain as after all he is bricks and mortar, but as the wind blows through his newly exposed rafters the house sinks a little into his foundations and does not stand quite so tall or quite so proud.

This new house, this interloper, sits awkwardly like a wedge of cheese stealing the unparalleled views the house previously had of the train line and of the people walking by on their way to work. The new house has stolen part of his footprint so the front garden is reduced in size and the back yard cut off at a strange angle. The new house has also plundered part of his upstairs passageway, creating a complicated flying freehold for solicitors to argue over whenever the house changes hands, but the builder does not care for he has lost interest in the house, lost interest in the street. He has new land to develop and his entrepreneurial eye is on the prize.

Eventually the house rallies around and tells himself that once he is lived in he will be happy and content once more. For everyone knows this is the 'raison d'être' of the house, in fact it is the goal of any house. For a house yearns to offer shelter and refuge. It is its reason for being, because an empty house is a shell, just a random pile of bricks and mortar. It is written in house folklore that a house cannot fulfil its destiny until it has secrets to keep. It is claimed that arguments and disputes need to be dissolved into its mortar and glad tidings etched into its brickwork for a house to properly come into being. These emotions must echo through the floorboards and bounce across the plasterwork until finally they settle, deeply entrenched into the very skeleton of the house. Then, when the house has had a chance to hold safe these memories it will have fulfilled its true fate and properly become a home. The house just needs the chance to make these memories.

23RD DECEMBER 1875, ST.CYNWYD CHURCH, MAESTEG

The wedding was a quiet sombre affair. Indeed there were no smiles, no back slaps of congratulation and no joyful choir to greet the entrance of the blushing bride. The bells of the church did not ring out throughout the valley proclaiming the joyful event and well-wishers did not line the cobbled streets straining their necks for a better view of the bridal procession. The father of the bride John Thomas stood poker straight at the front of the chapel and as he stared ahead towards the pulpit his stomach strained to escape the confines of his buttoned-up Sunday best vest. He let out an audible sigh of relief upon hearing the groom's carriage pull up at the church gates; for he was ten minutes late and John had been anxious he had had a change of heart. Sophia the bride – who had been sitting patiently in a side room - upon hearing the arrival of her intended began to make her way ponderously down the aisle to stand by his side. She was heavy with child and her gait adversely affected due to the baby lying low. Lewis her groom was a tailor by trade and had seen fit to alter the seams of her makeshift wedding dress to accommodate the growing baby, but despite the loose fitting attire her state of pregnancy was impossible to disguise. The Preacher averted his eyes as he began to read out the vows, almost spitting

4

out the words to further register his disapproval. The Preacher then asked if there was anyone 'here present' to object to the marriage. He raised his eyes and addressed the cavernous chapel as if half expecting a disembodied disgruntled voice to emit from an empty oak pew and when none was forthcoming he too exhaled loudly before continuing on with his arduous task.

Lewis, the groom was the only member of the tiny congregation to be smiling. Indeed to all intents and purposes, a casual observer would presume he had not a care in the world so nonchalantly did he repeat his vows. His bride, Sophia, did not display the blithe countenance that new brides should and she cradled her protruding stomach as if protecting her unborn child from both the Preacher and the good Lord above. She did not love the man she was about to wed, in fact truth be told she barely knew him, but in her position she realised that she has no choice and for the sake of her unborn child she knew she had to go through with the sham of a marriage. Her father had decreed that she must marry this man - who has so kindly agreed to take on her child as his own - so marry him she would. I will add that at this stage and indeed for the four weeks immediately preceding the ceremony Lewis had acquired an almost saintly status in the community. To such a degree that her father had taken to frequenting the same bar as Lewis- every night – with the sole intentions of buying him a pitcher of ale. This was not so much a case of John enjoying his prospective son-in-law's company – for the truth of it was he found him to be quite overbearing and arrogant - but more a case of John needing constant reassurance that the young man was not planning to back out of his betrothal promise. Sophia's parents John and Ann had previously hung their heads in shame at the spectacle of their rapidly blossoming daughter and indeed John would have taken the strap to her if it were not for Lewis' timely intervention. Lewis' offer of marriage had been grasped wholeheartedly, with both hands, for it took a special type of man to agree to take on another man's mistake. John was a simple honourable god-fearing man not normally given to such outbursts of violence but his daughter had brought the family name into disrepute. Lewis had alleviated some of the shame by asking for his daughter's hand in marriage and thereby offering legitimacy to her child. Although I suspect Sophia's father and mother would not be so welcoming of Lewis if they knew the child was actually biologically his.

The circumstances of the conception were shrouded in secrecy and with good reason for the child had been conceived while Lewis' wife lay dying in the adjoining room. I must hasten to add that Sophia was still a virgin when Lewis clumsily deflowered her on the scullery floor and in her teenage innocence she had naively believed Lewis' claim that it would help alleviate his crippling despair at witnessing the slow demise of his beloved wife. Sophia was only visiting Lewis' house at the behest of her mother, who had prepared a beef consommé for the sickly young woman. She had approached the house by the back door and upon receiving no answer to her tentative knocks had peered around the doorway only to discover Lewis sitting hopelessly upon the floor, slumped against a wall. She had hesitantly approached him to offer words of comfort and been understandibly taken aback when he grasped her outstretched hand and dragged her to the floor to sit by his side. She was further taken aback when he laid his weary head upon her lap and began to weep unashamedly for his young dying wife. There were really no words to fit such a situation so Sophia had simply held his shaking body until his frantic sobbing abated. It was a while until Sophia fully realised the significance of his wandering hands and it was not until they snaked towards her breasts and his fingers began to undo the tiny buttons of her bodice that she became aware of his true intentions. Yet despite the gravity of the situation she was momentarily flattered by Lewis' breathless passion for she knew she would be the envy of her peers. It must be said at this juncture that Lewis cut a dashing and romantic figure in the valley for he was well-groomed and quite the dandy. Lewis and his young wife had only arrived in the village a few years previously and had quickly ingratiated themselves into the community with their personable manners. He was held in great esteem amongst the tailoring fraternity for he had been commissioned by Queen Victoria no less, to stitch her soldiers' uniforms. It was also rumoured that due to his Royal connections he had once danced with her daughter Princess Beatrice but as Sophia later realised this rumour was in all probability spread by Lewis himself and quite impossible to prove or disprove. Lewis had borne his wife's recent illness with good grace even insisting on nursing her himself, when many a man would have baulked at partaking in such personal tasks. This alone had marked him a man amongst men and many a young lady was casting her eye his way even before his wife's actual sad departure.

It was barely ten weeks – after the intimacy in the scullery - that Sophia realised the true connection behind her constant nausea and the rapid swelling of her stomach. She had shyly approached Lewis to relay the news and he had brushed her away as one would an annoying fly. His wife had only recently been laid to rest so Sophia excused his behaviour, telling herself that his mind must be all over the place and he would need some time to come to terms with her revelation. But when he continued to ignore her attempts to converse and went to such great pains to avoid any confrontation she feared he was in denial. It was not until her pregnancy was the talk of the village that he had eventually approached her and laid out his well-thought-out plan. He declared that he would agree to marry her and legitimise his child but only after his wife had been in the ground a respectful further three months. Furthermore, he would only do this if she stated that she had been impregnated by a local youth, for if there were the slightest suspicion that the child could be his he would immediately rescind his offer of marriage. This way Lewis' grieving persona would hold fast and his wife's memory be respectfully honoured. He did not add that it would also ensure his bourgeoning tailoring business was not beset by the negative publicity. Sophia later found out that his dead wife's parents – who were not of modest means – had noted how tenderly he had nursed their darling daughter and as a reward gave him a small sum of money. This revelation was to be the final nail in the coffin for Sophia, and it served once and for all to open her eyes to the truth that the man to whom she had so casually lost her virginity was not worthy of her previous adoration. Nevertheless, Sophia held fast her vow to Lewis and refused to name the man who had 'taken' her against her will. She even concocted a highfalutin story in the mistaken belief that the village gossips – once word of the conception spread - would look upon her more as the victim in her sorry tale. But such was the hypocrisy of the time and the prevalence to blame the woman in such events, that even following this dark admission it was remarked upon that she would be more well thought of had she fought her assailant off. Surely this was what any good god fearing Baptist girl would have done? So the cruel consensus became that she had encouraged her hapless beau then cried wolf once the poor chap had reached the height of his passion.

It would be unfair of me at this point to paint Lewis as a thoroughly unsavoury fellow. Yes I concede he was a weak man who allowed his fate to be dictated by his sexual desires but he had neither a darkness of heart nor a cruelty of spirit. I do not want to portray him one dimensionally as the villain of the piece because one could even say that he was a victim of circumstance not fully realising that the circumstance was of his own making. But in his defence he was a product of his time, no more, no less and many a man who proclaimed himself honourable would have walked away and denied the child. In his eyes he did the right thing by eventually legitimising his child but in his relishment of the reverence this act afforded him and his continued vanity he once again loses some respect.

Not surprisingly following such a rocky start, the marriage was not to be an altogether happy union. Mary their only child was born to the world a red and squalling babe on 16th March 1876, a mere three months after her parents' nuptials. Her birth was neither easy nor straightforward and afterwards the midwife warned Lewis - in no uncertain terms - that unless he wished to become a widower again before the age of twenty-five Sophia must never bear another child. To give him his due, following this dark warning Lewis neither demanded his conjugal rights nor entered the marital bed for the entire duration of their marriage. I am desperately trying to find redeeming features in his nature so I concede he was honourable in this one respect but this is not to say he took a vow of chastity and throughout their short-lived marriage rumours would abound of his various dalliances and indiscretions.

And so Mary grew up, an only yet much beloved child. Both her father and mother idolised the ground she walked upon and she wanted for nothing. She was a pretty young girl with a mass of black if somewhat unruly hair and a tiny snub nose and it could be said that she knew no true sadness in her life until the day her father informed her that he was leaving for Colorado to seek his fortune. The year was now 1890 and Lewis along with thousands of other men his age saw the Gold Rush in Cripple Creek as a way to forge their own destinies. It was to be a dark day indeed for Mary and her peers as their beloved fathers and brothers closed the doors on their old lives and trudged up the cobbled streets in their hobnailed boots towards the glistening golden prize.

"I promise to bring you back a nugget the size of my fist fy mach," said Lewis clutching his precious daughter to his breast.

"I promise when I return we will live in a grand old house far from the valley and feast every day upon the finest sweetmeats."

"I promise that you and your mother shall wear only the finest silk and peacock feathers shall adorn your hair."

"I promise that I shall buy you two white ponies and a carriage and we shall all ride to St Cynwyds in style each and every Sunday."

Mary was never to see her beloved father again. Other fathers and brothers returned, some with fortunes some with none, but all returned. But not Lewis.

1876 THE HOUSE, ASHLEIGH GROVE, JESMOND

To the casual passer-by the house now appears so much more ordinary especially given its small town excuse for a garden, squeezed onto the small plot between the bay window and the pavement. The new garden is too small to cultivate properly and conversely too large to ignore but the builder insisted it be incorporated into the house design for he knew that vegetation was much prized as the suburban middle-class ideal. The house is walled by a knee high row of bricks and black iron railings of a gothic design in an attempt to reclaim back its importance. Many years later in the 1940s these iron railings will be removed to help with the war effort and recycled into munitions. The house will mourn the loss of its ornate railings as the stubs left in the brick wall will become constant reminder of his former glory. The empty stubs will fill with water and freeze in the winter and slowly the mortar will crack and the wall will bow.

A black and white geometric tiled pathway leads to the solid wooden front door with ornate carving and a brass lion's claw knocker. Above and to the edges of the door there are ornate leaded stained glass panels. Sometimes when the wind blows in a certain direction this stained glass rattles and threatens to fall to the ground and smash into a million tiny pieces, but the builder does not know this and the house has no way of telling him. The front door opens onto an adequate porch with ample space for coat hooks and an umbrella stand. The internal porch door is also panelled in stained glass and allows the setting sun to cast elaborate patterns upon the stairway and the hallway tiles. The stairs are to the right of the hallway and a passage to the left allows access to the lounge and the dining room. The fireplace is the main feature of the lounge as it is mahogany and elaborately carved. The fireplace like the house longs to be stacked with coal and lit. It is excited at the prospect of being able to emit puffs of smoke from its chimney stack and bring warmth to the bricks. The fireplace is constructed to be of a height that a gentleman may stand comfortably with an elbow upon its mantle and better survey the splendour of the room. With its deep skirting boards, dado rails and exquisite ceiling rose the room does indeed look grandiose. It is an ideal home for the aspiring gentleman to feel of an equal standing to his peers and once the house is lived in a maid will spend hours cleaning the fire and blackening the hearth before discreetly retreating to her rooms high in the eaves of the house. The dining room at the back of the house also has a fireplace but far less grand than the one in the lounge and the room is darker as the window is smaller and looks onto the yard with its high back wall.

The house is proud of the fact that the builder has seen fit to install a bathroom on his first floor because he views it as another reason he is superior, as the little flats have outside privies. The house had a fully flushing toilet and a claw-footed freestanding bath although it must be said that it still has an outside privy for the servant to use. Every Tuesday the house will hold his nose as the night soil men visit on their horse and cart to empty the privies. It is such a disagreeable acrid stench and the noxious fumes linger and seep into the very foundations beneath the cobbled yard. Every so often if the wind blows in a certain direction the house is reminded of the little outhouse, the blot on his landscape, the blemish on his otherwise pristine features.

1890, CRIPPLE CREEK, COLORADO

The date is 20th October and the year 1890. A ranch hand turned prospector called Bob Womack has just discovered a new rich gold seam near a place called Poverty Gulch. As a result of his timely discovery Gold fever spreads widely throughout the continent of America and spreads on into Europe and so begins the last major gold rush of the 19th century. Prior to 'Crazy Bobs' breakthrough, it had been widely assumed that Pikes Peak had been stripped of its gold bounty, and indeed when the drunken prospector had first staked his claim and set about building his cabin on the parched bank of the creek, the locals had shook their heads and laughed. They were to stop laughing when they found out about his amazing find just a few inches below the hard granite stone. More gold nuggets were soon discovered and the boomtown of Cripple Creek emerged from the shadows of its dominating mountain ranges. Two businessmen Horace Bennett and Julius Myers were the first to realise the area's true potential and they quickly mapped out a town and named it Fremont. The two entrepreneurs' oversaw and bankrolled the hastily constructed wooden buildings and had a mud gully dug out to form a road of sorts. As predicted, although the pavements were not paved in gold, its streets soon resounded with the heavy footfall of desperate men seeking their fortunes. Brothels, dance halls, gambling dens and saloons popped up on every corner to relieve the men of their fast- earned dollars. A notorious madam named Blanche Burton quickly moved a bevy of ladies of ill repute into one such brothel and with names such as Dizzy Daisy, Slippery Sadie and Greasy Gertie these good-time girls were very soon recognisable figures in the emerging town. What our feckless Lewis thought of this makeshift lawless community is anyone's guess but as he stayed a while I can only presume he availed himself of all it had to offer.

The period of time it took Lewis and his fellow villagers to find their way to Colorado I can only speculate on, but in early 1891 the motley crew were witnessed trudging into the town en-masse, tired and exhausted from their laborious journey. They had to a man been ill-prepared for their long trek across America, not fully realising the size of the country and the supplies they would need. They travelled across the continent firstly by train and then in covered wagons with the slogan 'Pikes Peak or bust' crudely painted on the sides. Many including Lewis were so inept that they could barely build a fire or erect a tent. Newspaper articles they read on their journey described Cripple Creek as *'A chance in a lifetime'* and *'A wealth resort not a health resort.'* The reporters wrote vivid descriptions of the yellow gold being so plentiful it was peeking from between the rock face. Gold fever was highly infectious and as the Welshmen travelled more men from other areas joined them and lifelong friendships were formed. When the men eventually reached the *'promised land'* a trio of men, including Lewis, broke away from the crowd to set up camp in an area called Broken Box Ranch. Once there, they quickly set up camp before spending the last of their cash on picks, shovels and prospecting bowls before making their way towards Battle Mountain to mine for gold. It has been reported that between the months of February and May a total of 18 men filed claims, but unfortunately Lewis and his comrades were not numbered amongst them. Although on July 4th 1891, a carpenter from Illinois named Winfield S. Stratton - who had travelled by train part of the way with Lewis - did strike the payload. Winfield was later to sink the Stratton Independence Mine and go on to mine the largest amount of gold ever discovered. Lewis is photographed around this time. He is part of a long queue of men waiting to sign up to work in the mine. The sad irony of this photograph is that when Lewis lived in Maesteg he had had little respect for illiterate colliers such as Sophia's father, thinking himself a cut above. As they say, pride comes before a fall and presumably in the interim time

Lewis had decided that a paltry wage was better than none. Once they had a basic income of sorts Lewis and his new found friends set about building themselves a log cabin. It was a very humble abode with just one central room, four small windows and a fire but it would offer protection from the cold harsh winter to come. One of Lewis' more enterprising fellow Welshmen, who had been a cook in Glamorgan constructed a makeshift tent on the edge of the town and named it 'Gethin's All American Kitchen' offering basic meals for 25c. This venture grossed the enterprising young man so much money that he later opened a hotel in the town, which he proudly named the Palace Hotel. I imagine that tailoring must not have been so much in demand or Lewis would no doubt have constructed his own tent and sought his fortune this way.

The coming winter of 1891 was predicted to be uncharacteristically bitter so many of the men, who had travelled to Cripple Creek with Lewis, took the decision to return to Wales and reunite with their families before it properly set in. But Lewis was determined to stick it out. He was vain enough to believe that he and he alone would find that precious nugget and return home the conquering hero. Although it must be said at this point that I am not really sure that returning to his wife and daughter was ever part of his plan. I make this assumption after finding out that that Cripple Creek's first post office opened in 1888 but Lewis did not see fit to write home and update his wife and daughter of his progress at any stage in this story.

Lewis goes off the radar during the autumn of 1891 so I will digress, if I may, then pick up his story in early winter 1891. The story of how Cripple Creek got its name is quite fascinating in itself because sometime during these months the nickname seems to have usurped Fremont as the town's official name. The stories are varied. One story tells of a clumsy drover accidently discharging his rifle near a herd of cattle and causing a frightened calf to jump the creek. The unfortunate calf landed in a gully and broke its leg, thereby effectively crippling itself and giving the creek its name. Another tale tells of a lumberjack felling logs near the creek, then being crippled when a log rolled and knocked him from his feet. Whichever story rings true, it is undisputable that sometime during this period Fremont became known as Cripple Creek and its two main streets were named Bennett Street and Myers Street as a sweetener to its architects. Brothels abounded on both the aforementioned streets to such an extent that it was decided they should be relocated to just Myers Street in an attempt to contain the 'red light district' to just one area. As a result, Myers Street went on to be generally known as the liveliest street in the old West. The street was open 24 hours, and the prospectors themselves coined the phrase 'there will be a hot time in the old town tonight' because it reputably, at one stage housed 300 prostitutes and 150 drinking saloons. In fact, by 1891 Cripple Creek was so overpopulated that two of the larger hotels, including the Palace, took to renting out 'sleeping chairs' for $1 a night and queues of men would line up as night fell to avail themselves of this offer.

We pick up Lewis' story in the latter part of the year 1891, because I have in my hand an old grainy sepia photograph from around this date. The photograph shows three men congregating outside a wooden shack. The shack is built of roughly hewn logs and it has two small windows to the front and a small window to the side. Smoke is coming from its tiny chimney to the back of its roof. Two of the men in the photograph are sitting on upturned barrels playing musical instruments whilst the other is standing by the open front door leaning on an upturned pick. The standing man is unmistakably Lewis. He is easily recognisable to me from his stance and the rather arrogant way he is staring into the lens of the camera. All three men are dressed in open-necked shirts with the sleeves rolled up to above their elbows. The high-waisted trousers have the hems tucked into scuffed leather boots. Yet despite their overall impoverished state of dress, Lewis still manages to stand apart from the group. This is in part because he is sporting rather spectacular sideburns which seem to run along the side of his face from hairline to jowl. His wide-brimmed Cavalry hat is worn in typical Lewis fashion at a rather jaunty angle. It is at this little interlude that we leave my great great grandfather Lewis for a while. An unforgiving winter may lie ahead but for now the sun shines briefly through the autumn clouds and Lewis continues to smile his narcissistic smile.

1891 THE HOUSE, ASHLEIGH GROVE, JESMOND

The house has been occupied for a good fifteen years but alas no one family has seen fit to reside within its walls for more than five. The house has had a somewhat complicated start after the 'cuckoo' house was so crudely built onto it. The foundations have needed more work and an alarming crack has appeared in the passageway and one of the attic bedrooms. The builder, as he saw the bills mount and the two houses lie empty, regretted his earlier greedy decision. But for now both houses are occupied and the floorboards ring with the sound of feet running up and down the stairs and the fire puffs smoke from the two large chimney stacks.

The house is concerned for he has started dreaming. He seems to have the same dream every night and wakes from the dream with condensation running down the glass of his sash windows, so he knows the dreams are not happy dreams. Dear reader until the house told me of his dreams I did not think it was possible for a house to dream but the house assures me that house folklore contains many tales of houses that dream.

On this particular night in October 1891 the house has a very vivid dream. He dreams he is not a house but instead just a patch of grass with a well-trodden track running horizontally through his land. On the edge of the track is a large rock and on that rock sits a man. This image seems to haunt the house and he suspects something sinister is afoot.

The house does not know this as he has no concept of time but the year of which is dreaming is 1181 and the man sitting on the rock is a pilgrim. He is travelling to Jesus Mound to kneel and pray upon the rock on which the apparition of the Blessed Virgin Mary has apparently been seen. Many years later a chapel will be built near the rock so that the pilgrims may visit and pray in comfort, but for now, the pilgrims can only visit the holy Jesus Hill on the edge of the river Ouseburn. The man is not well for he is weary from his travels and very soon he will tumble from the rock, crack his head and roll unconscious onto the ground. Night will fall and as the temperature drops the man will perish. Other pilgrims will follow in his path the following week and find his poor wizened body. They will pray for his soul before burying him respectfully beneath the rock. This is what the house dreams of and I will tell the house this story when he wakens from his slumber but I am confused why the house dreams of this, because the ground holds many bones and many secrets so why has this one chosen to surface? Soon the house will have more secrets to hide and each secret will etch itself into the very foundations on which the house stands.

OCTOBER 1891, CRIPPLE CREEK, COLORADO

The weather has turned a corner, the nights are colder but the days are still bright with the last of the autumn sunshine. Lewis is sauntering down Bennett Street with a customary swagger to his step and a few less dollars to his name for he has just visited 'Dirty neck Nell.' He is quite a regular visitor and Nell knows him by name. Unlike some of the other men who frequent the brothel, Lewis is invariably polite and respectful. He always takes his boots off beforehand and leaves a little extra on the plate by her bed. Nell suspects he has a wife somewhere but so in all probability have the majority of her clients for that is the nature of her trade. A little way ahead, coming out of Dobson's hotel, Lewis spies a young girl he recognises to be the proprietor's daughter. She is slim of hip with a well-shaped calf and Lewis appreciates the view as he strolls casually behind her. Lewis, as we well know, has a roving eye and his eye has settled on this girl numerous times in the past but her over-protective father has a reputation for being headstrong and 'trigger happy', so Lewis has kept a respectable distance from her thus far. The girl is struggling to carry a basket. It is filled to the brim with bed linen and on a particularly muddy part of the walkway she slips. Falling to her knees she drops the basket and it tumbles and rolls off the path directly into the sludgy quagmire below. The washing slowly submerges sinking into the mud and Lewis sensing an opportunity to orchestrate a meeting, races to her aid. He gallantly helps her to her feet before retrieving the sodden linen from the muddy mire. Always quick with a glib remark, Lewis jokes "My mother always told me that washing your laundry in public is not a good idea and now I know why." Despite the fact that she has turned her ankle and ripped the petticoat of her best dress, Dora, the young girl cannot help but smile at the devilishly handsome stranger. Realising she is limping; Lewis gallantly offers her his arm so that he can support her as she hobbles back towards the hotel entrance. Once they reach it, Dora smiles shyly into Lewis' deep brown eyes and thanks him for his help. "The pleasure was all mine," Lewis replies before adding "I see you have ripped your dress. Shall I mend it for you? Noting her look of confused bemusement, Lewis quickly adds "I should have explained I am a tailor by trade so I will do a very good neat job I promise."

Dora ponders on the offer for a moment before replying, "that would be very kind of you as my father will be most displeased by my clumsiness and it is my favourite dress."

"Your father need not know. If you wrap the dress in brown paper and drop it from your window later tonight it will be good as new tomorrow I promise. Even if I have to stitch till dawn's first light."

"How will I ever repay you? Dora replies, mimicking a phrase she has once heard Slippery Sadie say to one of her clients. From her young inexperienced lips this phrase is odd and incongruous but Lewis decides to play along with her nevertheless.

"Oh I am sure between us we will think of a way." Lewis says with a wink before carefully placing the basket at her feet. "Which window is yours? He asks before taking his leave, "I can collect your dress this evening at night fall."

Dora points to a window above the overhanging porch construction to the side of the hotel.

"I shall be watching from my window for your arrival."

"I will whistle so you know it is me but how shall I return it to you?"

"I suppose I could meet you somewhere."

"I have a cabin yonder on the bank of the creek near the lightening tree. I can meet you there tomorrow at five if you like." Then, not giving Dora a chance to ponder or indeed question how her father would respond to her arranging such a clandestine meeting, Lewis gives a tiny bow and strolls away.

Lewis is true to his word and later that evening he stands beneath her window and whistles a jaunty tune. The window opens almost immediately, and he sees Dora peering out into the darkness before dropping the dress to the ground. Lewis retrieves the parcel and makes his way back to the cabin, where, as promised, he sits by candlelight until the early hours of the morning invisibly stitching the fine lace material. When he is finished, he gathers the dress up and inhales the scent of her, deciding it to be almost as intoxicating as she. Lewis is quite smitten by the young girl, but he realises that due to her youth and shy demeanour, he must play the long game and not frighten her away. To this end, the next day he casually stands by the door of the cabin smoking a clay pipe and barely glances Dora's way when he hears her approach. She is nearly upon him before he exclaims, "Oh my word is that the time?" This exclamation has the desired effect for Dora had misgivings that his intentions were not honourable and now she tells herself that she has misread the signals. Lewis draws deeply on his pipe before tapping the ash from the bowl and placing it on an upturned barrel. He motions for Dora to follow him through into the cabin door and politely stands aside so she can walk unmolested, through the open doorway. The dress is lying on a wooden chair, its brown discarded packaging lies by it on the floor. Lewis proudly presents the dress to Dora and challenges her to find the rip. Despite holding it upwards towards the rapidly fading light at the window, Dora cannot find the repair. "That is astounding," Dora declares "I cannot thank you enough. I confess I was worried you would not be true to your word." Lewis takes her hands in his and proclaims "I am an honest man and, as you can see, I am master of my craft. Please come sit by the fire, your hands are so cold and I fear you may catch a nasty chill."

Dora wraps her cloak about her shoulders and joins him by the fireside where he takes both her hands in his and blows on them gently to warm them with his breath. Dora awkwardly pulls away, for she is inexperienced and understandably nervous to be in such close proximity to a strange man. Sensing her fear Lewis retracts and politely suggests she should leave before her father realises she is gone. "Can we meet again?" Lewis enquires, as she stands by the cabin door adjusting her cloak. Dora hesitates for she is afraid of her father's reaction if he were ever to find out. Her father is extremely protective of his only daughter and has already lined up prospective suitors for when Dora reaches the age of maturity. "I would very much like to meet you again." Lewis persists. As they stand so close in the shadow of the doorway, Dora feels her heart rate quicken, she feels herself drawn to touch the cloth of his shirt and imagines how his skin is stretched taught over his biceps.

"I suppose I could return again tomorrow," Dora suggests hesitantly. In response Lewis kisses her tenderly on the hand, then he watches as she makes her way along the bank of the creek, carefully holding her petticoat above her knee to protect it from the mud. He then turns and goes back into the cabin to collect his jacket. Lewis has a few dollars burning a hole in his pocket and a visit to Nell will keep him warm until his delicate wooing reaps rewards.

OCTOBER 1891 MAESTEG, WALES

Over a year has passed since Sophia had word of Lewis, or his whereabouts, so she is slowly coming to the conclusion that her erstwhile husband has no intention of ever returning. She has not yet voiced her fears to their daughter Mary as she knows it will break her heart. The money which Lewis left is slowly running out, and Sophia has been taking in laundry to make ends meet, but still there is a shortfall with the rent every month. Lewis's tailor shop now lies empty and the windows have been boarded up. The tenant they did have left the premises early in 1891 with unpaid bills in arrears, and Sophia has not been able to rent it out again. Selling isn't an option because legally the shop belongs to Lewis. Some days the food just doesn't stretch to two portions, and Sophia constantly goes to bed hungry. Sophia feels the shame of desertion and hasn't shared her concerns with anyone, even her parents. Ann, her mother, has remarked at Sophia's weight loss and is concerned that her daughter's clothes now hang like rags from her frame but Sophia is stubborn and refuses to acknowledge any problems. Her parents fear some terrible tragedy has befallen Lewis as they still

21

treat Lewis as her saviour and will hear no ill of him. The other men who returned early from Cripple Creek soon tire of Sophia's questions. When probed, they talk of Lewis working day and night in the mines so he can make his fortune and return home a rich man. It is a bizarre honour amongst thieves, as the majority of the men had acted out of character in Colorado and there are many incidents which they are glad their wives were not party to. The final straw comes for Sophia when her landlord visits and offers to renegotiate her rent in return for certain favours. She slaps away his intrusive hands and shows him to the door; then she sits by the flickering fire and bursts into hopeless tears. Later that evening she visits her parents in the next village and asks if she and Mary may move back home until her husband returns.

It is with heavy hearts that Sophia and Mary load their meagre possessions onto a wooden cart and travel the short distance across the valley back into the welcoming bosom of Sophia's parents. Her parent's house is small and cramped, so Mother and daughter will have to share a bed, but Sophia feels a heavy weight has been lifted from her shoulders as she crawls beneath the covers that night. It is not long before neighbours in the street begin to gossip and speculate that Lewis has abandoned his family. Sophia tries to rise above the title-tattle by not dignifying it with a reaction, but when her father John has a bare knuckle fight with another collier, and it transpires he was protecting her honour, she realises she will have to take action. So Sophia concocts a credible story that she has received word about Lewis. The news is not good, she tells her shocked parents, a doctor from Colorado has written to inform her that a support plank from the entrance of the mine has collapsed, and landed on Lewis, breaking his spine. The doctors are doing their best to make him comfortable but his breathing is laboured and they fear for his life. She cries crocodile tears as she waves the 'so-called' letter in front of her parents secure in the knowledge that neither of them are literate so have no way of reading it. She knows news of the incident will not be questioned by the local community, because mining accidents are so commonplace in Wales they are almost an everyday occurrence. It breaks Sophia's heart to lie to her daughter, Mary, and to witness her reaction is like a dagger to her heart, but she reasons that Lewis's broken promise and wanton desertion of his family would hurt her even more. At least this way her daughter can mourn and keep her father's memory safe. A few weeks later, Sophia declares she has had word her husband is dead and she asks the Preacher at St Cynwyd Church to hold a special service in his honour. With this declaration, Sophia dresses in black and transforms herself into a suitable grieving widow. She is barely thirty four and is exactly ten years older than Lewis when he was widowed. Such is the irony of life.

Mary is most disgruntled to be living with her grandparents, for she has become accustomed to the comparative luxury of being an only child. She has always enjoyed the privacy of her own room, and giving up such a privilege is not easy. Her grandparents continue to embarrass her with their old fashioned ways, to such a large extent that she avoids being in the vicinity of the house on a Friday night, for her grandmother's habit of standing on the street with her apron outstretched to collect her grandfather's wages seems both unnecessary and archaic. Mary yearns for her old life and weeps nightly for the father she has lost. Her saviour, my great grandfather Oshbert Le Britton, will ride onto the scene very soon, much in the manner of a 'knight in shining armour', albeit without the obligatory white steed, but more of this later in the story.

NOVEMBER 1891, CRIPPLE CREEK, COLORADO

It is now November 1891, and we find Mary's errant father Lewis alive, well and embracing his new life to the full. He has been romancing Dora for a good few weeks now, taking things really slowly and waiting for her to be fully comfortable in his presence before he takes her virginity. Lewis is now 39 so a good many years older than his belle – who has just turned sixteen - but he still cuts a fine figure of a man, and, if anything, his advanced years add a certain gravitas to his presence. It is a still clear night with a light frost settling on the mountain peaks and Lewis is waiting for Dora in their special place beneath the lightning tree, just a few yards from the cabin which he still shares with his two friends. Lewis has had a big promotion and is now overseeing the day-to-day running of the mine for his boss Winfield Stratton, so he has deliberately assigned both of his friends a shift so he will have a good chance of finally making Dora his. During the past six weeks, Lewis has grown increasingly fond of the young girl finding her zest for life both endearing and delightful. He has witnessed her blossoming into a very attractive young woman and her innocence and obvious adoration of him have served to be an added aphrodisiac. Once she arrives, they sit beneath the tree for a while and he pretends to listen as she chatters incessantly about her day. Lewis soon bores of her mindless prattling and abruptly gets to his feet snapping in an irritable voice, 'please pray be quiet, I tire of such trifles.' Lewis has never before spoken to her in such a fashion and Dora is understandably taken aback. She bustles to her feet and motions to leave, "as I bore you so I shall trouble you with my presence no more." All at once, Lewis is conciliatory and, in an attempt to placate her and explain his harsh words, he adds, "I apologise but I am bitterly cold and it affects my temperament so." Dora replies huffily, "I too am chilled but do not treat you in such an impolite manner." Lewis stretches out his hand to take hers, he then bends over and kisses her tenderly on the inside of her wrist before saying, "I long to go inside the cabin and smother you with kisses such as this." Dora is in a quandary as she knows that she cannot expect Lewis to wait forever, but she had hoped for a proper proposal or at the very least a declaration of love, before giving away her most precious gift. "Dora, my darling girl I can contain my passion no longer," pleads Lewis. His words are affectionate but Dora can still detect a tinge of annoyance in the tone of his voice.

"Surely we should wait until we are wed?" Dora intones.

"My darling, we shall be wed soon I swear. We shall leave the shackles of this life and set up home together. Have these last few weeks of my patient wooing not proved my honourable intentions towards you? Then, as a parting shot Lewis pouts like a belligerent child and storms away towards the cabin, fully knowing that Dora will follow soon after. He has tired of waiting to deflower her, for he has become accustomed to Dirty Neck Nell and instant gratification. As he presumed, Dora is soon standing at the doorway and it is not long before she is squeezing past him and entering the cramped confines of the cabin. She takes a moment for her eyes to accustom to the change of light, before crossing to what she presumes is Lewis' bed and then glancing shyly his way she reaches behind herself to loosen her stays. Lewis says nothing, but lazily stretches out an arm and closes the door with a resounding thud. The room is quiet and dark and he slowly crosses to Dora's side. Lewis proves to be a gentle yet persuasive lover, taking the lead when necessary, but allowing Dora to dictate the pace. It is only afterwards, as she lies quivering in his arms that she realises that Lewis has still not expressed his undying love for her.

Later, as she creeps out into the night, Dora fears that now Lewis has had what he wants he will not be so keen to seek out her company. Her fears, unfortunately, are well-founded for she has no word from Lewis for an entire week afterwards. When she tries to approach him, he is friendly, if dismissive, and blames the pressures of work, but she senses something in him has changed, his manner and demeanour are altered and the twinkle has left his eye. Dora is distraught and she questions if her inexperience has caused his ardour to wane, but her problems are to magnify a short while after when she discovers that she is with child. Very soon, her delicate condition is unmistakable and the shape of her is changing so rapidly that she knows she cannot hide it much longer. Fearing her father's wrath, Dora decides to swallow her pride and visit Lewis at the cabin. It is late in the evening when she arrives and she can hear drunken laughter and carousing from within its log walls. A man she presumes to be Lewis's friend, eventually answers her persistent knocks and informs her that Lewis will no doubt be on 'Sin Street.' Dora walks the short distance to the infamous Myers Street, all the while trying to cover her face with her cloak, for fear that reports of her whereabouts reach her father. Gangs of rowdy intoxicated men crowd the pavements jostling her, as she makes her way along, and in the upstairs windows of the various hotels ladies of ill-repute pose provocatively in their undergarments. When Dora finally locates Lewis, it is as she feared and he is not sitting at the bar table alone. Even from the relative distance of the saloon door, she can see Lewis' hand resting beneath the skirt of the woman sitting on his lap. Despite herself Dora recoils and gasps in disbelief for she had, after all, once believed him to be an honourable man. This realisation debases the very act which has formed their unborn child, but she reasons that perhaps she is slightly to blame for his action as she made him wait for so long and was so obviously inexperienced. At this crucial stage in the story I want to take Dora under my wing and explain that Lewis has done this before and she is not in any way to blame for his moral laxity and cavalier attitude towards women, but, no doubt, Dora will find this out in time anyway. For now she chastises herself for her hesitance and weeps silent tears of regret.

Dora's first instinct is to steal away into the night, but despite her tender age, she is a realist so she gathers her cloak about her and stands silently in the shadows of the building, waiting for Lewis to leave. When he staggers drunkenly from the saloon an hour or so later she steps from the shadows and opens her cloak so he may fully understand her desperation to see him. Lewis in his drunken state is pugnacious and they briefly bicker for a while, and he even questions if the child is actually his. But even he can see the truth in Dora's eyes, and some modicum of decency fights its way to the surface, and he declares that he shall honour his word and they will marry. He begs her not to tell her father, and arranges to meet her the following evening when, he claims, he will have organised a date for their betrothal. During this whole intoxicated exchange Lewis seems to have conveniently forgotten he already has a wife and daughter in Wales, and more importantly, that his poor deserted daughter was conceived in a similar fashion.

NOVEMBER 1891 MAESTEG, WALES

Mary bursts into the bedroom where her mother is modestly dressing. "Mother," she cries "I have great news which I have to share. I have been speaking to Aled Evans the tailor from Aberavon."

"Ah yes, I know of Aled the tailor for your father held him in great esteem. What of him?" Sophia was desperately trying to keep her voice even for she feared that Aled the tailor may have had word of Lewis. This was her worst nightmare, for if reports of his accident and subsequent death were proved to be a fabrication, the obvious conclusion would be that she had told a lie. The consequences of this most heinous of falsehoods had the potential to forever scar her relationship with both her daughter and her parents. Sophia was visibly shaking so she slumped down upon the bed to better hear the news. Her pallor, too, must have dramatically changed for Mary rushed to her side to sit by her mother, "Oh mother dear, I am sorry to have spoken so thoughtlessly, did you think Aled the tailor had news of father?" Sophia nodded as she couldn't trust her voice. "Oh mother dearest, if only he had but we both know from the letter that father is dead. I am so sorry to have caused you new heartache." Sophia sat a moment trying to collect her thoughts whilst Mary left the room to fetch a glass of water.

"Mother dear, do you wish me to tell you the good news now?" Mary said, as Sophia sat sipping from the glass. Sophia nodded her assent. "The news is that Aled the tailor has a boarder lodging with him who is very keen to set up on his own and he would very much like to look at father's empty shop." When Sophia did not answer immediately, Mary continued, "do you not see, mother, if we get the rent from the shop we may move back into our darling little house."

Sophia replied in a halting voice for she was still in a state of shock. "Yes my dear it is good news. Would you tell Aled the tailor that we are at his disposal and this man may view the shop at his earliest convenience?" Sophia had barely got her words out before Mary had grabbed her cloak and was fleeing from the house, such was her daughter's haste to impart the news to Aled the tailor and his new boarder.

It was barely half an hour later when Mary presented herself at Aled the tailor's front door. She had run part of the way so her hair had escaped from its ribbon. Her tunic too was in disarray. Had she known it was to be the first time she would set eyes upon Oshbert no doubt she would have stopped at the corner of the street to reassemble her plait and rearrange her clothing, but hindsight is a marvellous gift and in the scheme of things it mattered not a jot. Indeed, if love at first sight were not such a cliché, I would use such a description for their first meeting because both parties fell hopelessly in love that very afternoon. Oshbert, who was taller than Mary by a head was suave and debonair, quite the charmer with a look not dissimilar to her dear departed father. His handlebar moustache gave his features an air of sophistication so he appeared much older than his twenty-four years.

Oshbert was sitting at the table as Mary was shown into the room and he immediately jumped from his chair to guide Mary to the adjacent chair. Aled the tailor, who had been standing by the fireplace warming his hands walked across the room to introduce the pair. Once formal introductions had been made, Mary declared that she had spoken to her mother and she was most keen for Oshbert to view the property at his earliest convenience. Upon hearing this statement, Oshbert got up from the table and gathering together his overcoat and scarf declared, "Well there is no time like the present." He followed it up by saying, "if I may be so bold may I ask that you escort me there now. If nothing else, it will afford us a chance to get better acquainted." Mary was temporarily taken aback for she was not used to a prospective suitor being so forthright and decisive. The men she had so far had dalliances with were her peers, so just adolescent boys with all the awkwardness and angst which bellied their age. Pulling herself quickly together, she replied, "If you are not too busy Mr Le Britton I will happily walk back to Cwmdu with you now. We can collect my mother and the shop keys on the way there." And so the die was cast and their future written on the stars. I wax lyrical and presume their conversations, but I do know that as they walked along the shoreline that afternoon, Oshbert's knuckles accidently bumped and grazed Mary's causing a frisson of excitement pass between them. Later on, when they stopped to catch their breath and gazed out to sea, Oshbert took the opportunity to properly take Mary's hand in his and remarked her hand fitted his like a glove. Oshbert did not behave improperly in any way, although if he had, I feel that Mary would have been compliant, such were the strength and conviction of her feelings.

"It feels as if I have known you forever," said Oshbert, "you seem so familiar to me."

"Like an old shoe," Mary joked.

"I have many old shoes which I cherish," Oshbert declared.

"If you wish me to be an old shoe you can cherish me."

"Cherish you I shall. Will you walk out with me Mary Davies."

"Am I not walking out with you now, Oshbert Le Britton?'

29

"So is the answer yes?'

"Yes, my answer is yes," she teased with a mock exasperation to her tone, " a thousand times yes."

"May we seal our pledge with a kiss," Oshbert pleaded, for as we will soon find out, very much like her father he is not backwards in coming forward.

"No, we may not, Oshbert Le Britton, for we have but just met and I am not that sort of a girl."

"Not even one kiss?'

"Not even one," Mary replied flirting outrageously, "but ask me again tomorrow and I may say yes."

Then she jumped up and ran across the sand dunes towards the sea, lifting her dress as she ran for she did not want to explain to her mother how she had sand in her petticoat. Oshbert gave chase and she shrieked with excitement as he grabbed her around the waist and twirled her around to face him. "How happy I am to have met you, Mary Davies," he stated confidently. Mary was suddenly shy and dipped her gaze from his. "Are you blushing Miss Davies?' he asked.

"Are you toying with me, Mr Le Britton?" said Mary trying desperately to regain her composure and yet still match his jocular mood. Oshbert was all of a sudden earnest as he released his grip on her and declared "I would never toy with your affections. Let me prove my honourable intentions toward you for all to see." He then turned away and strode decisively across the beach. Then reaching down he picked up a piece of driftwood and drew a large lopsided heart in the wet sand. An arrow pierced the heart, and on the arrow tip and the nock he carefully wrote their initials. A passing gull squalled overhead and Oshbert raised his hat in a mock salute, "see my darling Mary our audience approves our courtship."

Now, dear reader I will divulge what precious little I know of Oshbert's early life. I believe him to hail from Guernsey but I am at a loss as to what has brought him to Wales. I can only speculate that it was a chance to board with, and be trained by, Aled the tailor, but saying that he had not a passion for tailoring, nor dare I say the patience to fully master the craft. Oshbert's father, James, had been a plumber by trade and when he died in 1879, records show that Oshbert returned to Kent the town of his birth. I imagine he stayed with relatives there, before deciding to move to Wales. James had left him some money when he died so no doubt in the intervening years the money had dwindled and Oshbert needed to earn a decent living. Oshbert had sown his wild oats, was ready to settle down and start a family, so meeting Mary in Maesteg was most propitious in its timing.

So we leave the young lovebirds to their coquetry and return to Cripple Creek and to Mary's father Lewis and his not so innocent courtship of young Dora.

JANUARY 1891 CRIPPLE CREEK, COLORADO.

Dora is standing at the back of Dobson's hotel waiting for Lewis to arrive. At her feet she has two carpet bags, the lighter of the two holds her clothes and precious possessions and the heavier contains the entire contents of the hotel safe. Although it was she who conducted the burglary, it was undoubtedly Lewis who had coerced her into doing so by insisting that she was only taking what was rightfully hers as 'a makeshift dowry if you will'. "We need money to leave Colorado and the only way is to elope because once father discovers you are with child he will have me shot," Lewis insisted. I interject that although this seems a rather dramatic statement it is actually quite accurate for Dora's father was well renowned for being quick to temper and would be much more likely to shoot first and ask questions later. Whether Lewis saw this as an easy way to make his fortune, I cannot say but he did undisputedly use the theft of the money almost as a pre-requisite to their impending marriage and Dora at this stage was so desperate to give their child legitimacy she would have agreed to anything. Lewis further declared to Dora, perhaps in an effort to sweeten the pill, that he had already arranged for his friend Preacher Joe to conduct the wedding ceremony once they had safely eloped. I must again interject and say that the aptly named Preacher Joe was not actually a preacher at all, and he had only earned the nickname from his habit of quoting liberally from the bible when intoxicated. Lewis no doubt realised that he would be committing bigamy employing the services of an actual preacher, and he presumed this would appease his young sweetheart who had her heart so set on marriage.

Dora turned her head quickly when she heard a low whistle and peering into the darkness she spied Lewis approaching in a canvas covered wagon. Lewis carefully pulled up alongside her then tugged swiftly on the reins so that the two horses came to an abrupt if juddering halt. He then jumped out and assisted Dora up onto the bench, before quickly clambering back aboard and snapping on the reins with a loud crack. The horses rapidly picked up their speed and were soon galloping towards Battle Mountain Pass and the Colorado border. It was not long into their journey before Dora became aware of a shuffling and the sound of muffled laughter coming from directly behind her in covered confines of the wagon. Turning to Lewis she questioned, "have we passengers?"

"Yes my dear." Lewis confirmed, "I have asked Preacher Joe to come along with us so that he can help me with the driving when I tire."

"I can hear two voices."

Lewis hesitated before replying in a deliberately dismissive tone, "Oh that's Nell one of the barmaids from the saloon. I thought it would be nice for you to have some female company on the journey and she was travelling back to England anyway."

"England?" Dora spluttered. "Why are we travelling to England?"

"Why to start our new life together of course."

"But what about father? What about my friends in Cripple Creek?"

"I'm sorry my dear, I assumed that you would realise we cannot possibly stay around here. Once your father discovers we have stolen from the hotel safe, I will be a wanted man. That's why I want to get as many miles under our belts before sunrise and why we must make haste."

Dora began to sob, so Lewis put his arm about her and gently draped the blanket over her knees. He was not a callous man and her tears upset him. He had not deliberately deceived her by omission and surely she must have realised that he was a dead man walking if they lingered in the vicinity too long.

"Please don't cry my dear, pray remember we will be married tomorrow at dawn," said Lewis in an attempt to placate her.

Dora stopped sobbing long enough to blurt out, "I thought it would be just the two of us, I am really upset that you never mentioned our travelling companions until now."

"It was always the plan. We will have more chance in a group and it will be safer should we encounter any vagabonds on the way. Please try to sleep, my dear, and I promise I shall wake you with a kiss in the morning." Sensing that further arguing would be pointless and suddenly overcome by an overwhelming tiredness Dora leant into Lewis and shut her eyes. Her sleep was fitful, for the night was cold and the bench hard and uncomfortable, but it was a blessed relief from her worries about the future.

Dora awoke as the wagon pulled to a halt by a little stream. Lewis leapt down and unbuckled the horses before leading them to the trickling water to take a drink. Once they had had their fill he carefully tied them to a tree before returning to help Dora down from the wagon. "Let me wake the other two so we may make camp here until daylight, for I fear it is too dangerous for the horses to go any further down the pass as I cannot see what lies ahead," said Lewis trying and failing to stifle a yawn.

It was not long before Preacher Joe had a campfire lit and Nell was collecting water from the stream. The hot steaming coffee was most welcome and all four huddled by the fire gingerly sipping it. Lewis was first to drain his cup and he threw the dregs to the ground before turning to address Dora, "my dear why don't you and Nell go back into the wagon to sleep some more? Joe and I will take turns at keeping watch for we are surely sitting ducks for any outlaw passing by." Dora needed little persuading and both ladies were soon inside the wagon tucked up in blankets and animal hide throws. The covered wagon was very dark and very cramped with not an inch of space wasted. Boxes of rations were lined up along its sides. Cooking pots, tools, rifles and a canvas tent hung from hooks attached to its bow like construction. The two bed rolls and blankets were squeezed into its centre alleyway in such a fashion that Dora and Nell had little choice of where to lie. Such enforced intimacy would have seemed strange at any other time but the two women were both so weary that they promptly fell into deep slumber. Dora woke alone the next morning and it took a while to become accustomed to her surroundings. For a brief moment she imagined she was still in her little bed at home in the hotel tucked under her colourful quilted eiderdown, her head resting on a soft down pillow. Nell must have heard her stir for she suddenly appeared, her hands parting the curtains of the wagon. "Good morning, I thought you could use this," she said stretching in and handing Dora yet another mug of steaming coffee. "I've just cooked up a batch of eggs and grits if you are hungry." Dora murmured a quiet thank you as she took the proffered mug. She was still at the sickly stage of her pregnancy and could picture the eggs swimming in oil, their yolks glistening and viscous. As a distraction she called out to Nell and enquired about the mens whereabouts.

"The men are yonder behind those rocks so that we may modestly get washed and carry out our ablutions in private," replied Nell. "Have you forgotten it is today you marry?" Nell then reached beneath the carriage and pulled out a small bunch of red twig dogwood tied in a red ribbon. "See," she said, "I have made you a bouquet of sorts. Can I braid your hair and make you ready, for we need to get going very soon?" Dora nodded. It was not how she had imagined her wedding day would be but she was thankful that at least it was going ahead as Lewis had promised.

And so, dear reader, they were married and there followed a rather chaste hurried kiss betwixt the bride and groom before the two women were once again ushered into the back of the wagon and the horses rehitched. "How does it feel to be Mrs Davies?" Nell asked her companion once they were underway.

"I confess it is not how I imagined my wedding day to be," Dora answered truthfully.

"Lewis is a man of good character," said Nell in a decisive tone, "he will do you and the child no ill."

"I just wish the circumstances were different and I do feel that baby has forced his hand."

"He is no better or worse in that respect than most of the men I know," said Nell reflectively.

"Have you ever married?" said Dora before adding "I am sorry if I seem bold but I am curious."

"Men don't marry women like me," declared Nell wistfully, "they marry women like you. They like 'em young and innocent. They practice on women like me then marry women like you ain't that the truth." If Dora had her suspicions as to Nell's profession before this declaration it was a mystery no longer, but now she felt compelled to address the elephant in the room. "I am curious, has Lewis ever had cause to visit you?" Dora hated herself for asking such a question but she had to know.

"I won't do you the discourtesy of lying to you for we have a long journey ahead so I will answer truthfully," said Nell, "so yes Lewis has made my acquaintance." Dora gasped for although she had suspected as much after seeing him that time in the saloon she had anticipated Nell would dismiss the question as irrelevant and try to change the subject. Realising the strength of her reaction, Nell quickly added "it was a bit of slap and tickle nothing more and I hasten to add I have no further designs upon him." If this was supposed to allay Dora's fears it had the opposite effect and she kept imagining Lewis and Nell engaged in acts which she had naively supposed would be special between he and she. I am sure she was not under the illusion that Lewis was a virgin, for at his advanced age that would have made him a very peculiar fellow indeed, but saying that, she had perhaps closed her mind to his past exploits.

"One more question if I may" said Dora. Nell nodded. "Why has Lewis asked you along on this trip?"

"He knew of my wish to leave my old life behind and he was concerned about your delicate condition on such a perilous journey."

"So you have had experience of childbirth?"

"Not directly but I have acted as a midwife many times for it is an unfortunate hazard of my job that these things happen."

The truth of it was that Nell, along with the other girls at the brothel, were regularly checked for venereal diseases as an influx of so called 'calamities' would inevitably cause an alarming drop in customers. Likewise any 'mistakes' were soon put right. It would be indelicate of me to go into too much detail, suffice to say that Nell's last 'mistake' had not been detected early enough and the subsequent removal had been misjudged and brutal. Blanche, the madam, had taken her aside once she had fully recovered from her ordeal and informed her that after such a procedure it was unlikely she would ever bear a child. Nell had put on a brave face but inwardly something in her died that day for her dream had always been to make money, move away and have a normal respectable life.

She yearned for a husband to treat her body with the reverence it deserved and not just as a vessel for his own pleasure and personal consumption. A short while ago she had imagined that man may have been Lewis but her dreams had been cruelly shattered when he confessed that he had impregnated a young girl. She felt the sting of embarrassment when she recalled her rather pathetic gaiety upon being asked to accompany him on this trip. For one memorable moment that is - until he fully laid out his plans and predicament - she had even foolishly thought he was asking her to run away with him. Now, here they were, and she felt strangely protective towards this young innocent girl and a rising anger at Lewis and at the casual arrogance of his sex. "I promise to travel with you until England so you may be safely delivered of child, then I shall leave," said Nell with a note of finality to her tone. Dora nodded then sat back against the sides of the wagon and closed her eyes. She needed some time to process this information and the motion of the wagon was making her feel most nauseous.

So we leave our motley crew of travellers and return to Wales and a much happier, and dare I add, traditional wedding ceremony.

FEBRUARY 1892 MAESTEG, WALES

It had been a crisp January morning in 1892 when Oshbert had fallen to his knees and proposed to his sweetheart Mary. The haste with which they met and married would be commented on in today's society but in the late 1800s it was normal to have a short courtship because, if nothing else, it prevented too many babies being born out of wedlock. With her mother's full blessing the couple visited the Preacher at St Cynwyd Church that very afternoon to set a date for the wedding.

They were married on the 13th February 1892 to a packed church and with all the bells and whistles of the time. They left the church for a small wedding breakfast in The Lamb and Flag, a local inn where Sophia had recently taken on a part-time cleaning job. The young landlord, Llewellyn Bevan, was much enamoured of Sophia and as a result had arranged the catering at a cut price to suit her meagre budget. Many glasses were raised to congratulate the happy couple and many a tear shed by both the bride and her mother. Mary's mother, Sophia, had decorated the back of the tailor's shop so the couple could set up their first home together there. It was small and spartan with only the most basic of amenities but Mary was so thrilled by it that she walked around the little room touching the surfaces reverently as if to prove they were real. Sophia had fitted it out with a square table, two chairs and a second-hand metal framed bed but to Mary and Oshbert the room was like a palace and their first proper chance to be a couple. Oshbert had proudly carried his new wife over the threshold, and once night set in, they shyly got undressed for bed. What possessed Oshbert to decide to confess to past encounters at such a time eludes me. But for whatever reason he marred, their wedding night by telling Mary of a letter he had received a few days before they wed. Oshbert sat at the foot of the bed in his dark red long john union suit and handed Mary the letter so she could read it herself. Mary sat up in bed and snatched the letter from Oshbert's clasp. It was not well written and barely legible but Mary struggled through to the flowery signature at the end. Oshbert sat with his head dipped and his hands placed upon his knees as he waited for Mary to speak. Her silence spoke volumes and once she had finished reading, she crumpled the letter up in her fist and threw it to the floor. Then she angrily got out of bed, holding the edges of her nightgown together with tensed hands.

"Have you read the letter?" Oshbert said eventually, directing his question to Mary's back, as she had turned away from him and was staring at the table in the corner of the room.

"You have just sat and watched me read it." Mary said quietly, "I don't understand why you waited until our wedding night to tell me of this."

"I was afraid that if I told you of this beforehand you would not agree to be my wife."

"You are twenty-four Oshbert; my mother warned me that it was unlikely that you were to be a virgin. But this, surely you can't expect me to agree to this."

"The child is my flesh and blood and the boy needs a father."

"The child is a bastard." Mary was so incensed she spat out the words.

"A bastard of my making, Mary, and therefore my responsibility. Now I am married Lemontina thought I would be better suited to care for him. The nomadic life she leads is no life for a young boy."

"Perhaps you should have thought of that before you had your way with her. I will not bring up a bastard Roma child as my own. I want our children to be part of you and me not some travelling gypsy you fell in with."

"Lemontina thought that.." Oshbert began, before Mary rudely interrupted.

"I do not care to hear Lemontina's thoughts on the matter and I would thank you never to utter her name in my presence again or this marriage will be the shortest union ever."

"I am taken aback by the hostility of your reaction, but can I ask that you at least think on it overnight and give me your answer in the morning?"

"My decision will not change. You must choose this child, or choose me, your wife, and now I will thank you to let me get some sleep for this argument has made me weary." Mary climbed back into the bed and turned to face the wall. After a while Oshbert got in beside her and he too turned his back to her in a similar fashion. Much later he woke enveloped in darkness and turned over to put his arm about her, unaware that Mary was still awake. She shrank from his embrace and it was at that moment that he voiced the decision he had made in the lonely dark hours, "I have been foolhardy in my affections so we will say no more on the subject. I shall write my reply in the morning. Now I bid you a goodnight." Mary did not answer but he felt the contours of her body shift slightly, so he knew she had heard and understood.

True to his word Oshbert wrote to Lemontina the next day. He gently explained that he had made his choice and he could not take on his son, for his marriage would be at stake if he did so. At this stage I will, if I may, interject for I fear I have depicted Mary as judgemental and uncaring without offering an argument for her defence. The strength of her convictions were based upon a common preconception and casual racism. At the end of the 19th Century, Roma were perceived to be a godless untrustworthy bunch of heathens, devoid of Christian morals and as a result a danger to civilised society. Mary was a young and immature sixteen year old, so to find out that her new husband had fathered a child with such a woman must have come as a terrible shock. Perhaps if Oshbert had timed his disclosure differently things would have taken a different path, but for some reason, known only to him, he decided to add discord to their nuptials with this confession. His relationship with Lemontina had been brief and the pair had never been star-crossed lovers nor ever seriously imagined a future together. For Oshbert it had been a sowing of wild oats without a thought for the consequences, much in the manner of Mary's father, the much derided Lewis. Indeed, I hazard to guess that if Mary had known the truth of her own conception she may have made a different decision, but all this is in hindsight, and once Oshbert replied to the letter it set in motion a whole series of events which would haunt their marriage and forever mar their lives.

Oshbert had met Lemontina in Kent during the six weeks the travellers encamped on a Kentish farm for the annual 'hopping'. He was at once entranced by her deep brown eyes, swarthy skin and brightly coloured attire. For her part she was flattered by the attention of one so well-educated and dashingly handsome. It was never a meeting of minds but the mutual attraction had been undeniably intoxicating and inescapable. When the gypsies had moved their wooden caravans away so they could spend the winter on the Hackney Marshes, north of the Thames, the relationship had died a natural death. Lemontina didn't tell him of the birth of his son Silvanus, until, the next year when out of curiosity he had again sought her out. Shocked to see her with a babe in arms he had waited until nightfall to approach her. At first she denied he was the father but eventually she had confirmed the child's true parentage, while stressing that she wanted nothing from Oshbert. Many a young lad would have counted his blessings to be absolved of such a responsibility, but Oshbert had a sense of honour, and when Lemontina refused his offer of money for the child, he insisted she at least had his address so they could keep up a level of contact. She had written sporadically with reports of his son's wellbeing but this was the first time she had ever asked anything of him and he felt a deep sense of shame at his discourteous and uncharitable reply.

It was to be quite a few weeks before Mary completely forgave Oshbert for his past transgressions and they lay as newlyweds should. But his joy at finally consummating the marriage was short-lived for the very next day he received a letter from Lemontina where she laid out her unsurprising disappointment at his cruel rejection of his son. She was so angered that she finished the letter by declaring that she cursed any future children he would have with his selfish young wife. Oshbert was so anguished at the acrimonious tone of her letter that he hastily tucked it out of sight in the tin box where he kept his important paperwork. There the letter lay until many years later when the family moved into the 'house' on Ashleigh Grove and Oshbert retrieved it and hid it behind a loose brick in the eaves of the attic.

FEBRUARY 1892, NORTH PLATTE, NEBRASKA

The wagon was making great progress and, by taking turns at the driving, Preacher Joe and Lewis had managed to travel on an average of ten miles a day. They had just crossed the border into Nebraska where they planned to stop the wagon outside North Platte, a town to the south west of the state. Lewis had originally arranged this stop so that they could buy train tickets to cross the states into New York in more comfort but, first of all, he wanted to check that they were not being chased by the sheriff from Cripple Creek. North Platte was quite an up and coming town. It had been sparsely populated before being designated the Western terminus of the Union Pacific Railway in 1867. The rapid creation of new jobs in the town saw a big influx of homesteaders, including the famous showman Buffalo Bill Cody. Buffalo Bill had bought a 160 acre ranch alongside its Dismal River in 1878 chiefly because the train connections were so good and he needed a central base for his travelling Wild West Shows. Lewis' old boss Winfield Stratton had visited the aforementioned Cody on more than one social occasion in his eighteen roomed mansion and happened to mention in Lewis' earshot that the new railroad ran right through the Scouts Rest Ranch. It was therefore a natural place for Lewis to head towards but he wisely decided that boarding the train there depended upon if they were being followed or not. Lewis reasoned that on board a train they were sitting ducks for any Bounty Hunter worth his salt, but travelling by wagon they at least had a fighting chance. Lewis had taken Nell aside earlier that morning and asked if she and Preacher Joe could go into the town for provisions. He was hoping that Nell could make discreet enquiries and find out if the theft from Dora's father's safe had been reported. Lewis decided that if he were a fugitive with a price was on his head it would be better know so he could be better armed and prepared.

Although just into her second trimester, Dora was now so heavy with child that she was finding it increasingly hard to get properly comfortable in the wagon. It had no springs so she constantly complained that she could feel every rock and every bump along the way, and the dust it threw up made her cough and splutter. Lewis pulled hard upon the reins once they reached the outskirts of the town. The horses came to juddering stop then he jumped out to uncouple them so they could rest and drink some water. Dora heaved a sigh of relief, while Nell helped her from the wagon for she was desperate to stretch her legs and relieve her bladder. "I will make a fire and prepare a meal for your return," said Dora once she had returned from her ablutions. She was conscious that she was not fully pulling her weight on the journey. "There's no need," Nell replied, "you sit and rest. I can do it when we get back. Hopefully we won't be too long." Nell had become very fond of the young girl during the last few weeks and watched over her with almost a maternal air. The four had become a family of sorts during the journey, a relationship forced by their close proximity but a relationship nonetheless. Preacher Joe remained the only fly in the ointment, and at this stage, in the story I must reveal that Joe was making a nuisance of himself around Nell. He seemed unable to grasp that she had left her old life behind and she had no wish to revisit their past encounters in the brothel. Nell had yet to voice her concerns to Lewis but she had been bathing in a stream earlier that morning and was sure that Preacher Joe had been hiding in the bushes watching her bathe. His constant pestering had now gone from being irksome to quite intimidating, most especially when he had a bellyful of whiskey. She deliberately kept her distance from him on the short walk into the town and once they reached the main commercial street they separated company. Joe had decided to check out the local saloons to see if there was any mention of Lewis in there, whilst Nell crossed the street to shop for supplies. Nell suspected Joe's true reason for visiting the bars was probably more an excuse to sample the whiskey than a quest for information but she said nothing for she was relieved to no longer be in his company. Once she finished the shopping, she crossed the street to where they had parted company an hour earlier. She stood waiting for a while, then as there were no obvious signs of Joe, she heaved the heavy sack of flour onto her own shoulder and began to make her way ponderously out of the town. If it had not been for the fact that the hessian of the sack chafed her shoulder Nell would not have stopped to rest at that particular spot on the outskirts of the town. It was most fortuitous that she had, for whilst sat there catching her breath, she happened to spy a poster nailed to a trunk of a tree. Leaving the sack where it lay she hurried across to look properly at the poster. She recoiled in abject disgust as she realised the poster related to Lewis. It read *WANTED DEAD OR ALIVE. WELSHMAN LEWIS DAVIES FOR HORSE THEFT AND ABDUCTION OF A MINOR.* It was not the fact that the pencil sketch of Lewis was such a good likeness that caused her acute reaction, it was more the wording under it which revealed that Dora was only thirteen years of age. Fuelled by fury, Nell grabbed the sack of flour from the undergrowth and swung it back over her shoulder. Her anger erupted when she came upon Lewis and Dora sitting laughing by the fireside. Lewis had his arm about Dora in a proprietary manner and Dora was leaning comfortably into his embrace. Not caring whether she made a scene or not Nell, dropped the sack at their feet then started to pound Lewis in the chest with her curled up fists. This display of rage was so unlike Nell that both Lewis and Dora were initially both so shocked that it took a while for either to react. Lewis eventually got clumsily to his feet and grabbed Nell by the wrists in an effort to restrain her.

"Coc y gath," he barked, reverting back to his native Welsh, then fearing the worst, he ordered Dora to go back to the wagon so she would be out of earshot. Turning to Nell he demanded, "what has got into you woman, are you possessed by demons?"

"It is you who is possessed by the devil, sir, not I," Nell snapped back.

"Pray explain yourself, you cannot declare such a thing and not explain," said Lewis in an infuriated voice.

"It is you who need explain. Please explain why you have impregnated a thirteen year old child."

"Are you mad woman? Where is this thirteen year old I have supposedly impregnated?"

"She is the girl you call your wife."

"Don't be silly woman Dora is sixteen and well of age to marry."

"She is thirteen." Nell insisted.

"This is absurd I shall fetch her this minute and we will have no more of this tomfoolery," Lewis said brusquely, as he made his way towards the wagon to get her. But Dora had not returned to the wagon as instructed instead she had hidden in the bushes so she could eavesdrop and that is where Lewis found her. She cowered from his touch as she could see the understandable anger in his eyes.

"Would you please explain yourself? Is this true?" he growled, after he had dragged her from her hiding place.

"Yes it's true," said Dora in a tiny voice, deciding that now the secret was out it would be pointless to deny the truth.

"Why in the name of God did you lie to me?"

"I haven't lied, you didn't ask me," Dora retorted in a defensive voice.

"That is still a lie and you know it. Get out of my sight; I cannot bear to look upon you. Your malicious lie will have me hanged or shot you silly, silly girl."

What Lewis didn't realise was that it was the other crime for which he would more likely be hanged. This was because horse theft was classed as the most serious crime in the old Wild West, and as such, carried a much more severe penalty than even murder. The argument was that horses were so integral to the survival of the pioneers that to steal their horses was basically the same as slowly starving them to death. But that is by the by and I digress.

Nell eventually calmed down and managed to relay to Lewis the full details of the poster. He felt a cold chill run down his spine as he realised that it was as he suspected and he was truly a fugitive of the law. It was now getting late, and Preacher Joe had still not returned, so Lewis decided that they should wait for him then leave at first light the next morning. In the meantime Nell's dormant maternal instinct had kicked in and even though she now believed that Lewis had been blissfully unaware of Dora's true age, she nevertheless put an arm protectively about Dora and stated that she was now the girl's guardian. She followed her statement up by declaring to Lewis that he could no longer lie with Dora. Lewis was so stupefied by the whole situation that he meekly nodded in agreement and stated he would instead sleep outside by the fire. He helped the women construct the tent under the wagon, then he returned to sit by the dying embers of the fire to wait for his friend Joe to return from town. Lewis desperately tried to stay awake but the glowing firewood was hypnotic and it soon sent him into an almost trance-like sleep. He was crudely awoken by a blood curdling scream which came from the direction of the wagon. Stumbling to his feet Lewis grabbed his rifle and raced across towards the screams. He feared the women had been attacked by a wild animal and he ripped open the entrance to the tent to find a petrified Dora hunched up in the corner and quite hysterical. There was no sign of Nell or of a struggle. It was most bizarre for she was nowhere to be seen. All of a sudden, he heard another anguished cry, but this time coming from behind the wagon. He raced around to find Nell lying spread-eagled in the undergrowth with her skirts about her hips, ripped and bloodied. Standing over her fastening his flies was Preacher Joe, who had the bare faced audacity to smirk in Lewis direction.

"Reckon she got what was coming to her," Joe slurred "putting on those airs and graces, acting like she's better than the rest of us. She's been leading me on with her wanton ways. I only gave her what she wanted, what women like her always want." He then started to quote liberally from the scriptures before being stopped in his tracks by Lewis, who had raised his rifle and pushed the muzzle threateningly into his chest.

"What the hell!" Joe exclaimed "Don't tell me you haven't thought the same. I seen you looking at her when little wife wasn't watching."

"Enough, I tell you,' Lewis bellowed, "get out of my sight before I shoot you down like the rabid dog that you are," Joe carried on smirking until Lewis fired a warning shot at the earth beneath his feet; then he cursed loudly before turning tail and disappearing into the night. Lewis heard him stumble away into the distance before falling to the ground, presumably in a drunken stupor. Lewis decided to leave him where he fell, because if he slept there it might just give them the chance to hitch up and leave at first light, before Joe had the chance to alert the sheriff of their whereabouts. After checking the two ladies were safely settled under the wagon, Lewis once again returned to his place by the dying fire but this time he kept his rifle tucked under his arm and he did not succumb to sleep. Instead he sat and planned their next move.

The next morning they quickly packed their belongings away and drove off but not in the direction they had originally intended because Lewis was in no doubt that Joe would sing like a canary for impunity. Instead Lewis turned the wagon and they headed towards Kansas, a journey which would add many weeks onto the trip but which would be their best chance to avoiding capture.

1892 SPRING, MAESTEG, WALES

It was now early spring and Sophia was still helping out at The Lamb and Flag public house. It would have been judged as unseemly for a recently widowed woman to serve behind the bar so instead she helped discreetly behind the scenes, washing glasses and sorting the orders from the draymen. Her parents, John and Ann, were not at all happy with the situation but her brother John was thrilled at the prospect of probable lock-ins. Sophia personally viewed her employ as a means to an end and what money she had left over - after giving her mother Ann board and lodgings - she squirreled away for her future. Now that her daughter Mary was married to Oshbert, Sophia longed to once again have a home to call her own. She had tired of her parents disapproving glances and mealy-mouthed ways. Llewellyn Bevan the landlord of The Lamb and Flag was eleven years Sophia's junior and proving to be a kind employer, mature beyond his years and respectful of her opinion. He was yet to declare his true intentions towards Sophia but he had made gestures to imply his attraction towards her. Unbeknownst to Sophia the previous week he had discreetly spoken to two military looking gentlemen who had marched into the bar enquiring about the whereabouts of her late husband Lewis Davies. It transpired that before marrying his first wife Harriet, Lewis had enlisted in the army, then after a brief year of service, had gone absent without leave. At this time this was a serious offence and deserters were arrested under a writ known as 'arrestando ipsum qui pecuniam receipt' which roughly translated meant 'for arresting one who received money'. Llewellyn deflected the men by stating he had read the letter sent by Lewis' doctor in Cripple Creek and could confidently confirm that he was indeed deceased. Now who fancied a nice glass of best ale on the house? Llewellyn had deliberately not mentioned that Sophia worked in the Public House because he had serious doubts as to how she would react under close scrutiny. He had realised quite early on during Sophia's employ that she was for the most part illiterate, which would no doubt bring up the question as to how she had claimed to have read the letter herself. This fact will come to light once again much later in this story when she and Llewellyn marry and she signs her name with a mark and Llewellyn will once again come to her rescue to diffuse the situation. At this point I must add that Llewellyn is unlike Lewis in every respect for he is loyal, true of heart and adores Sophia with every ounce of his being. Throughout their friendship and subsequent marriage he will never quiz Sophia regarding the circumstances of her first husband's untimely death and her hasty disposal of the letter. Llewellyn is very much an advocate of the old adage 'let sleeping dogs lie.' He has guessed she probably lied but he can still recall the desperate state she was in as a result of her husband's cruel desertion.

So we now return to Sophia's daughter Mary and her new husband Oshbert who are still in the first throes of romance and revelling in discovering new hitherto unknown facets of each other's personalities. Mary has discovered that Oshbert has dreams and aspirations of a bright, successful future and she is slowly coming around to his way of thinking and starting to contemplate a life away from Wales. It's a scary prospect for she has spent her entire childhood sheltered in the valley but Oshbert is an ambitious man and she understands that he has neither the interest nor passion for tailoring. He toils in the shop each day but she can tell he has no true enthusiasm for the craft for he is too quick to cut the cloth and often clumsy with his stitching. She is desperate to be pregnant before the year is out so that he will finally put all thoughts of his firstborn son Silvanus to one side. I can now divulge that more has happened on this front and Oshbert has once again had cause to conceal something from Mary. In his defence, this subterfuge does not sit well with him and he wears the guilt of concealment about his shoulders like a leaden cloak. The object in question was sent to him not long after he received the first hostile missive from Lemontina. There was no message with this parcel just a crudely made rag doll with a dressmaking pin in its stomach. No message was needed for the meaning of this humanoid effigy was crystal clear, and once again Oshbert has secreted it away, for whilst not a superstitious man he does not want to tempt fate by destroying it. So it lies beneath the letter in the tin box, a timely and constant reminder of his cruel rejection of his first born.

JULY 1892, NEW YORK

Lewis, Dora and Nell had eventually reached the emerging new metropolis of New York. It had been a hard slog which saw them travel through six states firstly by horse and wagon then later by train. Now they had at last reached their final destination but Dora was so heavy with child and so close to her date of confinement that they were compelled to rent an apartment on the Southern tip of Manhattan. In the 1890s Manhattan was not the desirable area of New York it now is, to the contrary it was filled with newly built overcrowded tenements and as a result a breeding ground for all types of vermin. These tenements had been hastily constructed from inferior building materials to house a growing population, and for the most part, they were dark and dingy with little light and no proper ventilation. Air shafts were later installed but still the only rooms with natural light were the ones which had windows facing the street. A majority of these five story walk-up tenements consisted of four apartments to a floor so space was limited, and, more often than not, two adults would sleep in a room which measured only thirteen inches square. The whole area was teeming with immigrants - who had just arrived via the newly opened immigration centre of Ellis Island located at the mouth of the Hudson River - yet despite the obvious poverty and desperation, the city still reeked of opportunity and the prospect of great wealth. The Brooklyn Bridge - which at the time was the longest suspension bridge in the world - had opened in 1883 and the shiny copper Statue of Liberty had been erected a few years later in 1886 as a symbol of hope and American independence.

The rooms in the apartment Lewis and the ladies rented were of slightly better quality than most, as at least they had a window to the street allowing fresh air to circulate and laundry to be hung out to dry. To the ladies the space seemed expansive, especially after the cramped conditions they had endured both in the wagon and on the trains. Lewis hung a makeshift curtain to separate the sleeping areas and they set out their precious few belongings on the floor. Their neighbours were a mixed bunch of individuals of Irish, German, Russian and Italian descent. These diverse nationalities normally settled in ethnic neighbourhoods because they faced discrimination 'nativism' from the older more established immigrants but some who had no relatives to meet them at the 'Golden Gate' settled in Manhattan. Lewis decided that he would seek employment for the duration of their stay in New York so that their stash of cash would not be further depleted. He soon found a kindred spirit in the form of a Yorkshire man called Timothy O'Dowd who was staying in the apartment above. Timothy had travelled to America to seek his fortune a few years after the death of his wife in 1885. He had left his children in the care of their maternal grandmother, Ellen Carter, but he planned to return to England with Lewis and the ladies – once Dora was safely delivered of her child - because his son John had reached maturity and was in need of fatherly guidance. Timothy had so far had no problem finding temporary work despite having an Irish name and a broad Yorkshire accent. He was only four years Lewis senior but much more used to New York ways so he took Lewis under his wing and together they left the apartment in search of work. Strolling through Central Park, swerving between the carriages and stopping to watch the brightly coloured carousels, Lewis felt like the king of the world. As he wandered further into the urban landscape he realised that he had finally found a place he would like to settle and call home. Perhaps it was at that moment that he made the decision to stay in New York and not bother returning to England, for after all dear reader, what was waiting for him back home? His marriage to Sophia was long over. It had been a marriage of convenience from the onset and his cruel desertion of both his wife and daughter was not surprisingly unforgivable. Lewis made up his mind to divide the remaining money fairly so that Dora and Nell could still travel to England if they so wished. He had no doubt that his new found friend Timothy could be called upon to keep a watchful eye upon the two ladies during the long and arduous voyage. It just remained for him to find gainful employment and tell them of his momentous decision.

Whilst Lewis was having this moment of clarity, his two companions Dora and Nell were standing chatting in the passageway to a group of Russian women they had recently befriended. The women were expressing their mutual dissatisfaction at the lack of decent sanitation facilities in the building when Dora first felt the stirrings deep inside her womb. The baby had been very active the night before and Dora at first put the twinges down to her body's reaction to the constant movement. She tried to ignore the pains and concentrate on the conversation but they became so intense that she was forced to bend double. It was as she let out the first groan that her waters dramatically broke then splashed and puddled at her feet. Nell and a Russian lady called Raisa quickly guided her back upstairs to the apartment so she might more comfortably and discreetly give birth. Dear reader, I won't go into elaborate details about the actual circumstances of the birth as it seems both indelicate and inappropriate, but Nell soon discovered that the baby was possibly breech. Between them Raisa and Nell tried to apply pressure to her uterus during the contractions but were not successful and the child was born bottom first. The umbilical cord was squashed during the delivery and the child entered the world in silence. Raisa tried to rouse it by smacking it briskly on the buttocks and when this didn't work she splashed it liberally with cold water from a jug. Both women yelped with relief as the newborn finally made a loud piercing disgruntled cry. I must now impart the heart wrenching news that Dora did not survive her painful ordeal. She lived long enough to briefly suckle her newborn daughter and name her Bertha, but she died with the child still in her arms. Nell was understandably distraught so it remained for Raisa to prise the tiny infant from her mother's embrace and reverently raise the blanket to protect Dora's modesty. This was the scene that Lewis walked into when he returned later that afternoon, brimming with excitement about his new job and eager to tell the ladies of the amazing sights he had seen. Nell's heart broke as she bore witness to the tears streaming down his cheeks, for no heart is so hard that it will not melt at the sight of a fully grown man cradling his new born child in his arms. Nell crossed the room to comfort Lewis while Raisa respectfully left the room to seek out a newly delivered Russian friend, who would hopefully agree to wet nurse the infant. To die at such a young age is always a tragedy and even though death was commonplace in the tenements a terrible hush fell over the building that night. Dora was interred in an underground marble burial vault in the New York City Marble Cemetery the next day, followed by a small religious service attended by Lewis, Nell, Timothy and a few of the women from the tenement block. The marble marker to her grave is still there to this day although it is now overgrown with moss and weeds. My daughter Claire who now lives in Brooklyn, New York visited it once a few years ago and told me that she sat a while quietly reflecting upon Dora's all too short life.

And so it came to be that Nell remained in New York, for how could she conceivably leave Lewis behind with such a young infant in his care? In time they even became a family of sorts, for what is a family but a group of people who are bound by blood or affinity with a commitment to care for one another? Lewis came to view Nell as his spouse, and although they never legally married, I can confirm that they did live out their days in a most conventional fashion. I can further confirm that as a result of this action my maternal great

JUST ANOTHER CENTURY

great grandfather has redeemed himself somewhat in my eyes and I find that I can now look upon him more favourably. Nell and Lewis did not produce any more children - for given Nell's pre-existing condition that was impossible - but as a result their beloved Bertha was showered in a deluge of parental love. I have lying on my desk a photograph taken when Bertha was about six years of age. It shows her standing with her parents on Bedloe's Island, alongside the base of the Statue of Liberty. They are waiting in a queue to climb the stairs inside Liberty's torch-bearing arm so they can take in the view of the skyline of Manhattan from its somewhat precarious balcony. Bertha has a red balloon clasped to her chest and standing protectively behind her with their arms linked are Lewis and Nell. All three look happy in each other's company and to the casual observer appear to be the quintessential model family unit. I will now impart what further facts I have in my possession. For I know that Bertha grew up to be a lovely young woman with a kind heart and sense of style inherited in part from her debonair well-attired father. I know also that she later married an Italian immigrant called Vincenzo Corasaniti and moved to Little Italy to help run the family restaurant there. Of Lewis and Nell I confess I know precious little but I like to imagine that they lived out their dotage in good health, surrounded by an ever increasing brood of grandchildren. Surprisingly, I know more of Timothy O'Dowd for his son John William went on to marry my maternal grandmother, Theresa Callender, thus proving that the statement 'seven degrees of separation' rings true. I can also confirm that whilst living in the tenements Timothy briefly had designs upon Nell but seeing how clearly devoted she was to his friend Lewis he did not make a move. Had he not so valued this friendship my story would perhaps have had a different conclusion. Timothy returned to England and, after reuniting with his children, they all moved into the house on Ashleigh Grove but more of this in the next chapter.

OCTOBER 1892 THE HOUSE, ASHLEIGH
GROVE, JESMOND, THE O'DOWD FAMILY

*It has been argued that a house has no emotions so therefore it
cannot smile but I choose to contradict this and as a consequence
I can confidently state that on the 2nd October in the year 1892 the
house smiled. Indeed its smile was so wide and broad that the lime
in the pointing between the decorative bricks cracked and the roof
joists groaned as the tiles clattered in merriment. The cause for such
joyous gaiety was the arrival of the O'Dowd family. John my paternal
great grandfather and his two younger siblings raced through the
rooms declaring each more astounding than the next. They paused
for a while at the top of the first flight of stairs and leaning from the
stairwell they shouted in unison their great approval at this choice
of new home. Timothy leant back on his heels gazing upwards at
his three children and smiled as broadly as the house he had just
purchased. The house had been a stretch to his budget and had used
up the majority of the funds he had amassed working in New York,
but he reasoned it had been necessary to make a grand gesture to
fully amend for his absence. He was astounded how much his three
children John William, Mary and Ellen had grown during the two
years he had spent apart from them. John his eldest especially had
noticeably sprouted skywards and was now almost a full head taller
than his father. Timothy had started laying the groundwork for his
new business almost as soon as he docked in Southampton and upon
his return to the North East had acquired premises behind a grocery
store on Salters Road in the Gosforth suburb of Newcastle. It had been
a proud moment indeed as he hung the sign 'Timothy O'Dowd and
Son Lithographers/Signwriters' above the door. This sign had been
John's first foray into the world of signwriting and with his father's
patient tuition he had practiced the brushstrokes for an entire week
before committing them to paint. Timothy had already obtained their
first advertisement commission for the Liverpool Victoria Friendly*

Society and other organisations were following suit and requesting advertising mock-ups. Their success was in part due to the purchase of a state of the art lithography press which was so much better at aligning the images for the characteristic poster designs of the period. Timothy was in fact a tailor by trade which was no doubt why he had so much in common with Lewis when they met in New York but he seems to have had an enviable skill for changing careers and excelling in anything he put his time and concentration into.

Yes, things were looking up for my great-great-grandfather and for the first time since the death of my great-great-grandmother, Elizabeth he felt hope in the future. The house in Ashleigh Grove was a major component of this brilliant fresh start, signalling as it did a new beginning for both Timothy and his family.

DECEMBER 1892, MAESTEG, WALES, LE BRITTON FAMILY

It was a jubilant time for Mary for she was at last with child, and at the stage where she deemed her pregnancy advanced enough to tell Oshbert the joyous news. Oshbert felt a chill run through his bones but he cleverly covered up his trepidation by swinging Mary up in the air and planting a kiss on the side of her cheek. The effigy doll still lay hidden beneath the letter in the tin box and the image of it imprinted itself into Oshbert's mind as he gently patted his wife on the belly and pretended to feel a kick. There had been no further communication from Lemontina, and Oshbert had managed to almost put the whole toxic business behind him but with this news it once again reared its ugly head. It was to his great regret but not altogether unsurprising that he had received no further communication from Lemontina regarding the boy's welfare. Silvanus was still in his heart and the last grainy photograph he had received just before his marriage to Mary still sat in his wallet in the breast pocket of his jacket.

Mary had yet to tell her mother Sophia the blissful news, for at this point of the story I must disclose that they are temporarily estranged. It seems that the gossipmongers had done their job well for they had gleefully spread the news that Sophia had moved into a house of her own, and promptly taken Llewellyn Bevan in as a lodger. Upon hearing this news Mary had marched immediately to Sophia's new home and asked her directly to her face if Llewellyn was more than just a lodger. Understandably, Sophia refused to answer so indelicate a question and as a result tempers flared and voices were raised. Later that evening, Oshbert further inflamed the situation by declaring that perhaps Mary should allow Sophia a personal life, for surely she deserved it after being widowed at such a young age. His apparent lack of support caused the couple to have the second major argument of their marriage and it was not until Oshbert retracted his badly timed opinion that Mary would deign to join him in the marital bed.

Despite this altercation with her daughter I must divulge that Sophia was of blithe spirit and to all intents and purposes Llewellyn and she were indeed living in sin as man and wife. Llewellyn introduced her to a tenderness and intimacy which had been sadly lacking in her marriage of convenience to Lewis. The first throes of a budding romance are always exhilarating, and the added forbidden aspect of this tryst no doubt added to its intensity. It would be churlish of me to pour scorn on this illicit relationship so I will affirm that I am delighted that my great-great-grandmother at last appears to have found a man worthy of her affections.

APRIL 1893 FELTON, NORTHUMBERLAND, O'DOWD FAMILY

It was the weekend before Easter and Timothy and John O'Dowd had been called upon to visit the Stags Head Commercial Hotel in

Felton, a village in the county of Northumberland. The hotel had originally been built in 1869 to cater for travelling salesmen but due to a slight dip in trade it was undertaking a major overhaul. The job promised to be lucrative and well worth the trip from Gosforth, as the two men had been asked to tender a quote for a comprehensive railway poster campaign and a total renewal of the hotel signage. It was a quite an accolade for a fledgling business so Timothy and his son John were appropriately suited and booted to meet their prospective clients. Builders had already started to work on the exterior of the hotel's new facade and it was while Timothy and John were walking through the foyer towards the main front door that a large piece of stone dislodged and hurtled to the ground shattering into sharp pieces. One shard bounced upon the pathway then ricocheted across the cobbles to impale itself in Johns' leg. John immediately fell to the ground clutching his thigh and the wound quite dramatically began to spurt a fountain of blood. Hearing the commotion going on outside, the Manager of the hotel rushed to Johns' aid but he was of a squeamish disposition and of little practical use. In the end it was Timothy himself who ran into the hotel to summon help. He had been told by one of the workmen that the local Dr William Callender could be found in the snug area of the bar availing himself of the hotel's hospitality. The clearly intoxicated Doctor staggered from the entrance of the hotel a few moments later, followed closely by a very concerned Timothy. After inspecting John's leg the doctor declared whilst it was not a terribly serious injury; it would need some stitches to aid recovery. He instructed John to follow him to his Surgery so he could perform the procedure and properly dress the wound. John flanked by his father and the Hotel Manager hobbled down the hill towards the Surgery all the while struggling to keep up with the good Doctors drunken stride. The door to the Surgery was quickly opened by the Doctor's daughter Theresa, a rather sour-faced young girl about the same age as poor John. Theresa quickly ushered them all through a side door and started to lay out the instruments required for the minor surgery. Then after observing her father the Doctor staggering about the room and struggling to form a coherent sentence, Theresa declared to the group that given her father's delicate state it might be prudent if she were to stitch the wound herself. John at this stage was too shocked by the whole event to utter a word or question her directive and he sat as directed in the chair opposite Theresa, wincing as she tore the ripped material of his trousers from his leg. After washing her hands and disinfecting the puncture with alcohol, Theresa confidently set to stitching his wound. Her father had poured himself and John a whiskey to drink prior to the painful procedure and despite previously being teetotal John swigged it back in one. As he swayed slightly in his chair, John concentrated on Theresa's dainty hands skilfully pulling the sides of his damaged skin together. Her brows were furrowed in deep concentration. At this juncture I will add that it was not the first time Theresa or any of her five siblings had been called upon to assist their father, nor would it be the last for unfortunately his drinking was getting out of hand. The previous week, while inebriated he had ridden his horse through the house and the maid had been so traumatised by the occurrence that she had promptly packed her case and left. I am compelled to add at this point that it is well recorded in the annals of family history that my great-great-grandfather was rather too fond of his drink, but in his defence the rural area in which he practiced was not affluent and payment for treatment was often conducted on a barter system. Instead of monetary reward for services rendered, the transaction was often brought to a conclusion with a side of ham or a bottle of whiskey, which I am sure you will concur, is not an ideal bartering tool for a character with such an addictive personality and a fondness for the hard stuff.

While Theresa gently dressed his leg John complimented her handiwork, declaring her an excellent seamstress and that was when Theresa smiled at him for the first time. When she smiled her whole face changed and looking into her eyes John saw warmth he had hitherto overlooked. With a courage possibly fuelled by the whiskey he boldly asked if he could call on her when he was next in the area. By way of an answer she shyly nodded her assent. Driving home in the carriage later that afternoon John turned to his father and declared "Father I have met the girl I will marry." Timothy brushed the comment off as the drink talking but by the time their work on the hotel was completed John was Theresa's swain and she his sweetheart. And that, dear reader, is how my paternal great-grandparents met, although due to circumstances beyond their control they were not to marry until ten years later.

15TH JULY 1893, MAESTEG, WALES, LE BRITTON FAMILY

There was much celebration in the Le Britton house on the day Evelyn Maud made her first appearance in the world. Her birth had been remarkably quick for a first child and she weighed in at a healthy 8lb 4oz. As Oshbert held his newly born daughter in his arms he was overwhelmed by a powerful surge of love for his wife, for although he had not witnessed the birth he had listened to Mary's cries of distress escaping through the thin walls of the bedroom. He had tried at various stages to enter the room and comfort his wife but the village midwife, a formidable lady in her mid-fifties had blocked his path at every juncture, stating that it was no place for a man to be. Mary for her part was grateful to have given her husband his first legitimate child and thankful the baby was not a boy for the spectre of Oshbert's first born son Silvanus was still a constant *elephant in the room*. Oshbert had not known Silvanus as a newborn so he could make no immediate comparisons, but still the guilt of refusing to give his son a stable upbringing remained a constant thorn in his side. Trying desperately to put such thoughts from his mind, Oshbert shrugged on his jacket so he could meet Mary's uncles and grandfather for a celebratory drink to wet the baby's head. Although he did not say as such to his wife he also planned to pop into the Lamb and Flag on his travels so that he could tell Sophia, Mary's estranged mother, of the birth of her first granddaughter. Oshbert was hoping the joyful news would perhaps encourage the two women to forget past arguments and build bridges.

APRIL 1897, FELTON, NORTHUMBERLAND, O'DOWD FAMILY

John O'Dowd was standing by the newly dug grave of Dr William Callender, the man he had hitherto hoped would become his father-in-law. John was flanked on one side by Theresa his betrothed and on the other by her mother Mary. Theresa's siblings Arthur, William, Mary, Francis and Agnes were standing alongside, embracing each other for comfort. As the priest read the eulogy John was suddenly struck by the realisation that now William was dead, and the older siblings had flown the nest, there would only be Theresa to comfort her mother through her bereavement. The couple had planned to ignore her father's objections and marry later that year but these plans were likely to be thwarted by the Doctor's untimely death. John had been constant in his four years of courting Theresa and despite her father's constant refusal to acknowledge his requests for permission to marry, his ardour had not dampened at all. Theresa throughout the long engagement had been similarly firm in her affections refusing to be swayed by her father's constant criticism of her intended. John had known from the onset of their relationship that he was not Theresa's social equal and her father had made no secret of the fact that he had in mind for her to marry a local Doctor of his acquaintance. Theresa's family were descended from a long line of doctors and surgeons going back well into the 1700s and, although John was now successful and the business was going swimmingly, William was constantly reminding Theresa of the fact that settling to become the wife of a lithographer would never match the prestige of being the wife of a doctor.

Dr William Callender had been thrown from a horse during one of his extended drinking binges and had died instantly from a broken neck. His wife Mary, whilst grieving for her lost husband, was also gratified that his death had come about before his date to appear at a General Medical Council Hearing. The doctor had been summoned on an accusation of medical malpractice linked to his excessive consumption of alcohol and rumours were soon circulating throughout the village that perhaps William had deliberately risked jumping the high fence in the hope that he would be injured and excused from attending. Mary herself suspected this was the case but strongly denied it as she didn't want to destroy what little reputation he had left. It grieves me to say this, but William's family had long since tired of his drunken shenanigans and far from being distraught at his death they saw it as a blessing to be spared the shame of their father being struck off. In fact, the only person grieving at the graveside was John and his grief was not for the man being lowered into the ground but for his own wedding which would once again be put on hold. It was to be six more years before John could finally call Theresa his wife but as he never tired of telling her, he would have waited an eternity to make her his own.

16TH DECEMBER 1894, MAESTEG, WALES, LE BRITTON FAMILY

It is with a heavy heart that I write this next chapter, so I will first start by imparting the good news and announce the birth of Mary and Oshbert's second child Gladys Martha on the 16th December

1894 and then follow on with the heartbreaking news that this happy birth took place a few months after the death of their dearly loved first born 'baby Evie'. Records show her death was attributed to a suspected case of measles but Oshbert in his distressed state convinced himself that it was linked in some way to the doll hidden in his tin box. Superstition is an irrational fear but even the most sceptical can be convinced supernatural forces are at large if enough *supposed proof* is set before them. A few weeks prior to 'baby Evie's' premature death Oshbert had received a cryptic message foretelling of a misfortune about to befall his happy family. He presumed this to be from Lemontina's mother and when he had hidden it in the tin box alongside the other letter he had noticed what looked like tiny pinprick spots on the torso of the effigy doll. Dismissing them at the time as an imperfection in the material their appearance took on a more sinister significance when it was confirmed that 'baby Evie' had perished with the deadly measles virus. From that day forward Oshbert blamed himself and his selfish actions for any misfortune that befell his family and his every waking moment was haunted by the tragic death of his first daughter.

On the 15th July 1897, the couple were blessed with another daughter who they named Lily May. Bizarrely she was to share the same birthday as dearly departed 'baby Evie' and this bad omen drove Mary to suffer from a complete nervous breakdown. Today, she would no doubt be diagnosed with postnatal depression and prescribed a mild tranquillizer and cognitive behavioural therapy but in the 1890s the normal treatment was incarceration in a Mental Asylum. Mental Asylums in the late 1800s were not the progressive places they are now and to be committed to such an institution carried a dreadful stigma for the entire family. Also the emerging treatments, such as lobotomies, were still in experimental stages so treatments consisted of restraint and little else. As a result once someone was placed in such an institution they rarely left. To his credit Oshbert had the foresight to fetch Mary's mother, Sophia, who once she fully realised the severity of the situation moved in to care for the children and her daughter. I am now happy to report that in the fullness of time Mary made a complete recovery and with love, rest and gentle encouragement she regained full mental capacity. Oshbert was bravely holding his precious family together although he did have a brief wobble himself when he peered in the tin box and saw the spots on the torso of the effigy doll had disappeared only to be replaced by a pin in its forehead. My great-grandfather must have had a Herculean strength of character for the sorcery dwelling in the doll might have caused him to question his attitudes and confirmed belief in the supernatural.

AUGUST 1899, MAESTEG, WALES, LE BRITTON FAMILY

A good few years had passed by, and Mary and Oshbert's two little girls were respectively now aged five and two. Mary was heavily with child once again and rapidly nearing her estimated time of confinement so she was grateful when one sunny Sunday late in the month of August, Oshbert offered to take his daughters out for the day so she might rest a while. Mary quickly packed a makeshift picnic for her little family then settled down on the bed to have some much needed rest.

Oshbert ambled up the cobbled street tightly holding the hands of his precious daughters, a constant smile playing upon his features. He was a man on a mission for unbeknown to Mary he had agreed to a secret assignation with Lemontina. There had been a slight thawing of hostilities of late and Lemontina had started to send him regular updates on his son Silvanus once again. It was in fact she who had proposed they meet at a designated spot by the side of a disused railway track. She had promised to bring their son so Oshbert could spend the day with him and Silvanus would have a chance to meet his half-siblings. Oshbert had been sceptical at first, suspecting foul play, but Lemontina had assured him that the previous letters and effigy doll were the work of her now departed mother and she personally wished him and his wife no ill. It was quite a hike to the place they had planned to meet and Gladys and Lily took turns having piggy backs from their father. When they reached the spot Oshbert laid a blanket on the grass verge and the two children ran off to play nearby. Shielding his eyes from the glare of the blazing sun, Oshbert grinned widely as he listened to the squeals of laughter from where the little girls were playing. He must have sat there a good hour before he slowly came to the realisation that Lemontina was not going to meet him, although at this stage I must confirm that he did not believe that he had been tricked and presumed that she had been held up somewhere. He laid out the picnic that Mary had prepared and called for his daughters to join him. When they did not appear he got to his feet and walked across towards where they were playing by the disused railway track. Oshbert let out an exclamation of horror when he realised they were playing with a dead cat. The two little girls were cradling it in their tiny arms like a baby and then showering its squashed dead face with kisses. They quickly dropped it when they saw how angry their father was and both children promptly burst into petulant tears. Oshbert kicked the dead animal away into the bushes and after collecting the untouched picnic the family began to make their way back home. I must remark at this stage that hygiene was not then the issue it now is and I fear the girls may have snacked on the picnic lunch as they wound their way back through the country lanes to the village. I make this assumption because the girls were soon taken very ill indeed with the acute and highly contagious disease of Diphtheria and I have no doubt that they caught it from handling the dead cat. I won't go into details about the disease save to say that it proved to be fatal and by the 4th of September both little girls had unfortunately lost their lives. This part of the book is heart wrenching to write, but I am compelled to disclose the details correctly, so I will add that on the 6th September poor Mary gave birth to her first son while her two little girls lay in their coffins at the foot of the bed. Oshbert junior was named after his father and was so alike the three girls they had lost that both his mother and father initially found it impossible to form a bond with him. Sophia took to the helm once again and sitting by the fireside she gently rocked the tiny infant to sleep as his parents sat side by side on the bed – with the two toddlers coffins in full sight - and cried until they had no tears left to cry.

It was not until after his precious little girls were buried in the graveyard alongside their older sister 'baby Evie' that Oshbert received his next letter from Lemontina. I can disclose that although I call it a letter, it was in fact just a scrap of paper and crudely drawn on the paper was an outline of a cat. It was upon its receipt that Oshbert knew the dead cat had been placed there by Lemontina herself. He further realised that he had never really known her at all, for theirs had been a brief courtship with no shared confidences or declarations of love. I can also confirm that it was at that moment that Oshbert made the decision that he would cut all ties with both Lemontina and Silvanus. He further decided to move his remaining family to a place of safety far away from Maesteg and Wales. A place where Lemontina and her cruel taunting would never find him or his darling wife and son.

JANUARY 1901, THE HOUSE, ASHLEIGH GROVE, JESMOND, LE BRITTONS AND THE O'DOWDS

It was moving day and Oshbert and his family were travelling from Wales to complete the purchase of their new home on Ashleigh Grove. The previous owner Timothy O'Dowd and his son John had just the previous day packed up the last of their belongings and said a fond farewell to the house. It had been a fine family home but once the girls had moved out – to marry and set up their own homes – it was just too large and too capacious. Their voices had echoed through the empty rooms and the upkeep of such a massive home was impractical. Timothy had briefly flirted with the idea of offering the empty rooms to lodgers but once he realised the extra housekeeping this would entail he quickly dismissed this idea. So it was after much deliberation that the men had cut their losses and moved into a Tyneside flat on Salters Road in the nearby suburb of Gosforth. The ground floor flat was just a stone's throw from their place of work so it was an excellent solution all around. Although he hadn't voiced this as such to his son, Timothy had only stayed in the house for as long as he did, because he had hoped John would take it over once he married his sweetheart Theresa. But despite the couple being engaged for so long, and Theresa's father being dead for four years, they still seemed to be no further forward in their plans. The fly in the ointment was Theresa's mother Mary who seemed to constantly throw a spanner in the works. Theresa was desperate to set the date – for she was worried John would tire of waiting patiently in the wings – but whenever she brought the subject up her mother would suddenly become violently ill with some new mysterious ailment. These ailments, which inevitably baffled the medical profession, had a habit of clearing up almost instantaneously once Theresa backed down and retracted her insistence to set the date.

Oshbert was thrilled to finally say goodbye to his old life in Maesteg. He had been offered a brilliant job at The Liverpool Victoria Legal Friendly Society in Newcastle upon Tyne, and as the icing on the cake, Mary was pregnant once again. Things seemed to be looking up for his family at last and Oshbert was hoping this fresh start would help to put the past few heartbreaking years behind them. Of course the effigy doll and the letters still remained and they were a constant thorn in his side. He had considered destroying these toxic manifestations of evil on many occasions – most especially after the deaths of his two little daughters - but an irrational fear of even worse repercussions befalling his remaining family prevented him from actually doing so. So the tin box was carefully removed from its hiding place and packed away, a constant reminder of how he had failed his precious family.

THE HOUSE, ASHLEIGH GROVE, JESMOND

Once again the house had reason to gloat as his new owners Mary and Oshbert excitedly walked from room to room - opening doors and peering inside his cavernous cupboards - all the while declaring how beautiful and grand he was. Later on when Oshbert lit a fire in the lounge the house huffed and puffed and bragged his joyful news to his sister at the other end of the Grove whilst the Tyneside flats sandwiched in-between secretly seethed with jealousy. Mary had been understandably gobsmacked at the grandeur of the house for she still couldn't quite believe that Oshbert's new job would sustain such a lifestyle. On the train journey across from Wales, Oshbert had hinted he was thinking of employing a maid to assist her with the day to day chores and help with the new baby once it arrived. Mary had never in her life mixed in the same circles with anyone who had cause to employ a maid, so it seemed a very wasteful thing to do, but Oshbert insisted that it would befit their new station in life and, as if to prove his point, hadn't the attic rooms in the eaves of the house been fitted out for this very purpose. Whilst Mary pottered about in the kitchen with Oshbert junior gurgling in her arms, her husband tiptoed upstairs into those attic rooms to try and find a secure place to hide the tin box. He was fortunate for one of the bricks high up in the eaves had worked slightly loose - no doubt while the house was having its interloper attached all those years ago - so Oshbert squeezed the tip of his penknife between the mortar of the joints and eased a corner of the brick out. There was just enough space in the wall cavity to tuck the tin box securely behind before replacing the brick. Hopefully if he put a dressing table or a wall hung mirror against the wall the missing cement would not be noticed or remarked upon. The very second the tin box was placed in the cavity the house began to shiver with a deep foreboding and unexplained trepidation. It felt as if a cancerous growth was spreading its noxious fumes deep into its very foundations and the bones of the pilgrim shifted in their resting place in acknowledgment of the presence of pure evil.

MARCH 1903, CHURCH OF ST. MARY, FELTON, O'DOWD FAMILY

John's grin was as wide as the Church doorway for it was finally the day of his marriage to his sweetheart Theresa. Timothy his father had tried his best to calm him down but nothing could stop John dancing a merry jig as he raced up the steps and towards the steeply gabled south porch. Later as he stood proudly at the altar, his heart beating wildly in his chest he could still hardly believe that in barely an hour Theresa would be his wife. He confessed at times that he had wondered if this day would ever come about. Ten years was a long engagement by anyone's standards but Theresa's mother was a stubborn old coot and had made it her life's ambition to put obstacles constantly in the couple's path. She had finally given her blessing upon the proviso she was allowed to move in with the newlyweds and John had reluctantly caved in.

As Theresa walked up the aisle on the arm of her sister's husband Dr Tom Dewell, John's breath caught in his throat. He had never wavered in his love and patient commitment throughout the years but if he ever needed proof that the long wait had been worth it, this was it. Theresa looked radiant, her carefully stitched dress emphasised the slim curve of her hip and the gentle slope of her breast. She was every inch the blooming bride. John's beaming smile spoke of his devotion and there was not a dry eye in the congregation. In fact, that's a lie for there were two dry eyes, those of Theresa's mother who even until the night before had been trying to get her daughter to change her mind and agree to marry a more suitable suitor. But just as she had been throughout the long courtship, Theresa was steadfast and firm in her intentions and her mother finally appeared to have conceded defeat. I like to think that she had slowly come to understand the deep love the couple shared but I suspect it was much more likely that she understood when she was beaten and realised that unless she agreed to the nuptials going ahead, she would lose her youngest daughter and faithful companion for ever. After the ceremony the couple spent their wedding night in the local Stags Head Commercial Hotel before moving into their newly purchased home in Jesmond with their mother-in-law in tow.

APRIL 1903 THE HOUSE, ASHLEIGH GROVE, JESMOND, LE BRITTON FAMILY

Time has moved rapidly on for the Le Britton family. Oshbert is now a firm fixture in the Liverpool Victoria office on Blackett street as he has rapidly climbed the ranks due in no little part to his hard work and diligence. The couple have now been blessed with three children, their daughter Anita having been born soon after they moved into the new house and their second son Lewis Isaac quite recently in February 1903. Their oldest son Junior is now almost four so the house is filled to the rafters. True to his word - just after Mary gave birth to their daughter Anita - Oshbert interviewed and employed a young housemaid called Susie. Susie lives in the two attic rooms high up in the eaves of the house and her happy demeanour has brought a joyful ambience to the building. The tin box is still hidden behind the loose brick in the wall and Oshbert himself has purchased a large dressing table with a high mirror to hide it from sight. Since they moved into the house Oshbert has had little reason to remove or check on the effigy doll and on waking each morning he sometimes even manages to forget its existence, but some random thought always invades his conscious mind and a dark shadow passes over his cheerful disposition.

Susie had never mentioned it to either of her employers - as she held no truck with the supernatural in any of its guises - but sometimes as she lay in her bed late in the evening she sensed a presence in the room. She had never actually seen anything untoward but as she lay in that state which is halfway between consciousness and sleep, she was aware of a pressure bearing down upon her chest. She always managed to wake up and persuade herself that it was a result of a gobbled late in the evening snack. Likewise she convinced herself that the strange groaning sounds which awoke her in the early hours of the morning were just the ordinary sounds of a house stretching and waking to greet the dawn. When she had visited her mother one weekend Susie made mention of these strange goings on - fully expecting her mother to wave them away as stuff and nonsense - but her mother had instead hotfooted away to seek the advice of the local priest. The priest had been sufficiently concerned to have blessed a string of rosary beads and instructed Susie to hang them where she felt the malevolent atmosphere was most present. And so the rosary beads hung from the corner of the mirror of her dressing table, swaying lightly in the breeze whenever she opened her bedroom door. The pilgrim's bones deep in the foundations of the house rearranged themselves to form the shape of a cross and between them these two factors managed to improve the atmosphere in the bedroom a hundred fold.

Susie had proved herself to be a godsend to the young family and was well worth her weight in gold as she had lifted Mary's spirits and avoided any repercussions of the baby blues. Oshbert had been concerned for his wife's mental health after the scare they had following the birth of their third daughter Lily May and so he had charged Susie with the task of nipping any potential meltdowns in the bud. As a result, Susie and Mary were now firm friends and occasionally Oshbert had reason to remind Mary that Susie was in their employ and they were paying her to do the heavy jobs around the house. The house was now filled with happy children's laughter and the patter of tiny feet charging through the hallways. Mary and Susie had woken especially early that crisp April morning in 1903. The older children had been washed and dressed in their Sunday best in anticipation of their special visitor and Mary sat nursing baby Lewis Isaac as Susie changed the sheets on the bed in the guest bedroom. The children were very excited as they were expecting a visit from Sophia, their Welsh grandmother. At this point I will disclose that mother and daughter were speaking again although part of this thawing of hostilities was due to Sophia making no reference to her lodger Llewellyn. Sophia always made a point of visiting alone and much to the children's glee, she would always arrive laden with special gifts. This visit was to prove no exception as she had brought some tin soldiers for Junior, a skipping rope for Anita and a brightly decorated wooden rattle for the new baby. Sophia had also stopped off in town - after alighting from the train - and purchased a jam filled Victoria sponge for their morning cup of tea. Susie quickly put the kettle on and the three ladies sat compatibly around the kitchen table in the parlour. Baby Lewis Isaac began to gripe so Mary gave him a little top-up feed before handing him to her mother so she could have a little cuddle of her new grandson before taking him into the next room to lay him down in his cradle for a nap. The two older children were playing quietly on the rug with Junior's toy soldiers and Sophia kissed both of her precious grandchildren on the top of their heads before returning once again to the parlour. As she sat down at the table she declared that two older children were playing quite happily together and the baby was fast asleep and 'dead to the world'. The three ladies sat chatting away and Mary professed the Victoria sponge to be quite the nicest she had ever tasted. They sat like this for quite a while – Susie getting up at some stage to warm the pot and fetch more milk – with the sounds of the children playing in the next room filtering through the open doorway. At first when Junior came into the parlour and pulled at his mother's skirt Mary had ignored him, but as he pulled more persistently upon it Mary turned and enquired, "whatever is the matter child?"

"Baby Lewis Isaac is making strange noises and he is spoiling our game mamma." Junior replied.

This sentence immediately filled Mary with dread and she raced into the next room followed closely by Susie and Sophia. I am once again at a heartbreaking stage in this story and I must disclose that baby Lewis Isaac perished that day. The general consensus was that young Anita had threaded the skipping rope though the bars of the cot and it had somehow got entangled in the baby's sheets. Mary was understandably distraught and in her anger banished her poor mother from her house. She needed someone to blame in the fallout from this dreadful accident and her mother had prophesised the baby's death by uttering the age old idiom 'dead to the world.' Sophia had also bought the skipping rope for Anita so in her eyes she was wholly culpable. It is very sad but from this dreadful day in April, Mary refused to have anything more to do with her mother. Oshbert still sent regular letters and photographs to his mother-in-law in Wales so she knew of their growing family and a little of their life, but the precious bond she had once shared with her only daughter was forever severed. Sophia went on to marry her lodger Llewellyn Bevan on 20th December 1905 and although deliriously happy to be Llewellyn's wife at last, she felt the pain of her daughter's absence. I wish I could finish this little chapter with a happier outcome for the Le Britton family but sometimes, dear reader, life is like this, it gives us lemons and they are nothing more, nothing less, than lemons.

1903, HIGHBURY, JESMOND, NEWCASTLE UPON TYNE, O'DOWD FAMILY

With financial help from his mother-in-law, John O'Dowd had just completed the purchase of his first home as a married man. The house was on a street called Highbury in West Jesmond and in those days cost the princely sum of £600. Today the house would be priced at over £600,000 but once again I digress. I must add that the house was a very desirable property in a very desirable neighbourhood especially for a newly married couple. Theresa's mother had loaned the couple the money for the deposit from the inheritance left to her from her husband's estate, and they were under the impression that the money came with strings attached. The couple duly converted the front part of the ground floor of the house into a granny flat for Theresa's mother and she would sit in her chair in the bay window watching the world go by. In 1905 the area was much less developed than it is now and she had an almost uninterrupted view right across the fields towards the Town Moor. When the travelling funfair 'The Hoppings' arrived in the last week of June she would have had a bird's eye view of Temperance Fair and would no doubt have spend the entire week complaining about the bright lights, noise and the throngs of working-class people strolling past the house en route for the West Jesmond train station. John had persuaded his father Timothy to relocate their business and they were now proud owners of a workshop located on the back lane behind bustling Brentwood Avenue. The parade of shops was a very popular shopping destination for the residents of West Jesmond as it housed an ironmonger, grocer, butcher and on the corner, just before the turnoff for Forsyth Road Bridge the Brentwood Tea Rooms. Theresa found it quite easy to persuade her mother to take the short walk down Ashleigh Grove if she suggested a visit to the genteel Tea Rooms, for her mother enjoyed the company of the other customers, who she referred to as 'women of equal social standing. The owners of the Tea Rooms were two elderly sisters who had grown up in West Jesmond and still lived in the original family house on Highbury. After baby Annie passed away, they would regularly visit their young neighbour Theresa, bringing with them a vast array of fancy cakes and scones in an effort to tempt her dwindling appetite. Mildred, the older of the two ladies, had been so moved by Theresa's state after the baby died that she had swept the young Theresa under her wing. To ease her through her bereavement Mildred had taken it upon herself to teach Theresa the delicate art of sugar craft. Theresa surprised herself and her tutor with her aptitude for the craft and in no time at all her dainty hands were creating the most marvellous icing designs. Occasionally, the twins would call upon her to ice a cake for a special wedding or christening and this was how she came to perfect her piping skills. Royal Icing was a most complicated icing to work successfully. It had become increasingly popular after Queen Victoria's bakers had used lavish amounts of it on her wedding cake in 1840 and it was still very much in demand as a result. Theresa's mother far from being glad her grieving daughter had a distraction made no bones about the fact that she did not approve of Theresa accepting employment in this way. She remarked more than once – deliberately loudly so John could hear – that it was hardly surprising given the social class her daughter had chosen to marry into. John was just grateful his wife had an interest beyond the housekeeping for he had been very concerned when she taken to her bed after Annie's death. His brother-in-law, Dr Tom Dewell, had declared Theresa's new found interest to be a life saver for her malaise had been so severe he had worried she may need medical intervention.

I've mentioned Annie in the last paragraph and now it is time for me to impart more heart wrenching news. Theresa had fallen pregnant within the first few years of their marriage. Annie was a sickly baby from the onset for she suffered greatly from colic. She developed a tendency to grizzle incessantly during the day then wail and cry throughout the night, causing both her parents and grandmother many sleepless nights. But despite this sleep deprivation both Theresa and John were overwhelmed with love for the infant and, often in the early hours of the morning, John would walk through the house rocking his daughter in his arms and whispering to the little girl about the brilliant future which lay ahead. One morning the couple awoke temporarily bemused that they had slept through the night. Annie was laid in the cot at the foot of their bed very still and very silent. Too still and too silent; for she had perished in the night as her parents slumbered. I am tearful writing this and so upset that both my maternal and paternal grandparents went through similar ordeals. Such ordeals are inconceivable to imagine and I am just grateful they recovered in time. After a suitable period of grieving, Theresa fell pregnant once more with my grandfather Lewis Joseph. Lewis was I believe a much more robust infant, but saying this, his parents were so anxious that he would suffer a similar fate to his older sister that, for the first few months of his life, they took turns to watch over him as he slept. The young couple did not properly relax until Lewis was toddling around the furniture for by then they had another son whom they named John junior.

John's father Timothy was now looking so much older than his years. He had undergone a particularly nasty bout of influenza earlier on in the year and never really recovered to full health. Theresa and John had tried to talk him into moving into the house on Highbury so they could look after him – the house was large so they had spare rooms. Whilst grateful for the offer, Timothy had replied honestly that it was hard enough being in the company of Theresa's mother on social occasions and he couldn't promise to hold his tongue if she belittled his son in his presence. So Timothy struggled on, living by himself in the flat on Salters Road. He walked the mile and a half to work then back every day, only once remarking wistfully on how helpful it would have been if they had decided to relocate their business whilst living in the house on Ashleigh Grove for he could have rolled across the road in his nightclothes if they had. Timothy had remained strong and steady when baby Annie had died. He had saved his tears for when he was alone in his flat and upon hearing the news he had hastily painted over the signage he had been working on as a christening gift for his granddaughter. The sign had read *'Timothy O'Dowd, son and granddaughter Lithographers/Sign writers'* and Timothy had planned to present it to his son and his new wife as a joke on the day of her christening.

The Signwriting business was going very well indeed and small jobs were proving to be the bread and butter of their workload. Just the previous week the chap who had moved into Timothy's old house on Ashleigh Grove had popped in and ordered a sign for a bench he was making as a surprise for his wife. I wonder what Timothy would have said had he known that the wife in question was the daughter of Lewis Davies his old friend from New York? We will never know for I seriously doubt such a conversation came up, for why should it?

1905, THE HOUSE, ASHLEIGH GROVE, JESMOND, LE BRITTON FAMILY

Oshbert was not by nature a practical man which is probably one of the reasons why the art of tailoring had never fully suited his skillset. He was much more at home with a ledger and fountain pen, finding a strange comfort in the predictability of numbers. But despite this, he had every evening for the last month been taking himself out of the house and walking down the backyard to the shed beside the outside privy and coal bunker. Mary and Susie had both taken the oath not to enter the shed and, as Mary later remarked to Susie, this strange request was easy to adhere to for why would either of them want to? Susie was curious as to what the strange hammering and sawing noises were but despite visiting the privy – which adjoined the shed - every evening before bedtime she too kept her promise. Oshbert was making his wife a special bench for the small front garden so she could sit in the sunshine watching their two young children as they played hopscotch on the pavement. The plaque he had ordered from Timothy O'Dowd the signwriter was a memorial for the four children the couple had lost at such tender ages. Oshbert could have paid to have had the bench made but he wanted to work the wood himself so the gift would mean more to his wife. Once it was finished it was very sturdy indeed and after he had screwed the plaque carefully to the back panel, he called Susie from the house to help him carry it around from the back lane to its final resting place in front of the bay window. Oshbert took one of Anita's ribbons and tied it in a bow before leading his wife gently into the front garden. Mary closed her eyes tightly and gasped with delight as she spied the brightly coloured bench. She later remarked to Susie that Oshbert could have spent a king's ransom on diamonds but nothing would have pleased her more than the wooden bench made with his own two hands. I have just this week been outside in my own garden and sanded this very bench. I have also repainted it in its original shade of canary yellow. I am so happy to report that it is still in regular use over a hundred years after my great-grandfather built it. Yes, it is looking worse for wear and the wording on the plaque is fading in places but like my great- grandmother Mary before me I would not trade the bench for all the tea in China.

MARCH 1906 SALTERS ROAD, GOSFORTH, O'DOWD FAMILY

Life was looking up for Timothy; his son John and wife Theresa were due to have another child in a matter of weeks and their business was going from strength to strength. He had left work early that day in March as his heartburn was playing up again and the tight feeling in his chest was getting worse. He had struggled on the walk home and the usual half-an-hour journey had taken him the better part of an hour. He was so breathless that he stopped for a while to sit on a low garden wall at the bottom of Salters Road, and that is where a passer-by found him a short while later. Timothy had toppled backwards into a rose bush and was lying among the thorny stems clutching his chest. My great-great-grandfather was only fifty eight which is ironically the same age I am today, as I sit at my computer writing this novel. Timothy was buried a week later alongside his beloved granddaughter Annie in All Saints Cemetery on Jesmond Road. Coincidentally, the same year that Timothy died, a baby girl named Kate was born in the Tyne Dock area of South Tyneside. I mention this young girl because when she later went on to marry, she took the name of Catherine Cookson. During the 1980s she and her husband Tom – a school teacher – lived in a house in Eslington Terrace in Jesmond. It was here that she penned a large number of her hundred and ten published novels. It is widely rumoured that when she couldn't think of a name for a particular character she would wander around the graves in All Saints Cemetery searching for inspiration, which I imagine is how one of the characters in her books is named Timothy O'Dowd. I myself lived in Jesmond around this time in the 1980s and it pains me to say - for I fear it may be sacrilege - but I would often sit and breastfeed my eldest daughter Katie in that very graveyard. I would always sit on a bench opposite Annie and Timothy's graves and even now I can clearly remember one morning smiling through the headstones at an elderly bespectacled woman, who was randomly wandering around reading inscriptions and jotting stuff in a notebook. It wasn't until much later on and after my children were grown-up and after I had read a couple of her books, that I realised the full significance of this chance encounter.

JUNE 1906, ASHLEIGH GROVE,
JESMOND, LE BRITTON FAMILY

It was the last week of June and almost overnight the Town Moor had transformed from an open expanse of grass with a few grazing cows to a veritable explosion of noise and colour, heralding the arrival of the annual Temperance Fair. Since the fair's first appearance in 1892 its name had slowly evolved and it was now generally known as The Hoppings. Apparently the new name came about as an indirect reference to the clothing the travellers wore because as the cloth was inevitably infested with fleas, the travellers would jump, twitch and hop around the fairground. The weeklong event was as popular in 1906 as it is today, and children would continually pester and plead with their parents for a chance to visit. Oshbert's children were no exception and they pestered and pleaded to such an extent that he decided to take a day's annual holiday so that the family could spend a sunny afternoon at the funfair. The children ran a few yards ahead of their parents, squealing in delighted excitement as they raced towards their favourite ride. When they reached the rope-operated 'Shuggy Boats' the two youngsters clambered into one side and Oshbert grudgingly climbed into the other. The 'Shuggy Boat' was essentially just a glorified swing but the children seemed to enjoy it and begged Oshbert to allow them to have another go. He felt a bit nauseous but the children had him wound around their tiny fingers so he reluctantly agreed. Mary shot him a sympathetic look before ambling off to wander around the rest of the fair. She stopped for a while beside the row of gypsy wagons. They were lined up on the outskirts of the field slightly removed from the actual rides. Elaborately decorated in rich tones of red, greens and gold many had tent-like awnings attached to the sides with handwritten signs advertising crystal ball and tarot card readings. Never having seen a fortune teller, let alone visited one, Mary was intrigued and she stood a while watching the women in headscarves standing outside their tents trying to encourage people to have a reading. Mary had not been standing there very long, before Oshbert and the children raced across to her side, the children frantically asking if they could 'please please' have a Candy Floss. Candy Floss was a new addition to The Hoppings having just been introduced at the St Louis World's Fair in 1904 and the children were desperate to try this sticky sweet treat. Mary told the children they could try one but she added if it spoilt their tea she would not be happy. The children promised they would clear their plates and quickly took the coins from Oshbert and ran across to the vendor before she changed her mind. A small group of scruffy looking urchins aged in their early teens were playing marbles behind one of the rides and seeing Oshbert with his hand in his pocket, one of the more cocksure boys decided to chance his luck and cheekily asked Oshbert if he too could have money for a candy floss. Mary waved her arms and shooed the flea ridden youngster away but Oshbert was in an altruistic mood so he reached further into his pocket for some loose change to give the youngster. The young lad grabbed the coins then darted off towards the wagons, his rowdy gang of friends swiftly following in his wake. The lads made quite a commotion whooping and caterwauling as they ran off into the distance. A swarthy looking woman in a brightly coloured shawl popped her head out of one of the tents directly opposite where Oshbert and Mary stood and she shouted angrily across at the young lads telling them to 'shut up.' Oshbert almost sank to his knees in shock as he recognised Lemontina. Fearing she would spot him and cause an embarrassing confrontation, he dipped his bowler hat further over his forehead before turning abruptly away to usher his family from the scene. It was not until they were walking away from the caravans that he realised, in all probability, the young cocky lad had been his own son Silvanus. Mary huffed and puffed as they walked away for she had been planning to ask Oshbert if she could have her fortune told – just for a bit of fun - but the suddenly stern look on Oshbert's face told her not to bother.

As he lay in bed that night Oshbert replayed the scene over and over in his mind asking himself if Lemontina's expression had altered at all when she saw him. By the next morning Oshbert had convinced himself that, of course, Lemontina had not recognised him, for she had not expected to see him and had no idea he had relocated to Newcastle. He left for work the next day at his usual time, checking his immaculately waxed moustache in the hallway mirror as he did every morning. Mary stood in the doorway and waved until he had turned the corner onto Brentwood Avenue as she did every morning. As it was such a lovely day Susie and she had decided to turn out one of the guest bedrooms, so she went straight upstairs leaving the two children to have their breakfast in the kitchen. Later on, the youngsters went outside into the yard to play with some tin cars while Susie and Mary put the bed sheets through the mangle so they would dry more quickly in the morning sunshine. It was Susie who first heard the persistent knocking at the front door, but it was Mary who answered because Susie was up to her elbows in dripping wet washing at the time. As Mary opened the door she jumped back in surprise as one of the Romany women from the funfair thrust a bunch of lucky heather wrapped in string into her hands. Once Mary had regained her composure, she realised that this would be an excellent opportunity to have her fortune told and asked the woman if this was possible. After setting her price the gypsy woman followed Mary into the hallway just in time to see Susie coming through from the kitchen drying her hands on a towel. Susie rolled her eyes and shook her head for she had no time for such nonsense, but Mary was adamant, so she went back into the kitchen to collect two dining chairs while Mary fetched a card table from the parlour. From deep in the layers of her shawl the woman produced a round glass ball which she placed reverently in the centre of the card table before she rested her hands upon its surface and began to chant. The words she chanted were not recognisable words – for she was speaking in the ancient language of tongues - neither Mary or Susie had heard it spoken before and they both presumed the women to be speaking in her native language. I will add that although the phenomenon of speaking in tongues is thought to have its origins in Christianity, it goes back to pre-Christian pagan practices, where it was believed it could summon the spirits of the deceased. As if to prove this point the effigy doll in the tin box began to rattle alarmingly behind the brick in the attic eaves but there was no-one in ear shot to hear its awakening. Then the bones of the Pilgrim shifted and altered, agitating the earth beneath the foundations of the house as they did so but again no one but the house itself was aware of this commotion. After what seemed like a very long time, but was in all probability less than five minutes, the woman stopped her incessant chanting and with no preamble to warn of her intentions she stretched across the table to grab Mary's hand in hers. Initially Mary flinched, for the gypsy woman's hands were icy cold and the abruptness of the actions had taken her quite by surprise. Once she realised that the woman planned to read her palm, Mary forced herself to relax her tensed fingers and allowed her hand to be turned palm upwards. This was even more disconcerting for after a quick glance at her palm the woman stared at Mary. Her stare was so intense and uncomfortable that Mary was compelled to dip her head. The woman started to speak. She muttered her words so quietly that at first Mary suspected she was speaking in that strange foreign language once again, but as she strained to hear, she managed to attune to certain precise words. Mary gasped with alarm and snatched her hand roughly away as she realised the woman was talking of the four babies she had lost and the ongoing curse which had caused their untimely deaths. The woman continued undeterred and her voice rose until she was almost shouting out her dreadful predictions. More heartbreak was to follow – she shrieked - and beware of the man who kept the secrets for he was the true instigator of the tragedies. It was at

83

this stage that Susie - who had been standing quietly observing the proceedings - intervened. She could see how upset poor Mary was becoming at these latest revelations and knew she must take action before they got even more out of hand. Firstly Susie, swung open the lounge door - and as the sunlight flooded the passageway the scene was not so sinister - then she scooped up the crystal ball and flung it in a most unladylike manner in the direction of the gypsy woman whilst simultaneously shooing her from the house. Mary was reduced to tears and had slumped in her chair, so Susie took her in her arms repeating over and over the mantra that it was all just 'mumbo jumbo' and not to read anything into it, these people were practiced actresses and it had merely been a stellar performance. Mary eventually calmed and nodded in agreement, before saying that emotions had got the better of her and she would go upstairs and sort herself out before the children came back indoors. Susie went outside to check on the children, relieved that they were still calmly playing with their tin cars. The back yard gate was swinging open on its hinges but when she questioned the children they shrugged and claimed they had no idea why. Deciding to let sleeping dogs lie, Susie ushered them indoors for a bite to eat.

When Oshbert returned home from work that evening, he went straight upstairs to wish his children good night as he did every evening, for Oshbert was not a typical Edwardian father and actually enjoyed the company of his offspring. Sitting with the children on his lap - after reading their favourite chapter from *Alice's Adventures in Wonderland* for about the millionth time - he enquired about their day. The children chattered as children do, then they mentioned the young boy from the funfair who had played 'cars' with them in the back yard that afternoon whilst his mother visited theirs. Oshbert could barely contain his shock as the youngsters went on to say that the boy had said he was their brother but had asked them not to say anything to their parents. When Oshbert fell silent, Anita piped up that perhaps her new brother had fallen down a rabbit hole and that was how their father had lost him. Junior followed up this rather vivid assumption by stating that he hoped their brother would come back to play the following day.

Later, as Oshbert sat in the dining room eating his dinner, he nonchalantly asked Mary how her day had been and noticed that both she and Susie were reticent and sheepish in their replies. Later on that evening, fearing Lemontina planned some further ill upon his family, Oshbert declared that he would be going out for a short walk around the block to settle his stomach. Striding up the Grove and along Highbury towards the Town Moor he had not a plan in mind, but he felt compelled to see Lemontina and plead with her to leave him alone. His furious anger at how she had placed the dead cat for his two daughters to find and play with was not diluted in any way, but he reasoned that begging her forgiveness was the only way he could protect what remained of his family. Oshbert reached the fairground site ten minutes later and squeezed under the makeshift fence which had been erected by the travellers. The fairground in darkness had an air of suppressed hostility about it and groups of men stood huddled, smoking by the rides and sideshows. One such group shouted across to him and when he ignored them they formed a posse of sorts and chased him through the field. At this stage, I will add that Oshbert was not an especially sporty man and like a majority of gentlemen of that era was unused to physical exercise, but that evening it was as if he had grown wings on the soles of his feet as he outran men half his age. He only slowed down as he reached the place Lemontina's wagon had been parked the previous afternoon. To his dismay the wagon and its occupants had disappeared and all that remained behind was a flattened rectangle of grass. Suddenly Oshbert was grabbed from behind by the angry mob and pushed backwards towards one of the rides. It was when he felt the pressure of a curled up fist hammer into his cheekbone that Oshbert turned tail and ran. To say he ran for his life would not be an understatement for he had quickly realised that he was hopelessly outnumbered so any retaliation would be foolhardy. When he finally returned home a quarter of an hour later, Mary gasped with horror as she saw his swollen bloodied face. His rather animated story of tripping up on a loose cobblestone was unconvincing and Mary was suddenly transported to earlier that afternoon and the words of the gypsy woman. For it is true, dear reader, that once the seeds of suspicion are sown, the trust in any relationship will be permanently and irreparably damaged.

JULY 1906, HIGHBURY, JESMOND, O'DOWD FAMILY

My grandfather Lewis O'Dowd made his appearance on the 23rd March 1906 just a short few weeks after his grandfather Timothy O'Dowd died of a suspected heart attack. Unlike his poor older sibling Annie who had been sickly from the start, Lewis was a brawny strapping baby with a hearty set of lungs. His name had been suggested in a conversation by his grandfather Timothy before he had passed away. Timothy had been chatting to John while they both worked the lithography press one day in the workshop. Timothy had been waxing lyrical about his time in New York and his great friend Lewis Davies from whom he had just received a letter. Later on that evening John had proposed the name to Theresa and whilst her mother who had been party to their conversation expressed strong dislike for the name, Theresa decided that she loved it. As Theresa later told her mother the name meant 'renowned warrior' and she wanted her second child to have a fighting chance at life. After this statement her mother found it hard to register further opposition towards it.

Lewis was unlike his older sister Annie in every way, he slept well during the night and fed greedily throughout the day; he was to all intents and purposes a text book baby. The family had been

at the fairground the same day as Oshbert and Mary but the two
did not meet as Theresa, being a staunch Catholic, had strategically
avoided the Gypsy wagons and the fortune tellers. John had seen
Oshbert stumble past his house on the night of his attack but by the
time he had opened the front door to call to him Oshbert had turned
up Ashleigh Grove and was out of sight. John mentioned it to his
wife Theresa the next morning as they ate breakfast and she said she
would make a point of asking Mary about her husband's wellbeing
the next time they met at the local shops. For although my two
great- grandmothers were not bosom friends they did apparently
have a passing acquaintance with one another.

JULY 22ND 1908, 'WHITE CITY' STADIUM, LONDON, LE BRITTON FAMILY

As I have alluded to previously, my great-grandfather Oshbert was
not a particularly sporty man but, along with the rest of Edwardian
Britain, he did during this period of time attempt to embrace more
physical activity, even if his particular participation was from the
sidelines. The 1908 Olympic Games had originally been planned to
be held in Rome but the eruption of Mount Vesuvius had caused the
Italian Government to back out and Britain had taken the mantle.
Hosting the Games was a terrific coup for Britain and they went on
to top the medal board with a grand total of 146 medals including 56
Gold's. The entire country seemed to get behind the Games and the
110 events went on for a total of six months although as a sign of the
times out of 2,000 competitors there were only 37 women. This went
against the growing popularity of the suffragette movement which
had just the previous month held a successful rally in Hyde Park
attended by almost 500,000 activists. I would like to think my great-
great-grandmothers were in support of this political movement but
I can find, unfortunately, no proof either way, although they would

no doubt have heard tales of Emily Davison who hailed from nearby Morpeth and was rapidly rising in the ranks of the WSPU.

Oshbert had decided to take a few days holiday so that he and his young family could travel to London to witness this momentous occasion. Mary had given birth to their third son Arthur Henri the previous year so Susie was tasked to mind the youngster while the two older children, Oshbert junior and Anita, travelled to the capital with their parents. From his contacts at work Oshbert had managed to procure tickets for the final of the Water Polo which Great Britain was rumoured to have a good chance of winning. It was with great excitement that the family took their seats in the newly constructed stadium that day. Junior and Anita were excitedly waving Union Jack flags and Mary was wearing the new bonnet she had purchased for the special day. The summer of 1908 had been particularly rainy and as a result the persistent showers had turned the area around the Olympic pool into somewhat of a mud bath. At times the water was so murky that the twelve field players in the deep end kept colliding with the goalkeepers but despite the muddied conditions Britain went on to take the Gold, with Belgium and Finland taking the silver and bronze. Oshbert and his young family were jubilant and as they made their way back to the boarding house they were triumphantly euphoric. Sometimes, dear reader, fate has a way of turning one's fortunes on a sixpence. The family were strolling through Trafalgar Square enjoying the jolly atmosphere when they stopped to watch some revellers having an impromptu dip in the fountain beneath Nelsons Column. Mary and Oshbert sat on a nearby bench and watched the gaiety as Junior and Anita alternated splashing in the water with chasing the many pigeons strutting and bobbing about the square. A scruffy looking street hawker stood by one of the four lion statues around the column occasionally letting out a cry of 'all 'ot' ches'nuts' so Oshbert gave the children some coins and they soon returned with a large bulging bag to share. Juggling the piping hot chestnuts between her hands, Anita announced that they had bought them from their brother. Without a word of explanation Oshbert leapt from the bench and ran towards the column but the young street hawker was racing away in the opposite direction his handcart scattering chestnuts as he ran. The intensity of the crowds and Oshbert's general unfitness prevented him from catching up with the lad and it was not long before he took a side lane and disappeared from sight. Oshbert half-heartedly searched for a short while, but he was worried for his wife and children's safety, so he soon returned back to the bench. As she watched him approach – holding his side as he had a stitch – Mary's expression was non-committal, but her body language spoke volumes as did her lack of comment regarding his hasty exit. Oshbert planned to broach the subject later on after they had settled into the boarding house, but his one feeble attempt was halted by a reproachful look and as a result things were left unsaid and allowed to fester unhindered. As she lay in bed that night listening to her husband's steady breathing, the words of the gypsy woman swirled around in her mind and it is safe to say she had little or no sleep.

I can now add that the family attended the Olympics once again the following year. I must make mention of the fact that Mary had raised a quizzical eyebrow when Oshbert had first announced to his family that he had managed to procure tickets. Mary knew that it was only held every four years so later that evening she verbalised her raised eyebrow to her husband. The pair were sitting compatibly in the parlour at the time – the children safely tucked up in bed – Oshbert lowered the newspaper he was reading onto the side table and answered enigmatically, 'my dear wife that is for me to know and for you to find out.' Mary let out an exasperated sigh before returning her attention to her rather complicated embroidery.

Oshbert was true to his word and the evening before the August Bank Holiday he informed Susie, the housemaid, that the family would be out the following day and would require a packed lunch. The two older children skipped around the room in mad excitement whilst Mary looked on bemused. She knew questioning her husband further was a waste of time as he seemed determined that the venue be a surprise. The family were up bright and early the following morning. This time though because Arthur Henri was older he too was dressed up in his Sunday best and allowed to go on the trip. Susie could not believe her luck. A whole day to herself with no-one to answer too would be pure unadulterated bliss. As she stood at the doorway waving the family off she mentally ticked off her plans for the day ahead. First on the agenda would be a long leisurely bath followed by – if the weather allowed it – a quiet afternoon in the backyard sitting in the sunshine and reading a good novel. She had noticed that Oshbert had recently purchased *The Hound of the Baskervilles* and was dying to take a browse through it. Oshbert had promised she could read it once he had finished but he was a slow and thorough reader much given to reading out amusing excerpts to his family and she was desperate he did not spoil the plot.

It was not long before the family reached the Central train Station in Newcastle city centre. It was here that they would board the train to their final destination. Once there, instead of waiting for his wife to catch up as he normally would, Oshbert instead strode off in a determined manner towards the railway bridge which crossed the patchwork of tracks. Mary tried to alert his attention because she could see that the London train was due on the very platform on which she stood but he seemed oblivious to her calls and as the children had followed in his wake she had little option but to do likewise. Huffing and puffing she crossed the first bridge then when realising they were not waiting for her on the next platform either, she pursed her lips and crossed yet another bridge. Finally, she found them. Oshbert had young Arthur in his arms and the two older children were playing an energetic game of tag around the skirts of some obviously disgruntled women passengers. Oshbert was staring into space quite oblivious to the trouble his children were causing. Mary called out and this time he heard for he raised an arm and waved in her direction. He shouted for her to please hurry as the train was due in a few minutes. To which she replied, perhaps if he had helped carry the hamper she would have been able to walk faster. But her words were lost as a passing train let out a loud whistle which she decided was a blessing for she didn't want the day to start with an argument. Mary had to quicken her step for the train was pulling into the station when she finally descended the ramp. Oshbert quickly took the picnic hamper from her outstretched hands then helped her and the children on board. Once seated Junior and Anita settled down to play a thankfully quiet and calm game of 'I Spy', while Mary gazed out of the window and jiggled Arthur on her lap. Oshbert smiled across at his family – not noticing or choosing not to notice his wife's earlier annoyance - then he shook open his newspaper and, taking his spectacles from the breast pocket of his jacket, settled down to catch up on the day's news.

The train chugged its way out of the busy station and in no time at all Oshbert was folding up *The Times* and announcing that the family must get their things together as they were alighting at the next stop of Morpeth. It was at that moment Mary realised Oshbert's plans and catching his eye they shared a knowing smile.

Once a year the normally sleepy market town of Morpeth was transformed for the Morpeth Olympics. The event had started in 1873 – a good twenty years before the actual Olympics – and had gained momentum ever since. Athletes now travelled from miles and miles away to take part in events such as the 'high jump', the 'pole vault' and 'Cumberland wrestling' all for prize money put up by local businesses. It was not as well organised nor as well advertised as the actual 'proper' Olympics – which was no doubt how Mary had not initially guessed their destination - but to the Northumbrians it was an event to be proud of and the crowds would flock to the designated field of Grange House to watch and cheer. As they approached the field and Oshbert noticed the 'hawkers' and 'vendors' lining across the entrance plying their wares his blood ran cold. For hadn't his own son Silvanus been one such 'hawker' at the previous year's Olympics in London. Feeling his wife's body language change and noting how she rapidly dropped his arm from his and scanned the crowd, Oshbert realised his wife had had the self same thought. I can now thankfully write that the day was not marred in the slightest, and once Oshbert had pulled himself together and rested a reassuring hand upon his wife's arm, the family made their way into the makeshift stadium. They went on to have a fantastic day, enjoying the picnic Susie had hastily prepared the previous day – which the children declared was the best picnic they had ever had ever! – and it was almost as if the previous year's fiasco was finally relegated to the past. But memories as we all know are unpredictable at best, and the more they are suppressed, the more likely they are to fight their way back to the surface when we least expect them.

MARCH 1909, JESMOND, O'DOWD FAMILY

Since his father Timothy had died John was having problems running the Lithography and Signwriting business alone. He had tried twice to employ an apprentice but soon realised that it was not so much the increased workload which was getting him down but more the lack of camaraderie that he missed. A rival business had offered to buy him out and, after discussing the proposition with his wife Theresa, he decided this would be a wise move. As luck would have it, the two elderly sisters who ran the Brentwood Tea Rooms had decided to sell up at the same time, and in gratitude for her help with the cake decorating, they had offered Theresa first refusal on the sale. After sitting up until the early hours of the morning and 'doing the sums' the couple discovered that with a small loan from

Theresa's mother – and if they tightened their belts – it would be possible. Theresa was beyond thrilled for she had never really taken to the role of just being a housewife and mother. She raced along the street early the next morning to ask Mary Le Britton's housemaid Susie if she knew anyone who could help watch over the children. Lewis my grandad was three at the time and his younger brother John Cuthbert had just turned one, so I imagine they were quite a handful. Theresa's mother had also been quite vocal in declaring that the loan was subject to her not being expected to take over care of her grandchildren for she was much too old to cope with their high-spirited behaviour.

The sale of the Brentwood Tearooms went through remarkably quickly and it was not long at all before John and Theresa were at its helm. Early on – when they had talked about it – they had mutually decided that John should be front of house and Theresa in the back room baking and icing the cakes. This would have worked well if John had been a natural raconteur but he found the social graces necessary for such a role difficult to maintain to such a degree that if a customer complained he did not grovel and apologise but instead fought his corner. Whilst he did not lose actual custom he did not gain it either. The stalwart customers still graced the tearooms in their droves but new customers took umbrage at his argumentative and often lackadaisical attitude and news soon filtered through to Theresa. It was a very difficult conversation indeed, but Theresa cleverly 'spun' the problem by suggesting that the couple expand their fledgling business and rent the shop next door's unused kitchen area to repurpose as a bakery. The couple had already encountered problems sourcing decent bread to serve in the tearooms, because at this time there were widespread problems with the general production of basic food. This ranged from unscrupulous shopkeepers drying out used tea leaves and adding them to fresh, to grocers adding water to the buttermilk. Some corrupt bakers in the area had recently been prosecuted for adding alum to their dough to make the baked bread appear whiter and add to its weight. The couple had once purchased baked goods from one such baker and their customers had complained that the sandwiches were dry, dense and more alarmingly had caused the most dreadful constipation. Theresa knew that, unlike her husband, she had not the necessary upper arm strength to knead the dough and this would be an excellent way of 'killing two birds with one stone.' Theresa was gratified that John was receptive to her suggestion for in his words he had tired of playing 'mein host' to a bunch of bored social- climbing housewives. He was very excited about the prospect of learning a new skill and one of the twins briefly came out of retirement to teach him the basics. Theresa still carried on with the sugarcraft and this new venture paved the way for the much larger confectioners/bakers named Hedleys, which the couple would later open on Salters Road in Gosforth.

28th APRIL 1911, ASHLEIGH GROVE, LE BRITTON FAMILY

This date is especially significant because this was the day that my maternal grandmother Dorothy Daisy Davies Le Britton was born. She was Mary and Oshbert's eighth-born child but, as four had unfortunately perished in infancy, their fourth surviving. Anita, her older sister, was now aged ten and was beside herself with excitement to welcome a new baby sister. She had been collecting her ribbons in a special hat box to present to the new arrival for months and months now. Arthur, her younger brother, had recently had his first proper 'boys' haircut and lost his baby-fine curls so she could no longer put pigtails in his hair. Arthur had also reached the age of three and to her dismay had reached the age where he refused to play nicely and participate in 'tea parties' with her favourite dollies. Brothers were such a pain and her older brother Oshbert Junior was surely the worst of the lot. Since he had turned twelve he had became even more impossible and insufferable. He was constantly teasing her and pulling her pigtails when no-one was watching, then calling her a 'telltale snitch' when she complained to Susie or their mother. He was also persistently in trouble at school with the Headmistress Miss Mowatt. Although, in his defence, Miss Mowatt was a formidable spinster with a reputation for being especially strict with her school leavers so his behaviour was probably no better or worse than a majority of his peers. Many a time – often as frequently as twice a week - Junior would be held back after the end of the school day and made to sit at a desk until he had satisfied her exacting standards and become better versed in the 3RS. Junior, I must add, was not a natural student. Indeed he found the majority of his studies to be pointless. He was constantly pestering his parents to allow him to leave school before his twelfth birthday, but Oshbert and Mary would not be swayed. They were both advocates of a good education and went to pains to try and convince their son of the glittering future which lay ahead if only he would knuckle down and concentrate in class. Anita, to the contrary, was an excellent student and popular with her teachers for she was both eager to please and willing to learn. Oshbert often wondered to himself how his two eldest children could have such differing temperaments and aspirations for the future. One evening he voiced his thoughts to Mary – but only once for her strong reaction took him aback – and suggested that it may have been better if his children's aptitudes had been reversed, as it was more mportant for a boy to be academically minded, as girls inevitably went on to become housewives. He immediately regretted his statement especially after hearing his wife's sharp intake of breath and witnessing the withering look she cast his way. Mary had recently taken on more of an interest in political events and Oshbert decided it might be prudent to keep such opinions to himself in future.

The Suffragette Movement was rapidly gaining momentum in 1911 and it had garnered much publicity after its Black Friday demonstration in London the previous year. The notorious November day had gained its name because of the violence, both physical and sexual, which was casually metered out upon the female protesters. The graphic reporting of the incident had shocked a nation and driven many more women to join the political movement as a result. Mary had not gone to the extent of joining the Suffragettes but had been vocal in her support of the women involved in fighting the cause. Oshbert would do well to hold his counsel going forward.

The 28th of April was a Friday and a surprisingly bright sunny spring day. Mary had felt the first stirrings of the baby's impending arrival in the early hours of the morning and Susie had alerted the local midwife to expect a call. Oshbert had a very important business meeting to attend with Rhys Williams his Divisional Manager, so he had gone to work as usual with a promise to return home as soon as was practically possible. Arthur had been dropped off at Highbury so Susie's friend could mind him along with the O'Dowd children, and the two older children were, despite their many protestations, going to school as usual. Susie had promised to walk along the avenue to the school playground to tell Anita of the new baby's arrival the second it was born. Junior didn't even feign an interest as he found the whole pregnancy a bit of a social embarrassment. Surely his parents were too old for that sort of thing?. Susie had asked Anita to pop into the bakery behind the Brentwood Tea Rooms on her way to school to ask Mr O'Dowd if he could possibly organise for their bread order to be dropped off at the house that day because she did not want to stray too far from Mary's side. Junior – despite being older by two years - could not be entrusted with the task because the last time he had been called upon to help in such a way he had collected some fish from the fishmonger, then left it rotting in his jacket pocket for an entire week. The resulting smell had been unbelievably offensive and, despite his jacket being thoroughly pummelled and scrubbed with carbolic soap, even now his mother still insisted it be hung on a hook in the outhouse.

Anita skipped along the back lane of Brentwood Avenue towards the bakery entrance of the Tea Rooms, her clogs clip clopping on the cobbles as she went. Mr O'Dowd was kneading the dough and the bread ovens were in full production, so the heat from the bakery was intense.

"Mr O'Dowd," Anita shouted through the open gate at the back of the Tea Rooms.

John stopped his kneading and wiped his floury hands on his apron.

"Whatever is the matter child?" John said.

"Mother has asked if you could deliver the bread order to our house later please, she would like two wholemeal loaves and a white cob please," said Anita, repeating parrot fashion word for word what Susie had instructed her to say.

"Of course that's fine, I will drop it off later. Are Susie and your mother ill?"

Anita giggled excitedly, delighted to have a chance to impart the groundbreaking news, "No, Mr O'Dowd, they are quite well but my baby sister is expected today so they are both in the house waiting for the postman to arrive."

Theresa, upon hearing this conversation, had walked into the bakery to better eavesdrop upon the exchange, and she let out a giggle as she noticed John's very serious face struggling to hold back a guffaw.

"Oh that's great news," he managed to eventually blurt out, "let's just hope the postman doesn't get the parcels mixed up and deliver a baby boy by mistake."

Noticing Anita's crestfallen expression, Theresa playfully slapped her husband on the shoulder and said, "Don't be daft John, you're upsetting the child, the postmen are very careful with such parcels so I'm sure they will do the very best to deliver a girl, but saying that baby boys can be great fun too."

Anita looked decidedly unconvinced but, nevertheless, she gave a polite little wave then skipped back along the lane towards school.

When she arrived at the gates the teacher Miss Hay had already blown the second whistle and the class was walking towards the classroom reciting their nine times table. Anita jumped to the end of the queue hoping the teacher hadn't noticed her late arrival. She tried desperately to blend in with the crowd of girls but was stopped at the doorway by an outstretched cane. Miss Hay was neither as old nor as set in her ways as some of the other teachers at the school but she was especially pernickety regarding punctuality. She was a firm favourite with the children's father's at 'open evenings' as she had a 'bonny face' and always dressed in the latest fashion. Although lately she had been sporting the most peculiar type of skirt, which had caused Oshbert to joke that the poor girl had become an unfortunate 'fashion victim.' This skirt was generally known as a hobble skirt due to the fact that it caused its wearer to hobble in an odd and unflattering way. Many cartoons of the time also alluded to the fact that their wearers were so seriously impeded in their stride that perhaps the skirt should be renamed the 'speed limit skirt.' It was probably due to this minor inconvenience that the skirts had such a short lived popularity and by 1914 they were deemed as old fashioned and quite ridiculous. It was rumoured that Miss Hay's infamous bicycle accident of 1913 - where she unfortunately broke her leg in two places - was a direct result of her being dressed in this dubious fashion item.

When Miss Hay stopped her progress into school with the outstretched cane, Anita knew she would be punished. Miss Hay held no truck with excuses and often it was better and, dare I say less painful, to accept the first punishment than to try and argue the case – annoy her - and have a more prolonged punishment metered out as a result. To this end Anita dipped her head and braced herself for the inevitable oncoming rap on the knuckles. Inadvertently, she recoiled her hand and the cane landed on the tips of her nails, which if anyone who has ever trapped their fingers in a drawer will know, is incredibly painful. Junior heard his sister's plaintive cry from the other end of the playground and, despite knowing he himself would be punished, raced across the cobbles to explain to Miss Hay why Anita had been late. Miss Hay, to give her her due, did apologise to Anita – for not giving her the chance to explain - before turning and hobbling away into her classroom. But Junior's form teacher, Miss White, was not quite so understanding and Junior was promptly sent to the headmistress for breaking the line without permission. Witnessing Junior's protective brotherly support and knowing of Miss Mowatt's aptitude with the cane, Anita decided that perhaps another baby brother would not be so bad after all.

It was much later that afternoon that my grandmother Dorothy Daisy Davies Le Britton made her entrance into the world. Oshbert, as promised, had returned early from work and was standing smoking his pipe in the back yard when he first heard the familiar wailing of a newborn. He punched his fist in the air, as Susie hurtled out to tell him that the baby was fit, healthy and blessed with a fine pair of lungs. The older children returned a quarter of an hour later and Anita burst into tears of joy to find out that her prayers had been answered and she at last had a baby sister. Although she did struggle to hold back the tears of disappointment when she held the baby and realised she was 'bald as a coot' so her collection of ribbons would not be needed for quite a while.

27th JUNE, 1911, WEST JESMOND INFANT AND JUNIOR SCHOOL, LE BRITTON FAMILY

There was much excitement in the school on that day in June as the school children were awaiting a special visit from Sir Haswell

Stephenson, the Lord Mayor. The distinguished gentleman was handing out souvenirs relating to the Coronation of King George V and Queen Mary, which had taken place earlier that month on the 22nd June. The children had been preparing for this great day for quite a while, and almost every subject they had been taught during the month of June included a reference to the momentous event to some extent. Lewis O'Dowd, my maternal grandfather was only five and still in the baby class so his recollection of the event was pretty sketchy but the older Le Britton children, Oshbert and Anita fully embraced the grand occasion. The junior school children had been tasked to decorate the main school hall and Anita was so proud to have stitched the central panel of the embroidered banner which now hung pride of place above the assembly stage. Indeed she was so proud she had spoken of little else for the entire month. Mary had taught her daughter some of the more common – yet visually effective stitches – such as the 'French knot' and the 'lazy daisy' but she and Susie had both struggled to master the more complicated 'couching' stitch, so Mary had called upon the services of Theresa O'Dowd from the Brentwood Tearooms. Theresa was well known throughout the area for her embroidery skills – a proficiency which she put into action all those years ago when stitching poor John's leg - and it was not long at all before Anita had also mastered the technique of laying a thread upon her work then carefully stitching it into the fabric. Mary declared – when effusively thanking Theresa for her help - that it was probably this one special stitch which had secured her daughter the prized central panel of the banner.

The children had initially tried to talk their father into organising a trip to London to watch the actual Royal Coronation Procession. Two of their school friends were making the trip with their father – and he was only a clerk at Oshbert's office – so Oshbert's 'excuse' regarding the unnecessary expense such a trip would entail fell on deaf ears. They tried to enlist their mother to fight their corner as she was often the easier to persuade, especially if a trip could be used as a legitimate excuse to purchase a new outfit, but frustratingly even she concurred with their father. As any parent knows, 'pester power' is a common ploy used by children from time immemorial the world over, and when even this normally successful ruse failed the children were forced to concede defeat and instead console themselves with the prospect of the Lord Mayor's visit. Oshbert's reluctance to allow his children to take part in this historical event puzzled me at first – for he was a man who prided himself on his modernity – but I now speculate that his disinclination may have been in part prompted by his fear of running into his illegitimate son once again. Although in a metropolis such as London this was illogical, for surely he must have realised that this coincidence was very unlikely to have happened again. I fear that Oshbert during this period of his life – his accomplishments at work not withstanding – appears to have been a man very much afraid of his own shadow and constantly aware that the family life he had so carefully constructed could so easily collapse, like a house of cards upon the whim of a curse. For the doll was still very much in his thoughts, and although he had no reason to dwell upon its presence for the last few years, its brooding darkness still invaded his consciousness.

When the day of the Lord Mayor's much anticipated visit came about Oshbert's children were not disappointed for Sir Haswell Stephenson arrived dressed in his full regalia and bearing gifts for the entire school. Anita was bursting with pride as he complimented her on her embroidery skills, but she was not so impressed when he went on to declare to her Headmistress that with such an amazing aptitude, 'this young girl would go on to make some man a fine wife.' It appears that listening in to her mother's frequent conversations with Susie about 'women's liberation' over the years had had an impact upon Anita's future aspirations. The Lord Mayor handed each child a specially commissioned china beaker memento that day, along with a catalogue describing details of the Coronation and a personally hand-signed letter. At this time Great Britain was basking in a surge of unprecedented patriotism and the Lord Mayor was keen to promote this emotion. In the letter he made a point of urging the children to 'please preserve the souvenirs they had received, not for their intrinsic value, but for their significance in the annals of history.' Stirring stuff indeed for a pre-war Empire, and a patriotism which would be tested to its limit during the rest of the decade.

ASHLEIGH GROVE, THE CURIOUS RIDDLE OF THE MAHOGANY WARDROBES, AUGUST 1911

I must at this stage again digress and make mention of the fact that in 1909 Oshbert had seen fit to move the tin box containing the effigy doll. He had moved the box into one of the pair of massive mahogany wardrobes which were squeezed into the alcoves of the master bedroom. This was because he had been nervous that Susie would find its hiding place when she decorated the attic room, so – using his bonus from work – he had purchased some new bedroom furniture. Mary had been thrilled when she first saw the oversized brown furniture, for it was very much in vogue at that time and the pair of wardrobes were of the most excellent quality and craftsmanship. They were so tall that they reached above the picture rail, and they appeared even higher again, due to the elaborate scrolled carvings atop their framework. One day, when Mary and Susie had taken a trip to the city to purchase new shoes for Dorothy, his youngest daughter, Oshbert had struggled up the stairway with the ladders from the shed then climbed up – petering alarmingly on the top rung – and hidden the box right at the back of the wardrobe nearest the bay window. He had stood a while at the opposite side of the room - on his tiptoes – until he was fully satisfied there was no way the box could be noticed, and even if Susie stood on a chair to dust the surface with a feather duster, she could not reach it. Although he doubted this piece of housekeeping was a regular occurrence, because just that morning he had ran his finger along the top of the doorway and almost suffocated in the dust cloud it created. After making a mental note to mention this lapse in household management to his wife, Oshbert struggled back downstairs with the ladders.

I mention this new hiding place because alarmingly once the box had been hidden the wardrobe had seemed to take on a life of its own. Whenever a relation - however distant - died, the doors of the wardrobe would start to rattle on their hinges for no apparent reason. The first time Mary had mentioned this phenomenon to Oshbert, he had managed to laugh it off by saying 'it would have nothing to do with us living adjacent to a busy railway line would it?' But secretly he was worried as his own explanation made little sense even to his ears, for there was also the glaring fact that the rattling pre-empted a death in the family. Things finally came to a head one day in August when the doors had rattled consistently for a full five minutes. Upon hearing the commotion both Mary and Susie had raced to the front gate to check the railway track, then returned declaring to Oshbert that no trains were on the line. Oshbert shrugged his shoulders and said he had no time, or inclination to discuss such a trivial matter. A few days later they received the devastating news that Mary's mother Sophia had died. Upon reading through the letter, Oshbert was shocked to discover that Sophia's death had occurred at the exact time and date that the wardrobe doors had rattled. Mary was understandably distraught - probably more so because during the intervening years since the death of baby Lewis Isaac, she had thwarted her mother's every attempt at reconciliation – and her grief resulted in an uncharacteristic outburst of anger. She too had made the connection between her mother's sad demise and the wardrobe doors and informed Oshbert, in no uncertain terms that until the wardrobes were removed she would no longer sleep in the master bedroom. Oshbert argued that the wardrobes had cost his entire quarterly bonus and the rattling was just an unfortunate coincidence but Mary would not be placated and, after a week of sleeping alone in the double bed, Oshbert conceded defeat. While Mary and Susie were at the Tearooms and the children were at school, he moved the tin box into a temporary bolthole. Then when Junior returned from school he and his son were tasked to take a hammer and axe to the construction. This was no easy job for the wardrobes had been craftsman built and the massive drawers in the bases were sturdy with dovetail joints. But Oshbert was resolute that no part of the wardrobe be left intact, so panel by unwieldy panel they struggled down to the yard. Oshbert had planned a makeshift bonfire and was about to set the pile of wood alight when he was stopped in his tracks by Susie who reminded him it was washday for the neighbouring flats so perhaps it would be wise to wait until the weekend. Women who had toiled all morning with poss-tubs, scrubbing brushes, bars of soap and 'monstrous' mangles were a force to be reckoned with, and only a foolish man would risk incurring their wrath by smearing their fresh laundered linen with dirty smoke. So instead, Oshbert and Junior trailed back up to the bedroom to tidy up the rest of the debris. It was then that Oshbert noticed the prominent black scorch mark, which had mysteriously appeared upon the wall directly behind where the wardrobe had stood. He stood scratching his head for a while as he was certain it had not been there earlier and, unless it was a trick of the light from the afternoon sunshine streaming in from the bay window the black shape to all intents and purposes resembled a coffin. Realising that his son was about to make the same assumption, Oshbert scurried him out of the room and told him to go quickly to the shed and bring back some white paint. He remembered he had some white distemper left over from when he had repainted the outside privy. It was not ideal as it would jar with the rest of the decoration in the bedroom but it would just have to do. Rather have Mary complain about the decor than get upset again. It took about three coats to completely hide the mark and even then Oshbert was not convinced it had disappeared from sight so he removed a mirror from the hallway and hung it over the patch. When Mary came to view the room a few hours later she let out an exasperated sigh and questioned why he had seen fit to only paint one alcove of the room. He feigned annoyance and stated that after destroying perfectly good wardrobes – which would need replacing – he could not afford the expense of hiring a tradesman to disguise one small patch of rising damp. Of course the problem of the box still remained, so the following week while Mary and Susie were out shopping in the city, Oshbert returned it to its original hiding place behind the brick in the eaves of the attic room, where he prayed it would lay dormant and cause no further mischief.

20th JANUARY 1912, HIGHBURY
JESMOND, O'DOWD FAMILY

West Jesmond Junior and Infant schools had been closed since the Christmas holidays due to an outbreak of Scarlet Fever. This dreadful contagious disease was very much the scourge of this period – pre the introduction of penicillin - as it primarily affected younger children and as such was one of the leading causes of infant mortality. My grandfather Lewis, who was then just shy of six, had been one of the first children in the school to complain of a sore throat and a red blotchy rash. Theresa his mother had – in a state of great panic - called upon her brother-in-law, Dr Tom Dewell and with prompt treatment and careful nursing the fever had thankfully not spread to his siblings. It did, however, claim the life of my great-great-grandmother, by prompting a reoccurrence of a prior medical complaint and culminating in her dying from congestive heart failure. My grandmother Theresa's grief was greatly magnified as she had only the previous day ignored her mother's complaints of chest pains. Although in her defence, her mother did have an annoying habit of 'crying wolf' when she felt she was not getting the attention she believed she deserved. Theresa made herself ill, so convinced was she that her negligence was partly to blame for her mother's death. Her belief in her own culpability was so profound that John was eventually compelled to call upon Dr Tom once again. He sat Theresa down and reiterated that her mother's death was in no way her fault and earlier intervention would not have changed the outcome a jot. Dr Tom went on to remind her that she should be grateful the consequences had not been worse, for although he had not said so at the time, he had been very concerned for her son Lewis' life as his fever took a long while to calm. In his clumsy way Dr Tom was no doubt trying to convince her to *count her blessings* that the disease had not decimated her family, but as his bedside manner was curt and laconic, I fear this fell on deaf ears. Her reaction that day could go some way to explain why she suddenly became so overprotective of her children – even into their adulthood – and why she was so reluctant to relinquish control and allow them to follow their dreams. It amazes me that for one so small in stature she remained the domineering matriarch well into her dotage.

My great-great-grandmother, Mary Hedley, was buried alongside her own granddaughter Annie in All Saints Cemetery on Jesmond Road, and yes, dear reader, her name is also used in a certain Catherine Cookson novel. But again, I deviate, so back to the story. After the interment the entire family congregated at the house in Highbury for the funeral wake. The local priest who had conducted the ceremony immediately downed a tumbler of whisky - as Catholic priests are wont to do – then went off in search of the 'funeral tea.' Theresa's five siblings and their partners – who with the exception of her sister Francis and husband Tom – had been conspicuous in their absence throughout their mother's later life were all in attendance. They were suitably dressed head to toe in black with their heads dipped and voices hushed as a mark of respect. In John's mind's eye he likened his wife's siblings to a flock of crows, feasting upon the carcass of their deceased mother's possessions. Theresa's older sisters, Mary and Frances, had already laid claim to various pieces of their mother's jewellery, and her other sister, Agnes, had taken Theresa aside to ask if she could take her mother's fur stole that very afternoon as it would compliment an outfit she planned to wear to the theatre later that weekend. To all intents and purposes, it appeared as if they viewed the wake primarily as an opportunity to procure as much as they possibly could, prior to the official reading of the Will. As John had feared, it was not long before Theresa's two brothers, Arthur and William, took him to one side to enquire about his plans for the house. This was because they were aware that their mother had helped the couple buy the house when they married in 1903 – with the caveat that she lived with them – and she had also helped them to finance the purchase of the Brentwood Tearooms. John had anticipated such questions, but he had assumed that the brothers would have waited a respectable time before bringing them up, so he replied that it was neither the time or the place to discuss such things, and no doubt their mother's Will would make her financial intentions crystal clear. Frances' husband, Dr Tom Dewell intervened at this stage and declared that he had been in touch with the Family Solicitor that very morning and the reading of the Will was scheduled for that Friday. The fact that the brothers did not seem surprised at this announcement convinced John that the siblings had discussed the whole affair prior to the funeral, and it was only himself and Theresa who had been left out of the loop. John had planned to broach the delicate subject with his wife when the wake was over, but upon seeing her distressed state he decided to leave it until the following day. Nevertheless, after she went upstairs to bed, he feigned a bout of insomnia so he could look through the Brentwood Tea Room accounts. He was relieved to find they were in profit, but despite this, he knew they had not enough in the coffers to fully repay her mother's loan or buy out the share in the house. Their only hope was that Theresa's mother had honoured her promise and left them the house in her Will.

It was Friday, and the day of the official read through of Mary Hedley's last Will and Testament. The extended family had all arrived early and were seated in the Solicitors Office on Larkspur Terrace. The Solicitor was making a great show of adjusting his glasses and clearing his throat, until Dr Tom Dewell urged him to 'please hurry' as he had Surgery that afternoon. Casting Tom a withering look the Solicitor began to read through the complicated legal document. From the onset John had been concerned and it very soon transpired he had due cause to feel so, for Theresa's mother had not honoured her promise and had instead left her share of the house on Highbury to her beloved sons Arthur and William. Further disappointment followed when it became apparent that Mary's equity in the Brentwood Tea Rooms had been bequeathed to her eldest daughter Frances. Her namesake was to get a string of pearls, Agnes an elaborate sapphire locket, and Theresa, to her absolute chagrin, would only receive a cameo brooch. Slim reward indeed for the fact that Theresa and John had cared for her mother for so many years. Theresa tried very hard to put on a brave face, and she managed to be quite convincing, until her sister Frances piped up that she and her husband Tom would be visiting the Tearooms over the weekend to check out their inheritance. Struggling to retain what little dignity she had left, Theresa turned tail and left the room before striding away along Acorn Road, desperately trying to fight back angry tears of disappointment. John collected his overcoat, shrugged a hasty goodbye, then followed his wife along the street, quickening his pace so he could catch her up.

True to their word, Dr Tom and Frances arrived at the Tearooms barely an hour after opening the following weekend and despite Theresa's protestations that the timing was inconvenient they sat at a table and asked to see the account ledgers. Desperate not to make a scene in front of her valued customers Theresa discreetly suggested that they take the ledgers home to peruse at their leisure, and, perhaps John and she could visit their house the following day to talk things through. This seemed to appease the couple and a time was arranged for the following afternoon.

Dr Tom and Frances lived in a very large house on Elmfield Road - a very desirable residential street just off Gosforth High Street - and a short half an hour stroll from Highbury. John and Theresa had discussed probable scenarios on the walk over, and both agreed it would be better for John to do the talking as he was less emotionally involved than she. The door was opened by the Dewell's maid, Maisie, and the couple were shown into the parlour where refreshments had been set out on a side table. It appeared that Dr Tom and his wife had had a similar chat to John and Theresa, for Tom led the conversation with barely an interruption from his wife. Her only input into the proceedings was to enquire where Theresa sourced her tealeaves as their local Greengrocer stocked an excellent brand, and she would be more than happy to have a word regarding a discount. Dr Tom seemed at pains to emphasize that both he and his wife led already busy lives so they would in essence be silent partners merely taking their fair share of the profits. John and Theresa left the house feeling that although not ideal, perhaps the arrangement had a small chance of working.

This was all to change dramatically during the following week with her sister as the chief protagonist. Frances appeared to assume that if she rendezvoused with her cronies at the Brentwood Tea Rooms, the afternoon tea would be gratis. She made a great deal of lording it over Theresa at these social gatherings, and addressed her younger sister as if she was the hired help. Theresa let this go the first few times it happened but after about the fourth time, in as many days, she decided to have a quiet word. But as we know sisters have a language all their own and old sibling rivalries came flooding to the fore. Voices were raised, tempers flared and past slights and misdemeanours recalled. It all became very ugly, very quickly ending only when Frances flounced off in a scurry of bustling skirts and clacking heels. Theresa was still visibly upset the following morning, and she notified John that after sleeping on the problem the only conclusion she had reached was that the arrangement was impracticable. She used well-worn adages such as *'I've burnt my bridges'* and *'I can't turn back the clock'* to argue her case, and long before she had finished her well-rehearsed speech, John verbally agreed with his wife that the situation was untenable. Perhaps sensing this was an opportunity to bring up a long forgotten conversation, John suggested that they should consider a fresh start. At this point, I will add, that John had long since been trying to convince Theresa that their future lay in New York. His deceased father Timothy had spoken fondly of the metropolis on more than one occasion and the only thing which had kept John from insisting they make this audacious move was Theresa's understandable reluctance to abandon her mother. For once, Theresa did not dismiss the suggestion out of hand and she promised to give it some serious thought as she went about her business that day. Later on that evening, after the two boys were in bed, John discovered his patient persistence had paid off for he had his answer. To use another adage, it was *'all steam ahead.'* The house on Highbury was swiftly put on the market, which greatly pleased brothers Arthur and William who had been silently waiting in the wings – for their fair share - out of respect for their sister. Then Dr Tom Dewell was approached and asked if he wished to buy the couple out of the Brentwood Tea Rooms, an offer which, I can confirm, he snapped up willingly with a view to inflating the price and selling the lease on with the goodwill attached. With the money this sale released, John purchased four tickets for a luxury steamship scheduled to sail from Southampton to New York on the 10th April.

The RMS Titanic was a brand new passenger vessel recently commissioned by the White Star Line and it was well reported to be the biggest ship afloat. Many wealthy passengers had already acquired their tickets, for its groundbreaking maiden voyage to New York as its opulence was rumoured to be boundless and there was allegedly a Veranda Cafe decorated with palm trees and a Turkish bath on board for the first class passengers to enjoy. Second Class tickets cost just under £50 and third class tickets were between £12 and £32. While tempted to go for the third class option and save more money for their start up in America, John still remembered his father's tales of crossing the North Atlantic in the 1890s and of the indignities he had endured in the cheap steerage class, so he decided the family would travel second class. Once the tickets were purchased and the date set the O'Dowd family began the preparations in earnest. John's two sons, my grandfather Lewis and his younger brother John junior were aged six and four respectively and, I can confidently assume that the children were beyond excited at the prospect of such an amazing adventure. The only fly in the proverbial ointment was that in all the chaos and confusion of the move Theresa had not kept check of her menstrual cycle and indeed it was not until she fainted and was examined by the doctor that it came to light she was well into her second trimester. She confessed to the doctor that she had noticed a slight thickening of her waistline, but in the haste of packing up her old life she had just loosened her corsets and ignored this most obvious of signs. Due to her previous conception problems, the doctor declared that the only way the couple could be assured of a happy outcome would be if Theresa was immediately confined to bed and remained there for the duration of her pregnancy. The entire family was distraught to see their much heralded plans shelved in such a way and Theresa swore that once the babe was born they could readdress the move. John went cap in hand to Dr Tom and Frances, but the lease for the Brentwood Tearooms had been negotiated and a Solicitor employed so it was no longer a feasible option. Likewise the sale of their beloved Highbury home was within a hairs breath of completion, so to back out would be financial suicide. They did, however, manage to get a full refund on the ship tickets which enabled John to put a down payment on a Tyneside flat in Bayswater Road, so thankfully the family were not homeless. Once they had moved into their new home John immediately set about searching for a business to invest their remaining capital. It was not long before he was given the heads up on a small shop on Salters Road. It was in an excellent position with plenty of footfall and crying out to be repurposed into an affordable bakery and cake shop. I further divulge that, to their credit Dr Tom and Frances, helped finance this new enterprise, so perhaps they did have a sense of guilt as to how John and Theresa's fortunes had turned out after all. Saying this but they did insist that the new shop be called Hedleys as a nod to their deceased mothers' maiden name and a lasting tribute to her memory. This insistence irked John somewhat as he still viewed Theresa's mother - and her actions regarding how she had worded her Will - as being the architect of the whole sorry affair.

I need not write the next chapter as the fate of the Titanic is well-documented but for the clarity of this story I shall. Needless to say, but if my great-grandmother had not found herself 'in the family way' my novel would have had a much different outcome, for I fear the family would have perished on that fateful night when the ship collided with the iceberg. Perhaps Theresa and the children may have survived - as the ship did adhere to a strict policy of women and children first - but saying that, there were limited lifeboats and they may not have reached them in time. I am just thankful that fate intervened but please, dear reader, may I ask at this juncture that you spare a thought and say a prayer for the poor souls who were not so lucky and did lose their lives on that most frightful night of nights. I will futher add that I have always felt a bizarre connection to the dreadful disaster and perhaps the connection was that, but for a twist of fate, my great-grandparents would have lost their lives all those years ago.

THE HOUSE, ASHLEIGH GROVE, SEPTEMBER 1913, LE BRITTON FAMILY

The weather in 1913 had been inclement to say the least. Winters are by their very definition cold and frosty but this winter had been exceptionally brutal. There had been such a severe and prolonged snowstorm in the January of that year that Miss Mowatt had taken the decision to close the school. Schoolchildren throughout Jesmond cheered as they collected their sledges and ran outside to take advantage of the impromptu extended Christmas holiday. They were not so jubilant when they returned to school a few weeks later and discovered that Miss Hays, and the other form teachers, had doubled their homework so they could 'catch up' on the studies they had missed.

The year did not improve and throughout September it rained and rained. The old Victorian drainage system struggled to cope with the constant deluge, and on September the 13th , after a particularly persistent downpour, Jesmond flooded. In retrospect, this was always on the cards as the village was on slightly sloping land, but the haste in which it happened took everyone by surprise. The Le Britton and O'Dowd children were at school when the first thunderbolt shot from the darkened sky. It took out a chimney stack on a house on Lavender Gardens and they ran to the windows – ignoring the pleas of Miss Hay to remain seated - and watched gobsmacked, as the water rose from the drains and streamed unhindered along Brentwood Avenue. The shopkeepers ran to their doorways frantically trying to hinder its devastating flow but the sheer force of it was too powerful to stop and they could only stand horrified as the water trickled over the doorstep – like a shy hesitant customer – then barged rudely through to lap at their ankles. Further down the street in Ashleigh Grove the house felt the ground beneath its foundations saturate and on nearby Bayswater Road – in their upstairs Tyneside flat – Theresa O'Dowd said a small prayer of gratitude that they were still not living in the old house on Highbury, for being closer to the Town Moor it would surely have flooded. Luckily, Oshbert had had the foresight to purchase sand bags early on when the rains first began. Mary, his wife had questioned the unnecessary expense at the time but knowing that Oshbert was a 'belt and braces' type of man she hadn't argued her case. Only that morning Oshbert had insisted the boys help him carry what furniture they could upstairs onto the first floor landing. Mary and Susie had followed with the rugs and soft furnishings, muttering to each other that it was a waste of time and energy, as the rain was dying out. Now, Mary was grateful for her husband's cautious and circumspect nature for with any luck, entirely due to her husband's – normally annoying quirks - they would be relatively unaffected by the flood. Later on that evening Mary and Susie trudged up the street offering dry blankets and hot food to their neighbours who had not been so lucky. Junior and Arthur the two older boys went across the street to help the shopkeepers save what remained of their stock. In the intervening years Junior had matured into a most compliant young man. He was now fourteen years of age, and earlier that summer he had finally finished his studies and officially left school. Junior had suggested his dream was to become a professional boxer but his father would not hear of such a ridiculous thing, and had instead found him employ as a clerk in the Liverpool Victoria Legal Friendly Society, where he was Branch Manager. Oshbert had been so desperate to avoid accusations of nepotism that if anything Junior was having to work harder than his peers to prove himself worthy of the job opportunity. Junior rightly felt that he had been steamrollered into the administrative career so he only paid it lip service. He had no interest in climbing the ranks like his father, and no wish to spend his working life confined to a stuffy office like a hen in a chicken coop. He still had secret aspirations to follow his dream and become a professional. He was an exceptional boxer, and as a result of his obvious talents, he had recently been taken on by a local boxing promoter and was swiftly climbing the ranks of the amateur league. His manager was convinced that his next big fight with the renowned Welsh boxer - the aptly named Johnny Basham – would be the fight which would make it a viable proposition for him to transition to professional. The *'Happy Wanderer'* Johnny had recently made headline news after an opponent he was fighting - and had knocked out – cracked his skull as he fell upon the canvas. When the poor chap later died, Johnny was arrested on grounds of GBH before being charged with the much more serious charge of manslaughter. Luckily, the magistrate decreed that it had been a fair fight and Johnny was duly acquitted but his confidence had taken a kicking. This 'friendly' with newcomer and amateur *'The Geordie Kid'* was to be Johnny's comeback fight. Junior had deliberately not told his parents of this latest development for he already knew his mother's views upon the sport. Mary had been vocal with her distain when the newspapers had reported upon Johnny's court case, so it was better all around if she didn't know that he would soon be fighting her eldest son. Junior was hoping – given his new fighting nickname – she and his father would remain blissfully unaware. His brother Arthur knew about the fight – as it was the talk of the village especially amongst the teenage boys – but the rest of the family were in the dark and Arthur had been sworn to secrecy.

At last the evening of the big fight loomed. Junior had gone to work in the office with his father that day for he was desperate to keep up the pretence that it was just an ordinary day. He had managed to pull a 'sickie' in the afternoon – by claiming he had taken ill with one of his headaches - so that he could rush to the gym for a last minute training session. I must at this stage mention that

Junior was prone to headaches. These headaches were not normal 'run of the mill' headaches, they were much, much worse and Mary was convinced they had worsened when her son first started fighting competitively. It is now well-documented that boxers suffer from brain-related illnesses later in life as a direct result of the constant knocks to their heads, but in the early 1900s this was unproven. Nevertheless, Mary had spoken to the local doctor and he had confirmed that, yes, such knocks would cause trauma to the structure of the brain over time. My grandmother recalls how upset she was watching her brother strike his head against the kitchen wall in an effort to get rid of these headaches, so Mary had good reason to be uneasy. That evening both Oshbert and Mary were concerned about Junior. Mary knew her son's moods well and she knew – by a mother's intuition - when he was hiding something, but when she expressed her disquietude to Oshbert, he brushed it off saying, 'at his age I'll wager a girl is involved somewhere along the line.' She was pleased when Junior came down from the bedroom later on that evening and announced that he was going out for a stroll. She hoped it would help to clear his head. It was when two hours had passed and her eldest son had not returned home that she sent Oshbert upstairs to have a quiet chat with Arthur. The two boys were as thick as thieves so if anything were amiss she reckoned that he would be more likely to discuss it with Oshbert than herself. She was not expecting Oshbert to come thundering down the stairs a few minutes later shouting for her to quickly get her coat. It took her a few moments to gather her wits about her, ask Susie to watch the children, then follow him out of the house. Oshbert raced up the street ahead of his wife - turning now and then to urge her to keep up - and all the while barking out a brief outline as to what Arthur had revealed. Once they reached the venue, there was a brief scuffle between the doorman and Oshbert regarding the fact that the 'fight' was sold out, and while Oshbert and this rather burly gentleman were engaged in their altercation, Mary grabbed the opportunity to slip inside.

Mary had read articles about such events but was not prepared for the acrid stench of predominately male sweat and tobacco. The noise too came as a shock, for the crowd of men were pressed up against the ring jeering, shouting and making rude mocking remarks. Mary was undeterred and elbowed her way through the unruly throng until she reached the ringside. She could just about make out the figure of her precious son. He was bowed with his fists raised. Blood was streaming from a rather nasty cut on his forehead and she watched in mounting horror as Johnny - his opponent - threw a well-aimed punch and knocked him clean from his feet. Junior collapsed in a heap in the corner – temporarily winded but still prepared to fight on – and as the referee stood over him counting down, he struggled to his feet. It was at this moment that his mother, inadvertently flashing her undergarments in the process and causing an appreciative 'whoop' to go up from the onlookers, crawled under the ropes and clambered clumsily into the ring. For a few seconds the crowd were confused, then they started to holler and clap as they assumed this was all part of a well-rehearsed performance because 'The Geordie Kid's' mum interrupting the fight fitted well with his persona. Mary walked across towards the referee and quietly but in no uncertain terms, demanded that the fight be stopped. It was at this stage that the mood of the audience changed, the bookies were working the room as the two fighters were so obviously ill-matched, and the crowd was baying for it to continue. The punters had tired of the 'pantomime' and wanted more action. The referee explained to Mary that to stop the fight midway would cause a potential riot, and worse than that, her son would be a marked man because an awful lot of money was riding on its outcome. He reiterated that men such as those in the audience had long memories and would not take a 'walkout' lying down. Mary was naive in many ways – for her husband had always endeavoured to protect her from the harsher realities of life, and indeed she would have left the decision to Oshbert, if he had been by her side - but as he had still not made an appearance she knew the decision would be hers, and hers alone. As a mother she was prepared to risk the onslaught, but she couldn't condemn her son to a life of constantly watching over his shoulder, for fear of reprisal, so she reluctantly nodded her assent for the fight to continue. The referee waved Johnny across so he could briefly explain what was happening. Johnny hadn't fully realised how young Junior was so he 'took a dive' and allowed 'The Geordie Kid' to throw the knockout blow and win. While I like to think his reasons for this were altruistic, I suspect it more likely that he was afraid of a repetition of his last fight, which had caused him to be arrested. Once the fight was over and Junior had completed his winner's lap of the ring, he and his mother quickly and quietly left by the side door in order to find Oshbert. It didn't take them long, for they followed the sounds of groaning only to discover Oshbert lying astride a pile of rubbish – in a most undignified manner - in a nearby back lane. It seemed that poor Oshbert had come off worst from his argy-bargy with the doorman, who was an ex-boxer and prone to settle spats with his fists, and even in the dim light shining from the street lamp, Mary could see the misshapen profile of his nose and his swollen left cheek. Junior and Mary helped him from the ground and then all three stumbled wordlessly back towards the house. Once there – and after Susie had fussed about making hot toddies and cold compresses – Junior profusely apologised to his parents and vowed to hang up his boxing gloves for good.

As a result of this incident Oshbert went onto adopt an even more uncompromising draconian attitude towards his family, and most especially towards his two sons Junior and Arthur. Perhaps he sensed that they were both independent of spirit and would benefit from reining in as World War One was looming on the horizon. Oshbert had always been a most fastidious man with a punctilious attention to detail, but this facet of his personality seemed to magnify with his advancing years. He also during this period extended this authoritarian attitude to areas of household management; areas which his wife Mary insisted were not of his concern. She constantly maintained that the house should be her domain, but he ignored her protests. Their marriage had always been a marriage of equals and in the past Oshbert had inevitably backed down and relinquished control, but something in him seemed changed. Such was his constant quest for perfection that he once disembarked from his train to work and returned home to tell Mary that the curtains in the master bedroom were not hanging straight. Then one day, when he noticed a tide mark on the inside of the bath, he again ignored his wife's well-balanced explanation that one of the boys had just bathed and she hadn't had a chance to scour it yet, and employed a part-time cleaner to help her and Susie with the heavier tasks. Although he was to rue the day he had ignored his wife's opinion, when he returned from work early one afternoon and found all three women sitting gossiping in the kitchen, eating tripe and 'tiddly' on stout. Oshbert's strict attitude thankfully did not extend to his precious daughters, as they both fondly remember being 'daddies little princesses.' Anita had just turned twelve and as well as her aptitude for embroidery, she was also proving to be a very competent piano player. Oshbert was so proud of his eldest daughter that he had promised to purchase a brand new 'state of the art' piano if she managed to successfully pass her final music exam. This promise spurred Anita on to practice and practice, much to Mary's chagrin for she seemed to 'go off key' at the same section of 'Fur Elise' again and again, causing Mary to whisper in an aside to Oshbert 'that Beethoven chap has a lot to answer for.' Anita's persistence paid off and it was during the November of that year that the family took delivery of the Kemble upright piano, and Anita was immediately tasked to master the popular tunes of the day before the Christmas holidays. That Christmas day was to prove to be, the most perfect Christmas day ever. They had feasted upon a fine lunch – prepared by Susie before she went to visit her own relations – then the entire family, even the boys, settled themselves companionably around the piano. And while Anita 'tickled the ivories' to 'Daddy Has a Sweetheart and mother is her name' – a much lauded tune of the time - Oshbert pulled Mary from her armchair and waltzed her around the room, much to the children's amusement. Then he stood, one arm resting upon the fire surround, and sang 'Too-Ra-Loo-Ra-Loo-Ra' in his deep baritone voice, beckoning his children – who were sitting cross legged at his feet – to join in the chorus. On days such as these Oshbert could almost forget the doll and the alarming damp patch in the shape of a coffin which had recently reappeared through the white distemper in the wake of the flood.

JUNE 28TH 1914, ASHLEIGH GROVE, LE BRITTON FAMILY

This date resonates through history, as it was the very day that Archduke Franz Ferdinand of Austria and his wife were assassinated in Sarajevo and the catalyst for what Woodrow Wilson would later in 1917 declare was the *war to end all wars*. Great Britain entered the war on August 4th 1914, and life changed irrevocably for the *lost generation* coming of age in the ensuing carnage. Patriotic fervour was heightened with an almost gung-ho attitude amongst the young volunteers who were keen to prove their mantle and give the Germans 'what for'. During the first year of the war the Services were forced to rely upon voluntary enlistment until an ardent warmonger named Admiral Charles Penrose Fitzgerald, hit upon a plan to boost recruitment by encouraging a group of thirty women in his home town of Folkestone to hand out white feathers to men wearing civilian clothes. Why these militant young ladies were so keen to send their brothers and sweethearts to their death beggar's belief, but the Press got wind of the group and dubbed them the "The Order of the White Feather."A popular poster campaign followed on as a result of this group's actions. One such poster addressed the young women of London and asked the question *'Is your "Best Boy" wearing khaki? If not don't YOU THINK he should be?'* Thousands of white feathers were handed out during the duration of hostilities, and to wear one was viewed as a sign of humiliation, for it marked one out as Conscientious Objector and a coward. The significance of the white feather as the emblem of shame was apparently based upon the myth that a cockerel with a white feather in its tail would lose a cockfight. I have no reason to presume this was why Oshbert Junior was so keen to , for at the age of fifteen he was too young to have been a target for these self-righteous women. His reasons were more likely linked to the propaganda spread by Kitchener, and his boredom for office work. Perhaps it was also in part rebellious, after being told what to do for so long by an inflexible father who demanded obedience. The need to escape such a constrictive lifestyle and seek adventure was undeniable. The criteria for enlistment were that a young man was nineteen years of age with a height of 5ft 3inches and a chest measurement of 34 inches. The problem was that many recruiters were prepared to turn a blind eye if a young man looked old enough, looked fit and claimed to have no birth certificate. By the end of the war in 1918 it was an alarming fact that 250,000 enlisted members of the military and navy were underage *'boy soldiers.'*

The night Junior chose to tell his parents that he had joined the Navy was the evening of 16th November 1914. The school holidays had been extended, due to the new school drains not yet being fully operational, and later that afternoon the Head teacher, Miss Mowatt, had received the devastating news that the military were planning to requisition the school building as an Army Hospital. Mary was not well pleased, for she had had four children milling around for weeks at this stage. Her youngest, Rhys John, was just a babe of two months, and between he and my grandmother, who was only aged three she had her hands full. Susie had done her best to take the strain – and the older children had helped entertain Dorothy - but Rhys John had colic so was constantly mithering and would only properly settle for his mother. When Junior walked in and sat down for his tea that evening, his mother's pained expression told him it would be prudent to wait a while before imparting his momentous news. Half an hour later he was just finishing eating his tea, when Oshbert stormed into the kitchen demanding to know why his son had gone absent from work after his lunch break. Seeing his son sitting calmly at the kitchen table Oshbert senior was further incensed and let loose with a long angry tirade.

"Where have you been all afternoon young man?' he barked, following it up with, "I have gone against my better intentions and made an excuse for your absence. I will not be put in this compromising position again. Do you hear me boy? I will not be looked upon as a fool and forced to lie for your laziness. Actions such as this will have consequences and, unless you have a suitable explanation, I shall have no choice but to formally reprimand you in my office tomorrow."

Junior waited a while until his mother was out of earshot for he did not want her to have to hear his news in such a fashion. He spoke very quietly and said, "I have joined up."

"Joined up where? Speak sense my boy, I am in no mood for childish riddles."

"I've enlisted in the navy."

Oshbert seemed not to fully comprehend for he continued shouting, "You will have to make a better excuse than that my boy, to get out of this pickle. Just wait till your mother hears of you playing wag this afternoon."

It was at this stage that Mary walked back into the kitchen with a freshly changed baby Rhys slung over her shoulder.

"What pickle is this then Junior?' Mary asked addressing her eldest son.

"He claims to have joined the Navy, daft lad. You must take us for fools. You are far too young."

"It's true I have. I've joined up." Junior was tearful with frustration for he had been expecting back slapping and congratulations rather than ridicule.

Seeing how upset her son was, Mary suddenly realised he was telling the truth. She fell back into her chair, the sudden jolt causing baby Rhys to let out a disgruntled vexed cry.

"Get out of my sight boy, upsetting your mother with your silly stories. Come back when you have grown-up and changed your tune," Oshbert snapped.

"Perhaps he is telling the truth Oshbert?" Mary intoned as her son stomped from the room, "the newsagent was telling me about a boy he knew who had joined up, and this lad was a good year younger than Junior."

"I'll give him joining up when I get my hands on him. Upsetting his mother like that. What in heaven's name does he think he is playing at? Are you alright my dear? I will go and have a word with the boy now I've calmed down a bit. I am sure it's all just a storm in a teacup and I can sort it out."

Oshbert came back into the kitchen about ten minutes later and immediately crossed the room to take his wife and baby in his arms. Mary knew before Oshbert even shaped the words that Junior had been telling the truth. She could see the distress in her husband's eyes.

"Whatever will we do?" she pleaded, "Junior is far too young. I still have to remind him to comb his hair in the mornings and he's not even properly shaving yet. Whatever will we do? Oh Oshbert I am so worried. He is still my baby boy."

"Hush hush, my dear, try not to fret so," said Oshbert in an effort to placate his wife, 'I promise that I will do my very best to sort it out. I will go down to the recruiting office first thing tomorrow. I am sure by this time tomorrow it will all be sorted out. There is no way any son of mine is risking his life in this fake and fabricated war."

True to his word, Oshbert was up bright and early the next morning in order to visit the Recruiting Office but it proved to be too late, for Junior and his friends had already boarded the train in the middle of the night and were on their way up to the big naval base in Rosyth. Undaunted Oshbert still stood in the Recruiting Office for the better part of an hour, fighting his son's corner and arguing his case, but the Navy were so desperate for ratings that his words fell on deaf ears. I will add at this point that a few years later in 1916 the War Office, who had then tired of being criticised with regard to these 'boy soldiers' declared that if parents could prove a boy's true age with a Birth Certificate, they would immediately be removed from the front line and demobbed. But by then it was too late for Junior, for by 1916 he was a seasoned sailor, having thankfully survived his ship being torpedoed at sea. But I must add that Junior had not escaped entirely unscathed, for following the bombing he had been medically discharged from the army with what is now called Post-Traumatic Stress Disorder. I am happy to report that with peace, quiet and patient nursing he went on to fully recover from his ordeal and was allowed to return home. Although this was not without its own problems, for on the very first day he plucked up the courage to leave the house alone, he was hesitantly strolling across the Tarry Bridge onto Thornleigh Road and was accosted by three young women, who mockingly forced a white feather into the lapel of his jacket. Junior was so shamed that he would have gone to the recruiting office and re-enlisted there and then were it not for the sudden appearance of his mother, who happened to be passing by on her way to the Acorn Road shops and had witnessed the whole event. In actuality – unbeknownst to Junior - Mary had followed him that day at a discreet distance for she was worried how he would fare out and about, after being cooped up in hospital and home for so long. As Mary sat crouched on the ground holding her son – until the tremors and shaking abated – she gave the girls 'what for' and totally forgetting her social status in the community, she scolded the girls for their unspeakable cruelty, much in the manner of a fishwife on North Shields Quay. One of their neighbours from the nearby flats took great pleasure in waylaying Oshbert on his way home from work that day, and casually dropped into the conversation how surprised and shocked she had been at the 'uncouth language' Mary had used. Oshbert was overcome with embarrassment, and immediately raced home and demanded his wife told him "what on earth was going on." To give him his due once Mary had explained he hotfooted back up the street and after braying upon her door told the neighbour in question "in future he would thank her to keep her views to herself and refrain from her tittle-tattling." To end this chapter I will add that the one positive thing to come out of Junior's time in the Navy was that the bang on his head - when the ship was torpedoed - seemed to cure his terrible headaches, although saying that, he did still suffer with tinnitus from time to time.

APRIL 1915, BAYSWATER ROAD, O'DOWD FAMILY

The O'Dowds were still living in the Tyneside flat on Bayswater Road. Initially, both Theresa and John had assumed the living quarters would be too squashed - especially with three still quite young children - but in no time at all they had become accustomed to the lack of space and were actually enjoying the quality family time such close proximity afforded them. My grandfather Lewis had just turned nine years old, his brother John junior was nearly seven, and baby Dolly - whose untimely conception had stopped the family perishing on the Titanic - was almost three.

The war had impacted on all walks of life and the O'Dowds were to prove no exception although saying this their new bakery venture, Hedleys, was just about managing to stay afloat and had even registered a small profit. Theresa's sugar crafting skills were beneficial in keeping the wolf from the door, for despite many wedding cakes being nothing more than hollow cardboard shapes, they still benefitted from decorative icing. When a bride insisted on an actual cake John had perfected the recipe for the aptly named 'Trench Cake'. This popular wartime cake had no eggs in the recipe instead using vinegar to achieve the necessary rise but it still needed dried fruit and this was getting scarcer by the day. John was gaining a great reputation as a Master Baker and at weekends his two sons would help him in the bakery and then go around the local streets delivering baked goods in a handcart. This was no easy task and the boys would frequently stop to argue over whose turn it was to push because the handcart was so difficult to manoeuvre, especially around corners and up inclines. The boys also constantly complained about their schooling, because since West Jesmond School had been taken over by the Military; both boys had quite a long walk along Osborne Road to neighbouring Sandyford and the school there. They developed a habit of dawdling so their timekeeping was problematic. The lateness also frequently resulted in their teachers administering the strap as a punishment. One would think that being aware of the corporal punishment which would inevitably be metered out, the boys would hurry but it seemed they had good reason to tarry. John would hop onto Lewis shoulders and they would stop to 'scrump' apples from overhanging trees in a garden on Lily Crescent. Once they had collected a dozen or so they would gather up the apples in their school sweaters then sell them on to their classmates at school. Despite their hands often still smarting from the strap, the pleasure of walking home then stopping in the grocery store on Brentwood Avenue to purchase a quarter of sweets made the pain worthwhile. Both boys had inherited a sweet tooth from their father. Lemon Sherbets and Pear Drops were the boy's particular favourites although it was always risky sucking on a

Pear Drop just before going home as the boiled sweets had a very particular aroma and more than once their mother had sniffed the air and questioned the distinctive smell.

Lewis, my grandfather, at the age of nine was a bright and inquisitive boy. His most frequent question around this time was undoubtedly "why?" Theresa always tried to explain things properly because she was proud of his eagerness to learn, which I will say went against the grain of a lot of mothers of this time who would simply snap, "because I told you so, that's why." One day pair were walking along Acorn Road when Lewis noticed a group of pretty girls thrusting white feathers into the faces of some of the older boys. Lewis was confused by the boys angry reaction for surely attention from such pretty girls would be something to appreciate. He asked his mother 'why?' and he was taken aback at her brusque explanation. 'It is because those lazy boys should be in uniform.' She followed her statement up by adding, 'there is no bigger shame for a man than to be branded a coward.' This declaration was to stay with my grandfather throughout his life and her words would come back to haunt him most especially during World War 2 when he toyed with the idea of registering as a conscientious objector. But more of this later, as for now he is only a young boy aged nine, mindful of his mother's opinions and with a mind like a sponge.

APRIL 1915, ASHLEIGH GROVE, LE BRITTON FAMILY

In this next chapter I shall impart the facts as I know them, but may I take the opportunity to add that they are subject to hearsay? I shall endeavour not to contrive situations (although this goes against the grain for a novelist) as I promised myself while constructing this novel that I would travel back in time and try my best to resist the urge to tie up the loose ends.

I shall start by mentioning that during the month of April in 1915 The Cavalry moved en masse into West Jesmond. Their horses were housed in makeshift stables all along Highbury – right in front of John and Theresa's old house which would have so angered her mother if she had still been alive. Horse troughs lined the streets and Sentry posts were positioned at each end of Forsyth Road to guard this most precious of commodities. Anita Le Britton and her best friend Rita had taken to strolling up Ashleigh Grove after school each afternoon on the pretence of feeding carrots to their equine neighbours. Both schoolgirls had recently turned 14 and were in the delicate state poised between girlhood and womanhood. Their heads were brimming with romantic dreams, fuelled by the tawdry cheap novelettes of the period and they had set their sights upon a couple of young grooms who were tending the horses. It was not too long before mild flirtations in the form of shy smiles and hesitant waves had progressed to the two couples walking out together. Their first 'foursome' date was a trip to the duck pond on the opposite side of the railway track. This duck pond was a regular spot for canoodling couples during the war years, to such an extent that some keen romantic soul had constructed makeshift benches out of fallen logs and evenly spaced them around the pond. After the war ended the pond was drained for the erection of the Jesmond Picture House in 1922 – but the 'pit' still regularly flooded as the pond had been fed by water draining from the town moor. I suspect the girls' courtships were innocent by today's standards but they were scared their parents found out about them because soldiers had a bad reputation. It was not until a good few weeks into their burgeoning wooing that Anita's relationship went up a notch. The night in question Anita had taken the trip up the street to feed carrots to the horses alone because her friend Rita had been kept back at school for extra studies. Van, the soldier Anita was so smitten by, could not believe his luck to have her all to himself at last. He was not normally so inhibited in such matters but he had sensed from the onset that he was much more experienced than Anita, so it would be wise to take things slowly and not scare her off. I must at this stage also add that Van was not a natural soldier and to be honest he cared little for the King and country he had sworn to serve. His reason for joining up was purely because he could not bear to be parted from his horse Queenie, who he had nurtured since a foal. When the war had first began the previous year the Army only had 25,000 horses so they had made a concerted effort to procure another half a million from the length and breadth of Great Britain. Van was heartbroken when his precious mare was requisitioned, and rightly so, for the unfortunate fate of these poor creatures was well known even this early on in the military campaign. The requisitioning officer had taken pity upon the heartbroken young man and promised that if Van enlisted as an infantryman he would ensure the two remained together. Van's sole intention was not to fight but to protect his precious horse although he had been wise enough not to voice this to anybody else. His troop and the horses were due to be shipped out the following week so emotions were understandably heightened which goes some way to explain why Van found himself professing his undying love and asking Anita to wait for him to return. Rumours abound as to what occurred between the two lovebirds that evening following this declaration, but suffice to say that when Rita visited the house that evening Anita was keen to confide in her best friend. The two chums chatted on the front door step blissfully unaware that Oshbert had returned early from work and was standing in earshot. Oshbert waited until the coast was clear before strolling into his house that evening. When he passed his daughter on the stairs a short while later, he held fast his countenance and acted as if he had heard nothing untoward. He similarly held his composure with his wife Mary for he reasoned that with their son away fighting at sea she had enough on her plate already. It was later on that night as the other inhabitants of the house had settled down for the night that Oshbert quietly redressed on the landing before making his way up the street and towards the Cavalry Stables. Once there, he stood silently in the shadows watching and waiting as the groomsmen settled the horses down for the evening. It was not long before someone called out the young infantryman's name and Oshbert could ascertain who he was. I cannot suitably express the shock or horror which struck Oshbert when he made the connection and realised that Van was his son, grown up, now a man but still undoubtedly his son Silvanus. The novelist in me yearns to write how Oshbert called out to his long lost offspring and father and son shared a glorious reconciliation and long overdue reunion. But I have promised not to sway from the facts and the truth as I know it is that a heartbroken Oshbert shrank away from the scene like a thief in the night. He then spent the remainder of the evening sitting upright in his armchair internally debating what action to take. He knew his daughter was young and would not take his interference at all well, but likewise she would be truly shamed to know she had been romanced by her half-brother. Oshbert initially held no anger towards his son, for he reasoned that Silvanus would not have known who Anita was when they first met, but a little nagging thought preyed upon his mind. The thought that surely Anita's name would have sparked some alarm bells because the boy had made her acquaintance when he visited the house in Ashleigh Grove many years previously in 1906. I surmise that perhaps Van did have his suspicions but it is well documented that half-siblings often share an instant attraction so perhaps emotions overtook common sense.

I do know that the following morning Oshbert visited the Cavalry Officer in charge of the temporary Barracks and discussed with him his concern about his daughter having being romanced by the young groomsman. I am certain he made no mention of the 'half sibling' problem but focused instead on his daughter's reputation and tender age. The Officer for his part dispensed with protocol and promised Oshbert that he would see to it that Silvanus and his beloved horse Queenie were on the first deployment overseas, rather than the second as originally planned. I am forever thankful that Oshbert never discovered that he had condemned his son to a certain death because his interference that morning caused Silvanus to be deployed to Gallipoli to take part in one of the bloodiest battles of the entire War. Gallipoli was later remembered by veterans as one of the worst places to serve during the First World War. The casualties were exceptionally heavy and due to the risk of snipers the bodies were left to decay on no man's land for the duration of the battle. I have found out from Military Records that Silvanus perished in the July of that year and I can only presume his loyal companion Queenie suffered a similar fate. Van's meagre belongings were returned in due course to his mother Lemontina. His wallet contained very little bar a photograph of his sweetheart Anita and a lock of her auburn hair. His mother was too heartbroken to realise the significance of the girl's name for she had long since tired of seeking revenge upon Oshbert. If only Oshbert had known this, it may have offered him some comfort in his final years. But hindsight is a wonderful thing and Oshbert took the knowledge of what he perceived was an unbroken grudge to his grave.

I end this chapter by saying that I suspect this ill-fated love affair may have cast a shadow upon Anita's future relationships. Anita could not forget her young soldier lover and even after the dreadful war had run its course she would still search crowds for a glimpse of him. She never for one moment believed he had willingly abandoned her, for she was so resolute in the conviction of the feelings they had shared. As a postscript to this chapter I will add that a couple of months after Van's hasty deployment, Anita was sent away to Maesteg in Wales to stay a while with her mother's cousin and his wife. When she returned she had aged a decade and the innocent flame of youth had forever left her eyes. She never spoke directly of Van to either of her parents, so one small blessing is that she never knew of her father's involvement in her lover's fate.

JANUARY 1916, BAYSWATER ROAD,
KITCHENER'S ARMY, O'DOWD FAMILY

The World War was rapidly gaining momentum and it was clear from the vast number of casualties that the Services could no longer rely on volunteers alone. This was despite Lord Kitchener the Secretary of State for War's iconic recruitment campaign which had encouraged millions of volunteers in 1914. But despite this concerted effort, there was still a massive shortfall so in January 1916 the Military Service Act was passed through parliament to boost the numbers. This compulsory conscription targeted single men between the ages of 18 to 41. A second Act in May 1916 would include married men, but as my great-grandfather John O'Dowd worked in food production as a baker, he was classed as 'starred' and thankfully exempt. Likewise, my other great-grandfather Oshbert was then aged 48 so well over the age for compulsory conscription.

John O'Dowd and his wife Theresa were still running Hedleys the Bakery on Salters Road, although acquiring flour was getting increasingly more difficult. By 1917 there was food hardship all over Great Britain as the Germans, realising that we imported half of our food, were making a concerted effort to bomb supply ships. It has since been reported that alarmingly by the spring of 1917 Great Britain had only three weeks' supply of food left. Yet despite this, the Government was still reluctant to introduce rationing and instead declared that in future it would be illegal to have more than a two-course meal in a restaurant, and furthermore people would be fined if it was discovered they were feeding stray dogs or pigeons. When this did not make enough of a difference, the Government backtracked and introduced compulsory rationing to basic foods, and as most of Great Britain's wheat was imported from America, this rationing also included bread. This was the death knell for many a bakery but John and Theresa quickly cottoned on to using potatoes as a substitute for flour. The resulting bread was surprisingly palatable and sacks of the potatoes were delivered to the bakery on an almost daily basis. John's two sons, Lewis and John Junior, then had the unenviable task of peeling them so they could be boiled and mashed. This was my grandfather's abiding memory of growing up in the shadow of war. But other things too were changing because people were having to come up with even more inventive ideas. When all the horses were requisitioned by the Cavalry, a local grocer in Sheffield even took ownership of a circus elephant to assist with his deliveries, although I can find no evidence of this having happened in Newcastle.

Another problem my great-grandparents encountered during this time was the growing antipathy towards anyone of Irish descent, which was due in part to the much publicised Easter Rising of the Irish Republicans in the April of 1916. I believe it was around this time that my great-grandparents may have initially discussed dropping the 'O' from 'O'Dowd and the saving grace for the business was probably that the bakery was named Hedley's in a homage to my great-grandmother. It was not until the family relocated to Canada in 1923 that I can find the first written evidence of the family finally dispensing with the 'O', although my grandfather's brother, when he was ordained a Catholic priest, appears to have reinstated the missing 'O'.

FEBRUARY 1916, ASHLEIGH GROVE, THE GREAT POTATO DILEMMA, LE BRITTON FAMILY

Junior was returning home for a short leave and the entire household was in a state of excited anticipation. Mary had been marking the days off on the calendar in the kitchen and Oshbert teased that she had spoken of little else for over a week. She and Susie had been taking it in turns to make daily visits to the greengrocers so they could stock up on ingredients for Junior's favourite 'childhood' meals. Knowing of her son's love of warm bread, sliced fresh from the oven, and thickly spread with homemade jam, Mary had planned have a loaf baking in the oven to coincide with the time of his expected arrival. At this time flour was still in short supply but thankfully potatoes were still plentiful and she had - after much practice - finally perfected the 'potato' bread recipe. Therefore her dismay was understandable when - on the day before Junior was expected home - she discovered that the greengrocers on St George's Terrace had adopted a 'one potato per family member' policy. Oshbert returned home from work that night to find his wife sobbing quite unconsolably in the kitchen and for a brief and shocking moment he feared the worst. Ever since Junior had first signed up, he had lived in dread of the knock on the door and the visit from the Telegram Boy, so his relief when his wife had calmed sufficiently to explain the 'potato' dilemma was palpable. Once he had calmed her – and calmed his own still rapidly beating heart – he called the family into the lounge for one of his regular 'family meetings.' Arthur was last to descend the stairs. He was dragging his heels because the local shopkeeper, Mr Monroe, had caught him trying to pinch a gobstobber only that very morning and he was worried his father had got wind of it. He breathed an audible sigh of relief when his father laid out his hastily thought out plan to combat – what the family would forever after refer to as the 'great potato dilemma'. Striving to be more avant-garde, Oshbert had only recently started holding these family meetings, although as the Chairman, he still of course held the deciding vote. Once his family were seated, he put forward the proposal that they should all forego their potato rations so that their mother and Susie could have a 'bumper baking session' for Junior. Looking around the table at the sea of raised arms, Mary clapped her hands with glee and jumped from her chair to do a little impromptu jig – much to the amusement of the children who were more used to their mother being quiet and subdued. Then Oshbert added to the levity by remarking upon the large pile of socks – stacked on the sideboard - that his wife and Susie had spent many a winter's night knitting for Junior and his shipmates, and joked that during his time as a boxer Junior had surely received his fair share of socks already. Mary groaned at her husband's bad joke whilst the children giggled so incessantly and so loudly she had to threaten an early bedtime to get them to calm down.

Mary was still up to her elbows in flour and mashed potato when Junior arrived home. He was earlier than expected and after dropping his kit bag in the hallway he ran through to the kitchen to hug his precious mother. Despite telling herself she would not and must not, Mary burst into tears of distress, quickly disguising them as tears of joy for she was so shocked at the change in her darling boy. He had lost his former youthful exuberance as he stooped slightly as he raced towards her, and she could feel his shoulder bones jutting through the thin fabric of his shirt as she hugged him. Junior's lips had made the motion of a smile but the smile had not reached his eyes and they no longer twinkled and teased. But the unbridled euphoria of having him safely home and in her arms soon overpowered every other emotion.

"I've missed you mother," Junior managed to say, after eventually escaping her clutches.

Mary sobbed by means of a reply, before giving herself a little shake to help regain a modicum of composure.

"That smell is amazing mother. Are you baking bread? I've so missed your bread, the stuff I've been eating on Pepperpot is so blinking dry, I swear it's like eating sawdust."

"Pepperpot?'

"Oh that's what us lads call Penelope our ship. She's been shot at so much the poor girl's backside is now like a pepperpot." Junior said this as if getting shot at was a normal everyday occurance, before he noticed his mother's distraught expression and realised that gallows humour and profanity did not travel well and perhaps his colourful language would need to be put on the back burner for the duration of his leave.

"Any chance of a cuppa and a slice of warm bread and jam before the rest of the brood get back from school?"

"The bread's still proving, Junior, so how about a slice of cake and a cuppa instead? Why not go up and run yourself a nice hot bath and I will bring it up to you once it's brewed."

Junior was upstairs soaking in the bath when Susie walked into the house with the rest of the children. Leaving Rhys in his pram on the front path, she followed Junior's other three siblings into the kitchen.

"Is our Junior back yet mother?" Anita spoke first, nearly tripping over her words in her haste to ask her question. She was desperate to speak to her brother and find out if he had news of Van. She had written to Junior just before Christmas and his reply had given her false hope. Junior had not wanted to regail her with tales he had heard about the full horrors of the battles the Cavalry were fighting on the front. Like many of his peers, he strongly believed that such truths were not for the sensitive ears of loved ones at home. He had promised he would make enquiries when he had the chance, in the hope that it would help her sleep easier at night. He did not know of her 'holiday' in Wales, for the family thought it was not the kind of thing to put in a letter and were deliberately only writing morale-boosting news in their communications with their son.

"He's upstairs taking a bath so let him have some peace you lot. I am sure there will be plenty of time for chatter later on. Who wants a nice cup of tea and a slice of cake? But just a small piece mind, you don't want to spoil your dinner." Then Mary turned to address Susie, "Junior's left his clothes on the landing. If you have the time, would you be an angel and do a quick wash and I will carry on with the baking before Rhys wakes up and needs feeding again."

Arthur rushed to the hall shouting back over his shoulder 'I'll get them for you Susie, wait at the bottom of the stairs and I will drop them down."

The clothes landed with a resounding thud and after collecting the remainer of his laundry from his kit bag, Susie began to sort it in the scullery. She baulked when she realised the clothing was crawling with lice but decided it better not to spoil Mary's good mood by telling her, reasoning that a hot wash and carbolic soap would hopefully sort the problem out.

Oshbert returned early from the office that night, alighting from the train with a jaunty skip to his step. The younger chidren met him on the street and half-pulled half-dragged him towards the house to where Junior was sitting like the *Lord of the Manor* in their father's special chair. Seeing his father come into the room, Junior made to get out of the chair, only to be stopped by his father's firm hand upon his shoulder.

"You stay there son, you've earned the privilege of the best seat in the house. I'm quite happy to sit at the table with this merry band of vagabounds."

"I would have run away to sea much sooner if I thought I would get this kind of treatment," Junior joked much to the amusement of the rest of the children.

Later on that evening, Oshbert offered his son a glass of whisky, much to the disgruntlement of Mary but his reproachful look reminded her that things were changed and she must acknowledge that her precious son was grown-up. The two men took their drinks and stood for a while on the front step so they could chat and enjoy a smoke away from the ladies. Oshbert offered his son a puff of his pipe but Junior shook his head and reached deep into his trouser pocket for a packet of cigarettes instead. Junior lit his cigarette and inhaled deeply, spluttering as the intensity of the smoke hit his lungs. "Damn that hit the spot," he declared leaning back against the doorframe.

"Better not let your mother cuss like that young man. She would have my 'guts for garters' mithering on about what the neighbours would say.'

"All the lads on the ship swear father, it's what keeps us going through the bad times, that and the beer, although I must say I could develop a taste for this whisky. It's going down a treat. What's the story with our Anita and this lad then? She seems pretty smitten by him."

What possessed Oshbert to open up to his son on that night I shall never know. After keeping his secret for so long, perhaps the feeling of being on an equal footing, and the whisky played a part, for Oshbert found himself telling his son everything. He left nothing out even telling him the devastating story of Lemontina, the dead cat and the effigy doll. It was a long time before his son spoke, for he needed time to properly digest what his father was telling him.

"I understand why you can't tell Anita this," he said eventually. "My God it would break her heart. I swear I shall never tell a living soul what you have confided in me tonight. Can I ask if the blasted doll is still in the tin box in the attic?"

Oshbert nodded "Yes, I've tried to get rid of it many times. I always stop because I am afraid the curse may reignite if I do. I have no illusions that it is cursed, for Lemontina's mother was a black blood gypsy so well versed in the practice of witchcraft."

"Try not to read too much into it father. From the things I've seen, men can do far worse to each other than some cursed doll ever could, and there is nothing more fearful than fear itself."

"You could have a point there son, perhaps it is time for me to bite the bullet and get rid of it once and for all."

When the men returned back into the parlour, Mary raised her eyes from her knitting and sniffed the air casting Oshbert a reproachful look as if she suspected he had encouraged Junior to drink too much.

"What have you two been chatting about out there for so long? You appear thick as thieves." Mary said addressing her question to Junior. Oshbert quickly caught Junior's eye and they both shrugged.

"And they say we gossip? Bit like called the kettle black," Susie interjected and both women giggled.

"Man's talk if you must know," said Oshbert cryptically, winking in Junior's direction, "far too lewd and vulgar for your sensitive little ears."

"I'll wager it was about a girl," joked Susie, "So are you a typical sailor then our Junior? Do you have a girl in every port?"

Junior blushed a bright beetroot red and Oshbert, afraid that in his semi-intoxicated state he might blurt out the truth, jumped in to his son's rescue. "Susie, that's for you and his mother to speculate on, and for us men to know. Now who fancies making us both a nice cup of tea?"

During the entire week of his leave Susie ironed Junior's clothes on a daily basis with the hottest iron she could bear and still the dreadful lice remained hidden in the stitching.

On the day Junior was due to return to his ship, a deep sadness pervaded the house. Junior's kit bag sat heavily upon his shoulder as the numerous pairs of hand knitted socks had been squeezed inbetween his clothes. Wrapped up tightly and hidden in the toe of one of the socks was the effigy doll. His father didn't know that Junior had taken it, for he planned to write and tell him after he had thrown the blasted thing into the vast expanse of the North Sea. Junior and Oshbert's previous tenuous relationship had turned a corner during this leave, for Junior finally understood his father's obsessive need for control, as to live with the knowledge that his past actions had caused these terrible catastrophes must have been an intolerable cross to bear.

25TH APRIL, 1916, JUST OFF THE NORFOLK COASTLINE, LE BRITTON FAMILY

On 24th April, the previous night, Junior had clambered upon the deck of HMS Penelope 'Pepperpot' and with no preamble at all flung the damned effigy doll as far as he could into the black abyss of the sea. He had then returned to his bunk and settled down for the night assured that he had done this one little thing for his father. HMS Penelope, the ship on which Junior served, had been sent to sea to track down the German ships which had recently attacked Lowestoft. It was a dangerous mission and the crew were on high alert, but the torpedo from the UB-29 which struck the stern of the ship the following day came out of nowhere with no prior warning. Junior was below deck in the Engine Room when the torpedo exploded and he suffered a heavy blow to the back of his head and was catapulted backwards against the steam turbine. He was badly concussed and only survived because he was dragged to the poop deck by one of his shipmates. The steering gear and rudder of Pepperpot were both badly damaged in the blast, but thankfully Commodore Reginald Tyrwhitt managed to guide the stricken ship back to shore. Junior was immediately taken in an ambulance to the local hospital. His hasty departure was followed by his kit bag a few days later, after it had washed up on shore and been retrieved by a local fisherman. The kit bag was emptied and the contents placed in a bedside chest alongside Junior's hospital bed. During the night Junior persistantly complained of a disturbing noise coming from the drawer. No-one else could hear this noise so Junior was told it was most likely a result of his eardrum being damaged in the explosion, but he would not be appeased, and the noise which he described as a cackling continued to haunt both his waking and sleeping hours. When it reached the disturbing stage whereby Junior had started to sit muttering to himself with his hands pressed hard against his earlobes, the Matron decided she needed to take decisive action and called for the Porter to help her empty the drawer in a heap upon his bedclothes. She was to regret her actions when it took the strength of both herself and the Porter to restrain her patient, for after seeing the effigy doll staring up from atop his pile of belongings, Junior had quite lost his mind. The next day he was moved to a more secure room, and after being visited and assessed by the Doctor, it was unanimously decided that, due to his delicate mental condition, he was no longer fit for active service and he was medically discharged into the care of his family.

Upon returning home Junior suddenly became irrationally obsessed that his kit bag must never leave his side. One night Mary had crept into his room to try and remove his clothes for washing – this was because Susie had mentioned that on his previous leave his garments had been infested with lice – but as she inadvertanly stepped upon a creaking floorboard her son abruptly awoke, realised her intentions and became quite hysterical. So hysterical in fact that even his father could not manage to calm him, and eventually the local Doctor was called to administer a mild sedative. Mary decided there and then that given his extreme reaction it would probably be best to leave the clothes where they were for the time being as any lice were at least contained. A few weeks later when she and Susie were busy baking in the kitchen, Junior struggled from his bed – for he was still weak after the accident – and climbed the stairs to the attic with the sole intention of returning the cursed doll back into the tin box. As he tentatively dipped his hand into his kit bag to retrieve the doll, he felt a pincher like nip to his finger and he fell clumsily back upon Susie's bed in a state of shock. The commotion his fall created, alerted his mother and Susie and hearing them racing through the hallway and up the stairs, Junior tightly closed his eyes and steeled himself to try again. This time taking the precaution of grabbing the doll by its throat he managed to heave it from the bag then roughly thrust it into the tin box and slammed the lid shut. He had just enough time to hide the box back behind the loose brick in the eaves before the two women came thundering into the room. Witnessing the sight of her son lying there, an expression of abject horror playing upon his face, Mary cried out in despair, "oh son whatever are you doing in here?" Then noticing the wet patches on his striped nightshirt she quickly deduced that in all likelihood he had been searching for the bathroom and lost his bearings. Between them Mary and Susie managed to help Junior back to his bedroom, into clean dry clothes and settled him back into bed. Then Mary laid his kit bag at the side of his bed – grateful that in all the confusion Susie had seen fit to remove the dirty clothes from it. Junior was exhausted by his ordeal and fell into a fitful sleep. It was not until he woke a few hours later that he remembered that the doll had been dripping wet while the rest of his clothes had been bone dry. Alarmingly, the finger where the doll had nipped him throbbed like the steady beat of a drum. More alarmingly still, during the next few days it became dangerously infected and as poor Junior – fever raging thrashed about in his bed – the Doctor fearing the early onset of sepsis lanced the wound in an attempt to remove the infection. Mary and Susie were at a loss to understand how Junior had been injured and Junior himself was too delirious to cast any light upon the accident, but thankfully due to the Doctor's prompt action, and their constant nursing, Junior made a full recovery. Physically he was fine - but much like it had his father – the doll preyed upon his mind. For how had it still been wet when the rest of his clothes were dry? And stranger still, how had it returned to his kit bag? He vividly recalled throwing it overboard into the North Sea then watching it bob and sink beneath the waves.

The house too felt the return of the accursed doll and a familiar heaviness seeped though its brickwork. The bones of the Pilgrim meanwhile shifted once more to form the shape of a cross.

Sophia Davies and her second husband
Llewellyn Bevan, Maesteg, Wales. 1905

Oshbert Le Britton – mid 1890s

Dorothy Le Britton and
Rhys John Le Britton 1915

Mary Le Britton nee Davies and
Arthur Le Britton 1910

John O'Dowd, Lewis O'Dowd,
Dolly O'Dowd about 1918

John O'Dowd, Gosforth, 1922

Theresa O'Dowd/Dowd 1925.
Port Alberni, Vancouver Island

Lewis and John O'Dowd/Dowd painting the
Church of the Holy Name, Port Alberni 1923

Dorothy Le Britton 1927

Jimmy Monroe 1927

Liverpool Victoria Works Outing to Blackpool 1930. Dorothy far right with her best friend blanche and Lewis (kneeling).

Dorothy and daughter Joan 1941

Lewis Dowd 1941

Dolly Dowd and her niece Joan Dowd 1942

Dorothy at Wolveleigh Terrace, Gosforth with granddaughters' Leonie ,myself and son Martin in the pram 1964-65

Dorothy and Lewis with son Martin and grandson Ben. Mid 1980s

AUTUMN 1916, HEDLEYS BAKERY, O'DOWD FAMILY

Times were hard and meeting the rent on the business was increasingly difficult. The business relied upon supply and demand. The demand was there but the supplies were not. Sugar had nearly doubled in price, and with flour and latterly potatoes in such short supply, the couple were on their knees financially speaking. After a lengthy discussion - which went on well into the night - John eventually convinced Theresa that the only option was to go to her sister Frances and her husband Dr Tom Dewell to ask for a futher loan. The following afternoon, after leaving their eldest son in charge of his two siblings, the couple walked the short distance to Elmfield Road. With heavy hearts they knocked on the door and waited patiently as Maisie the housemaid rushed off to tell her employers that they had come to call. Frances eventually emerged from the drawing room and ushered the pair inside out of the drizzling rain. After enquiring about their general health she turned to Masie to ask if she could organise an impromptu tea. Frances took pains to emphasise the word 'impromtu' and this had the desired effect of 'prompting' her sister to apologise for turning up unannounced. Confident she now had the upper hand, Frances sat down and waited patiently for the couple to speak. No doubt she had a vague idea why they had called as the plight of small businesses was well recorded in the press and many bakeries had found themselves in similar predicaments. She could have led the conversation and eased the subject in to allow her sister and brother-in-law to retain a modicum of self-respect, but instead, for reasons known only to herself Frances chose to sit silently, arms folded, not resorting to any further small talk. John took the initiative and clearing his throat spoke up, "No doubt you realise we are not here purely on a social visit, although saying that it will be lovely to catch up on the family news. May I add we are not here 'cap in hand' but we have found ourselves at the mercy of this blasted war and wondered whether you and Tom could see your way to helping us in the form of a small loan. I understand this is a lot to ask, especially after you were so kind to help us out last time, but we are finding it increasingly difficult to make ends meet."

Frances leant back in her chair and nodded sagely, "I can't say I'm surprised you find yourselves in this unfortunate situation, Mother always did worry you would not be able to sufficiently provide for Theresa, which is probably why she tried to delay you marrying all those years ago. I'm casting no aspersions but perhaps if you had stopped at one child instead of going on to have three you might not be in such a desperate position. Tom and I manage to provide very well for our darling Winifred and we see that she does not go without the finer things in life." John felt his wife stiffen in her chair and he laid a placatory hand upon her knee. They had spoken of this very scenario the previous night and agreed to keep calm heads in the face of provocation just like this. John realised it was one thing to talk about keeping one's cool, but another to actually do it, and he dearly wished he could wipe the smug self-righteous expression from his sister-in-law's face. He could only imagine how Theresa was feeling and he was immensely proud of his wife for holding her patience so. As he was undoubtedly the cooler headed of the two, John once again took the lead.

"I am sorry that you view our circumstances so; we are trying very hard, and I honestly think how many children we chose to have is up to us and us alone. We were providing very well for our family before this happened and had the country not been in a state of war we would not have found ourselves in such an unfortunate position. We do not ask this favour lightly and have debated long and hard before approaching you and Tom. We realise you helped us once before and, as you know, we repaid that debt as soon as we were able so we had hoped that as you were family you would be willing to help once again. But we totally understand if you don't have sufficient funds to do so."

This parting shot had the desired effect for Frances was a proud woman and to insinuate that she and Tom were also struggling was something she would rather die than admit. Frances relaxed into her chair and with this change of stance her whole demeanour seemed altered and she added in a more concilitary tone.

"I tell you what? If you leave this with me tonight I will try my best to sweet talk Tom. As you know, we have an old fashioned marriage and I leave the complicated monetary decisions to my husband." This was an obvious dig at her sister's more modern relationship of equals, but as promised, once again Theresa did not rise to the bait. Instead she stood rather briskly up from her chair and motioned to leave, only to be stopped in her tracks by Frances insisting they stayed for tea.

"Oh no don't rush off, please stay a while longer. Maisie will be in with the tea any moment now. Let's catch up on happier news. Did I tell you Winifred has been accepted into the Medical School at Oxford?" And with that, she started to brag and brag and brag about her clever daughter and her amazing aptitude for the sciences and how proud their poor dead father would have been at the prospect of another Doctor following in his footsteps. She stopped her lengthy encomium briefly in order to pour the tea, and that was when John took the opportunity to catch his wife's eye and feign 'dropping off to sleep.' Theresa tried her utmost to suppress a fit of giggles and managed to disguise the ensuing guffaw as a loud dry cough. Suddenly, Frances was most concerned and forced a cup of tea into her hands declaring, "my dear sister that is a very bad cough you have there, remind me to ask Tom to take a look tomorrow."

"Or you could ask the future doctor Winifred to take a look," John quipped, causing Theresa once again to collapse into a hopeless fit of coughing. Thankfully, the sarcastic comment went right over Frances' head and she replied in a confused tone.

"Oh John, surely you realise it will be quite some time before she is anywhere near as qualified as her father and grandfather."

As they walked back home later that afternoon, John and Theresa were in much better frames of mind for laughter had the effect of making things seem far better than they actually were. Theresa even had to stop and lean against a garden wall on more than one occasion – and succumbing to further fits of giggles - as she kept reliving John's comedic act. John always had the capacity to see the humour in a situation; it was one of things which had so attracted Theresa to him in the first place. It was while they walked – and quite out of the blue for John had presumed that particular ship had sailed - that Theresa declared that she had not forgotten her promise of starting a new life abroad, and once this dreadful war had passed perhaps they should reconsider this. John was so overjoyed that he grabbed his wife by the shoulders and kissed her right there and then in the middle of the street, not caring who was twitching behind their net curtains. Propriety went out of the window. The only proviso was that they did not seek their fortune in New York, as they had originally planned for, since the near miss on the Titanic, it felt like bad luck. Then, still in a jovial mood, Theresa added, "I suggest you don't get me pregnant before we leave either." John twirled her around then looking deep into her eyes he said, "that promise may be harder to keep for I have never seen you look more radiant or loved you more. I shudder to think how I would feel if I had ended up with a stuffy wife such as your dear sister."

"Or I with the equally obnoxious Tom," Theresa retorted, then they both had to stop and lean against a wall for a while until their laughter subsided.

The next day, as promised, Dr Tom came to call. He announced that he had spoken to his wife the previous evening and she had made mention of the small loan. Unfortunately, they could not be overally generous as they had Winifred's education to think about but they could offer them half the amount they had asked for on an interest-free basis, to be repaid once the War had taken a turn for the better. Theresa was so grateful she crossed the room to hug her brother-in-law only to be stopped in her tracks when he declared, "better not get too close my dear, Frances mentioned you had a severe coughing fit at the house yesterday, and I am forever wary of catching germs. How are you now?"

"I'm fine thankyou Tom, think it was just a case of something going down the wrong way," desperately avoiding her husband's eye incase it sparked another coughing fit.

At this point in the novel I will mention that Winifred did indeed go onto become a Doctor, which was a great achievement for a woman at that time, for while nursing was seen as a suitable role for women to undertake, the very prospect of women becoming doctors was seen as beyond their 'limited capabilities.' A few notable women, such as Elizabeth Garrett Anderson, had successfully overcome the prejudices, but they were to prove the exception rather than the norm. Winifred's saving grace had bizzarly been the outbreak of war, as with the lack of men available to take places in Medical Schools, the Universities were short of funding. To this end in 1916 Oxford welcomed its first female medical students, a move which was unprecedented and on the whole extremely unpopular with the 'old school lecturers.' This first pioneering enrolment included Winifred, and her parents were understandably overcome with pride, although Tom did have a brief moment of hesitation as he realised the total cost of this academic sojourn. Winifred went on to excel in her class and once qualified, she became a School Doctor, with overall responsibility for the North East of England, which I am led to believe, was quite an accolade. My grandfather always referred to his cousin reverently as 'The Doctor', in deference no doubt to her hallowed status. For her to succeed on an even playing field with male counterparts was an achievement in itself especially because women did not attain voting rights until 1928. My mother remembers her 'auntie' as being a no-nonsense type of woman with mannerisms perhaps more suited to a man. She lacked the more feminine traits of the fairer sex and held no truck with young women just settling for the role of wife and housemaker. She tried to instil this ideology into my mother but it fell on deaf ears. My mother remembers that Winifred's cheeks burned red with frustration when she discovered that my father had proposed and she had accepted. Winifred went out of her way to persuade her favourite 'niece' to reconsider and weigh up her options. She offered my mother the job as her companion, sugaring the pill by promising to introduce her to her good friend and fellow bridge player the dashingly handsome Omar Sharif. My mother was a great fan of the movie magazines - so this must have been a most tantalising prospect – and at this time Omar was very much the 'star on the rise', poised on the brink of a Hollywood career with rumours abounding that the Director David Lean was scouting him to appear in Lawrence of Arabia. But my mother was blinkered by love and couldn't wait to start her new life as a 1950s suburban housewife.

My own memories of Winifred are sporadic, but I do remember visiting her and her companion Elizabeth quite often in the 1970s. They were rattling about the family home on Elmfield Road, living in one room, and despite Winifred's Doctor's Pension, surviving on a diet of tinned baked beans and custard creams. Two rather dotty old ladies surrounded by relics of the past. I was an avid reader of Dickens at the time and always likened Winifred to Miss Haversham and Elizabeth to her much maligned adopted daughter Estella, for the old family pile did have the feel of a ruined mansion with clouds of dust settling on almost every surface.

NOVEMBER 11TH, 1918, ASHLEIGH GROVE, JESMOND

The 'war to end all wars' had finally run its course and with the final death toll for England alone standing at almost a million people, thereafter discussing the Great War would forever include reminisces about a 'lost generation' of young men. But on the day that peace was declared, the whole country seemed to unite to celebrate Armistice Day. The children were granted an extended holiday from school and, despite the inclement weather, people took to their streets to commemorate the momentous day. Tables decorated with homemade flags were dragged from back kitchens and laden with a vast array of pies, cakes and homemade biscuits, while neighbours who had previously only been on nodding aquaintence, hugged and kissed while dancing around the tables and drinking copious amounts of alcohol. Oshbert Le Britton feigned a smile and pretended to join in the jollification along with his family, but his heart was not really in it because he kept recalling the Rudyard Kiping couplet from Etipaphs of War. Again and again the same two lines – almost as a mantra – repeated in his mind, invading his conscious hours.

'If any question why we died/ Tell them, because our fathers lied.'

No doubt the words resonated more, as Oshbert empathised with Kipling, who in a surge of patriotism, had encouraged his own son John to enlist, only for the pitiful boy to perish in Loos in 1915. Rightly or wrongly, Oshbert believed he had similarly sealed the fate of his estranged son Silvanus, by insisting he be deployed as soon as possible. He told himself he had spoken out that morning purely to protect his daughter's good name, but in truth he knew he had, in part, also done so to save himself from a potentially damaging argument with Mary. His past was still a major bone of contention in their marriage and, although not spoken about directly, it was always there brewing just beneath the surface. To have to choose one child's life over another is a thing which no parent should ever have to contemplate and for poor Oshbert it must have been a harrowing decision. Of course Oshbert could only speculate upon the fate of Silvanus, but knowing as I do, that Oshbert was a well read man, he would surely have kept abreast of the situation abroad and known of the true horrors of trench warfare.

The war had touched the entire population and, despite most of the fighting having taken place away from home, there were very few families who were not directly affected by bereavement. A rare exception appears to have been my paternal great-grandparents, the O'Dowds, who although impacted financially were otherwise untouched by the mass sorrow surrounding them. For this, both John and Theresa were eternally grateful and they said a special prayer at mass each week at thanking God for sparing them the heartbreak of sending their two beloved boys abroad to fight. As Theresa was want to say on an almost daily basis, "but for the grace of God we would be walking in the shoes of the wretched souls grieving for their lost children."

1919, THE SPANISH INFLUENZA OUTBREAK, LE BRITTON FAMILY

It seemed that no sooner had Great Britain emerged from the spectre of World War 1, than she had a new and potentially more deadly enemy lapping at her shores. This invisible enemy had first showed its face in Europe, Asia and USA in the Spring of 1918, barely six months before Germany had signed the Armistace Agreement which ended the dreadful war. Wartime censorship at the time forbade the sharing of the rapidly increasing statistics regarding the fatal pandemic – as it was feared it would damage morale – but Spain, being neutral, had no such restrictions in place so the rest of Europe dubbed it the Spanish Flu. This annoyed the Spanish who persistated in calling it the French Flu as they were convinced it had originated in France. The first wave of the pandemic erupted in the Spring of 1918, and it was basically no more than a severe case of the flu, but the second wave which peaked in the autumn of the same year was much more indiscriminatory. It has since been reported that the lethal flu claimed more than 40 million victims, and that more US soldiers lost their lives to the deadly disease than actually died in battle. This pandemic is all the more relevant as I write this chapter, because the world is now in the throes of the Coronavirus 2019 pandemic and the similarities between the two virus outbreaks, are becoming more evident. Covid 19 has - despite the advances in medical science - spread more quickly than the virus of 1918, but this may in part be attributed to advances in air travel, which have made otherwise desolate parts of the world accessible, and as a result, more vunerable. Only the most isolated areas escaped the deadly virus in 1918 and likewise, a century later, it appears that the more populated areas of the world are the worst affected. The world in 2020 is filled with trepadation in expectation of the much more severe second wave. It is praying that this latest pandemic will peak, burn out and disappear before it has a chance to mutate. Scientists everywhere are working day and night to perfect a vaccine as they fear that, as it was then so will it be now, a case of survival of the fittest.

Throughout the long and arduous war years Oshbert Le Britton's health had taken a dramatic turn for the worse, but Oshbert being Oshbert, he had soldiered on and steadfastly refused to take even a day off work. When Mary mithered around and fussed over him he would brush her ministrations away by saying, " if men can fight in trenches knee deep in mud, I am sure I can pull myself together enough to sit at an office desk all day." I have no doubt the cursed 'effigy doll' played a major part in his final demise because Oshbert was subjected to mental strain on an almost daily basis due to the latest mischief of the doll. I am loathe at this stage in the novel to carry on calling it an 'effigy doll' for such a description conjures up a mental vision of a child's innocent plaything, and I can no longer pretend it is not the manifestation of evil, in its purest form, so I shall if I may – despite my former scepticism - rename it the 'creature'. The 'creature' had once again reared its ugly head this time taking its pleasure from stalking the entire household but most particularily poor Junior. It was as if it sensed his delicate mental state and thrived upon tyrannizing him. A sudden unexplained draught, a clattering of hangers in a closet, the lightest of touches on the shoulder, a whispered name in an ear, were its calling cards of choice. Oshbert took his usual stance of dismissing such phenomena with logical explanations, in the same manner he had previously when the wardrobe doors had rattled on their hinges to predict a death in the family. Mary, however, was all too aware of the effect this 'poltergeist' - as she called it - was having upon her shell-shocked son, and when her plea's to Oshbert fell on deaf ears, she decided to take matters into her own hands. Without his knowledge she implored Susie to ask her local priest if he could conduct an exorcism of the house. Mary's reasons for asking Susie were twofold. On the one hand, she reasoned that given the Catholic faith's old fashioned belief in the fire and brimstone concept of Hell, the priest might be well versed in such practices and, secondly, she knew that by not asking her own preacher, Oshbert would be less likely to discover she had gone behind his back. It was at this stage that Susie decided to confess to the fact that some years prior, after being scared witless by the feeling of a presence in her bedroom, her mother had asked the Catholic priest to bless her Rosary Beads. Knowing of the old priest's unfortunate demise in the Zeppelin attack upon Great Yarmouth in 1915, she wondered out aloud if perhaps as a result of his death the Rosary Beads had lost their healing powers. The actual attack hadn't harmed Father O'Neill directly - although it did claim two other lives that night - but the shock of the house opposite his sister's collapsing in the blast, had caused the old priest to suffer a devastating stroke. His successor was a much younger and much more progressive man, so Susie was unsure if he would agree to carry out an exorcism but she promised Mary she would ask that Sunday after Mass.

Oshbert had been drawn to the 'creature' with an increasing frequency ever since Armistace Day, and his obsession had grown to such an extent that he had taken to checking upon it every Sunday, whilst the rest of the family attended Chapel. His own children were now sporting bags of camphor around their necks - because Oshbert had recently read an article in a Medical Journal which claimed that it might help ward off the dreadful virus - and he had noticed the 'creature' smelt of camphor the very last time he checked upon it. Oshbert thought it strange at the time, because he knew for certain that the 'creature' had been in the tin box in the attic when Mary had placed the oily cubes into the jute bags the previous morning.

One day in February - while the school was closed in a desperate effort to slow the epidemic - Oshbert stood straightening his tie in the hallway mirror, in the same way he did every morning before leaving for work. Mary had just come out from the parlour to wave him off and she was shocked when she noticed how grey and drawn her husband looked. When she expressed her concern, Oshbert as usual dismissed it out of hand, and declared his pale pallor was most likely because he had not slept well the previous night. Mary was tempted to remind him that she had more than once during the night had reason to nudge him awake, so he would turn over and stop his infernal snoring, but thought better of starting the day on a squabble and let his comment go. However, she had also noticed how slowly he rose from his chair and how little of his breakfast he ate that morning, for he had pushed his porridge to the sides of the bowl with his spoon and barely sipped his tea. Before she had a chance to say anything else, the younger children raced down the stairs to walk their father to the train station, as they normally did when they were off school. They could not believe their luck when after reaching the platform their father reached in his overcoat and took out his wallet so he could give them each a few pennies to spend on sweets. He gave his youngest daughter, Dorothy, a few extra pennies and asked if she could buy her mother a nice bright bunch of flowers to cheer her up. He then asked the children to give their mother a special hug and tell her not to worry so much. He chuckled as Dorothy recited in a parrot fashion the little saying he had taught her, 'you die if you worry, you die if you don't, so why worry?' Patting her gently on the head, he climbed onto the train then he jauntily tipped his hat in the direction of the youngsters before gingerly settling down into his usual seat. This was the last time any of the children were to see their precious father alive.

Oshbert returned from work early that afternoon and he went directly upstairs to the master bedroom closing the door firmly behind himself. When Mary – who had worriedly followed him upstairs – knocked at the door to ask if he was alright, he told her she must not under any circumstances come into the room. Then in a very weak voice he asked if she could possibly leave a chamber pot by the door, so he could collect it later to carry out his ablutions. Mary immediately knew that it was something serious, so she and Susie quickly and quietly moved the children's bedding to the ground floor so they could all camp out in the lounge. The children were understandibly distraught as it was unheard of for their father to come home poorly from work. Two laborious days went by and Oshbert got progressively weaker and progressively worse. Mary could only stand at the doorway, wearing a mask about her face as he forbade her to enter. On the evening before he died, he managed to croak a request to hear his favourite tune played on the piano one more time. The older boys dragged the piano into the hall, which was no mean feat as pianos are notoriously heavy and unwieldy, and this one was no exception. Anita, his eldest daughter, positioned herself at the bottom of the stairs and started to play 'Too-Ra-Loo-Ra-Loo-Ra'. She played it again and again, on a loop, with tears coursing down her cheeks and until the tips of her fingers smarted and stung. She played it until her mother leant over the banister and motioned for her to hush as Oshbert had finally drifted off to sleep. Mary later told Anita that Oshbert had smiled as she played, but I suspect that Mary was saying this to ease her daughter's pain for from her position at the doorway she could barely see her husband, let alone his expression. It was in the early hours of the next morning that Oshbert struggled to take his last gasping breath before sinking back into his pillow for the final time. He was just fifty one years old and another tragic victim of the devastating second wave but thankfully due to his quick actions at containing the virus, his wife and children were all mercifully unscathed.

The piano was dragged back into the parlour the day after he died, and it sat untouched gathering dust until the family moved house many years later. Anita never played another note. At family parties the others would try and cajoal her into playing a tune, but she steadfastly refused, for she could not bear the memories it dredged up. As far as I am aware until the day she herself died, at the ripe old age of seventy nine, she never again laid her fingers upon a piano key.

My grandmother Dorothy was still only a young girl of seven when her precious father died, and her beloved father's passing, had a profound effect upon her too. It is not until now, with the benefit of hindsight, that I realise how this manifested itself. I always remember thinking it was strange that her Hollywood 'crushes' were as opposite as chalk and cheese for whilst she idolised Rudolph Valentino for his swarthy Latin good looks, her other Hollywood hearthrob was the rather effeminate actor Clifton Webb. We used to tease her that surely he must have been gay for there were never any reports of his romantic assignations and he lived with his domineering mother until she died in 1960. When Noel Coward made his famous quip, 'it must be terrible to be orphaned at the age of seventy one', it reinforced the longheld suspicion that Clifton - the mummy's boy - had no interest in any other ladies. My grandmother however would not be swayed in her affections, no hunky beefcake Clark Gable, or suave Cary Grant for her; no, it was the slight, fey, effete, moustached Clifton Webb all the way. I've come to realise since writing this novel that her father Oshbert had a look of Clifton Webb about him. Likewise both men were fastidious about their appearance and fussy to the point of being pernickety, so the similarities were always there, but they appear even more evident when I think of Clifton playing the role of Frank Bunker Gilbreth, the patriarchal father to a large brood of children in *Cheaper by the Dozen*. Another altogether more unfortunate similiarity, can be found in the film's sequel *Belles on their Toes*. The film tells the tale of how the bereaved family struggle to make ends meet after the death of their father. This must have also resonated with my grandmother because after Oshbert died, Mary discovered that despite being a Branch Manager for a large Insurance Company for a large part of his adult life, he had neglected to insure himself and as a result his family, whilst not destitute would need to seriously tighten their belts. Bizzarly, this problem was to manifest itself again fifty years later when my grandmother discovered when moving house, that my grandfather had also neglected to insure both himself and his home. As he worked for the same Insurance Company as his father-in-law had, it was very much a case of 'history repeating itself.'

For a short while at least, as Junior and Anita were still working, Mary realised that she could remain in Ashleigh Grove although, however she tried to tweak the finances, there was no way they could afford to keep Susie in their employ. To her credit, Susie was so worried how Mary would cope with the young children, that she offered to work only for board and lodgings so she could stay in the family home. It was not long after Oshbert's death that the 'creature' decided to once again rear its ugly head. The Catholic Priest's exorcism – conducted a few weeks after the funeral - had suppressed it for a while but the strength of the 'creature' was such that it would not be quelled for long. It seemed to 'up its game', almost as if it was bored with being sidelined and ignored. Its haunting reached such an extent that the younger children started to refuse to go to the toilet or bathroom alone and would insist either their mother or Susie escort them, then wait upon the landing until they had finished. Susie made a joke of the whole affair so as not to feed their fear but even she felt a trepidation late in the evening as she made her way up the attic stairs to bed. She took to sitting by the fire in the kitchen until the early hours of the morning, often falling asleep in the armchair once almost setting alight to her embroidery which slipped from her hands as she slumbered. In the end, it was Mary who took the initiative and declared that enough was enough and the family would no longer be subjected to live in fear. First of all Mary enlisted her two oldest sons, Junior and Arthur, to construct a makeshift bedroom with curtain partition in the master bedroom so that Susie and she could share, yet still retain a modicum of privacy. Susie had argued that she felt it unfair that she was depriving Mary of a bedroom, but Mary waved her concerns away by saying the room was too empty and spacious now anyway with Oshbert gone. Then, when the younger children were at school, and Junior and Anita had left for work, she coaxed a reluctant Susie up the attic stairs so they could make a start on emptying the rooms. Between them that morning the two women managed to lug the furnishings down the rather narrow stairs and pile them up on the landing to sort through later that afternoon. It was not until they moved the rather cumbersome dressing table squeezed under the eaves, that Mary first noticed the wall. The loose brick was probably more visible because the sunlight was filtering through the dormer window and shining in an arc light fashion upon it. Mary instinctively leaned across and prodded the loose cement work around the dislodged brick, then jumped back hollering a loud cry of pain. Quite bizarrely the brick and the surrounding area had been scorching hot and as she cradled her hand wincing in pain, Susie noticed that the flesh was already puckering and starting to blister. Seeing how distressed Mary was, Susie decided it would be quicker for her to race downstairs and fetch a large bucket of cold water than to try and help Mary down the narrow stairs so she raced from the room. Once she returned she persuaded Mary to open her clenched fist and thrust her whole hand right up to the wrist into the icy cold water. Mary initially cried out in shock for the water was freezing cold but after a short while it seemed to be starting to soothe, so Susie left her sitting there and approached the brick herself. She had taken the precaution of picking up Oshbert's old winter gloves when she fetched the cold water so wearing this basic protection she gingerly prodded and poked at the edge of the brick. The brick scraped against the cement moving slightly so she pushed it with more force and it fell to the floor – thankfully narrowly missing her feet - with a resounding thud. The hidden cavity was suddenly exposed, and peering in, Susie could see pushed far into a corner a rather rusty tin box. She cautiously leant in and shuffled the box to the edge before grasping it in both hands and bringing it to where Mary sat cross legged upon the floor, her hand still in the bucket of water. Both women held their breath as Susie, using one of the hairclips from her bun, prised the top of the tin box open. They both jumped apart as the lid swung off and they saw the grinning 'creature' staring up at them.

"Whatever is it Susie?" Mary managed to finally whisper in a tiny voice. Susie guessed immediately because the Priest had persistently questioned if they had such an object in the house when he performed the exorcism and she had most adamantly declared no.

"I don't want to scare you Mary, but I believe it is what they call an 'voodoo doll."

"Is it cursed do you think?" Mary hesitantly asked, although in her heart of hearts she already knew the answer.

"Well it would certainly explain a lot if it were. But how long has it been here and whoever hid it in there in the first place?" Susie replied.

Mary outstretched her leg and with the tip of her shoe tipped the box over so its entire contents spread on the rug between them. Pushing the doll to one side with the hairclip, Susie lifted out one of the letters trying not to gasp out aloud as she realised the envelope containing the letter was addressed to Oshbert.

It was at that moment Junior bounded up the stairs and barged into the room causing both women to jump with surprise as he was not expected back from work until much later that afternoon. Something had prompted Junior to leave work early and until the day he died he could not say what had prompted him, but he just knew he was compelled to go home straight away.

Without thinking and somewhat stating the obvious he said "You've found the box then."

Mary jumped to her feet almost upturning the bucket of water, which dramatically sloshed at her feet. She was incredulous with rage as she stood in front of her son and demanded, "You knew it was here?"

Susie stopped her in her tracks by handing her the letter and saying, "You need to see this first Mary." Both Junior and Susie stood silently by while Mary read the letter. Mary read the letter with tears of rage coursing down her cheeks and once she had reached the signature at the bottom of the page she crumpled it into a ball and threw it to one side.

"Who is letter from Junior?" Susie demanded.

"It's from a woman called Lemontina. She was my father's fancy woman before he met mother."

Mary turned to stare incredulously at her son, "I cannot believe my ears. You knew of Lemontina? Of all of this?" As she spoke, she gestured her arms towards the tin box before adding, "and yet you chose to keep it secret. You chose to deceive me and keep your father's dirty little secret?"

Junior hung his head low, he could not look his mother in the eyes as he desperately searched for the right words to explain his actions. Eventually he mumbled his answer, which even to his own ears was pathetically inept, "father told me of it many years ago when I was home on leave. Those letters and that bleeding doll had ruined his life. He made me promise to keep them both a secret for he knew how it would upset you. He was trying to protect you, to protect all of us." As he said this, Junior forcefully with the heel of his boot, kicked the doll into the corner of the room, trying not to grimace as it seemed to inexplicably nip at his ankle.

It was as he did this that Mary noticed the crude drawing of a cat, which had been hidden by the torso of the doll. Turning and glaring at her son she snapped, "you seem to be the expert on all of this, what's the significance of this child's crude drawing then?"

Junior shrugged his shoulders before replying in what he hoped was a convincing voice, "I have no idea what it's about." Junior lied, for he knew he could never and would never tell her what it really meant for that knowledge would surely tip his mother over the edge into the vast abyss of madness. For a while the room fell silent before Susie took the initative and interjected, "I suggest we take this rubbish and burn it all in the fire, including that stupid doll." After saying this and without waiting for Mary to agree, she roughly gathered everything up and stuffed it back into the box before firmly snapping shut its lid. The trio made their way downstairs with all the slowness and solemnity of a funeral cortege. Once they reached the kitchen Susie stoked the fire, then while Mary and her son stood aside and looked wordlessly on, she tipped the entire contents of the wretched box into the coals. As the fire licked and danced around it the 'creature' let out what could only be described as a blood curdling scream and Junior dipped across towards the flames as if to rescue it. Mary pushed her son roughly away snarling, "don't you dare try and protect that foul thing or it will be the last time you set foot in my house." Susie fussed around the pair in an attempt to diffuse the situation. She made a pot of sweet tea and gently guided Mary from the fireside towards the table so that she could dress her wounded hand. "There there, that should make you feel more comfortable," she said as she fastened the bandage carefully with a knot, "just try and remember that Oshbert was a good man and he did what he thought was best to protect you and protect his family. You know as well as I that your husband did not have a malicious bone in his body, God rest his soul." With these words Mary seemed to settle into her chair and took a tentative sip of her tea. But her calm state did not last and a few minutes later, quite without prior warning, she jumped to her feet and declared that she needed some air. Junior made to follow his mother from the room but Susie shook her head in his direction and said, "give her some time to think it over lad. Come sit by me and have some tea, you've had a bad shock too."

It was much later that same evening, after the rest of the family were settled and sleeping soundly in their beds, that Mary suddenly awoke and knew what she had to do. She stumbled down the stairs and made her way through the kitchen and out into the yard. Once she reached Oshbert's shed she pulled the wooden door open so sharply she nearly pulled it from its hinges, then lighting a candle so that she could see more clearly she reached in and grabbed a large axe that Oshbert had used to chop firewood and kindling. The axe was heavy. It was so heavy that she had to drag it behind her for she could not bear its weight. She struggled into the house only to come face to face with her shocked son. "Whatever are you doing mother? please put it down and go back to bed," he said haltingly for he was not convinced that she was not sleepwalking. For the second time that day, Mary pushed her son away – and for a second time he was taken unawares and stumbled and fell against the door. Ignoring his pathetic plight Mary carried on through the kitchen, through the hallway and then on through the porch before reaching the front of the house. Once outside, she clambered over the tiny wall surrounding the front garden and made her way decisively towards the hand crafted bench which Oshbert had so lovingly constructed for her all those years ago. With the strength of ten men she then hauled the axe above her shoulders and started to chop indiscriminately at the seat of the bench. Junior eventually managed to grapple the axe from her grasp and taking her in his arms; he half dragged her into the house and away from the prying eyes of the neighbours – who hearing the commotion in the street were all now standing in their nightclothes at their front doors. Between them Junior and Susie managed to settle Mary down with a large glass of medicinal brandy, which thankfully had the desired effect and knocked her quite literally from her feet. Susie took Mary back upstairs while Junior, after trying to help but being pushed away, declared that he would stay downstairs for a while to clear things up. He stood in the hallway patiently listening until he heard the sounds of his mother and Susie settling into their beds, then he returned to the kitchen and crossing towards the dying fire he bent double so he could rake amongst the ashes and retrieve the 'creature.' Junior was not altogether surprised as he realised that it was barely scorched, for he knew from past experience of its ability to defy logic. Holding it carefully aloft in the palm of his hand he made his way towards his father's shed. Then once there he squeezed the 'creature' into the dark depths, secreting it under a wooden box of nails. Junior knew he was defying his mother's express instructions by doing this, but much like his father before him, he felt it was now his responsibility to watch over it and protect the family.

1923, THE BIG CANADIAN ADVENTURE, O'DOWDS

Theresa O'Dowd had been true to her word and once the dreadful war and deadly flu had run their devastating apocalyptic course, she honoured her promise to reconsider a new life abroad. After much deliberation, the family decided on Canada and more particularily on the island of Vancouver in British Columbia. I confess that I have often wondered why they had made the decision to move there - for after all the world was their proverbial oyster - but from investigating this further I have discovered that a first cousin of Theresa's mother had emigrated there many years earlier. Ada and her husband Thomas

Hutchinson appear to have taken advantage of a Government scheme whereby settlers were enticed to Canada by a promise of a free Land Grant. The couple initially settled between Ucluelet and Tofino on the west coast, setting up a homestead on the allotted 160 acres and cultivating their newly acquired land, but some time after the birth of their eldest daughter, they upped roots and moved across the Island to make their home in Port Alberni. I have no doubt that encouraging communication had taken place between the two cousins over the passing years and this probably, more than anything, else convinced John and Theresa that their future lay in Canada. It must have been incredibly daunting to plan to travel such a distance so to know that there was a friendly face awaiting you at your final destination must have made the journey so less intimidating.

Lewis, the couple's eldest son, had just turned seventeen. Both of his parents had tried their best to encourage him to fully embrace the family bakery business but Lewis had a longheld dream of becoming an artist. When he had tentatively told his parents of his artistic dreams, John had tried his best to fight his son's corner but Theresa - who even then was the stronger in character of the two - was not one to take a back seat regarding her eldest son's future. At some stage during the deliberations she had voiced her concerns to the local priest, who had told her that under no circumstances should she allow Lewis to pursue such an aesthetic career. His primary concern - which he discreetly shared with Theresa - was that such training would involve him drawing nude models in a life class and this would surely turn his head to impure thoughts. It had always been his mother's expectation that her son would eventually enter the priesthood so when Lewis – aggrieved at not been allowed to follow his dream's snapped that he had no wish to 'become a stuffy self-righteous priest' it was probably the main decisive thing that spurred his mother on to agree to finally set the wheels in motion for the big Canadian adventure.

John senior had initially suggested he travel out alone to 'check the lay of the land as it were' but Theresa was adamant that the family stay together. This disinclination to spend time apart, if nothing else, confirms that theirs was a marriage of soulmates and not only of convenience. Theresa's other concern at this time appears to have been John's declining health, for during the long dark years of the war his constant worries regarding the family finances had manifested itself in many ways. John was suffering from what we now refer to as *obstructive sleep apnea,* which is a condition whereby your breathing stops and starts as you sleep; it is directly linked to obesity and getting older. Often, late in the night, Theresa awoke in their bed slightly disorientated for she was so used to his constant loud snoring that, when it suddenly stopped, it inevitably woke her. She developed an almost subconcious habit of nudging him awake and his constant complaint during this time seemed to be that he never seemed to get a full night's sleep. Her constant retort was that due to his loud snoring nor did anyone else in the household. His weight too had been steadily increasing ever since they opened the bakery on Salters Road, and many was the time Mary had caught her rather portly husband with his hand in the 'cookie jar' sampling the biscuits she had baked. It must be said that John had a sweet tooth so running a confectioners was perhaps not the wisest of career choices. Rather similar I imagine to employing an alcoholic to run a Public House. One evening his snoring had been so loud and so persistant that the neighbours two doors down had seen fit to comment upon it, joking that they had been convinced a 'steam train was pulling into the station.' Theresa was also worried that John may have inherited heart disease from his father Timothy, who had died at the age of fifty eight with similar symptoms. She took it upon herself to ask her brother-in-law Dr Tom if he could check John over before they fully committed to the big move. Tom expressed concern as he monitored John's slow heart beat and suggested it might be prudent that they consult a more experienced doctor, for he was not specialised enough to make a proper diagnosis. John brushed off his concerns and promised he would make a concerted effort to lose some weight before they travelled, joking in an attempt to lighten the mood, that he was as fit as a somewhat overweight fiddle and it was most probably working in the bakery in a constant cloud of flour that caused his breathlessness. Somehow he managed to talk Tom around to declaring him as fit as an average man of his age. Theresa was unconvinced by John's seemingly clean bill of health but when she later questioned Tom, he rather vaguely reminded her it was between John and himself and he had taken the Hippocratic Oath to respect patient confidentiality. Although he did suggest it might be prudent if Theresa served her husband slightly smaller portions in the months leading up to their final departure date.

Finally, the momentous date arrived and John's only regret that day was that the family had not made the move while he was younger and in more rude health, but he consoled himself when realising that at least his offspring could fully avail themselves of the opportunities this brave new world had to offer. John had a few sleepless nights before they left because he had sensed his wife's previous zealous enthusiasm was wearing thin. Perhaps as the big day approached, she fully realised that she would never again set foot upon English soil. It wasn't as if she could pack a suitcase and take a quick trip home to visit her relations. To the contrary this move was momentous and final. They were embarking on a new life and once she climbed upon the ship there would be no turning back. No time for second thoughts. But Theresa had made a promise to give this her best shot and she was determined to see it through. She might have been swayed if she had discovered that John was deliberately withholding information from her by not showing her the actual tickets. This was because he felt that after their lucky escape from sailing on the Titanic in 1912, Theresa would decide that fate was trying to tell them something. Even he confessed to a brief moment of hesitation when he realised this ship was also part of the fated White Star Line and this trepidation was

169

greatly intensified when he found out it had been built by the selfsame Belfast shipbuilders, Harland and Wolff. John had always known that his wife did not share his dream, and she would have been quite content to live out the rest of her days never venturing more than a few miles from her own front door. It was proof of her devotion and love for him that she had even agreed to contemplate it in the first place. He had to pinch himself that this longheld dream had at last been realised and the rolling waves and wide blue horizon in the distance convinced him that, at last, he had a chance to charter new waters and forge a wonderful future for his family. Canada was a vast country of opportunity. It was there for the taking and John had never been afraid of hard work. He held a firm belief that his children would thrive on the outdoor life there too, for unlike Theresa he had never been convinced that either of his sons were suited to the priesthood. He had noticed Lewis' eyes light up as a pretty young girl wandered into the Bakery. With his pale blue eyes and charming manner, girls had flocked to the bakery like bees to a honeypot. John also felt that Lewis had great potential as an artist for he had witnessed his steady hand as he taught him calligraphy. Lewis' writing was a work of art, every delicate curve, every carefully placed dash and dot carefully and patiently crafted. His drawings too, especially the charactures he did of the local priest, had John chuckling in the aisles at Mass every week much to Theresa's annoyance.

The journey overseas was arduous and John was constantly glad that he had opted to buy third class tickets, for at least this way he and his family had a modicum of privacy, unlike the poor souls who were consigned to the steerage. He felt quite unwell for the duration of the journey but he put it down to a bad case of sea sickness as he had never travelled by boat before and the sea was particularly choppy at many stages of the journey. When they eventually reached dry land on 24th April 1923, they all breathed a collective sigh of relief, for despite the fact that the children had found their sea legs and quickly adapted to strolling throughout the ship whatever the weather, it was nice to walk without constantly adjusting one's centre of gravity and grab at handrails. Seeing how ill and drawn her husband looked, Theresa insisted they spend a few nights in a guest house in Halifax, Nova Scotia, recuperating before they purchased the train tickets for the next part of their journey. John spent the next few days resting wrapped up in a blanket in the boarding house while Theresa made arrangements for the next stage of their big adventure. Theresa wondered if they should perhaps enlist the advice of a Doctor as John was constantly complaining of a tightness to his chest and a dreadful heartburn but he insisted he was fine and his body was merely adjusting to being on dry land. John had waited so long for his dream to be realised he was not going to let a bad bout of indigestion stand in his way.

I have in my possession the Declaration of Passenger to Canada forms which all five of the party would have needed to complete before being allowed to enter the country. They all appear to have entered the country with a small sum of money in their possession, the three youngsters have each claimed they had £10 each and the two adults £15, which totals £60. Today this would have been worth about £3,000 so I hazard a guess this was their life savings or perhaps they had more stashed undeclared in their luggage or about their person. They all mention that they are travelling to Port Alberni to stay with Theresa's first cousin once removed, Ada Hutchinson, and their intention was to take up a similar occupation of farming. Interestingly, they all enter the country stating their surname was Dowd but when John unfortunately died a few weeks later his Death Certificate stated his name as O'Dowd which if nothing else proved that this dropping of the 'O' was discussed between the family but not legally changed. To this day the confusion remains as various branches of the family have reintroduced the 'O' whilst others have dropped it.

17th MAY, 1923, COCHRANE, ONTARIO, O'DOWD FAMILY

It was whilst on the sleeper train and travelling through Ontario that John William O'Dowd, my maternal great-grandfather fell into a deep sleep from which he never woke. Theresa, upon finding her beloved husband cold and still by her side, ran into the passageway frantically screaming for help. A fellow passenger who was first to race into the compartment thankfully had the foresight to gently usher her youngest daughter Dolly from the scene. Theresa was hysterically unconsolable so it remained for Lewis my grandfather to race up the corridor to find the Ticket Inspector, whilst his brother John leant across his mother and gently pulled a blanket over his father's contorted face. The train pulled into the Station of Cochrane a few minutes later for its scheduled stop of twenty minutes and Lewis quickly jumped from the train to find the Station Master. The Station Master, Claude Proulx-Chedore, was sitting at his desk having a much needed cup of coffee, the first he had actually managed to drink hot that day, so when Lewis hammered on his door he was not best pleased and threw the door open in an angry manner. He snapped a question at Lewis who despite his better intentions of acting like a grown-up promptly burst into tears. Claude, seeing how distressed the young lad was, immediately changed tack and ushered him into the warm confines of his office. Cochrane at this time was just coming out of the the worst typhoid outbreak to darken the Province in recent history, so outpourings of grief such as this were unfortunately commonplace. The outbreak had only began in March and was later discovered to be the result of a water supply contaminated by sewage which had been pumped from Spring Lake. In ordinary circumstances the water supply would not have come from the lake, but instead from nearby springs, but due to an exceptionally dry season, the previous fall, the springs had dried up so water was instead taken from the lake. The lake, prior to the outbreak, had always been deemed a safe supply because it was several feet higher than the adjacent series of lakes – into which the town's sewage ended up - but the weather had dramatically changed the direction of its flow. The unfortunate consequence was the dreadful outbreak which had so overwhelmed the hospitals and cemeteries. Lewis eventually calmed enough to blurt out the details of his own family tragedy and Claude - to afford him his due - immediately took control of the situation. Claude, it must be pointed out, thrived in situations such as this for he had an inflated sense of his own importance and to have the chance to demonstrate his competence was almost God-given were it not for the tragic circumstances which surrounded it.

"I am so sorry for your loss. I shall,of course, arrange for a horse and cart to collect your father but I must first inform the doctor so he can pronounce the death and complete the necessary paperwork. I must point out that all of this will take quite some time due to the typhoid outbreak, so perhaps it would be wise for your mother and the rest of the family to alight from the train as she is leaving in..." he stopped for a moment to check the watch which he had dangling on a gold chain from his regulation waistcoat pocket, before adding self importantly, "precisely seventeen minutes."

"Is there any way you could delay the train for a while longer?" Lewis asked the question, painfully aware that the Station Master would probably be unable to, but deciding it was worth asking nevertheless. Lewis was right in his assumption because Claude promptly replied, "I am so sorry but that is out of the question. The trains have a strict timetable to adhere to and I really cannot delay it more than a few minutes or it will mess with the signals. I can, however, complete the paperwork in the office if your mother comes straight across now, or if she is too upset I suppose I could bend the rules and you could sign for it. I presume you are of age?"

Lewis nodded to confirm that he was indeed old enough. This was to be his first lie but he knew that his mother would be in no fit

173

state to sign paperwork.

"Unfortunately I have just remembered that Dr Fenwick is out of town today at the Prior smallholding, so it will be much later this evening before I can release your father's body to the undertakers. I must also remind you that if you choose to leave the train at this station you will need to purchase new tickets to continue your journey. It is Company policy and completely out of my hands. If it were my decision I would make allowances but......" Claude paused to give Lewis the opportunity to could collect his thoughts before making a decision. Claude had no doubt taken note of the bedraggled state of my grandfather's clothes for - despite his mother's best efforts - after weeks of travel they were not in the most pristine or cleanest of condition. This was to become my grandfather's second lie for he knew the family had not the surplus money to buy new train tickets and the undertaker and burial would use up what little contingency cash they had.

"I shall be honest with you and admit that we have not the wherewithal to purchase more tickets. I would appreciate it if you would not tell my mother of this decision as it would break her heart. If I leave what cash we can spare, could you possibly arrange for the undertaker to collect my father and ensure he has a Catholic funeral and burial plot?" As my grandfather said this, he realised that there would not be enough money left over for a headstone but even as he spoke he also knew that he would later lie and tell his mother there had been. The Station Master made a point of looking once again at his watch, and clearing his throat before stating that if they were to complete the paperwork they would need to do it now to allow time for Lewis to transport the body from the train. He confirmed that he would do as Lewis wished and promised that he would ensure his father had a decent Catholic funeral. So it came to pass that after completing the paperwork, Lewis clambered back upon the train and with the assistance of his younger brother John, the two boys managed to carry their father across the platform. It was there that they left his body. Propped up in a sitting position by a bench on a station platform many miles from home, draped by a blanket looking to all intents and purposes like a discarded pile of rags. This image would haunt my grandfather to his dying day as would the shame he felt as he had lied into his mother's trusting eyes and assured her that he had given the Station Master enough money to pay for a headstone to properly mark their father's grave. It is remains for me to add that we believe my great-grandfather was buried in an unmarked grave in a Cemetary named Potters Field, which was apparently where the penniless and destitute were interred. I can only hope that he received a decent Christian Funeral and that his poor soul rests in peace. My grandfather and his brother made a pact that day to never again speak of the indignity of their father's temporary resting place. Instead they contrived a rather elaborate story whereby they claimed they had themselves transported his body by horse and cart to its final resting place.

Many years later John's granddaughter Pauline had reason to travel through Ontario and was compelled to make an impromptu stop at Cochrane when her daugher Claudia, then a babe in arms, was inexplicably taken very ill. Claudia was so poorly with an unexplained high fever that her anxious parents saw fit to visit a doctor – who diagnosed a virus - before they checked into a local hotel. That night the couple slept fitfully as they watched over their feverish daughter and Pauline describes waking to a vivid vision of her grandfather John entering the room with his arms outstretched. He did not speak as he approached the cot but Pauline sensed he was not at peace and yearned for a member of his family to stay behind and keep him company. She remembers shaking her head vehemently before placing her hand protectively over the baby's chest. John smiled as if in gentle acceptance before disappearing into the darkness. Pauline's husband Cyril, normally sceptical of such things, later confessed that he too had witnessed the vision and he similarly believed there had been no malevolence to the spirit just a deep loneliness and a need to reconnect with his loved ones. Bizarrely, when they left the town the next morning and the train pulled from the station, the baby miracuously recovered. Hopefully this novel will prove to be a fitting epitaph and my great-grandfather John, will finally accept that he was never recklessly abandoned, nor forgotten, and realise that his memory lives on in his family forever.

PORT ALBERNI, VANCOUVER ISLAND, BRITISH COLUMBIA, 1923, O'DOWD FAMILY

Ada Hutchinson was beside herself with excitement when she finally spied the train – on which her mother's cousins were travelling - approaching in the far distance. Her unbridled joy that morning had been so contagious that her husband, Thomas, had also taken the decision to take the morning off work so he could join his wife in greeting the new arrivals. The Hutchinson's stood on the edge of the boardwalk platform - with their five young children - craning their necks for the first sight of the O'Dowds. It had been arranged that the family would stay with Ada and Thomas for a few weeks until they found their feet. Thomas had made enquiries in the local community and had lined up a couple of smallholdings for John to take a look over and he was quite looking forward to sharing what knowledge he had gained since first emigrating all those years ago. He planned to be both mentor and friend to John for, although they had only met the once in England they had forged a friendship of sorts over the last few months of shared correspondence. Ada stretched an arm in front of her eldest daughter and with a moist finger slicked her son Arthur's hair back from his forehead as he squirmed out of reach. She had dressed the children in their Sunday best so they would make a good first impression and the children fidgeted and wriggled as they were unused to wearing the heavily starched, uncomfortable clothes outdoors in such warm weather.

Lewis was first to alight from the train, followed closely by his brother John. Once on the platform the boys reached upwards to take the luggage from their mother, Lewis offering his arm so Theresa could balance as she climbed down the steps. Dolly, the youngest, followed next with her head dipped. She clung to her mothers' skirts for despite being twelve she was suddenly shy and awkward. The Station Master blew the whistle and the train pulled effortlessly from the station leaving the family of four standing forlornly in its wake. Ada looked questioningly across, not sure now how to greet the family in such circumstances. This was not the grand welcoming committee she had planned and even her children had noticed the absence of the head of the family and were uncustomarily silent as a result. Thomas had been about to make a quip along the lines of "where have you hidden that husband of yours", but noting Theresa's disconsolate state he thought better of such frivolity. No doubt Ada would fill him in on the details later, although he did not think from the short aquaintence he had shared with John, that he was the type of man to desert his wife and children, so surely this could only mean that some terrible tragedy had befallen the family on their journey. Thomas was a quiet man who avoided confrontation both physical and emotional, so once he had helped pile the family onto the cart he made his excuses and left under the pretext of having urgent work to attend to. His wife Ada was more than competent driving the horse and cart; years of farming had ensured that she had had plenty of practice, so he felt no guilt at abandoning her so. They made for an ominously silent group that morning as they travelled up Harbour Road before turning left towards Ada's home on 5th Avenue. Once they had lifted the luggage onto the front stoop, Ada asked her eldest son, Thomas Junior, if he could unharness the horse so she could settle Theresa and her family into the room she had prepared for their stay. Ada had shuffled her own children around so that the O'Dowds could have the privacy of a large bedroom at the front of the house and Theresa – aware of the inconvenience of their arrival - made the appropriate sounds of appreciation and she thanked her cousin for her hospitality. Still painfully aware of Theresa's mournful expression, Ada then turned to her own children and suggested they show their new cousins around the town while she and Theresa sorted lunch. As the children trudged en masse from the confine's of the house, Ada motioned for Theresa to sit down.

"Please sit, dear cousin, and tell me whatever is the matter and where is John?" Ada was so distraught at her cousins obvious discomfort that despite her better intentions she blurted out the question with no preamble.

"John has gone." Theresa answered in a quiet voice.

"Gone. Gone where?" Ada felt bad for pressing for more information but she was still not convinced that John had not cruelly abandoned his family.

"He has gone Ada, we lost him on the train in Ontario. I only pray that he has gone on to a better place. God Rest his Soul."

Theresa then made the sign of the cross on her chest before collapsing into tears. Ada suddenly understood, there would be plenty of time to find out the circumstances later, but for now she sat by Theresa and took her gently in her arms. When the children reappeared at the door half an hour later, Theresa was still sobbing so Ada waved the children away again. A few moments later there was a tentative knock and the local priest Father Joseph Bradley popped his head through the open doorway. Father Bradley was the town's first permanent priest and a very keen young man with a disconcerting, over zealous attitude towards promoting the Catholic faith and recruiting oblates.

"Sorry to disturb you ladies, I just wanted to be the first to welcome the O'Dowd family to my Parish. I hope we will see your lovely family at church this weekend." Father Bradley was about to carry on with his welcome but was stopped in his tracks by Ada's expression. It was then that he looked properly at the new arrival and fully realised her distressed state. Ada discreetly took him outside and quickly explained the unfortunate news of John's death and Theresa's understandable worry that her husband had not received a proper Catholic funeral.

"Oh blessed Mother of God we cannot let the poor man go to his maker with this uncertainity hanging over his immortal soul. Can I suggest we hold a requieum mass for him as soon as possible?

Father Bradley sat with the two ladies at the kitchen table and taking their hands in his he started to pray to God for a speedy resolution to their many problems, for they all realised that without John it was out of the question that the family could go ahead and buy a shareholding. Even with the best will in the world the two boys were far too young and inexperienced to undertake such an endeavour. It was Ada who first piped up and suggested that as the young priest had been looking to employ a housekeeper perhaps he might consider Theresa for the role. Ada made her suggestion in such a way that the priest would seem churlish and unchristian if he did not agree to at least mull over her proposal. The following day Father Bradley returned to the house and offered Theresa the role with the implication that he himself had first thought of the idea. Theresa gratefully accepted his kind offer, and the following weekend the family moved into the upper floor of the little house adjoining the wooden church.

SEPTEMBER 1923, PORT ALBERNI, VANCOUVER ISLAND.

My grandfather Lewis and his brother John were both fit and able-bodied young men so they quite quickly found employment in the local Saw Mill situated on the edge of the Somass River. The Island of Vancouver was rich in Western Red Cedars and Douglas Fir so large logging operations such as this had recently been popping up all along the Somass. The river - whose name meant 'washing' - had been named by the indigenous people of the Pacific West Coast of Canada who were collectively known as the *Nuu-cha-nulth*. It is shocking to learn that the population of these tribes was decimated by 90% when European explorers first landed to colonise, because they brought with them infectious diseases to which the tribes had no prior immunity. Port Alberni itself was named after Pedro de Alberni, a captain in the Spanish Army, who had commanded a military outpost on the West Coast in 1790. The Canadian government had created small Reserves for the *Nuu-cha-nulth* tribes in the late 1800s, then swiftly and cruelly curtailed their hunting and fishing rights - including outlawing their salmon weir traps - thereby depriving them of their 'hunter gatherer' way of life.

As Lewis and John were still comparatively young they were initially employed in the role of caring for the horses, alongside the *Hupachasaht* men from the nearby reserve of *Asw'win'is*. This indigenous tribe had been compelled - like many other tribes in the area - to seek work at the Mill when their hunting and fishing was restricted. The *Asw'win'is* Reserve was located on the north side of the Somass River and the *Hupachasaht* men ironically travelled to work each day in the very same canoes which they had previously used for hunting parties. Whilst their native language *Wakashan* was still spoken on the Reserve, the men had taught themselves a basic form of French Canadian dialect so they could understand and more importantly be understood. My grandfather and John were befriended by an older *Hupachasaht* man named Mikom, who had recently 'lost' his own son and took pity on the fatherless boys. It was Mikom who taught my grandfather Lewis the age old skill of driving the logs. This was an incredibly dangerous practice, especially bearing in mind that one log could be 20ft long, so a careless slip could easily result in serious injury or death. Lewis, along with the other men from the Mill, envied the awe and respect afforded to the *Riverjacks* who each spring - once the ice on the river had sufficiently melted – transformed into the undisputed '*kings of the wood*', hopping across the logs as if it was the easiest thing in the world. The *Riverjacks* regularily worked in ankle deep icy water brandishing their pikes and peaveys - the tools of their trade - like weapons and showing off to the crowd by clambering onto a chosen log then *birling* it by turning it with just their feet. Lewis was desperate to master this sure-footed skill and one day in the Spring of 1924 after carefully calking his boots as instructed by Mikom, he took a first tentative exploratory step onto the rapidly moving half-submerged logs. These logs proved so slippy and difficult to balance on that it was not long before he found himself plunged head first into the freezing water and scrambling, shamefaced, to the safety of the river bank. The other *riverjacks* caterwalled and yelled across that he had now '*closed the door*', which was the term they affectionately used if the water had gone over your head. Mikom reminded him that it was a rite of passage to fall in many times before mastering the skill, and the best advice was to get dried off and get back out there. This is what Lewis did; urged on by the other *riverjacks* he jumped across, fell off, climbed back on, nose dived off, then clambered back on again. He thrived upon the adrenaline as young men often do, and during that spring he went on to become '*one of the elite*' both a *lumberjack* and a *riverjack*. Athough despite being skilled in birling, he was never called upon to find the key log as this was a specialised job which often required laying dynamite, and he was much too young to be allowed access to this despite his protestations to the contrary. It is frightening to note that no one including Mikom had at this stage thought to ask my grandfather if he could actually swim, and it was only later on that this omission came to light in the most tragic of circumstances.

Theresa, during this transitional period, had taken to the role of housekeeping like a duck to water for after all it wasn't that what she had spent the vast majoring of her life doing anyway? She had proved something of a confidente to Father Bradley for he had already had cause to call upon her calming advice on more than one occasion. The boys too had been a godsend as they had undertaken the painting of the wooden church in the summer of 1923, then Lewis had both constructed and painted a tabernacle for the altar. I have a photograph of this wonderful ornate golden box sitting pride of place as a centrepiece to worship, but I fear it may have become lost over the years. For upon investigating, I have discovered the old wooden church of the Holy Family fell into disrepair in the '60s and various reports to its fate abound, the most ubiquitous being that it was sold on to a motorcycle gang. Although I personally prefer the more dramatic presumption that it was washed away in the tsunami of 1964 which struck the Island six hours after a massive earthquake in Alaska. Whatever the truth of the matter is, a new church was built nearby and named The Holy Family and Notre Dame Parish Church. The present parish priest is trying to find out if the tabernacle is still in existence.

I have already alluded to Father Bradley and his dependence upon Theresa for her sober sangfroid, but I now have reason to believe that he became so reliant upon her, and would gaze at her with such intensity, that she was obliged to avert her eyes. This delicate shift in their 'friendship' had not gone unnoticed among his congregation and rumours soon started to circulate that theirs was not a completely chaste kinship. For a priest this was to ring the death knell upon any relationship, for the practice of celibacy was non-negotiable and to be suspected of not abstaining from one's sexual urges was tantamount to being accused of a heinous crime. The young priest was compelled to discreetly broach the matter with Theresa, and her reaction was of such abject horror, that he, for one brief second, felt the sting of rejection - despite the fact that he had not in his opinion behaved with any moral impropriety so he had no logical reason to feel so. Theresa argued that her three children were settled in their new home and surely to move them again would confirm rather than dampen the rumours, but Father

Bradley was adamant that his credibility as a man of the cloth was at stake and it was not up for any further discussion. So it came to be that the family were decamped en masse to live with a very well-to-do family called the Luke's in their massive mock Tudor mansion, The Hermitage. Dolly was upset, as it meant a much longer walk to school for her, but the boys were thrilled as the ten-bedroomed house was closer to the river so much nearer to the Mill where they both worked. The house had been built on the 14 acre site around 1912 for the English millionaire and big-game hunter Cluny Luke and his family. The oak panelling was imported from England and the bricks from Italy so, in a *frontierland* such as Port Alberni, it was the very epitome of good taste and twenties glamour. The plumbing was imported from France so the taps were marked chaud and froid although a hapless plumber had fitted them incorrectly so it was a constant surprise whether one would be scalded or frozen to the bone. Mrs Luke, who was French by nationality, was prone to complain and nitpick for she was used to getting what she wanted from her overindulgent husband. She was constantly pointing out to their houseguests that the fireplaces were still unfinished because the ship bringing the final fittings had been sunk at sea. This was a source of constant annoyance to Cluny, who never tired of reminding her in a patronising voice that if she had not pointed out the imperfections they would not have been remarked upon. The trophies of Cluny's game-hunter days also adorned the home with alarming regularity and a vast stuffed Kodiak bear guarded the entrance way. Much to young Dolly's dismay, for she was so afraid it would magically come to life and grab her, she adopted a habit of running through the hall with her eyes tightly closed to avoid its outstretched claws. This fear was intensified on the day her brother John decided it would be fun to hide behind the bear and jump out growling as she reached the front door. Theresa, his mother, was so angry she swore that if he had been younger and not so tall she would have tanned his hide and laid it out on the floor with the other animal pelts. My grandfather Lewis held the display of taxidermy trophies in great distain for the indiscriminate slaughter of these once noble beasts disgusted him to the core. He was not overly squeamish - for living in a farming area he was used to the sight of dead deer and the such - but this killing seemed to have a purpose as it was for the provision of food. It was the photographs of Cluny standing triumphantly over some poor felled critter that filled him most with revulsion, for what chance could any creature have against a rifle such as that? It was hard to keep his counsel but his mother, knowing of his strong opinions, had begged he try, for she could not bear the thought of the family becoming homeless once again.

Dolly along with her two older brothers had fully embraced her new life. She had been enrolled in the local Smith Memorial Catholic school and had very quickly become best friends with a girl called Agnes. Agnes was of a similar background as her family and had also recently emigrated from England. The two bosom pals relished their newly found freedom exploring outdoors, and more often than not - after the school bell had rung for close of day - they would grab their school bags and run towards the river to splash about and cool down. Unfortunately the Somass river, like most rivers, was not an ideal playground for the weak swimmer, as beneath the gently rippling surface lurked unseen currents and eddies. Never has the age-old adage of 'still rivers run deep' been more relevant than on the day when the girls were playing catch and Agnes in an effort to escape slipped on a rock, lost her balance and fell backwards into the water only to be swept away by the undercurrents into the rapidly flowing water beyond. At this point, below the dam, the river was particularly turbulent and Agnes was quickly dragged downwards towards the rapids, which although short were deadly, due to the many submerged rocks. As her head dipped under the water for the third time and her arms waved frantically above her head, Dolly took to her feet to run for help.

At this stage,, I will add that Dolly, like Agnes, and the majority of the recently arrived English children, had never had the chance to learn to swim. Dolly's screams for help alerted Agnes' father who was walking along Falls Road after finishing his shift at the mill. He, and a few of the other men, dropped their tools and raced to her rescue, forming a human chain across the breadth of the river, but it was too late and as they dragged her poor body towards the river bank it was plain to see that the child had drowned. Her father crouched over her still, sodden rag doll of a body and let out such a cry of anguish that Dolly fled from the scene with her hands tightly clasped over her ears. As she raced from the river, Agnes' mother ran past her screaming at her husband that she wished it had been him that had drowned and not her darling daughter. It was a while before the shock of witnessing the terrible tragedy wore off and Dolly could finally speak of the terrible accident. From that day on and for the remainder of their stay in Port Alberni, the poor girl would wake in the night with the most terrifying of nightmares as she relived that afternoon again and again. It is ironic that this terrible tragedy took place on almost the same spot where Mrs Luke's brother Ernest Henri DeBruyne had lost his life about nine years earlier in 1916. Ernest had been 38 and apparently a strong swimmer when his canoe overturned. He had knocked his head when falling into the water and his unconscious body had been drawn downstream into the dam. Cluny Luke, his brother-in-law, bravely leapt in to save him and he too would have drowned if he hadn't managed to grab onto some overhanging branches. Cluny was trapped in the freezing water for two hours, before a Chinese cook in his employ managed to successfully launch a flat-bottomed skiff to rescue him. The men from the Paper Mill then dragged the river for two weeks trying to find poor Ernest's body before it was eventually washed up downstream. I have since discovered that in the year 1916 Vancouver Island was hit with the 'snowfall of the century', so by the April when Ernest drowned, the runoff from the neighbouring mountains would have caused the Somass to swell at her banks, so despite his being a competent swimmer he did not stand a chance once he had been dragged towards the rapids. He was buried in St Peter's Cemetary in a plot near where poor Agnes would be interred almost ten years later.

The entire town turned out for Agnes' funeral, for there is nothing so sad as a child-sized coffin, and nothing so wretched as a death that could so easily have been avoided. Theresa blamed herself for the tragedy, for she had never checked where Dolly and her friend were playing after school and she had never thought that her children would need to be taught to swim. Of course, if John had been alive he would have made it a priority to teach this important lifeskill to his children, but Theresa had been so set on forging a decent lifestyle for her family that she had taken her eye off the ball, and she was forever thankful to God that her own daughter had been spared. Mikom felt a similar guilt when he found out, for he had actively encouraged Lewis to join in the log drive and just assumed that he knew how to swim, because a *Hupachasaht* child would learn almost at the same time as learning how to walk. Mikom, with permission from Theresa, made it his priority to teach the Dowd family to swim and even brought his own daughter Leonore along to help and encourage the children. Leonore at eighteen was the same age as Lewis and she was strikingly beautiful with a slim build and jet black straight hair tied back in a braid. Needless to say Lewis fell helplessly and hopelessly in love. Leonore's free spirit of adventure and lack of pretension being all the aphrodisiac he needed. Being young he never once considered his mother's great plan for him to enter the priesthood, he was just driven by a compulsion to get closer to her and breathe in her very essence. Mikom, standing on the river side witnessed the magical transition from boy to man. He took note as Lewis puffed out his chest, smiling adoringly whenever Leonore congragulated him on a particularly well-executed swimming stroke. Mikom decided there and then that he must do everything in his power to discourage this budding romance, for his people on the Reserve muddled along quite well with the general populace of the town by adhering carefully to an unwritten code of conduct. It was what one would now call a 'casual racism', although it was often on the cusp of flaring up into full blown 'racism'. Casual racism is probably one of the most unpredictable, for on the surface, rather like the Somass river, all could seem calm and tranquil but beneath the surface there skulked deep-held beliefs of an implied superiority. The 'racism' manifested itself in forms of denigration and marginalisation which had the desired effect of undermining the dignity of the native peoples, while reinforcing social barriers. It upsets me to write that this 'casual racism' and 'anti-indigenous racism' still exists in society today, despite the argument that we are more 'politically correct' and all inclusive, so a hundred years ago it was unsurprisingly more ubiquitous. Mikom was canny enough not to forbid the pair to socialise, but he did spread the word throughout the Reserve that if a young *Hupachasaht* boy was to show a romantic interest in his daughter, he would not obstruct such a friendship. But star-crossed lovers have always found a way to meet - indeed from the dawn of time this has been so - a few stolen hours here and few precious moments there and Lewis and Leonore were no exception. Once Lewis had made his romantic intentions known to Leonore, and she had succumbed to his charms, he took to hiding love tokens in a tree trunk near the Reserve and as a secret code known only to the couple, Leonore would remove them and leave a feather in their place. They managed to spend many an afternoon together away from the watchful eyes of their parents. Leonore taught Lewis to fish for salmon, by rubbing their underbellies as they swam through the shallow waters, then as they entered a trance-like state quickly flip them onto the dry rocks. Theresa accepted his proffered gifts of fresh salmon for tea, never asking how and where her son had learned this skill. Lewis in turn would read to Leonore from his compendium of the works of Shakespeare, her favourite being Romeo and Juliet, as no doubt their ill-fated plight mirrored her own. The names of these doomed lovers soon become their pet names for each other and whenever they had planned a secret assignation Leonore would reach their rendezvous and quote 'O Romeo, Romeo wherefore art thou Romeo,' then Lewis would spring from his hiding place behind a tree. Communication between the two had been basic initially because as English was a second language to Leonore, particular nuances were often lost in translation, but with Lewis' patient tutorage Leonore soon became quite the scholar. Their first kiss was chaste by today's standards but it was a stolen kiss, so tender and shared with such feeling and promise that it would never be forgotten even in the passage of time. The couple's budding romance would have continued unhindered in a similar vein were it not for the intervention of fate on the day Lewis was in the woods logging, and he inadvertently missed the tree trunk and instead with a heavy swing of his axe took a chunk out of his own thigh.

In the ensuing panic - for the blood loss was considerable – a horse pulling logs had been swiftly unsaddled from its skidding chain, and reharnessed to a cart, so that Lewis could be ferried quickly back to the Hermitage. When he reached the house one of the Japanese gardeners was dispatched to fetch the local doctor and Lewis was gently lifted into the parlour where Theresea had constructed a makeshift bed. The doctor came swiftly, for he was used to injuries such as this and knew time was of the essence if the laceration were not to become life threatening. Once the blood flow was stemmed, stitches were administered and the leg dressed, then Theresa stood back to assess the damage to the Luke's bear-skin rug, before taking note of Lewis' deathlike pallor and deciding that under the circumstances washing the rug could probably wait, as it was more important to get her son settled and comfortable. The Luke family were out of town visiting the mainland in their new automobile, so there was no desperate hurry to see to it being cleaned, although she did know the longer she left it the more likely it was to stain and catch the eye of Mrs Luke. In the end the Chinese cook's wife came into the parlour and removed the rug stating that she had just the compound to make it good as new.

It was in this parlour that Lewis lay for many days, his temperature raging, as he drifted in and out of conciousness. The doctor visited daily, shaking his head as he removed the bandage then gently swabbed the wound before replacing it. The gash was deep; there was no denying its severity and the only hope was that it would start to show signs of healing soon. One day Mikom's visit coincided with that of the doctor's, and he overheard his hushed tones as he expressed his concern to Theresa. Once the doctor had taken his leave, Mikom took Theresa to one side and pleaded that she allow her son to visit the Reserve so the Shaman could perform a Doctoring Ritual. Despite her scepticism, no doubt entrenched in Catholicism, Theresa was so concerned for her son's health that she reluctantly agreed. After all, she reasoned that conventional Western medicine had proved woefully inadequate, and after assisting her father in his surgery all those years ago, she knew that if gangrene were to set in the outcome would be catastrophic. So that very afternoon Lewis was collected by a small group of tribesmen and carried on a makeshift stretcher towards the Somass River so he could continue the rest of the journey by canoe. This access to the Reserve was a privilege afforded to very few, for the *Hupachasaht* were fiercely protective of their heritage and as a result non tribespeople were not normally welcome, but both Mikom and his daughter Leonore had begged so fervently that eventually the Chief Gitkinjuaas Cumshewa had agreed. At this time in 1924, Reserves were overseen by an Indian Agent who was exclusively in the employ of the Canadian government to keep the indigenous peoples in check. From 1910, onwards the Indian Agent was a very unsavoury character named Alan Webster Neill who lived in a house on River Road just across the river from the Reserve. He was instrumental in enforcing the federal government's policies of assimilation and the residential 'Indian' school system before going on to to be a member of parliament. The tribesmen knowing of Neill's previous dependence on alcohol orchestrated a way to get the Agent 'rip roaring' drunk that night, by using means which it would be indelicate of me to go into, but they had the desired effect of ensuring the Ritual could go ahead unhindered. The infamous Indian Act had banned all such Rituals as being anti-Christian because the Christian Missionaries feared their pagan implications. The Act had then gone even further and outlawed the Potlatch ceremony, thereby taking away from the indigenous peoples the very foundation of their culture. The Canadian Superintendant General of Indian Affairs, John A MacDonald, had dismissively decribed the Potlatch as being *the useless and degrading custom in vogue among the Indians..at which an immense amount of personal property is squandered in gifts by one Band to another, and at which much valuable time is lost.* The Government administered Draconian laws which prohibited singing, dancing, because they believed that such measures would eventually encourage the tribesmen in the Reserves to turn their backs on their very cultural traditions.

It was as night fell that the secret Ceremony began. Lewis had been propped up by the campfire and was flanked on either side by a concerned Mikom and his daughter Leonore. The Doctoring Ritual began in earnest when the Shaman dressed in an elaborate headdress and loose fitting heavily decorated robes entered the circle. As he made his approach, the rest of the tribe started to drum on large carved plates and chant in unison. Then all of a sudden and quite dramatically the Shaman fell to his knees. With his arms flaying he rocked to and fro in an almost dream-like state, not unlike someone suffering from Oneirophrenia. "He is entering the spirit world," Mikom whispered to Lewis, "it is good that he is hallucinating. Let's hope the spirits are receptive tonight." Lewis grimaced in reply, for quite bizarrely his leg had began to twitch uncontrollably and the wound seemed to be pulsing in a rhythm to match the chants. Suddenly, with no preamble at all, the Shaman ran towards Lewis and with one swift motion ripped the bandages from his leg before leaning across and laying the open palm of his hand directly onto the weeping laceration. Lewis flinched in grim anticipation of searing pain, then relaxed gratefully back into his seat when he realised that bar a slight pressure there was none. The sound of the chanting got louder and louder and louder until it reached a deafening crescendo, then, just as abruptly as it had began, it stopped and it was immediately silent. The only audible sounds being the crackling of the fire and the howls of wild wolves in the distance. The Shamon lifted his head, flicking the headdress skywards, and he smiled at Lewis - which was most disconcerting for the few teeth he had were needlesharp - then slowly removing his hand he danced away from the circle and disappeared theatrically into the enveloping darkness. Lewis looked questioningly towards his mentor Mikom, who whispered, "it is done, you are healed. Now lets gather the men together and get you back home to rest up for a while."

Theresa was waiting anxiously at the doorway of the Hermitage as the party of tribesmen approached. They slowly lowered Lewis to the gravel ground infront of his mother, and he tentatively took a baby step with his injured leg. The flesh on the wound felt tight and constrictive but other than that he felt no pain, and even managed to walk haltingly into the house. Theresa followed, silently praying upon the rosary beads she wore around her neck. Turning to Mikam she said, "how can I ever repay you? I will be forever in your debt."

"The debt has been repaid in full dear lady for my good friend is healed. The Spirits have looked favourably upon we poor mortals tonight and his life has been spared," Mikom replied enigmatically.

"Come, sit with us a while. I have prepared a small meal." Theresa said, ushering the tribesmen into her rooms as the other housestaff, who had heard the commotion and come to evesdrop, looked on agape, for it was unheard of for a lady of Theresa's breeding to offer such hospitality to the men from the Reserve. It was a complete reversal of roles, and one which the rest of the staff were not comfortable witnessing, so they skulked away back into their own private quarters. Theresa had not noticed Leonore at first for she had been hidden slightly in the shadows, but Lewis reached across and took the young girl's hand in his so he could introduce her to his mother. Their relationship was plain for all to see but Theresa was thankfully in such a euphoric state that she was blissfully unaware of anything untoward and accepted Mikom's explaination that he had brought his daughter because she had always wanted to see inside the famous Hermitage. Leonore shrank back into the shadows, searching for Lewis in the crowd. Seeing him creep from the room she followed in his wake and together they walked outside.

It was as the couple stood at the far end of the circular drive - their visibility from the house shrouded by the holly bush which marked its border - that Lewis first pledged his love to Leonore and she to him. He boldly announced his intention to speak to his mother - when the time was right - and to tell her of his intention to marry as soon as it could be arranged. Leonore promised she would have a similar conversation with her father. They both unintentionally used the word tell rather than ask, for they knew that the objections to their union would be considerable and Lewis further realised that his faith would neither condone nor perform the ceremony.

"Now that I am well and my leg is healed I think we should buy some land to farm," Lewis enthused before adding, "it was after all what my father had planned for the family when we first came to Vancouver Island and I know that it would make him proud."

"I shall enjoy being a farmers wife. Can we have some animals too?" Leonore asked, matching his jubilance with her own. "Yes of course," Lewis replied, "I was thinking of four cows, eight sheep, twelve chickens and..." he paused dramatically before finishing his statement with a flourish, " perhaps one baby."

Leonore grinned, she was well used to this English humour by now. "Only one?"

"Only one at first then.... if I find it pleasing we may have more.'"Lewis joked but before they could discuss it further the couple heard Mikom calling out for Leonore. It was time to go - Theresa had asked more than once where her son had got to – so Mikom wanted to leave before she realised that Leonore had disappeared from the room a few minutes after her son, and she too was missing. The couple shared one last precious kiss, little knowing that it would be their last for once they parted that night they would never see each other again.

The next morning Lewis woke with a *joie de vivre* he had not experienced since his accident and he cadged a lift into town with one of the gardeners, who had business to attend to there anyway. Once Lewis reached the town, he headed towards the Holy Family Church for it had been many weeks since his last confession, and as a devout Catholic, he needed to seek contrition. A confessional is anonymous with the priest representing God and, rather like a doctor signing the Hippocratic Oath, a priest should never divulge what he has been told during the course of the Sacrament of Penance. There is the often spouted ethical question of, 'if a priest is told of an impending murder and the murderer is in his confessional, can the priest report it and stop it happening? The answer bizarrely is that the priest is allowed to urge the murderer to confess but he cannot do so on his behalf for if he does so the priest himself will be excommunicated. There is also the altogether more alarming conundrum which poses the question, if a priest is told a time-bomb is planted under his bed to explode the second he alights the bed, is he allowed to remove it? The answer is yes, but only if he normally looks under his bed before climbing into it, otherwise he cannot and he must climb into bed and be blown to smithereens. Lewis, as a practising Catholic would have been well-versed on the Sacred

Seal of a Confessional and so he entered the tiny booth knowing that Father Bradley would recognise his voice but was bound by his ministry to keep his confession secret. Lewis began by saying a small prayer then followed this by stating the time it had been since his last confession. Lewis knew that he had committed a mortal sin by lying to his mother about his whereabouts, when he was secretly meeting Leonore, and it had prayed upon his conscience throughout his long convalesance. Once he had made this act of contrition Father Bradley chanted the Prayer of Absolution and Lewis left the confessional booth to kneel by the altar to conduct his penance. What Father Bradly did next, whether well-intentioned or with an ulterior motive is inexcusable. I call his motives into question because I know the rumours of his 'supposedly inappropriate' relationship with Theresa was still being remarked on, despite her having moved out of his house and into the Hermitage. Father Bradley was the first permanent priest Port Alberni had ever had so he did not want to 'upset any apple carts' but he also knew of Theresa's wish for her son to become a priest. None of this excuses what he did next. For he hotfooted to the Hermitage under the guise of visiting Lewis to offer the sick boy the Sacraments, then in a flurry of well-timed and deliberately leading remarks left her in little doubt of Lewis' true relationship with Leonore. When Lewis eventually managed to get a lift back to the Hermitage later that afternoon, Father Bradley had orchestrated his dirty deed and scuttled back to the town. Theresa was incensed, and in the height of her fury, she forbade my grandfather from ever seeing Leonore again and made him swear on the Bible that he would not disobey her wishes. Much like Father Bradley perhaps, her motives for this outright ban on the relationship were mixed for we know she never really settled in Vancouver after losing her beloved husband, so this, if nothing else gave her the perfect excuse to insist the family return to England.

Lewis respected his mother, but despite swearing upon the bible, he knew he couldn't just leave Vancouver without explaining his plight to Leonore and saying goodbye properly, so using their secret code he arranged a final tryst the day before they left the island. But this time when Lewis reached the clearing it was Mikom who stepped out of the shadows rather than his precious Leonore. Mikom explained that Leonore was too distraught to meet him, but emphasised that Lewis must never doubt the strength of her love for him. The truth of it was that Mikom couldn't allow the situation to get out of hand, for the alliance between the town and the Reserve was a tenuous one and as a result was a tinderbox. He also knew there were hotheads in both camps who would use this as an excuse to wage a fight. Much like in the couple's favourite Shakespeare play where the Capulets and the Montagues were constantly searching for reasons to escalate the smallest of smites. Also Mikom - although he never voiced this fear to Lewis - was afraid that emotions would get the better of the two erstwhile lovers, and they would get it into their heads to elope. Lewis begged Mikom to take pity on him and allow him to at least see Leonore, but Mikom was firm and steadfast in his refusal - even though it broke his heart to see the boy he had thought of as a surrogate son reduced to such a state of emotional turmoil - for he had to look at the bigger picture, and long after Lewis had left the Island and memories of him ever being there was forgotten, the two communities would still need to exist side by side. Mikom's own precious son had been lost to him when he was taken from the Reserve by the priests from the United Church many years earlier. The boy was now being taught in the notorious Alberni Indian Residential School which was positioned just across the Somass River opposite the Hermitage. Mikom still had nightmares about the dreadful day when the Police and the priests had arrived unannounced, and had snatched the 'innocent' child from the bosom of his family. He and his wife never got the chance to even say goodbye to their precious son as he was whisked away. Mikom still recalled with shame how he had restrained his wife from attacking the priest. He did this for one reason and one reason only. It was because he knew the devastating punishment which would be metered out to the reserve if she had been able to register her objection in this way. The brooding sinister red-brick building of the Indian Residential School had been constructed as a means to control the native parents and assimilate the children quicker into white society. The argument the Canadian Prime Minister John A McDonald had used at the time was that if the school was situated on the actual Reserve the children would learn French and English then revert back to being 'savages', communicating in their native tongue once school was over. Unfortunately it has now come to light the terrible acts of abuse, both sexual and physical, which the poor children suffered. They were subjected to constant beating for the slightest of misdemenours and had needles poked into their tongues if they accidently spoke in their own native language. The buildings are now razed to the ground and forty-five years after it finally closed its doors the day was marked by an event hosted by the Tseshaht First Nation to celebrate the bringing home of their children, and as a means of closure for the many children who had been wrenched from their families and installed there. Mikom must have felt the agony of separation from his 'lost' son daily and knowing of the participation of the Christian Missionary fraternity in all its guises, he was understandably scared that the wrath of the church would be rained upon his Reserve should the relationship between Lewis and his daughter ever come to fruition. That night, which was the night before Lewis left Vancouver, he enlisted the help of the other women in the Reserve to watch over Leonore and ensure that she was not even allowed to go through the most personal of abolutions without a watchful eye upon her. A week after her beloved Lewis left, Leonore returned once again to their special tree where she found the final love token he had left her. She carried this token in a little leather purse, wherever she went, to the day she died, always hoping that one day he would return for her.

As the train pulled out of the station – on the day they left Port Alberni - Lewis felt as if his heart was broken in two, and he had left a large piece of it behind, blowing in the gentle breeze across the glorious mountains and weaving through the sprawling forests of trees. He was convinced he would never love again and so sure was he in this assumption that while on the train travelling back across Ontario, he told his mother that once they were safely back in England he would enrol in the Seminary and train to become a priest. I have the records from the Canadian Pacific ship the *Minnedosa* showing that they travelled back to Southampton on 14th May 1926, and it so sad to see my great-grandfather John's name missing from the passenger list. The family must have looked a sorry sight indeed as they disembarked from the ship in Liverpool – a widow and her three children - their dreams and hopes shattered by their Great Canadian adventure.

While writing this chapter, I have had great assistance in my research into the Hemitage and have been contacted by the daughter of the family who bought the mansion in 1954. Daphne Dobie's story is a sobering one for her parents, Bill and Phyllis Taylor, loved the house so much and had dreams of restoring it to its former glory days of the twenties. For many years the couple refused to sell it, but their dreams of restoration were dashed when health issues concerning Daphne's father forced their hand. Reluctantly, they sold the house under the assurance that it would remain intact and the new owner even went to great lengths to explain how he planned to breed horses on the land. Unbeknownst to Daphne's parents the new purchaser was part of a consortium and in 1961 the house was demolished, because the gravel pit on which it stood was actually worth more than the building itself. All that now remains on the land are the two holly bushes which marked the edges of the once grandiouse circular driveway and I like to believe that the spirits of my grandfather and Leonore still haunt the grounds, desperate to be reuninted in their teenage love. The old adage 'time is a great healer,' was to ring true for Lewis, as he went on to fall in love and marry my grandmother, but saying that, he never forgot the girl that Catholicism and Racism had forced him to leave behind. As to the fate of Leonore I know little. I do, however, know that up until the late 1980s she was still living in the area, so I am hopeful one day I can find her descendents and tell them more details of this ill-fated romance.

THE HOUSE, ASHLEIGH GROVE, ENGLAND, 1926

The house and its residents had recovered - in time - from the loss of its patriarch Oshbert to Spanish Flu in 1919 and a new 'normal' had fallen into place. Mary Le Britton had allowed herself a reasonable period of grief then 'pulled up her britches' and knuckled down to restoring her reconstructed family. Her two youngest children, my grandmother Dorothy and her brother Rhys John, were aged 15 and 12 respectfully, and still in need of a mother's guidance, so she confined her widows tears to the private sanctity of her bedroom. The house too had been adversely affected by the loss of the head of the household and for a while it was all at sea, navigating choppy waters, unanchored, and drifting aimlessly. It was brought abruptly back to the present by the recent stirrings of the 'creature'- which even though concealed beneath the box of nails in the backyard shed – still thrived on being a constant thorn in its side. Every so often 'the creature' would seem to bore of its surroundings and the tentacles of its uncurling fingers would crawl along the back wall and creep between the bricks, creating cavities in its wake. It was as if it had an insatiable appetite for mischief and would feed hungrily on the fear it instilled in its prey. Junior, Oshbert's and Mary's eldest son - who had placed it there not long after his father had died -had left home to seek his fortune a few months after hiding it in 1919.

No-one else in the family knew it still existed, for both his mother and Susie had witnessed the flames lick around it and presumed it destroyed. It had been Junior who had retrieved it from the burning embers and Junior who had recoiled in horrified disbelief as he realised it was undamaged. Junior had debated taking the wretched 'creature' with him when he moved away, but he reasoned that since it had been hidden in the shed its power had diminished so the family were safe from its peversity. It held many bad memories for Junior - not least the part he believed it played in infecting his father – and his part in hiding its existence had caused his beloved mother to hurl some hurtful abuse at him. Although she had later tried to understand his dilemma, and mother and son had made amends, the hurtful words were not forgotton but instead confined to the back recesses of his memory. For it is true that, once words have been voiced aloud, they cannot be quietened and many, many years later they will again rise to the surface and reopen old wounds. Junior still made a point of returning home at regular intervals and he and his mother - to the casual observer - rekindled their old relationship, but every phrase and shift in mood was carefully measured and the spontaneity lost. For once the boundaries are blurred and unclear, the enmeshment results in dysfunction and constant misunderstandings. The last time Junior had returned home he had brought with him his new wife. This gave rise to much debate, because both his mother and siblings had not even realised he was courting, such was his detachment from his family. Mary, for fear of provoking an argument, had held her tongue, and it made for a very uneasy and unnatural visit. After the couple had left, Mary and Susie shared a knowing look for it appeared they had both noticed the telltale swell of his young bride's stomach. Much to Mary's joy her first 'acknowledged' grandchild, Dennis, made an appearance quite soon after their visit and what a beautiful baby he was, almost the perfect textbook baby if there was such a thing. He slept when he should sleep and when he was awake he lay and gurgled, happily grinning toothlessly at his adoring grandmother's expression of wonderment. Because his young parents were still finding their feet, and possibly as a way to build bridges, Mary had suggested her young grandson stay for prolonged periods of time. The joy the entire house experienced from one small little being was tantamount to a miracle and all focus was on his wellbeing and welfare. Anita took to rushing home after work so she could have a 'nice cuddle' before Dennis settled down for the night, and my grandmother Dorothy was obsessed with helping to change and feed him. Even the boys grudgingly agreed that he was 'quite sweet', although, as Arthur pointed out, a puppy would have been just as sweet and a lot less troublesome. "Also a lot less smelly," Rhys John added looking pointedly at the baby's nether regions as both boys rolled about laughing.

It was probably due to the arrival of her first grandchild that Mary had not fully noticed the dramatic change in her youngest son Rhys John. He had recently turned a teenager and almost overnight transformed from a pleasant personable and biddable boy into a truculent rebellious youth. It seemed as if her every request was answered with a grunt and he would sneak from the house at every opportunity be it dawn or dusk. But it was not until a policeman turned up at her door that she discovered the full truth about his nocturnal misdemeanours. For it appeared that while his mother and Susie were 'all hands on deck' administering to the baby's every need, Rhys had found himself ungainful employment. The policeman was quickly ushered into the house before the neighbours could see him and speculate on the reason for his visit. To have a policeman turn up at your door unannounced was a thing of great shame in the street, and Mary, still harbouring illusions of grandeur thought herself to be a 'cut above' the rest of the inhabitants of the street. The policeman gratefully availed himself of her hospitality, for he had been plodding the beat for the better part of an hour in a persistant drizzle, and within a few minutes he was settled comfortably in the parlour, a cup of tea perched rather precariously upon his knee. PC Creigh was 'old school' and upon discovering exactly what Rhys was up to he had taken it upon himself to visit Mary. He was technically off-duty, so therefore despite his uniform the visit was strictly *'off the record'*. He began by reassuring her that Rhys was not the first boy he had seen to get in with the wrong crowd, and nor, he declared, would he be the last, but once a youngster's parents were involved and the lad's were *'reined in',* the problems were normally nipped in the bud. It appeared that Rhys had been earning himself a small fortune acting as a go-between for a bookie's runner and his punters. Rhys would relay the details of the odds and receive the bets. He even had a little notebook tucked in his trouser pocket so he could issue receipts. The bookie's runner would give Rhys a small commission for each bet placed, so as this racket seemed to have been carrying on under the radar for quite a while, Rhys had probably amassed a sizeable sum of money for himself. Albert, the runner in question, was notorious throughout the neighbourhood and his pitch in a doorway on Lyndhurst Avenue near the entrance of the newly opened Jesmond Picture House was well known to the local bobbies. Perhaps becoming a Bookie's Runner was not the best career choice for a man with a wooden leg and the very title of his employ was ironic in that he could not run but merely hobble from oncoming law enforcers. This was no doubt why Albert had seen fit to pay a 'middle man' or 'middle boy' to do the actual *running* around, because when he had his 'collar felt' there would be no incriminating evidence upon his person. Between them, Albert and his young protégé Rhys John were making a tidy packet and no doubt they would have gone on doing so if the police had not recently got wind of their little scheme. When the police had approached the pair, Rhys had raced off into the distance but Albert as usual had been easy to catch. The mere mention of a custodial sentence had been enough to encourage Albert to 'grass up' his young employee. What Albert didn't realise was that the threat of jail was just that, an idle threat, for unbeknown to him the police never offically reported his various captures, as they knew he had fought bravely in the Great War and then fallen on hard times. But whilst Albert himself was small fry, he worked for some frankly nasty individuals, and PC Creigh was worried that Rhys would get involved by default. And that would be a very slippery slope indeed. Mary was shocked speechless - so much so that Susie went to fetch her a medicinal brandy from the larder – she had never imagined that any of her children would bring the 'police to her door.' She knew that if Oshbert were still alive Rhys would not have dared to act in such a way for Oshbert had always been of the opinion that *idle hands were the devil's playthings*. Once the policeman had said his piece and left, Mary and Susie raced up the stairs together to the bedroom which Rhys shared with his older brother Arthur. It was not long before they found the envelope stuffed full of money hidden under his mattress. Clutching it carefully to her bosom Mary descended the stairs and positioned it pride of place upon the sideboard in the parlour. Then without another word, she and Susie went back into the kitchen to see to baby Dennis and prepare the tea. When Rhys came home from school a short while later, Mary did not say a word. She merely placed the plate of food in front of her youngest son then went about her normal business as he ate his meal. After he had eaten, Rhys pushed his chair away from the table and asked if he could be excused so that he could go upstairs to the bedroom to 'do his homework'. Suspecting he was going upstairs to check on his money, Mary stood at the stair well and listened carefully. She heard the mattress flop to the floor as it was dragged from the bed and in her minds eye she could clearly see Rhys' panicked expression as he searched in vain for his envelope of money. Still she did not say a word and instead she pulled the parlour door to, then returned to the kitchen to nurse baby Dennis. Later that night - as she suspected he would – Rhys crept from the house under the cover of darkness. Treading carefully upon the stairs to avoid the creaking boards he stealthfully made his way towards the front door. What a fright he must have got when he opened the porch door and found his mother, all dressed for bed, her hair in curlers, sitting silently by the hatstand in the hallway. After muttering an expletive - which he knew he would be reprimanded for later - he desperately gathered his wits about him to formulate what he thought was a good and believable excuse. "Me and some of the chaps from school are going ratting."

"Did I ask you where you were going?" Mary quickly replied.

"No but....." Rhys sentence dwindled away as Mary stood up and ushered him back into the hallway and towards the parlour. She motioned that he take a seat by the fireplace, and it was when he sat on the chair and glanced towards the sideboard that he noticed his envelope of cash, and realised with a start that the game was up. Mary's anger that night was a sight to behold for she did appreciate being taken for a fool and lied to. She let loose a tirade of angry words and Rhys was immediately contrite. To his credit he did not try to apportion the blame in anyway and took his punishment on the chin. What a punishment it was for Mary 'suggested' he volunteer to help out at Chapel every weekend, then ask the Preacher what would be a suitable charity to donate the money to. She also proposed that he take up a hobby to keep himself occupied after school. His father's tools were all still lying untouched in the backyard shed and there were many odd jobs to be done around the house, so perhaps that would help keep his idle hands busy.

It was whilst Rhys was rummaging about in the shed searching for a suitable project to appease his mother and set her on the path to forgiveness that he came upon the wretched 'creature' lying squashed beneath the box of nails. Despite its great age – for his father Oshbert had first received the dreadful effigy doll in 1892 – the 'creature' had somehow renewed itself. Its cloth was now as soft as velvet and a delicately stitched welcoming smile played upon its face. Rhys immediately had the bright idea of presenting the doll to his nephew Dennis, for surely that would please his mother and go some way to persuading her that he was not an altogether 'bad egg.' And so that is what – with the very best of intentions – he did, and Baby Dennis fell upon his new toy with gusto. He sucked and chewed at its tiny velveteen feet and squeezed its little potbelly with great glee. It was quite a while later that Mary checked upon him and discovered the toy lying disguarded by the foot of the cot. Mary let out such a blood curdling scream, that Susie almost tripped headfirst down the stairs as she came racing from the attic. Seeing Mary's distress Susie snatched the 'creature' from her grasp and swore to immediately take it from the house and destroy it. Mary was distraught, for like Oshbert before her, she suspected that pure evil dwelled in that piece of cloth. Fearing for her precious grandson she began to watch over Dennis like a hawk, his every murmer giving her cause to rush to his side and indeed she did not properly relax nor sleep until his parents, Junior and Kitty, collected him that weekend. Once he had left the house she allowed herself a moment of reprise and even managed to convince herself that the family had dodged a bullet and that no harm had come to her only grandchild.

But unfortunately, it was not to be so and a few days later she got word that Dennis has died in his sleep. The cause of his death was never voiced and by the very omission of a recognisable cause, Mary took the blame upon herself. She decided she was solely responsible for the 'creature' being in their lives and nothing could convince her otherwise. Infant mortality was frighteningly high in the early 1900s and the causes were manifold - statistically out of every 1000 live births 86 would go on to perish - so it is very likely that the baby died from a group of symptoms we now collectively call *Sudden Infant Death Syndrome*. Mary never told Junior of the sudden reappearance of the 'creature', for she knew it would upset him too much and what good would it have served? I can now write that Junior and his wife Kitty - in the fullness of time - came to terms with their bereavement and went on to have three more children, all of whom lived to ripe old ages. Oshbert was their second born son – named after his father and his grandfather before him and known in family circles by the nickname of Sonny – and he was swiftly followed by two sisters Olive and young Anita, to complete the family.

As to the fate of the 'creature'? Well Susie finally got rid of it for good. She ran all the way across Jesmond on that fateful afternoon and once she had reached Grosvenor Avenue – a road leading off from Osborne Road - she searched for and found *The Grove*, a long forgotten ancient footpath hidden behind the avenue. Squeezing through the many branches and nettles overhanging from the gardens which backed onto to the narrow lane, she trudged determinedly downhill along the muddy track until she reached the site of St Mary's Well. Being a Catholic Susie knew of the existence of the Holy Well and had visited it many times in the past. The ancient Well was thought to have healing powers and so strongly entrenched was this belief that the the pilgrims of Middle Ages had even stopped there on their pilgrimage to nearby St Mary's chapel. Susie descended its old worn stone steps - slipping slightly on the damp moss on the ground surrounding the well – and struggling to regain her balance. Once she reached the lip of the well, she bowed her head in a guesture of religious humility and reached into the pocket of her skirt to retrieve the damned 'creature'. Since leaving the confines of Denis' cot it had reverted back to its previous guise. The smiling stitched grin was now an angry scowl and the velveteen material a course scratchy hessian, smelling of mould and mothballs. Holding it gingerly between her hands she thrust the wretched 'creature' under the steady flow of water - which ran from a chamber in the wall of the well - then watched transfixed as it dropped into the pool of water. It bobbed about for a while as its material became sodden then all of a sudden it was dragged deep down into the depths of the well water by an inexplicable extreme swirling vortex of boiling steaming water. For a brief moment the floating green sediment in the water flashed a crimson red, then just as quickly it settled and reverted back to a calm still opaque. A bright ray of sunshine peeped from behind the clouds and shone like a beacon into the dingy secret shrine and Susie felt a lightness wash over her entire body. It was then she knew for certain that the 'creature' was no more and good had finally conquered evil. The dreadful curse had been quashed. *The house too sensed the final destruction of the 'creature', as did the Pilgrims bones which shuffled to a final resting place beneath its foundations.*

ASHLEIGH GROVE, JESMOND, 1927, SUSIE AND THE GROCER

Susie at this time was still lodging in the rooms of the attic of Ashleigh Grove, and as Mary had not been able to pay her since Oshbert died, she had found it necessary to take employment at the local grocery. The grocers, which was located on nearby Brentwood Avenue, was a most salubrious place to work and the grocer himself had taken quite a shine to Susie. For whilst Susie looked in the mirror and saw a Plain Jane spinster, beauty is in the eye of the beholder, and the grocer gazing in her direction saw a congenial woman in the prime of her years, who was not at all displeasing to the eye. The grocer was a recent widower and he soon discovered that Susie to be everything his wife had not been. Susie was a good hard worker, eager to please with a calm and collected temperament. His recently deceased wife had possessed none of these qualities and, although the grocer made a convincing show of mourning her untimely departure, he did not miss her cruel cutting remarks and constant lack of good humour. Their son Jimmy had fortunately taken after himself, and for that he was grateful because the boy - despite having a job as an apprentice engineer - was more than happy to help his father in the shop most evenings after work. If nothing else, the grocer soon realised that having his son helping out in the shop was an asset customer-wise for many a young girl would siddle into the shop just to engage with him and flirt outrageously. But the lad seemed to have his eye cast upon a local lass called Dorothy Le Britton. Dorothy was the younger sister of Jimmy's good friend Arthur and in a twist of fate she lived in the very house on Ashleigh Grove where Susie lodged. At first the grocer had assumed his son had fallen for Arthur's older sister Anita, for she was quite the siren and the hearthrob of many a local lad, but when one day Dorothy popped in the shop with a message for Susie, the Grocer realised that it was in fact she who had stolen his son's heart. Jimmy's whole demeanour changed as he served the young lass, and he leapt from the chair behind the counter to rush to open the door when she made to leave the shop. Then he stood in the doorway staring at her departing figure until his father discreetly coughed and he moved reluctantly back inside. Susie witnessed the entire exchange and when she returned home later that night she gently teased Dorothy about her secret admirer. Mary was quick to interrupt and remind her that Dorothy was just turned sixteen, and despite holding down a full-time job, her daughter still had a lot more growing up to do, but Susie had noted Dorothy's shy smile and realised that the attraction between the two was probably mutual. And indeed it was not too long after this very exchange that Jimmy sought Dorothy out and confessed that he had taken a fancy to her. He followed his admission up by boldly asking if she would care to walk out with him and from that day forward the two were inseparable. Jimmy was so taken with his new sweetheart that a few weeks later he carved a heart in the railing of the wooden tarry bridge, so everyone could see that their names were interlinked and know that she was his girl. I have walked across that very bridge and even now, almost a century later with a tip of a finger the heart is still discernible.

The grocer was not so forward as his son for he had yet to declare his romantic intentions towards Susie, and she for her part was so blinded to her own attributes that she had no idea he thought of her that way. The grocer became so convinced of Susie's suitability as a future wife that a short while after his son had started to woo Dorothy, he decided perhaps it was time he to made his feelings known to his sweetheart. Being a shy hesitant man by nature he had tried many times to bring it into the conversation and time after time he fell at the first hurdle. When he did finally blurt out that he felt he had mourned his wife for long enough and perhaps it was time he found himself a new one. He did it in such a confusing out of context manner that Susie completely misunderstood and thought that in his own inimitable distinctive way he was trying to convey that he had developed feelings for Mary. So that night - as she sat quietly reading in her room before turning the lights out - she devised an ingenious and sneaky way to engineer an impromptu date for the two. Not one to sit on her laurels, Susie put her plan into action the very next day when she asked Mary if she fancied a leisurely stroll in the Dene once her household chores were done. She then raced to the grocer's shop and suggested exactly the same scenario to the grocer. He could not believe his luck and quickly before she had a chance to change her mind he affixed the shut sign to the front door of the shop - much to the dismay of his regular customers – who would prove to be quite vocal in their disapproval the next day. Ever the gentleman the grocer suggested calling upon her so they could enjoy the walk across to the Dene together, but she had anticipated just this and had a ready excuse to hand. She went on to use the self same excuse to Mary a few minutes later when she suddenly remembered she had ugent business at the church so it would be better to meet her there too.

Jesmond Dene was a haven of tranquillity, nestled within the urban sprawl of Newcastle and a very popular destination for an afternoon stroll as a result. In the beginning of the 19th Cenury the naturally wooded gorge had been home to watermills and quarries but in the 1850s Lord Armstrong – a local entrepeneur – bought a large area of the valley with the intention of landscaping it for his own private use. He added waterfalls, rock islands and idyllic stone built bridges to compliment the vast network of pathways meandering through the carefully chosen imported shrubs and trees. Armstrong had a strong sense of philanthropy so he opened the parkland to the public twice a year with the profits going to help the upkeep of the local hospital. This altruism came into play once again in 1883 when he kindly donated the park to the people of Newcastle so they could continue enjoy its recuperative merits into perpetuity.

It must have made for a very uncomfortable assignation indeed when the grocer and Mary slowly came to the realisation that Susie had set them up on a blind date. They were both standing on the bridge overlooking the waterfall at the time, and when it became evident that they were both waiting for the same person and had been 'stood up', the grocer gallently suggested that rather than wasting such a splendid afternoon they should perhaps walk a while. They crossed the bridge towards the old Mill and wandered companiably along the narrow paths enjoying the vista of Rhodedendrums which were in full bloom and quite glorious. As they walked and talked they discovered that they did indeed have a lot in common not least their love for Susie. The grocer was usually shy in talking of such things but he sensed an ally in Mary and asked her if she would 'put a good word in for him' once she returned home. Mary did as promised, and rather than chastise Susie for her well-intentioned trick she instead made a point of singing the grocer's praises. Susie was taken aback for she had never in her wildest dreams imagined herself as wife material and had presumed that she was destined to live out her remaining days as a lodger in someone else's home. She agreed to give the matter proper consideration but would not be drawn on what her decision would be. The next day she calmly prepared the breakfast, sorted the washing, then went to work as usual with the intention of giving the grocer her answer. It gave her quite the start when he took her hand and there and then issued his marriage proposal. Whilst not the most intimate of settings, nor the most romantic of proposals, it was a scene which Susie would lovingly revisit for a long time after the two were wed. Jimmy went on to make much of his father's lack of romantic finesse in his best man speech a few weeks later, much to the couple's embarrassment and their guest's amusement. It was a sad day for Mary when her good friend moved out of Ashleigh Grove, but Susie reassured her that she was after all just a stone's throw away and would pop in daily for a cup of tea and catch up.

USHAW COLLEGE, DURHAM, JULY 1926, THE DOWD FAMILY

True to his word my grandfather had enrolled in Ushaw Seminary College and - due to the high dropout rate - he had been able to start mid-term, just a few short months after returning to the UK. What prompted him to agree to such a drastic future of celibacy was without doubt his doomed love affair with Leonore and I know it was with a reluctance that he agreed to it at all. Once he had voiced his agreement on the trip back from Canada, the wheels must have been put into motion with the utmost of haste – in case he had a change of heart. Within weeks the Diocese of Hexham and Newcastle had been approached for help with the fees and he had passed the necessary interview with the Bishop. As he approached the imposing Pugin inspired buildings on that balmy July day in 1926, he must surely have realised the dramatic difference between his new life of monastic study and the carefree farming life he had once envisioned for himself and his former sweetheart. For never before had two such views so differed. The grey stoned theological college - very much at odds with the surrounding lush green rolling hills - were in stark contrast to the mighty forests of cedar and fir near his old home on Vancouver Island.

Uhsaw College in those days was very much a self-contained community, for it had its own kitchen garden, bakery, tailor and even cobbler. Looking through old photographs of the College, the buildings and the Refectory Hall in particular seem to me to be reminiciscant of a latter-day Hogwarts. As Lewis was studying theology and classed as an older student, he was referred to as a Divine, and one of the tailors from the nearby village of Hill Top and in the employ of the College – at one time in the 1880s there were 17 – was immediately tasked with stitching his special 'outfit' of Cassock, clerical collar, biretta and black knee-length coat. It was not only the 'outfit' which was overly restrictive but also the monastic life he had signed up for. His new life was ruled by the bell. It seemed to signal every significant occasion, not least the Magnum Silentium – a silence strictly adhered to, running from Benediction at 9.15pm to Mass the following morning. The President of the College at that time was the Right Reverend William Henry Brown, affectionately christened by the students with the nickname of 'Bob or Mons Bod.' Bob was very much an integral part of the institution as he had arrived at the College in 1865 at the age of 12 before becoming President in 1910, an office which he went on to hold until 1934. He, and a door porter, met Lewis at the door on that sunny August day, then escorted him into the cavernous hallway before leaving him in the capable hands of his mentor, another fellow Divine or Cod – old codger – by the name of Geoffrey Duffy. Geoffrey's first instruction to Lewis was that whenever he passed by the statue of Our Lady 'Sedes Sapientiae'-which was positioned opposite the main doors on the front ambolacrum - he must always stop and remove his biretta. Lewis dipped the checked cloth cap he was wearing, then quickly followed his new companion as Geoffrey raced him through the vast array of buildings, stopping briefly to show him the Divine's Playroom (Common Room), The Refectory Hall, The Library and finally his cell-like room where he was encouraged to leave his suitcase upon the narrow bed so that they could better continue their tour unhindered. The grounds of the College were far stretching and Geoffrey told him that a great emphasis was put upon outdoor recreational games such as Cat's. Cat's was a most peculiar game – it had originated in France – and Lewis had never come across it before. From Geoffrey's brief explanation Lewis surmised it to be a cross between cricket and baseball with two opposing teams of seven players striking a ball with a 'cat stick' then rushing madly around a gravel ring. Geoffrey was quite enthusiastic in his descriptions so Lewis presumed it to be more fun than it sounded. No doubt he would soon find out for it seemed almost mandatory to participate in the game.

The next morning, Lewis' reverie was rudely interrupted by the sound of the loud resounding bell. He peered, bleary eyed out into the corridor just as Geoffrey raced passed his doorway barking out instructions over his shoulder.

"Hurry up old Cod, it's morning prayer at quarter to, then breakfast at eight. It's first come first served at breakfast in the ref' and there's bacon on the menu for us Divines this morning, so shake a leg."

The Morning prayers in St Cuthbert's Chapel were led by one of the chap's, a fellow Divine, who Lewis had briefly been introduced to in the Playroom the previous evening. The prayers rolled on into a Morning Mass but despite the warm weather outside, the Chapel was cold and draughty, so much so that at one stage Lewis involuntary shivered and nearly dropped his prayer book. As he shuffled to keep a hold of it, a rather stern looking Professor at the end of the pew glared across in his direction and loudly hissed "HUSH." "Well that's a good start to my time here," Lewis thought to himself as he more firmly grasped the book and dipped his head in prayer. Breakfast in the Refectory proved to be a much warmer affair and the promised bacon was a welcome addition. Whilst they dined, another of Lewis' fellow Divines shuffled behind the Lecturn at the head of the room - just below the portrait of Cardinal Allen the founder of the college – and read a poem by a former Ushaw pupil Francis Thompson. Lewis mused that this seemed a very sombre and serious tome for so early in the morning, as it was full of fire and brimstone in its evocative description of God pursuing a young man through the years. Even its title 'Hounds of Heaven,' seemed entrenched in Victorian symbolism and imagery. The other Divines seemed almost oblivious to the gloomy vocal accompaniment as they greedily wolfed down their bacon and bread.

The remainder of the morning was taken up in lessons and Lewis was most perturbed to see that one of the teachers lecturing in Moral Theology was none other than the man who had 'hissed' so eloquently at him during the Mass earlier that day. It seemed Professor Mitchell recognised him too for he once again glared in his direction, and pursing his lips, declared in a somewhat menancing tone, "I trust you will have more success holding onto your books in my lectures young man for I do not suffer fools lightly and shall be keeping a special eye upon you." Thankfully, the rest of the lesson was unremarkable although Lewis did struggle from time to time with various catholic indoctrinations but thought it prudent not to voice his opinions for fear of rebuke.

After a rather meagre lunch, there followed a brief foray outside so the students could partake in recreational games. Lewis requested that he be allowed to watch from the sidelines, in the hope that it would help him grasp the rather peculiar rules of Cat. Lessons recommenced and continued until seven that evening. Afterwards, there were more prayers in St Cuthbert's Chapel then a most welcome tea. The younger boys (minors) had a strict bedtime of 9pm and it fell to the Divines to make sure they strictly adhered to 'lights out.' Lewis was alloted a specific dormitory and, after popping in to make sure all the boys were tucked up in bed, he switched the lights out and left the room. Standing outside the door for a few moments to make sure there were no whispers or loud giggling, he was just about to walk away when he became aware of a gentle sobbing. Going back in the room he soon ascertained which bed the crying was coming from, and knelt by the boy's bed, in an effort to find out what the problem was, but before he could ask, one of the other boys shouted across the room, "just ignore him sir, he's a Scouse baby. He was flogged by Professor Fiddler this morning sir, and he's just feeling sorry for himself." At this statement, the rest of the boys in the dorm immediately fell about laughing and jeering in mock Liverpudlian accents. Lewis was incensed, for he could not abide bullying, and switching on the light he shouted, "Enough I tell you, enough." The room immediately fell silent, although the young boy still sobbed, his shoulders heaving and lifting the bedclothes as he gasped in a desperate attempt to retain composure. Lewis decided to take the boy into the corridor away from his jeering classmates so he could better find out what the problem was, and hopefully calm him down. It was quite a while before the boy stopped sobbing enough to form a coherent sentence, and in a juddering voice he said, "I'm sorry for being a pest sir. I haven't been here long and the others tease me all the time. My backside is really sore too. It was my fault. The Prof gave me the choice of the Cat stick or his hand and I chose the hand thinking it would hurt less... and it didn't." Lewis was lost for words, he had been caned at school and while it smarted at the time it had soon wore off. How hard had this so-called man of God struck the poor boy?

"What did you do to be punished so severely," he asked the boy, expecting to hear of some serious misdemeanour.

"Me and some of the other lads were chatting at the urinals this morning and we hadn't realised the Prof was hiding in the showers to catch us out."

"So were the other boys punished too?" Lewis asked.

"Yes sir, Potts and Monty were but they knew better and chose the Cat."

"What's your name boy?"

"Paul sir. Paul Murry. I'm from Birkenhead. I hate how the other boys call me a Scouse baby whenever I say I miss my mother."

"I miss mine too," Lewis confided, "I'm also new here. What say you look out for me and I look out for you? Have you told anyone about this taunting?"

Paul nodded his head vehemently, "Yes sir I have. I tried to tell Professor Fiddler before he flogged me and he said to grow up and then he called me a Scouse baby too."

Lewis was shocked. So much for Pastoral Care and teaching the boys the true meaning of their Christian Vocation. What signal did it send out to his classmates if a teacher condoned their actions by joining in the bullying, and surely the punishment he had metered out was disproportionately severe for such a small wrongdoing?

"I tell you what. I will try to have a quiet word with the Professor myself and let's see if we can't knock this silly nonsense on the head once and for all shall we? Now are you alright to go back to bed?"

Once the young boy was settled back into the dorm and the dorm had properly fallen silent, Lewis left to search for Professor Fiddler. He had every intention of having a discreet word in the hope of making him see the error of his ways. Surely as a man of God once he fully realised how much he had hurt and upset the poor boy, he would be at pains to make it right again? Lewis was just descending the main stairs when he collided with Geoffrey going the opposite way.

"I say Geoffrey," Lewis began, "would you point me in the direction of Professor Fiddler's rooms. One of the young lads in the dorm was flogged by him this morning and is in a proper state."

Geoffrey smirked before pulling Lewis aside. Speaking in a whisper he said, "firstly old cod don't let him hear you calling him that or he will have your guts for garters. The honourable Professor

Fiddler is the nickname we lot give to Professor Mitchell. I wager this lads a new starter is he?"

"Yes but what's that got to do with anything," Lewis replied, still trying to get his head around the Professor's bizarre nickname.

"Fiddler is infamous for giving the new lads the choice of the Cat or as he phrases it the more gentle hand. That's how he got his nickname. The man's a sadist amongst other things. He gets the lads to drop their drawers and the slap of the hand on a bare bottom is far more painful than the Cat stick I can tell you."

Lewis was temporarily lost for words, "but surely if everyone knows of his perversion he would be stopped?"

"It's an open secret which everyone knows but Fiddler's first cousin is a Bishop somewhere down South so it's swept conveniently under the carpet."

"Well I for one won't be sweeping it under any carpet. Where are his rooms? I want to give this bully a piece of my mind."

"I wouldn't old cod, just let sleeping dogs lie. This lad won't make the same mistake twice, of that I am sure, and making the Fiddler your enemy won't bode well for your time here I can tell you that."

Lewis was incensed at the injustice of the situation and strode determinedly off in the direction of the Professor's rooms. Once there, he hammered on the door and when it was swung open, he barged rudely in. But true to form, the Professor was not remotely contrite. Firstly he admonished Lewis for interfering, then he demanded to know why he – a lowly Divine - dared to think that he had a right to preach to a superior. Corporal punishment, he reminded Lewis, was a normal part of school life and if he chose to administer such floggings, Lewis could rest assured that he had the full support of the rest of the faculty. Lewis bravely fought Paul's corner which was probably not the best idea for this only suceeded in angering the Professor even more and it was with great venom in his voice that he issued a warning to Lewis that he would make it his mission that his every waking moment was pure Hell. And from that moment on that is exactly what he did. Whenever Lewis turned a corner, the Professor would be there. Watching and waiting to jump upon him for the slightest error or tiny violation of the rules. It was as if he had eyes in the back of his head, such was his constant brooding presence. Lewis kept calm. He had made his mother a promise to see this through. It would be four long hard years but he had sworn he would try his hardest to make her proud of him once again. So every insult, every disparaging slur the Professor threw his way, he turned the other cheek and refused to be riled. The fateful day he finally gave in to his temper was the day he was wandering aimlessly through the grounds and came upon the 'minors' partaking in a very energetic game of Cat. He stood by the sidelines for a while before he realised that young Paul Murry was part of the team of seven players. Lewis watched as Paul – not a natural sportsman - tried to strike the ball, and witnessed his embarassed wince, as the opposing team jeered his every missed shot. In the background, on the opposite side of the ring, Lewis spotted a figure dressed in a similar manner to himself and it was then he realised that the mocking was being actively encouraged by the aptly named Professor Fiddler. Lewis and the Professor locked eyes, they held this position for a long while and in the end it was Lewis who – eager to avoid yet another confrontation - dropped his stare and walked away. Lewis had barely walked more than a few paces when a heartrending scream rang from the sports field. It appeared that young Paul - due to his incompetence as a batter - had been moved off- field behind the new batsman and as a result had been struck quite violently in the face by the hard wooden Cat Stick. It was as the mutilated boy was being helped from the field - his face streaming with blood and his nose broken - that Lewis instinctivly realised that the boy had become injured on purpose, in all probability to escape the constant bullying and probable abuse. Lewis was so enraged that he raced across the field and almost with battering ram action, he knocked the sneering Professor clear off his feet. Lewis was a gentle soul and not naturally an aggressive man but that day he saw red. As the professor lay helplessly on his back like an upturned dung beetle - his black clad legs and arms uselessly flaying - Lewis nudged him roughly in the crotch with the tip of his shoe. "You are not worth the dirt on the sole of my shoe," Lewis declared before calmly strolling from the scene to await his fate.

The very next day, as he had anticipated, Lewis was called to 'Bob's office and politely asked to leave the premises with immediate effect. Lewis had thought of fighting his corner, but in reality being sent home was a good result. He was now certain that this life was not for him and he had lost all respect for his teachers and his religion in general.

The following day his younger brother John made the short train journey to Durham to take Lewis' place in the Seminary. I can now add that John went on to become a fully ordained priest, serving ministries in both India and San Francisco, before settling back in England and penning a Spiritual novel called *You Cannot Hold Back The Dawn*. It is undeniable that John was much better suited to life in the Seminary than his older brother, and it should have been he who had been sent in the first place. Lewis returned home, tail firmly between his legs, to his very disenchanted mother who would at regular intervals reiterate and remind him of her great disappointment. Paul Murry, the young boy that Lewis had befriended, also returned to his own mother in Birkenhead and I am happy to report that he went on to lead a quite unremarkable but nevertheless quite pleasant life. Paul qualified as a Geography teacher - with a lifelong aversion to corporal punishment of any kind - and when he later married and he and his wife welcomed their only son into the world they named him Lewis. This may be just a coincidence for at the time Lewis was a popular name and I may be reading too much into it, but I like to think this was in gratitude for my grandfather's bravery that day.

ST CHARLES CHURCH PRESBYTERY,
GOSFORTH 1927. THE DOWDS

My great-grandmother Theresa during the time her son Lewis had been holed up in the Seminary, had taken up residence in the Presbytery adjoining St Charles' Catholic Church on Church Road in Gosforth. She had returned to England a penniless widow so it had been a priority to find paid employment which included a home for her and the children. No doubt, she was initially fearful that this experience would turn out like her previous one in Port Alberni, but Father Adam Wilkinson was so much older and more experienced than his Canadian counterpart, Father Bradley, and this gravitas and his state of blindness would hopefully ensure no talk of impropriety was ever imagined nor uttered. And so it was to this vast house in the centre of the village of Gosforth that my grandad returned. He swiftly moved into his brother John's recently vacated bedroom in the attic, and set about finding a job and worthwhile career. It just so happened that at this time Liverpool Victoria was having a big employment drive and, after successfully passing the interview, Lewis was offered a post as a door-to-door Insurance collector. Unbeknown to him on the floor below, beavering away as a Junior Clerk sat my grandmother, Dorothy Le Britton, his future wife. As Lewis was escorted through her office, after successfully completing his interview and accepting the post, Dorothy had glanced up from her desk and smiled in his direction. His very appearance had caused quite a stir amongst the young girls in the office, for he was a handsome man of marriageable age, with striking ice blue eyes, a confident deportment and impeccable manners. My grandmother was still much enamoured by her sweetheart Jimmy Monroe so I don't think for one minute she imagined this was to be the first time she would set her eyes upon her future husband. But she, like the rest of her young female collegues would have appreciated the new addition to the firm, and been aware of his more charismatic qualities. At this time in 1927 Dorothy was classed as an Office Junior. She had left school a few years earlier at the age of 14 and much like her older sister Antia, and indeed her brothers Junior and Arthur, a career at Liverpool Victoria had been a foregone conclusion. For although their father Oshbert had died in 1919, his legacy to the Company lived on and to this end, and because he had been held in such high esteem, his offspring were guaranteed a career once they reached employable age. Anita was newly married and Oshbert had recently moved away, but Dorothy and Arthur were still holding up the family name as loyal Liverpool Victoria employees. Their mother, Mary had once joked that her children had Liverpool Victoria written through them, rather like a stick of rock has Blackpool written through it.

Dorothy had not really given much thought to her career choice after leaving West Jesmond School, for she saw it as a stop gap between education and marriage to her sweetheart Jimmy Monroe. Although Jimmy had not gone down on his knee to actually propose, it was an unspoken assumption that they would eventually marry and the two lovebirds would often sit in the 'pit' of the Jesmond Picture House, watching a silent movie and whispering plans for their future. The Picture House was a favourite destination for many a courting couple as the close proximity to their beloved, coupled with the darkness made for an excellent canoodling opportunity. Dorothy and Jimmy were regulars at the Picture House and the only bugbear was, while talkies were the new sensation – The Jazz Singer starring Al Jolson had premiered in October 1927 - the movies shown at that time in Jesmond were silent, so a vast majority of the plot was missed or misinterpreted as constant smooching tended to take their eyes away from the screen. In fact the Jesmond Picture House was one of the last movie theatres in Newcastle to make the conversion to 'talkies', because the Manager wrongly presumed it to be a short-lived fad. The only movies Dorothy insisted on sitting and watching intently were the ones starring the recently deceased

Italian heartthrob Rudolph Valentino. Valentino was very much the 'Latin Lover'. Most girls swooned over his good looks in the 20s and his popularity had prompted many a young man, including Jimmy, to replicate his greased back hair – the vaselino – in an attempt to impress their girlfriends. When Valentino died in August 1926, such was his stardom and popularity, that there was an outbreak of mass hysteria among his female fans, including some reported suicides. The Manager of the Jesmond Picture House was a canny businessman and he knew that running any Valentino movie would guarantee a full house, so he looked upon Valentino's death as a blessing in disguise and an excuse to re-run the favourites, such as *The Shiek* and *Blood and Sand*. Watching the movies now, when we are so used to realism, they seem melodramatic and over-the-top, but to the twenties moviegoer they were the very epitome of Hollywood glamour, and when Valentino dressed up as the smouldering Shiek and entered Agnes Ayres' tent with the intention of making her his own, his female fans fainted in the aisles at the breathtaking passion of the moment. As ill-founded rumours of Valentino's homosexuality and his 'lavender marriages' began to abound, Jimmy, along with many of his chums quickly changed their hairstyles and grew moustaches in the style of the other major Hollywood Hearthrob Douglas Fairbanks instead. Dorothy remarked it suited him, although she was to change her opinion when the constant chaffing gave her a rash on her upper lip.

Mary was not so keen on her daughter's relationship with Jimmy, as she had wanted more for her younger daughter than marriage to the son of a grocer. Despite the fact that she had encouraged her former housemaid Susie to marry Jimmy's father, she had hoped for a better-educated and well-connected suitor for her daughter. Dorothy found this snobbery most disturbing, and had said as much to her mother on the numerous occasions that Mary had voiced her feelings out aloud. But Mary was undeterred for she was adamant that Dorothy could in her words 'do better.' Jimmy was painfully aware of the frosty reception he received whenever he visited Dorothy's house, and if nothing else it motivated his desire to strive for a better life than his father's mundane nine to five existence. Jimmy's dream was to emigrate to Canada with Dorothy by his side, but Mary would not entertain such a proposition. Dorothy could not openly defy her mothers wishes, so eventually Jimmy declared that he would go alone and return for Dorothy once he had made his fortune. She tearfully agreed to wait. The day that Jimmy left, Dorothy was distraught. She sat in her bedroom all night long, staring at his photographs and re-reading the letters they had shared during their long courtship. Mary thought it best to keep her distance, so she stayed in the parlour quietly knitting as her daughter's soulful cries descended the stairs. With the three precious photographs of her beau propped up on her nightstand, Dorothy eventually fell into a fitful restless sleep.

For the next few months, Dorothy would return home from work and rush through the porch to the hallstand to check if any letters had arrived from her sweetheart. But every day it was the same, and the shelf below the motley collection of hats and scarves remained empty and bare. Occasionally, an unopened letter would be lying there, and for a brief moment Dorothy's heart would soar, only to fall and shatter to the ground when she realised it was not addressed to her. Day after day. Week after week. Month after month. No letter arrived. She began to play tricks with her mind, telling herself that one day it would arrive when she least expected it and the mere expectation of it being there when she walked into the house would stop it arriving. Pride stopped her from going to Susie and the grocer for news. Pride and a fear that her mother's words were in fact true, and Jimmy had left her with the intention of never returning. In her mounting insecurity, she convinced herself that some pretty Canadian girl had caught his eye and stolen his heart. In time even his words and promises became hollow in her memory and she struggled to even remember his voice. Then she reflected upon the conversations they had shared, and reading between the lines of his earlier love letters, imagined a hesitancy and reluctance to his replies. At this stage, I must add that she had herself written numerous letters to Jimmy. Letters which her mother had assured her she had posted as she went about her day-to-day errands, but which Mary had actually ripped up and deposited in a bin as she crossed the tarry bridge to the shops. I have also since discovered that Jimmy had been true to his word and he had written his first letter to Dorothy the minute he set foot upon Canadian soil, but Mary had intercerpted this letter, and the numerous others which followed, and had burned them en-masse and uncerminoniously on the kitchen fire. For this was how desperate Mary was that her daughter not marry Jimmy. Whilst she had claimed the reason to be his social standing, I suspect it was more to do with the fact that she did not want to be left alone in the big house on Ashleigh Grove. For despite the two boys Arthur and Rhys still living in the house, she knew that when the time came they would leave her without a backward glance. She often quoted the old adage *a son is a son until he takes a wife but a daughter is a daughter for the rest of her life*. I cannot find any evidence to support the claim that Mary even felt any guilt for the emotional pain and turmoil which she inflicted upon her daughter. It appears that she was so sure of Jimmy's unsuitability as a son-in-law that she had convinced herself that she was being cruel to be kind. When Susie and she met for a cup of tea and a catch up, the talk often fell upon Susie's stepson Jimmy, and Mary would quickly change the subject. Although I feel I must add that Mary did make a particular point to mention what a brilliant social life her daughter had, and how popular she was at the dances she attended, fully knowing that this information would be imparted to Jimmy when his father the grocer wrote to him.

BLACKPOOL 1930, LIVERPOOL VICTORIA WORKS OUTING

As the coach neared the outskirts of Blackpool, the young men sitting at the front of the vehicle lowered the windows and craned their necks for the first glimpse of the famous Blackpool Tower. The Tower which sat on the Fylde Coastline had been the iconic backdrop to Blackpool ever since its construction in 1894. The town's Mayor at the time, a Mr John Bickerstaffe, had attended the Great Paris Exhibition in 1889 and been so impressed with the Eiffel Tower that he commissioned the Blackpool Tower upon his return to England - even investing £2,000 of his own money into the enterprise, so firm was his conviction. When it was first built it was the the tallest man-made structure in the British Empire, although it has now, with the passage of time, been relegated to the 120th tallest in the world. A cry of elation reverberated throughout the bus at the first sighting of the pinnacle of the Tower, and one of the more exhuberant young men leapt from his seat, punched the air and whooped in anticipation of the day ahead.

The morning had started drizzly - cleared up - became overcast, but thankfully now as they finally pulled along the famous Promenade the sun peeped its head shyly from the clouds. The chatter of excitement reached a fever pitch as the young girls adjusted the angles of their hats and checked their lipstick in the small compact mirrors they had hastily retrieved from their handbags. Lewis was at the front of the coach with the other *door-to-doors,* and Dorothy was holed up in the rear with the Accountancy Office girls as she had made the transition from Office Junior the previous year. There was a heirachy in place even in the seating on the coach. The Office Manager, the rather bombastic Mr Farrar, had thankfully elected not to attend - using his wife's rather frequent and convenient migraines as an excuse - so the younger men on the coach had been all the more high-spirited and boisterous as a result. Lewis sat in the middle of the crowd of lads, trying hard to join in with the friviolity, but finding the coarse language his work colleagues used most inappropriate.

"Hey I say Lou," said one of the more vulgar lads addressing Lewis with his office nickname,"did you hear the one about the fellow who went into the bar and the barman asked him how many wives he had had?" Lewis shook his head, hoping the punchline would not be too crass, and hoping the young ladies in earshot were not party to the conversation. He was shocked when a girls voice piped up from behind him and she recited the punchline of, "he said I've had many wives but only one of them has been mine," It seemed as if the entire coach fell into spasms of raucous laughter even though they had probably heard the joke many times before. The girls suprisingly seemed to take the innuendos in good nature and there was already a natural pairing taking place. This outing was the highlight of the office social calendar. Much discussion had gone on before this actual day. The girls flustering about the perfect outfit for the probable inclement weather, and the chaps ensuring they had enough money to show their chosen girl a good time. Dorothy, like Lewis, was trying desperately to blend in with the crowd and join in the frivolity but she felt removed, as if she was trying too hard to match their gaiety. She had missed the works' outings the two previous years, as she had still been pining for her sweetheart Jimmy, and truth be told, she had taken some convincing to attend this one. But her every possible excuse had been ignored, and eventually she had given in to peer pressure and agreed to 'perk up old girl.' Now they were almost at their destination and she was actually starting to quite enjoy herself. It had been quite a merry journey, as they shared fizzy pop and handed sandwiches along the aisle. Unlike the other single girls she had no interest in 'finding herself a fella,' but her best friend Blanche had whispered in a deliberately loud voice – no doubt hoping he would hear - that she intended to 'bag' the enigmatic Lewis Dowd. Lewis was the office charmer, but seemed blinkered to the flirting and batting of eyelashes his presence inevitably prompted, and his total lack of interest made the prospect of 'bagging' him quite the challenge. Dorothy promised to help her friend in her quest and to endeavour to engineer a meeting between the two, because as she reconciled the *door-to-door* books, she was on a nodding aquaintance with most of the collectors.

Blackpool was a confusion of colour, and the crowds who strode along the pavements seemed to match its joyful mood. Dorothy made a decision that by *Hell or high water* she would enjoy the day. She had given enough of her time to mourning her lost love, and perhaps now, today, was the day she could start to feel happy again. But the happy prospect did not bode well as she hopped too energetically from the bus, and unused to wearing heels, lost her balance on the cobbles below. She was startled yet relieved to feel a steady firm hand under her elbow saving her from an embarrassing tumble. Dorothy turned gratefully to thank her rescuer, and was momentarily lost for words, as she stared into the most striking and mesmerising blue eyes of Lewis Dowd. Not trusting her voice, she shyly instead smiled her gratitude while Lewis, ever the gentleman, tipped his hat and replied in a joking manner, "the pleasure was all mine Miss Le Britton. I only hope the rest of your trip is just as memorable." The brief interlude between the two was disturbed when Dorothy was roughly prodded in the back by her friend Blanche, who it seemed was not at all happy that Dorothy had missed the chance to *sing her praises.* Blanche huffed and puffed for a while before finally forgiving her friend, when she renewed her promise to introduce Blanche to Lewis, when next their paths crossed. Linking arms the two girls were soon drawn along the promenade by the merry throng of daytrippers. The girls ducked from the crowd and after a brief wander under the Central Pier and along the sand to stroke the donkeys, they made their way towards the famous Noah's Ark on Blackpool Pleasure Beach. This self-dubbed 'rocking fun house' was based upon the biblical boat, and as it had only opened in 1922, it was a popular destination. There were apparently similar Ark's as far afield as Venice Pier California and Kennywood Amusement Park Pennsilvania. After parting with their 6d's the girls dawdled through its meandering corridors and passageways, jumping and giggling as the compressed air blew their hats clean from their heads, then shrieking at the mild electric shocks they received from the metal banisters and door handles. Dorothy nearly lost her balance for the second time that morning on the moving staircase. Unfortunately the gallant Lewis was not there to save her this time, but thankfully Blanche managed to grab a hold of the hem of her jacket and pull her back to safety. After all the excitement of the 'fun house', Blanche declared that an ice cream would be a most welcome treat and they wandered back off onto the Pier, stopping briefly to chuckle along with the 'laughing policeman' on their way. It was there that Dorothy once again set her eyes upon Lewis. Throughout the morning it seemed that wherever they wandered they would walk into the '*door to doors*', and Lewis who was a good head taller than the majority of his co-workers would seem to seek her out and smile in her direction. Despite her previous promise to Blanche these distant interactions became so frequent that Dorothy herself began to seek out his distinctive hat in the crowd and will him to look her way. After enjoying the ice creams – which were so soft in their cones that they were rapidly melting before they could be eaten - the two girls met up with a group of the '*secretaries*', and joining their merry gang, they ran back onto the sand to peel off their stockings and dip their toes in the chilly North Sea. But no sooner had they started to plodge and splash about in the waves than the weather dramatically changed and as a sharp wind raced across the beach, swirling the sand and raising their skirts, the girls decided to cut their losses and visit the Tower instead. As they scurried along the promenade, Dorothy paused briefly by a tram stop to gaze at a poster advertising Louis

Tussaud's Waxworks. She had dearly wanted to visit the attraction but Blanche had declared it boring, stating who wanted to stare at a 'pile of melted candle wax.' Dorothy's attention had been drawn by the poster primarily because it depicted Valentino in a famous scene from his most famous movie *The Shiek*. Although peering at the waxwork model in his arms, she decided it looked more like Mary Pickford than Agnes Ayres, so the modeller had obviously not been a true Valentino aficionado. It was as she stood there, staring transfixed at the poster, that a stray dog wandered past and cocked his leg up against her skirt. Dorothy let out a cry of distress coupled with embarrassment, but her friends were by now out of earshot and wandered on oblivious to her plight. Luckily for her, Lewis was walking by at exactly the moment the dog decided to do its dirty business and quickly excusing himself from the others, he once again raced to her aid. Shooing the dog away, he poured the drink of fizzy pop he had been holding upon her skirt in a desperate effort to wash off the offensive urine. He then proceeded to apologise profusely as her skirt began to bubble and froth in a most alarming manner. Lewis grabbed her hand – giving her the second electric shock of the day but a much more pleasurable one – and half pulled, half dragged her from the promenade and back onto the beach. "We can soon wash it off in the sea," he declared. As they ran, Lewis turned to smile at her, and just at that moment, a sudden gust of wind blew his jacket over his head. Dorothy had a sudden image pop in her head of her hearthrob Valentino 'overcome with passion' pulling Agnes Ayres across the desert sand dunes. But this brief romantic vision was soon blurred because Lewis stumbled over a child's sandcastle and they both fell in a clumsy indelicate heap upon the sand. Lewis was about to burst out in apology once more, but he noticed Dorothy's shoulders heaving and realised that she was in a fit of the most contagious giggles he had ever witnessed. It was not long before he joined her and they were both lying spread-eagled upon the sand, laughing so hard at the pure absurdity of the situation. They laughed so long and so energetically that Dorothy was soon struggling to catch her breath, and Lewis' sides ached, but everytime they managed to contain themselves they would glance across at each other and the giggling would start afresh. I like to think that the laughter was all the aphrodisiac the couple needed, and it was at that moment that they fell hopelessly in love, but their romance was more of a slow burn and all the more precious for it. Once the giggling was finally spent, Lewis helped Dorothy to her feet then proposed that, as they had appeared to have both lost contact with their friends, they might as well spend the rest of the day together. He went on to suggest that perhaps they could even visit the Waxworks she had been so enthralled by on that fateful poster. Dorothy jumped up from her sitting position upon the sand and clapped her hands in glee,"Oh please, that would be marvellous."

What a jolly time they had, wandering around the Exhibition Hall trying to guess the identity of the wax models based only upon the actual recognisable likeness, then standing astounded as they scrutinised the name plaques and realised how wrong they had been. Buster Keaton and Charlie Chaplin were easily recognisable from their outfits, but Harold Lloyd had them completely flummoxed for quite a while. When they came upon the tableau of Valentino crouched in his Bedouin tent, Dorothy involuntarily let out a gasp of recognition. Screwing up her eyes so she could see more clearly in the half darkness, Dorothy declared with satisfaction, "I was right that is Mary Pickford. I knew it wasn't Agnes Ayres. The jawline is all wrong and the hairstyle too." Lewis nodded sagely, although truth be told he had no idea who either actress was, for he was not a great fan of the movies. But he did sense an opportunity to get closer to the delightful Dorothy and hopefully get to hear that sweet giggle once more. So in a gesture quite unpremeditated in any way, he dramatically flicked his freshly laundered hankerchief from his breast pocket and draped it across his head in the manner of the

Shiek. Then again - in a similar bold move he took Dorothy into his arms and swept her from her feet - whereupon she fell into a fake swoon. Lewis was rewarded with a bewitching Dorothy giggle. A passing Custodian of the Museum – upon hearing the commotion - curtly stopped them in their tracks and directed their attention towards a sign above the doorway which stated that there was to be *No lewd or boisterous behaviour / the consumption of alcohol on the premises is strictly forbidden.* His point made, he stuffily wandered off into the other room allowing Dorothy to stand up straight and hastily rearrange her outfit.

"Oh my," she said "I do hope he doesn't think we are intoxicated?"

"He would be right in that assumption," Lewis declared, pausing for effect before continuing, "I confess that I am intoxicated but not with the drink. I'm intoxicated with you and laughter, and the wonderful time we are having today."

Dorothy smiled. She was unexpectedly shy in his presence once again, and also suddenly aware of her growing attraction to this lovely, kind man who had made her laugh so uproariously.

When they left the Waxworks it was still drizzling. It was the light sprinkling type of rain which despite its innocuous appearance soaked one quite to the skin. Lewis was about to suggest they risk it and wander along to the Tower, but just as he was about to speak he spotted Dorothy's pals just across the street. Quickly before they looked over, saw her and the moment was lost, Lewis twirled Dorothy around to face him.

"It looks like this rain is set for the afternoon. What say we try and find a Picture House so we can stay moderately dry?"

"Oh please," said Dorothy smiling broadly, "I am sure we passed one earlier, near the Pier. But only if you are certain you wouldn't rather spend the remainder of the afternoon with your friends?"

"I assure you Dorothy there is no-one I would rather spend my time with than you. I am just so glad we have had this chance to get to know each other properly at last."

Without further ado, Lewis took off his jacket, outstretched his elbow so Dorothy could link arms, then draping the coat over both of their heads the couple made a run in the direction of the Picture House. Once there Lewis - ignoring Dorothy's protestations - insisted on paying and they were very soon being ushered into the middle of a row of damp picturegoers as it seemed they were not alone in their impromtu cinema trip to escape the inclement weather. The film showing that afternoon was a musical western called Montana Moon and starred Joan Crawford in the leading lady role. As they squeezed into their seats, Dorothy turned to Lewis and declared, "I have been wanting to see this for ages. I'm not normally a fan of westerns but I've heard its really good." Lewis just nodded. The few times he had previously been to the movies he had not really taken with it, but if Dorothy was keen he was more than happy to give it a try. Lewis really hadn't taken much notice of the film showing as he paid at the kiosk - for he was so desperate that Dorothy not change her mind that he would literally have paid to 'watch paint dry' that afternoon - so he was pleasantly surprised at how much he enjoyed the strange genre of a musical western. In the interval, while Dorothy visited the 'powder room' he quickly raced back to the kiosk to surprise her with a box of chocolates. Once the lights dimmed after the intermission, he was rewarded by Dorothy passing him a heart shaped strawberry cream. Trying not to read too much into it, he then gingerly snaked his arm along the back of the seats and was further rewarded when Dorothy relaxed into his embrace.

All too soon the movie was over, and it was time to meet up with the rest of their workmates at the coach point for the long journey back to normality. As they strolled companiably along the promenade, Lewis peeled away from Dorothy and raced into a shop making Blackpool rock. He came out of the shop doorway a few minutes later proudly brandishing a pink and white stripey stick of rock poking out of a similarily striped paper bag. He handed the rock to Dorothy, declaring, "a small momento of our glorious day together." Seeing that they were nearly caught up with the rest of their collegues, Dorothy quickly thanked him and stuffed it into her handbag. All of a sudden she had realised how it must look. The two of them walking in such close proximity and turning up together. The office gossips would have a field day on this one and what of her best friend Blanche, how would she feel when she saw them both together? She fell back a few paces, letting Lewis take the lead and then when they reached the others, she sidled across towards her co-workers. She was surprised to find that Blance was not amongst the crowd, but the talk was all of her best friend. Apparently, Blanche had met a local lad in the Ballroom beneath the Tower, and she was still missing. One of the young lads from the postroom was delegated to run along the street to see if he could find her and it wasn't long before he let out a cry, "it's alright chaps here she comes." Blanche came into their sight on the opposite side of the street, she was running along, her hat askew, swinging hands with a rather handsome young lad. Dorothy let out a sigh of relief. Firstly, her good friend was safe and secondly, she seemed to have found herself a really nice boyfriend into the bargain. They clambered back onto the coach in preparation for the long journey back home to Newcastle. Dorothy made her way along the aisle towards the back seats, but as she squeezed past the bags – which were now strewn haphazardly along the walkway – Lewis reached out his arm to block her path, then he shuffled across his seat to make room for her to sit by him.

"I've saved a seat for you," he said with a smile to his voice, "rather that than have you take another unfortunate trip."

Answering with a bravado which was quite out of character Dorothy replied, "there's me thinking it was because you liked my company."

Lewis was quick to reply, "'Oh I do, I like it very much Dorothy Daisy Davies Le Britton. Very much indeed." Then he took her hand in his and they travelled home that way. Her hand firmly clasped in his.

Dorothy alighted from the coach before Lewis, for she still lived in the house on Ashleigh Grove so her stop was before his. Feeling empowered by the darkness of the coach she leaned across the seat and pressed her lips to his cheek. Lewis in turn took her hand, and with the lightest of touches pressed his lips to the underside of her wrist. When she had managed to regain her composure Dorothy said – in almost a whisper for she could sense the other passengers on the coach watching and listening - "thankyou for a very pleasant day." To which Lewis replied, in a similar barely audible voice, "the pleasure was all mine. Do tell me your answer soon." It was not until Dorothy had wandered along Highbury and was strolling along Ashleigh Grove in the direction of home that she began ponder on Lewis' last statement. Whatever did he mean? What question was he referring to? As she turned the corner into the Grove she saw Mary, her mother, watching from the bay window, waiting for her safe return. "Hello my dear," Mary said as Dorothy slipped off her coat and followed into the parlour, "I do hope you have had a lovely time today. I've really missed you." Then noticing the stick of rock poking from her daughter's handbag she added excitedly, "Oh lovely you've brought some rock back with you. It's been so long since I last visited Blackpool and they do make the most delicious rock." Dorothy handed her mother the rock. She was sure that Lewis would understand, and it had been purchased on the spur of the moment after all. It was as Mary bit into the rock that she said questioningly,"thats strange Blackpool Rock normally has the word Blackpool running through it but this seems to read *Be my girl*. How quaint, but I do declare it is as lovely as I remembered. Here have a piece." And she handed it back to Dorothy, not noticing how her daughter's hand shook slightly as she took it from her. So that was what Lewis had meant earlier. What a lovely gesture and what a romantic way to ask her to walk out with him. She would give him her answer the next day at work. Before she climbed into bed that night, Dorothy decisively crossed the room towards her chest of drawers and removed the three framed photographs of Jimmy. Turning them upside down, she carefully tucked them under her sweaters in the drawer. She wasn't quite ready to throw the photograph's away, but she had turned a significant corner.

ANITA LE BRITTON, 1931, THE RETURN OF THE LONG LOST SON

In the spring of 1927 Anita, my grandmother Dorothy's older sister, had eventually consented to marry her long-term boyfriend James Young. Both parties were honest enough – albeit only to each other - to admit that theirs was a marriage of convenience rather than one borne of deep passion; but Anita was 26, and James at 34 considerably older, so perhaps they both realised that time was running out if they wanted to settle down and start a family. Another contributory factor in Anita accepting James' half-hearted proposal was that he had agreed that her distant relation from Maesteg Wales could come to board with them, once the young lad left school. James' reasoning was that the extra 'board money' would not be an unwelcome bonus for the slight inconvenience of offering temporary hospitality to young Alun. James knew that Anita was very close to the offspring of her late grandmother's brother and his wife, for she had visited the family so regularly throughout the boy's childhood that the lad apparently looked upon her as a second mum. Early on in their courtship, James had viewed these frequent sojourns to Wales almost with a suspicion, but for the last year or so, the visits had proved a godsend as they allowed the couple time apart and a brief respite from the constant bickering. If nothing else,

James hoped the presence of a third party in the flat might improve Anita's moodswings. Sometimes, he felt as if he was walking on eggshells and his new wife was constantly looking for an excuse to engineer an arguement. Also the spectre of their childless state sat like an elephant in the room and, more often than not, the mere mention of a friend being pregnant would be enough to unleash Anita's inner demons. The clattering of the saucepans as she made the tea was always an indication of what was to come. James had been known of late - to stand in the hallway listening out for the telltale clashing – then, if he suspected it was 'one of those days,' he would turn tail and seek refuge at the local Public House *The Cradlewell*. This inevitably incensed Anita even more but was often the less of the evils. If James timed it right, he could stagger between *The Cradlewell* and its sister bar *The Punchbowl* availing himself of liquid sustenance in each, then by the time he returned back to the Tyneside flat – two sheets to the wind – Anita had usually retired to bed. The bedroom door would be firmly closed, and he would settle down instead on the armchair in front of the dwindling fire. Despite the dying embers and the cold draught from the ill-fitting sash window, it was still a much warmer proposition than the icy reception he would have received from his wife. By the next morning her temper had normally improved and they would carry on as normal, never speaking of the very thing that so upset them both so much. James hoped that once her cousin Alun arrived, Anita might be more occupied with housekeeping and less likely to sit and brood upon her problems conceiving. Also the second bedroom was all kitted out for the *baby which never arrived* and seeing the empty cot on a daily basis wasn't helping either of their mental states. The bedroom with is permanently ajar door seemed to mock James - and his inability to father a child - whenever he climbed the stairs up into the flat, so God only knows how Anita coped walking past it time and time during her day as she went about her household chores. Once her cousin arrived, the room would have a purpose and perhaps afford them both some breathing space.

Bronwen from Maesteg had fallen pregnant with Alun very late in life, and his sudden appearance on the very last day of 1915 had taken the local villagers by surprise, for Bronwyn had barely shown throughout her confinement, and his arrival also coincided with the arrival of a young female relative from Newcastle. The newly-born boy was born with a fine head of inky jet black hair and his deep brown eyes and somewhat swarthy complexion marked him out from the rest of the Thomas family from the onset. A brief rumour had circulated that perhaps the babe was not the couples' natural flesh and blood, but it was soon quashed by the boy's father John who had a reputation in the valley for punching first and asking questions later. Anita, the young female relative from Newcastle, and the subject of the earlier speculation, went on to spend long stretches of the summer months in Wales. From the second she arrived she would take over the care of the young child - to allow her much older relation some well-earned respite - for having such an active child so late in life must have been a tiring task for dear cousin Bronwen. Ever since Alun was a mere babe in arms, Anita would pack a bag and take him out from under her cousin's feet for the day. Strolling along the winding country tracks, Anita would find a grassy verge and gently sing him lullabies, tenderly rocking him until his tiny eyes closed and he drifted off to sleep. As she cradled his slumbering body in her arms, she would gaze down and instantly be transported back in time to the summer of 1915 and a young Infantryman called Van. Time had not dimmed her love for Van, nor her desperate dream that he would one day return for her. When Alun had been a toddler he and she had played a little game – at her bidding – whereby when they were alone she told him to call her 'mummy.' The rules of this secret little game were that he must never call her by this name when others were in earshot, as it was only to be used during their special time. Only once had young Alun forgotten and the look that Bronwyn shot her way, reminded Anita that she should respect the choice which had been made all those years ago. Now Alun had reached the age of 15 – bizzarly the age she had been when she last saw his father – and he had expressed a wish to move from the valley and broaden his horizons. With barely a thought for his poor parents, Anita swiftly found him a position at a stables on the outskirts of Jesmond, then suggested he move in with her and James. I must add that Anita did this without the knowledge of her mother Mary, for she knew where her opinions lay. More than once during the early stages of Alun's childhood, Anita had begged she reconsider her position, but her desperate pleas had fallen upon deaf ears. This time Anita was undeterred. She had missed out on such a large chunk of Alun's life already, and was not prepared to miss out on any more. James must never know or indeed Alun either – for with the passage of time he had forgotton the special game they used to play - but this was a secret Anita was happy to keep for the unadulterated joy of having her son under her own roof. I think that perhaps Mary was still worried that people would put two and two together and deliver shame to her door. Mary, of course, knew only part of the story of the boy's parentage as Oshbert had been canny enough not to impart the full details all those years ago. In fact the only living soul who knew the whole sorry truth was Junior, but he had sworn to his father that he would keep the secret to his grave. And keep the secret he would, for he was a man of his word, and he also knew the devastation it would cause if it were ever to get out.

It was a warm muggy day when Alun climbed from the train at Newcastles Central Railway Station. The journey had been long and laborious, with many changes and he was grateful to be at last alighting upon the platform of his new home town. As arranged, Anita was there to greet him at the station. She was still dabbing at her eyes with a handkerchief, as he strolled towards her – blaming a particle of dust from the steam engine for her tears – for his likeness to his father was alarmingly more pronounced, as he had matured into adulthood and for the briefest of moments, it had caught her off guard. After a brief hug, which in typical teenager fashion Alun shrugged off, they went for a 'nice cup of tea and a stottie' before boarding another train towards West Jesmond and home. When they reached the flat, Alun ran up the narrow stairs in a state of youthful excitement such was his haste to see his newly decorated bedroom. It was a room 'fit for a prince', which were the exact words James had used, when he discovered how much she had spent on the various new pieces of furniture which encircled its four walls. James' grudging disgruntlement had fallen upon deaf ears, and after saying his piece, he had decided it would be wise to keep his own counsel in future for never had his young wife appeared so animated or been so keen to complete a project. He did, however, remind her of her promise that once she was pregnant she would ask the lad to make other arrangements, and return the room to its earlier guise of a nursery. A look of irritation - at being reminded of this pledge washed across Anita's expression - but it was so brief that James did not even notice the change in mood. That evening he was so confident in her continuing good humour, he even went so far as to address the 'darned elephant' and was duly rewarded, when Anita agreed to make an appointment with the local GP to get 'herself' checked over. Such was the extent of male sexism at the time that the problem of infertility was inevitably 'blamed' upon the wife.

DOROTHY AND LEWIS 1934

It had been quite early on in her son's courtship that Theresa had found out about Dorothy and Lewis, and she had been most insistent on meeting this young girl who had stolen her son's heart. No doubt remembering how she had intervened in his last relationship with Leonore, Lewis was not surprisingly hesitant for the two to meet, but eventually social protocol forced his hand. So one afternoon in the Autumn of 1930, Lewis invited Dorothy for afternoon tea at the Presbytery. Theresa had hosted the tea with the help of Lewis' younger sister Dolly and in Lewis' eyes it had been a resounding success. There had been no awkward silences and his mother had been congenial company and on her very best behaviour. Indeed, it had been quite a pleasant afternoon all round, made all the more memorable because it was while they were walking home afterwards that Lewis confessed to harbouring growing feelings towards her. He was prattling on about buying a motorbike – indeed he had spoken of little else for weeks, and Dorothy had been desperately trying to muster interest as she stood by listening to Lewis and her brothers waxing lyrical about their various merits. 'Boys and their toys,' she had said in an aside to her mother who was similarily unimpressed by the cumbersome oily machines. He had been working up the courage to tell her of his intentions, and in a typical Lewis manner he worked it into the conversation by saying he would need a nice bike to transport his 'special girl' in style. It was the first time he had put anything like that properly into words. Yes, he had remarked upon her appearance, planned future dates, and told her he loved being in her company, but to be told she was his 'special girl' was all the proof she craved that the relationship was progressing as it should. Dorothy felt a reassuring warmth race through her veins as Lewis went on to talk of the lovely picnics they could take on their bike rides into the countryside. When Lewis stretched in to kiss her goodbye, later that afternoon, even their kiss was changed. He had been expecting the usual chaste kiss upon her cheek, but she responded in a way which quite took him by surprise as she upturned her face so her slightly open lips met his.

Lewis was full of the joys of spring when he returned back to the Presbytery later on, but he did still feel a slight trepidation as he walked into the parlour, and found his mother sitting patiently waiting to speak to him. He had expected her to present a full assessment of his new girlfriend, but not quite so soon, as she normally liked to mull things over and make enquiries as to their backgrounds. Theresa had already met two of his past dalliances – quite by accident – and had been vocal in her dismissal of them both as 'unsuitable' future wives. Bunty she had declared to be too 'fast and loose with her affections' and Maud - a girl Lewis had met at a Catholic social dance – she dismissed as a classic 'church mouse', impoverished and far too scared of her own shadow to be a suitable contender. Lewis was therefore gratified when Theresa declared Dorothy to be quite quite charming, but she countered her approval by adding that the sticking point would always be the fact that she was not a Catholic. Lewis had never really considered this a major problem, but now it had been remarked upon, it seemed to swell in proportion and whilst a proposal of marriage was not immediately imminent, it was all part of his future plan. Surely it would be easily rectified if Dorothy agreed to convert to Catholicism, but it was a discussion to have at a later date, and in the meantime, his mind flitted back to which model of motorbike would best suit his needs.

It was barely a few weeks later when Lewis roared up Ashleigh Grove on his newly purchased motorbike. Dorothy's mother, Mary, stood at the doorway of the house barely managing to conceal her concern, as her son Arthur manhandled his sister upon the rather narrow pillion seat behind her beau. Mary raced up the path to help Dorothy modestly arrange her skirt, then gave her a quick kiss upon the cheek, just as Lewis kicked the throttle and they roared off into the distance, a cloud of dirty smoke following in their wake. Arthur followed his mother's departing figure back into the house, all the while chatting to his younger brother, Rhys John, about the new motorbike he was planning to buy once he had saved up enough money. Mary turned quickly and snapped 'over my dead body my lad,' and Arthur – tired of being told what he could and couldn't spend his own money on - disresectfully poked out his tongue in her direction as she stormed away. This, of course, caused his younger brother to collapse into helpless fits of laughter and prompted Mary to once again turn swiftly and bark, "you two are each as bad as each other. I don't know why I bother sometimes."

Whilst her mother had made no bones about her feelings regarding the 'infernal machine', Dorothy had promised Lewis she would reserve her judgement. But by the time they had driven up Jesmond Dene Road, then turned at the Blue House to make their way towards Gosforth High Street, she had decided she did not like the 'crazy contraption' one bit. The wind had whipped around her ankles for the entire journey and her carefully styled hair was now a bird's nest of tangles. The perisistant drizzle had done little to improve her mood, and now, just as they pulled off the High Street and onto Church Road, the sky grew even darker and the heavens opened. Poor Dorothy was now soaking wet into the bargain. However, the state of her newly purchased chiffon skirt was of most concern, as the hemline seemed to be creeping up at an alarming speed towards her waistband. It must have shrunk quite dramatically, for although Lewis declared the short length flattering he nevertheless still raced into the Presbytery to collect an overcoat of his sister's so he could protect her modesty. The couple were leaving the motorbike in the Presbytery porch before heading straight back out to see a film at the nearby Royalty Picture House, and Lewis was so worried that his mother was watching from an upstairs window, that before Dorothy even had a chance to squelch her arms into the sleeves of the coat, he unceremoniously bundled her through the garden gate and back onto the street. The couple ran up the street, suddenly aware of the time and the fact that the film at the newly opened Cinema was just about to start. Thankfully, they made it just in the nick of time. The lights were just beginning to dim as the disgruntled usherette shone her torch to show them to their seats. They had opted for the Circle - as a special treat - but the Cinema was packed to the rafters, so there were more than a few objections as they shuffled along the aisle tripping over handbags and overcoats, while politely asking people to move their feet. They eventually gratefully plopped down onto their seats. Both still dripping wet - despite Lewis' valient battle with the now sodden towel – but as they sat in the warm dark auditorium, Dorothy became convinced people were staring at the steam rising from their rapidly drying clothes. She whispered as much to Lewis who patted her gently on the hand and told her that it was all in her imagination, although he feared, it was not. To improve her anxious mood and get the romantic date back on track, Lewis dug into his jacket pocket to retrieve a paper bag of boiled sweets which he had purchased earlier that afternoon as a 'cinema snack.' He offered the open bag to Dorothy and, as she reached in to retrieve a 'melting sticky mass', the bag loudly ripped and the remaining sweets rolled out onto the floor, gaining momentum and volume as they rolled down the sloping floor towards the balcony. Dorothy did not know whether to laugh or cry. Lewis, for some reason known only to him, decided he must chase after the sweets, so he squeezed his way along the row of seats then dropped down onto all fours and crawled down the aisle. Dorothy was mortified with embarrassment. Even more so when the usherette came along and shone her torch illuminating Lewis' trouser clad bottom for all to see. The rest of the audience saw the funny side and the entire circle erupted in laughter, with people at the back standing up so they could get a better view. Lewis turned and stumbled to his feet, temporarily blinded by the glare of the usherettes torch. Not knowing what to do, he gave a little bow and the audience slow clapped as he made his way back to his seat, the knees of his trousers adorned with sticky sweets. He was fully expecting recriminations from Dorothy, but to his surprise she took his sticky hand in hers and kissed his rapidly reddening cheek. They managed to settle back into their seats just a few seconds before the main feature movie started. What an enjoyable romp it was. The latest in the ever popular Tarzan franchise, starring Olympic swimmer Johnny Weissmuller as the leading man, with the altogether more genteel Irish American sweetheart Maureen

O'Sullivan playing the supporting role of Jane. When Johnny swung through the trees and gave his distinctive 'Tarzan' yell, the whole audience erupted in joyous claps of excitement. Later on as they walked from the Cinema, Lewis stopped under a streetlight to strike a Tarzen-like pose and thump his chest, only stopping when curtains from the house opposite began to twitch, and a porch light was switched on a few doors up. They ran off up the street giggling like teenagers. All too soon, they were back at the Presbytery and Lewis was wheeling the preposterous bike from the porch. This was the moment Dorothy had been dreading the entire evening. The motorbike ride home. This time, Lewis popped in the Presbytery to collect his sister to assist Dorothy onto the pillion. Lewis began to *'rev the throttle'* just as Dorothy stretched a tentative leg over the motorbike. His sister held Dorothy's free hand, whilst she struggled to arrange her very short skirt into a more ladylike fashion. Dorothy was just about to lower herself finally onto the pillion - when all of a sudden Lewis pulled away - leaving her stranded mid-air for a few seconds before she made the inevitable slow descent into a muddy oily puddle. There she sat, her skirt almost around her midrift, as Lewis' younger sister, who found the whole thing quite hilarious, rolled around on the pavement in hysterics. Eventually it was Lewis' mother, Theresa - who had witnessed the whole sorry scene from the lounge window - who raced to her aid and helped her to her feet. Lewis was nowhere to be seen. He had sped off into the distance oblivious to his poor girlfriend's fate. Actually, it was not until he took the turn into Osborne Road, that he even realised she was not sitting behind him. In a fit of panic, he swiftly turned his bike around and sped back retracing his route, fully expecting to find Dorothy injured and sprawled out on the road. He inwardly cursed himself for putting her precious life in danger. It was as he raced back towards the Presbytery that he realised how much he loved her. He decided there and then that he could not live without her in his life, and if she was spared, he would prove his love by proposing that very evening. He was not even daunted when after returning to the Presbytery, he ran into the kitchen only to find the three most important women in his life all glaring accusingly in his direction. He was so happy to find Dorothy alive and unharmed, that with no preamble at all he dropped to his knee at the foot of her chair. Taking her hand in his, he firstly apologised, secondly promised to get rid of the motorbike, then thirdly asked her if she would do him the honour of becoming his wife. The room fell silent. It was so silent that he wondered if he had in fact spoken out aloud or just imagined the whole thing. It was Dolly, his sister who first found voice. She jumped up from her chair and gave a little whoop.

"Congratulations. Can I be your bridesmaid? Oh please say yes Dorothy..oh please do," she pleaded.

Theresa was next to congratulate the couple, but she swiftly followed up her good wishes by adding that she would to speak to Father Wilkinson the very next morning, so the 'conversion to Catholicism' classes could start as soon as possible. No-one, bar Lewis seemed to notice that Dorothy had yet to acknowledge or indeed accept his proposal. Dorothy was still very angry and still very annoyed, but seeing Lewis looking up at her with such hope and love in his eyes, her bad mood slowly evaporated and she stretched down to kiss the top of his head as a way of acceptance.

Dorothy and Lewis meandered slowly back to Jesmond later that night – as Lewis knew better than to suggest a motorcycle ride. Swinging hands in a carefree way, the couple stopped every so often to stare at the night sky and wonder at the stars, because despite the inclement start to the evening, the sky had cleared and the stars shone brightly in the black sky. As they walked, Lewis must have reflected upon the unromantic way he had proposed, for he suddenly stopped Dorothy in her tracks and twirled her around so they faced one another. Then he once again dropped to his knees – little caring that he landed in a puddle from the earlier downpour – took her hand and properly declared his undying love for her. To cap the gesture off, he pointed towards an exceptionally twinkling star and proclaimed, "that star up there shining so brightly is our special star, and if we are ever parted for whatever reason we can both look out into the night sky and we will know that our star is always there, and somewhere we will both be looking at the same star." This was the most romantic statement Dorothy had ever heard. Yes, movie stars spoke this way in romantic films but in real life most men just grunted and expected you to know this meant they loved you. She was temporarily lost for words so as means of a reply she leant in for a long and lingering kiss. Once they reluctantly pulled apart, Lewis spoke with a tremble to his voice, "Oh Dorothy, my darling girl, please don't let's dither long over this engagement. I am desperate to make you mine. If I were not such a gentleman....." His words faded but Dorothy knew what he was trying to say and felt empowered. Much like the actresses on the silver screen whom she so admired. It was very late by the time they eventually arrived at Ashleigh Grove, and both mutually decided it was probably too late to wake Dorothy's family to tell them the good news, so Lewis turned up his collar and strolled away. His mood was such that he little cared when the sky clouded over and it once again began to drizzle. Nothing could dampen his spirits that evening, his future was after all written in the stars, and what a wonderful future it would be with his Dorothy by his side.

Lewis was true to his word, although he did try every trick in the book to change Dorothy's mind about the many merits of the Royal Enfield 250cc motorcycle. But once she had made up her mind, my grandmother was stubbornly tenacious and she steadfastly refused and refused until he eventually got the message and sold the motorbike – for a loss - to her young brother Arthur. As you can imagine this did not endear him in any way to his future mother-in-law Mary. Mary was not thrilled in anyway to hear of the impending marriage, although being canny, she made a great show of acting pleased. Her reluctance was in part due to her daughter's decision to convert to Catholicism, for whilst she had never been as religiously zealous as her own mother, Mary still regularly attended Chapel. Her other reason was that she knew her 'sons' would soon be finding wives and leaving home and she was scared of being left alone rattling around in the big old house. If truth were told, even as it was – with her and her three children – living in the house, no-one had ventured up into the attic rooms for any reason, other than 'dumping' stuff, since Susie had moved out to marry the Grocer in 1927. This fact, had unfortunately, bode well for a most unwelcome visitor who had snuck back in the dead of a stormy night and was now securely hidden in the eaves. I suspect the arrival of Alun had lured it from its hiding place in St Mary's Well, but I doubt it meant to do him any ill, for after all it had been his own great-grandmother who had cursed it into existence in the very beginning. I do wonder how the dreadful 'creature' transported itself back to Ashleigh Grove, but knowing of its supernatural powers I doubt I will ever know the full truth of this. But back it was and what a terrible calamity it had planned for poor Mary. The house, I must add, had sensed its return in 1931, but as the house had no voice it had no way of warning anyone, but it did do what precious little it could and coaxed the Pilgrim's bones into once again forming the shape of the cross. But the bones were crumbling from the constant friction of the toing and froing through the soil so were not the effective deterrant they had once been.

ANITA FALLS PREGNANT, SPRING 1937

At last I can reveal the joyous news that, in late March 1937 Anita discovered that she and James were going to have a baby. Anita had a skip in her step as she left the Doctor's on that glorious day in spring, as she raced to meet James from work - for she felt it only fair that he be the first to know. He had been so patient throughout their long struggle to conceive, and despite her constant nagging, had never lifted a finger in anger towards her. It seems strange to write this eighty years later but during this time 'domestic violence' was never talked about and was even more of a taboo than it is today, which is not in any way denying its existence, but rather highlighting that it was seen to be the norm. A way for a husband to 'rein his wife in' and correct her behaviour. Anita's best friend from her schooldays had the misfortune to have married a man who was '*handy with his fists*', and many was the time that she had sought refuge at Anita's when he had had '*one too many*,' or had a '*monk on.*' In fact during the early part of the 1900's 'domestic violence' - on the rare occasions it was even directly addressed – was widely acknowledged to be a private family matter and it was not until the influence of Womens Liberation in the 1960s that it became a topic of any discussion at all. The adage 'rule of thumb' apparently derived from a long-held belief that English Law stated that a man must not strike or chastise his wife with any rod/stick thicker than his thumb. James was not an ill-tempered man for he was slow to anger and during Anita's 'tirades' he would choose to walk away, more often than not seeking refuge of a liquid kind. But one thing had really irked him during the last six years, and that was Anita's utter reliance upon her cousin's son Alun and his upon her. James often felt like the spare wheel in his own home, and more than once he imagined the conversation had promptly changed when he entered a room. It was certainly time for the boy to move on and move out, but his every attempt to suggest this to Anita had been vehemently discouraged.

As Anita had anticipated, James was as jubulent as she and, as they wandered back towards the train station, he even stopped complete strangers in the street to impart their happy news. On a whim he further insisted that they buy a fish and chip supper. This was quite the treat as they were normally too skint to afford this luxury, so Anita decided not to spoil the mood by mentioning the meal she had prepared before her Doctor's appointment, which as she had left out on the stove would now no doubt go to waste. They travelled home with their 'priceless', supper wrapped tightly in yesterday's newspaper and squashed under James' jacket to keep it warm. Once they reached Myrtle Grove, Anita raced up the stairs ahead of him, for she had noticed Alun's boots in the porch - so knew he was home - and was desperate to tell him about the new baby. Alun leapt from his chair to give her the biggest bear hug ever, for although they had never spoken directly of her problems conceiving – for that would have been indelicate and inappropriate – he must have sensed the atmosphere change each month as her 'curse' arrived. Initially after the euphoria of having her pregnancy confirmed, she had worried about the problem of space in the tiny flat, but she put such thoughts aside, because after all they had six long months before the baby would make an appearance. It was later that night – after Alun had gone to fetch something from his bedroom – that she quietly broached the impending problem to James, no doubt remembering her former promise that she would ask Alun to leave once a baby was on the way. Hoping to capitalise upon his good mood, she put forward the suggestion that when the time came that the baby needed its own bedroom, perhaps they could section off a part of the lounge for Alun. Reminding him that she was a most proficient seamstress, she said running up a curtain would take no time at all, and she could probably buy the material in the market for next to nothing. James nodded, not agreeing with her impractical solution, but not wanting to mar their special day by pouring cold water upon it. He held his counsel until Anita had retired to bed, then he sought out Alun and told him in no uncertain terms that he expected him to vacate the room well before the baby arrived. The manner in which he said this was bordering upon the aggressive, for he secretly hoped to provoke a reaction from the boy so an argument would ensue and then perhaps Anita would prioritise her marriage for a change. Alun had always suspected that James was only pleasant to him as a means to court favour with Anita, but to hear it proclaimed in such a manner, he instantly took offence and a brief scuffle broke out between the two. Upon hearing the rowdy commotion, Anita struggled to find her dressing gown, before stumbling from the bedroom into the passageway. She arrived huffing and puffing just in time to hear the front door of the flat dramatically slam. Tripping down the stairs, she raced out on to the dark street. Peering into the distance, she could just about make out Alun's departing figure in the half light of the dusk. When she eventually returned to the flat – after calling and calling Alun's name in vain – James was standing in the doorway. His hands were cupped together as he tried to light a cigarette. She pushed past him hoping for a reaction but he just shrugged and said "I figure it's best all round that the little sod ran off. The ungrateful bugger went for me. I swear if I see him around here again I will do for him, so I will." After saying this, he stubbed out his partially smoked roll up with the heel of his boot, and strode of up the stairs. Anita stood in the doorway a while longer, listening to the sounds of the night, then she sank down onto the front step – not caring who was watching from their windows – and collapsed into floods of tears. The next morning she deliberately burnt James' breakfast, and then, without apology, plonked the scorched remains unceremoniously in front of him. Then she flounced from the kitchen and back into the bedroom, where she remained until she heard the front door slam shut and his heavy footsteps walking down the street.

For the next three months of her confinement, Anita searched the length and breadth of the North East in her quest to find her missing son. Her rapidly expanding girth hindered her somewhat but still she carried on, following up every probable sighting of him. Alun had left his job at the stables the day after he had run away from the flat, so she had no other means of finding him, bar endlessly plodding the pavements. Indeed it transpired that he had covered his tracks so well that she did not find him until she was well into her second trimester. She had almost given up all hope when purely on an off-chance she decided to check out the local bars near the Central Station. The Public Houses in this area were 'rough' and not normally frequented by a woman of Anita's social standing, nor her advanced state of pregnancy, but she felt inexplicably drawn towards one in particular for no other reason than gut instinct. The insalubrious Victoria and Comet Public House was nicknamed the 'spit and vomit', because it had sawdust on the floor to soak up the spit and was the backdrop to many a bloody drunken brawl. Its usual clientele were the Irish navvies who worked on the Quayside, so it was purely by chance - or fate - that she came upon a fellow who worked as a stablehand at Alun's previous employ. The young lad claimed he hadn't seen Alun around for a few weeks, but had heard a rumour that he had taken rooms in a house on the notorious Pink Lane, while 'oddjobbing' on the Quayside.

Pink Lane was a narrow lane which ran from Neville Street on the one end to Clayton Street West on the other. It had derived its name from its now demolished 'Pink Tower', which had been one of the 17 towers which had formerly linked medieval Newcastle's 25 foot high Town walls. The lane had initially been part of a system of narrow lanes (the pomerium), which ran along inside the town walls, although now it was infamous for another reason altogether. For its narrowness, dark alleyways and close proximity to the Central Station made it an ideal 'hunting ground' for the many dubious ladies of the night.

Despite the lateness of the hour, Anita immediately took her leave and rushed straight to the address the lad had given her. She did not really expect to find Alun still there, but the hope in her heart propelled her to almost run from the 'spit and vomit' and across towards Pink Lane. The houses on the notorious lane were interspersed with 'hotels' and shop frontages, which gave the whole street an air of dangerous desperation, and prompted Anita to clutch her handbag firmly to her side, as she peered at the ramshackle numbers affixed to the front doors and shopfronts. When eventually she reached the given address she, without preamble or indeed any actual plan, knocked heavily upon the door. She was taken aback at the speed with which the door cracked open; it was almost as if the occupant was expecting the knock. A young girl of no older than seven years stood there. The poor child had no shoes upon her feet and her greasy lank hair fell about her shoulders like rats' tails. Despite her bedraggled appearance, the girl politely answered Anita's query, and pointed a dirty finger towards a door at the rear of the hallway and beckoned Anita to follow her. Anita half fell, half stumbled into the dimly lit hallway. There was an overriding stench of stale urine and cooked cabbage and Anita had to struggle to stop herself – in her heavily pregnant stage - from retching. She nearly jumped from her skin when a door to her left flew open, and a rather dubious looking character blundered from the room, fastening his flies in a nonchalant manner. "Oh my giddy aunt," thought Anita as she stopped for a moment to compose herself. She had heard rumours of such places being up this way, but in her 'middle class' innocence, believed it to be an urban myth. The young girl tugged at her skirts impatiently urging Anita to follow her slight figure towards the rear of the building. The lass stopped suddenly in front of a door, which Anita presumed to be Alun's, then she turned to Anita with her palm outstretched, obviously expecting a fee for her assistance. Anita burrowed her hand deep into the recesses of her handbag and brought out a sixpence, which the girl fell upon greedily before departing even further back into the shadows. Anita knocked tentatively on the door, then when there was no answer, she knocked once again but this time in a much brisker fashion. Again, there was no answer, so she turned the doorknob and hesitantly entered the dimly lit room. At first she presumed it empty, but once her eyesight became more accustomed to the darkness, she made out a shape slouched in a chair by the bed. As she approached the propped up body it appeared to not be breathing, but as she got closer she recognised Alun and let out a cry of shock, causing him to jolt upright in the chair and splutter up a stream of blood and saliva. Anita quickly shook off her coat and wrapped it around Alun's shoulders, for the boy was now shivering and twitching in a most alarming manner. Anita then dropped to her knees and crouched by the side of his chair – without a care for her own welfare or the wellbeing of her unborn child – and took her precious son in her arms. He raised his eyes to hers in scant recognition, but even the effort of this seemed to cause him such fatigue that he all too soon dropped his exhausted gaze and fell back into the confines of the chair. Taking in the sight of the blood stained sheets strewn in piles around the room, Anita suspected that her son had caught the dreadful disease Tuberculosis. She knew if he had any chance of a recovery, she must get him out of this damp house and into warm surroundings as soon as possible. This decision brought about a whole new problem of where to take him. James had been all too clear about his feelings towards Alun, so taking him back to their flat was out of the question. This only left her mother and the big family house on Ashleigh Grove. Despite her mother's previous reluctance to acknowledge her illegitimate grandson, surely even she could not turn away her own flesh and blood under such dire circumstances? Reluctantly leaving Alun's side, Anita ran out of the house and back out onto the lane, then grabbed the arm of the first burly looking man she encountered departing from the nearby North British Hotel. Initially the half-intoxicated chap pushed her aside as he presumed she was plying her trade, but when - even in his drunken state - he realised how eloquently she spoke, he decided to himself that she must be a woman of some substance and worth a bob or two. Propping himself up against the wall for support, he listened to her plea as she begged that he help her to carry her son to the nearby train station. The chap had been trudging back to his cold unwelcoming lodgings near the Quayside – because he had no more money left for ale and the landlord had refused to chalk more up on his slate – so Anita's offer to pay for his services was most welcome. Between them they dragged and carried Alun along the hallway and out into the street. Luckily, the chap was too worse for wear to realise the full significance of Alun's illness or he may have refused to help. Once they reached the entrance to the train station, the man rudely snatched the cash from Anita, then stumbled off without so much as a backwards glance, such was his haste to catch last orders. Anita bundled Alun upon the train, silently thanking God that there were some spare seats near the door. Once seated, she wound her scarf about her son's neck and cuddled him protecively to her bosom. To the casual observer the pair must have looked like canoodling lovebirds, which was exactly the image Anita was trying to promote, for such was the general population's fear of catching the dreadful disease, she may have been ordered to leave the train immediately if the full extent of Alun's illness was even suspected. It was not long before they reached their stop at West Jesmond. The fresh air seemed to encourage Alun to temporarily regain his wits, and with Anita's arm supporting him by his waist, they managed to make their way in a crab like fashion towards the sanctuary of Ashleigh Grove. Once there, Alun slumped upon the garden wall - clutching his chest and persistently coughing in such a raucous fashion that Anita feared they would alert the neighbours - as Anita knocked frantically upon the front door. It was opened by her brother Arthur who had been downstairs in the back yard having a nip of whisky, away from the disapproving glare of their mother who had just retired to bed. Arthur had met Alun socially more than once at his sister's flat - so he immediately recognised the lad, and helped his sister to manhandle him into the porch so they could close the door from prying eyes. It was not long after, that Mary made an appearance - her long hair tightly wound Medusa-like in makeshift curlers - for she had been kneeling by the bed saying her nightly prayers when she heard the commotion on the street.

She let out a cry of anguish when she saw the emaciated state of the boy, and another when she saw the bedraggled state of her heavily pregnant daughter. Making an instant decision, she asked Arthur to summon Rhys John and Dorothy, so they could carry poor Alun up into the bedroom in the attic. Once he was safely tucked up there in Suzie's old bed, Mary turned to Anita and told her to go home to her husband and she would sort things out from here. James had already called at the house twice that night searching for his wife, and Mary suspected they had been rowing. Anita reluctantly left her precious son in the care of his grandmother, but not before tenderly kissing his cheek and reassuring him that she was only a stones throw away.

All that long, long night Mary sat wide awake in a chair by Alun's bedside, alternately wiping his fevered brow, and holding his head steady as she urged him to take a drink or have a bite to eat. The next morning at first light, she wakened Arthur and asked him to dress quickly and fetch the local GP. Alun's breathing was becoming more laboured by the hour, and the poor boy was now in such a state of delirium, drifting in and out of consciousness, that she feared he would not make it through the day. Alas, I must now relay that it was too late for poor Alun, and he perished that very afternoon, although as a faint consolation he did have his grandmother and birth mother weeping by his bed as he passed. I must now also add that a short two months later on 6th August Mary also fell victim to Tuberculosis, no doubt caught that night as she nursed her illegitimate grandson. The rest of the family, Arthur, Rhys John, my grandmother Dorothy, Anita and her unborn child were all thankfully spared, but only for a while, because a disease as contagious as Tuberculosis will lie dormant for a long time, before striking again. It's as if it waits for a weakness, then pounces to do its worst and reek the most havoc. Much like the cursed 'creature.'

Upon their mother's death the family scattered to the wind. Arthur and Rhys John moved out soon after the funeral – hurt and annoyed that their mother had left the small amount of money she possessed £595.16s, *in probate* to be shared between their sisters - to make their own way in life. Anita who was now in the final stages of pregnancy went back to stay in the tiny flat with James her husband. Only my grandmother Dorothy remained in the house, but not for long, for it soon transpired that Mary had given up the deeds for the house when she faced penury after Oshbert's death. As a result the house was quickly repossessed by the bank which effectively left my grandmother homeless. Her wedding to Lewis was swiftly rescheduled to take place just after Christmas, and in the meantime, she was sent to board with a local family who bizarrely also bore the name Dowd – they were not blood relations of her fiancé but they were good God-fearing Catholics and as such deemed suitable landlords – in Woodbine Road, Gosforth. The family took Dorothy to their heart and hearth, feeding her so frequently and so well that she worried that, if the wedding were delayed her dress would not fit. The more obvious solution would have been for Dorothy to stay with her future husband and his family for the few short months leading up to their nuptials, but Theresa declared that would happen over her dead body. And the house. Well he felt the excrutiating pain of the untimely demise of his matriarch Mary and her illegitimate grandson. And the 'creature' felt it even more so, because the death of Alun was an unfortunate consequence of its cruel actions once again. In its haste to spread the disease throughout the house, the creature had not realised that the host was in fact its 'creator's' own great-grandson. So the 'creature', ashamed of its failure to correctly carry out the curse, somehow found its way back to its damp hiding hole in St Mary's Well. It still lies there just beneath the surface, occasionally bobbing to the surface – and looking to all intents and purpose like a brand new doll. It is desperate to entice a curious child to reach in and retrieve it. The house has told me that the creature was 'helped' on its way by the Pilgrims' Bones, which although crumbling, had finally managed to claw themselves to the surface of the mud. They 'transported' the 'creature' as they made their own way to their final resting place of St Mary's Chapel. The house was anxious as to how he would function without the reassurance of the bones but the Pilgrim assured him that he was no longer needed as the curse had finally run its dreadful course.

THE HOUSE, 1986

Many many years later in the late 80s my young family and I moved into the house, little knowing of chequered history, until the day my grandmother Dorothy visited. She was suffering from early onset Demetia at the time so no-one took her seriously when she clapped her two hands together and expressed her unbridled happiness at returning to her childhood home. We all suspected that she had confused the past and the present as she often did, but now in hindsight I know she was telling the truth. I call to mind her cry of utter joy when she spied the ghosts of her beloved parents, Oshbert and Mary, strolling arm in arm along the hallway. My grandmother – on that day - rose from her chair with an agility she had not displayed for many a long year and raced along the hallway towards the parlour. Once there, she stopped quite abruptly and stood at the doorway with a look of such utter contentment playing upon her face. My daughter Claire who was only two years old at this time had toddled in her great-grandmothers wake – I remember thinking how alike their gait was because they both looked ready to stumble and fall at any time – and when she reached the parlour door she pointed excidedly into the empty room. As I tried to usher the two of them back towards the kitchen - where I was serving tea - Claire started to chatter in her infant like 'gibberish' about a pretty lady playing the piano for the little girls and boys sitting on the mat with their mummy and daddy. My grandmother bent down and we all anxiously gasped as she hauled Claire into her arms – Dorothy was so frail at this time and had recently recovered from a badly broken arm – and, clasping young Claire tenderly in her arms she reeled off the names of her many siblings, before stating how wonderful it had been to see them all again.

It was around this time too that I began to have the most vivid of dreams – which I put down at the time to being heavily pregnant – where I would waken from my sleep to the sound of soft melodic piano playing. I would struggle from my bed and pace the vast house but I could never quite place where the sound came from, and would eventually retire exhausted once more to my bed. The next morning I would awaken and wonder if I had in fact dreamt the entire thing. The dreams/hallucinations stopped quite abruptly when my youngest daughter Ami was born and it was around this time too that my Grandmother Dorothy unfortunately died, so perhaps the two incidences were linked? I never previously held much truck with 'superstitious nonsense' but I confess my hitherto scepticism is slowly diluting as a result of researching this novel.

It was much later on whilst conducting in depth research for this novel that I first discovered the true history of the house on Ashleigh Grove. In a way, I suppose, it explains why I was so drawn to the place in the first place, for apart from its low price it had very little going for it. With its odd shaped rooms and flying threshold I recall it proved quite a nightmare for our conveyance solicitor. The house had been inhabited since the early 1940s by a middle-aged couple who despite having no children of their own often spoke to neighbours of the 'children's laughter resounding through the hallways.' This reference to ghosts was no doubt why the neighbours described them as an 'odd couple,' perfectly fine to say hello to but probably not 'quite the full shilling bless them.' They had both been in poor health, so the house when we moved in was very much as it had been when my great-grandfather bought it over a hundred years ago. The old ramshakle shed was still 'just' about standing at the bottom of the yard and the bench which Oshbert had so carefully handmade for Mary was still sitting there under the front bay window. The attic room which had for so long been the domain of Susie the housemaid, and where poor Alun had struggled to gasp his last breath, still had the loose brick hidden deep beneath its eaves. I remember we noticed this particular brick when stripping the wallpaper and we excitedly checked behind it – hoping to find some long lost treasure or clue to the house's history – but all we found was an empty dusty hole housing a particularily large and particularily scarey, but thankfully dead, housespider. I will, however, add that during the many years we lived there, the house always retained a happy welcoming ambience – even taking into consideration how exhausted he must have been from the many alterations we made to his internal structure – and whenever we returned from a holiday or similar short absence he always felt like our sanctuary from the outside world. My three daughters grew up, then flew the nest - much as Mary and Oshbert's children did all those years ago – and we, much like William and John O'Dowd moved out when the house became too large for us, but saying that, we all fondly reminisce upon that special family home and will all - when passing through West Jesmond Station - peer from the train window to catch a fleeting glimpse of the 'family' house standing proudly 'almost' on the end of the Grove. One day, who knows, history might repeat itself and a member of my family may move back into the house and start a saga all of their own. This is what the house yearns for as he girds his rafters for the return of the loud and somewhat obnoxious student boarders who presently call him home. They run along his hallway playing their loud music – ironically classed as 'house' - and hammer nails and tacks into the stucco plasterwork without a care for the damage these cause. And the parties!! The smoke chokes his chimney and the constant beat of the infernal synchronised drums make his roof tiles throb. The house still dreams every night, as he has always done, but now his dreams are always of the past and happier times when Oshbert and Mary were so in love and their childrens' giggles filled the rooms and warmed his foundations. Now, dear reader, let's *leave the house to his slumber and transport ourselves back in time to the 1930s to catch up on Lewis and Dorothy and their impending nuptials.*

THE WEDDING DECEMBER 29TH 1937

Lewis and Dorothy tied the knot just after that Christmas in the year of 1937, with the marriage being conducted by Lewis' younger brother Rev. John Cuthbert Dowd at St Charles Roman Catholic Church. Dorothy's only bridesmaid was Lewis' sister Dolly, and his Best Man was his good pal and cousin Arthur Kinghorn. One of the many sad facts which marred this otherwise perfect day – apart from of course, that Dorothy was still grieving the loss of her precious mother Mary - was that none of Dorothy's relations attended the ceremony at the Church for they could not condone her marrying a Catholic man. It's hard to understand now how deeply entrenched religious beliefs were during this time, and likewise difficult to comprehend that to marry at all, my grandmother had to consent to convert to her future husbands religion. Dorothy's mother Mary had died in the August so we will never know if she would have eventually relented and attended. As she had such a close bond with her youngest daughter, I like to think she may have or at very least witnessed it from a discreet distance, but we will never know. Dorothy's brothers Junior, Arthur and Rhys John had all moved away by this time, and Anita had just recently given birth, so they all had valid excuses for not attending, but I can only imagine the hurt my grandmother felt on what should have been the happiest day of her life. Looking at the photographs now that I know the true circumstances her smile seems almost forced, for she must have felt quite abandoned and adrift and in all probability scared – for becoming an 'orphan' at any age is a scarey prospect.

Lewis' relations had all rallied around to make her feel an integral part of their extended family but nonetheless the day must still have been tinged with sadness. My grandfather in this photograph looks as if he has won on the 'horses' – and he really believed that he had. In his own words, he had spent a long time waiting for Dorothy and finally to be able to call her his wife was beyond his wildest dreams. His only fear now was that he would not be able to make her equally as happy. He had at this stage heard many whispered conversations, alluding to the 'infamous' James Munroe and suspected that the 'cad' had broken Dorothy's heart – although she had never been as indiscreet or as cruel to confirm this – and throughout their marriage he would always worry that if this 'first love' were to turn up would Dorothy regret her decision to become his wife? I imagine Dorothy felt the same way about his lost love Leonore, and no doubt nursed insecurities similar to his own. But I do know that they made a mutual decision to 'make the marriage work', and that it was based upon a deep love and respect which is after all the best and strongest foundation for any union. As a postscript I will add that over 20 years later when his oldest daughter Joan (my mother) married, my grandfather Lewis could still fit into the very same wedding suit - and look just as smart and just as proud.

The couple had made plans to spend their wedding night in their newly purchased home. A charming little bungalow on King George Road in Fawdon, so named because King George himself had apparently once walked up the road, although I have not been able to substantiate this claim so in all probability it is an urban myth. Like many couples during these pre-war years they could not afford a proper honeymoon, so after a 'nice little family tea' at the Presbytery they took themselves to the Royalty for a 'nice night out.' This was not as romantic or as intimate as it should have been for cousin Arthur, who had been Lewis' Best Man – upon hearing of the couples intentions – declared that he would like to join them. This was despite Theresa taking him to one side and suggesting that it would be tad inappropriate. Lewis and Dorothy were both too polite for their own good and neither had the heart to tell him that perhaps he should allow them - as newlyweds - to have a little private time together. Then, as if to add salt to the wound, just as the final credits rolled, Arthur suddenly 'remembered' that he had no way of getting himself back home and asked if Lewis could borrow a motorbike and drop him off. This left my poor newly married grandmother to walk herself back to Fawdon and 'her new home', the cold empty bungalow. As Dorothy fumbled in her handbag for her doorkey, her diamond engagement ring glinted in the glare of the streetlight and all of a sudden she felt woefully sorry for herself. So sorry for herself that she burst into floods of tears. It was not so much the present situation which prompted her tearful reaction – although it was undoubtedly the catalyst – but more the realisation that this was it. This was now her life. She had made her proverbial bed and now she must lie on it. Then, as she peered into the lounge and switched on the lamp, her sorrowful mood improved in an instant and she felt a glimmer of hope for the success of her new marriage. This change of mood and change of heart came about as her gaze fell upon a glass milk bottle placed somewhat off centre and somewhat unceremoniously upon the mantelpiece. The bottle was brim full of cloudy water and overflowing with a lovely display of vibrant pink tinged heather and cheerful yellow witch hazel. This simple yet heartfelt gesture made the troubles of the day melt away because she realised that Lewis must have visited the bungalow early that morning and picked the flowers from their new garden before placing them in the only vase he could find. They served to remind her that this was the first day of the rest of their lives and give her faith that things could only improve. So in a typical decisive 'Dorothy' action she 'pulled herself together', shrugged off her 'posh' coat and set about locating the coal store so she could at least set the fire 'away' in the bedroom. Lewis would probably be chilled to the bone by the time he eventually returned and she meant to start as she meant to go on, as a dutiful and caring wife. It was not too late to turn the day around and, if she could, she would. As it turned out, it was ridiculously late by the time Lewis did finally return home, for Arthur and he had stopped off for a cheeky pint in Morpeth en-route to Felton. Lewis had been understandably reluctant to dither, but Arthur, a much more experienced 'man of the world' had convinced him that it was 'de rigueur' for all new bridegrooms. By the time he returned Dorothy had become so chilly that she had changed into her night clothes and hopped under the covers in an effort to keep warm. She had then drifted off to sleep. She awoke with a start upon hearing Lewis at the front door fumbling to find the keyhole, and she instinctively pulled the covers protectively over her breasts, for although her new mother-in-law Theresa had tried to talk her through what 'to expect' she was still both confused and nervous. It was faint consolation to realise that she was not alone in her trepadation and that both she and Lewis were unexpectedly shy in each other's company that night. For despite his 'dutch courage', Lewis was bumbling about the bedroom, tripping over his shoe laces and almost strangulating himself as he tried to remove his tie. Once he had partially undressed and calmed a little, Dorothy suggested they have a nice pot of tea then sit on the bed a while to talk through their eventful day. This dear reader is exactly what they did. They sat and chatted and then in the early hours of the morning as the birds began their dawn chorus the couple finally turned off the light, climbed under the covers and Lewis took his new bride into his arms.

They awoke the next morning with their arms still wrapped tightly about each other. The day seemed brighter and the bird song sweeter and their future blew in the cold frosty breeze. Dorothy clambered from the confusion of tangled sheets to open the bedroom curtains and the room was dramatically flooded with winter sunshine. With a jaunty spring to her step, she declared she would wander around their new home and make a list of what needed doing. Once Lewis had pulled on his trousers and followed her from the bedroom, they strolled hand in hand from room to room creating a neatly written list of how to make it more homely and put their individual stamp upon it. Lewis was thankful that Dorothy was finally taking an interest in her new home. He freely admitted that he had jumped the gun and bought the little bungalow without properly consulting her. The truth of the matter was that he had become so excited after securing the mortgage that he had surged ahead with negotiations, rather patronisingly dismissing her reluctance as foolhardy, and instead seeking counsel from his own mother. It was not until he had signed upon the dotted line that he realised the seriousness of her deliberations but by then it was too late. As his mother had pointed out, he would be silly to hesitate, as the bungalow was a bargain and Fawdon was so much more affordable than both Gosforth or Jesmond, despite being but a stones throw away. The two bedded bungalow was something of a tardis for it had a substantial lounge to the front of the building and a similarly spacious dining room to the rear – once children came along the lounge would be repurposed into a third bedroom and the dining room a lounge – but for now the couple could enjoy the luxury of two reception rooms. It sat on a third of an acre plot giving the illusion it was far more rural than it actually was. The bungalow had charmingly been named by the previous owners, an elderly couple called Renwick and Winifred who had amalgamated their names to form the word Renwinn. This now paint-faded nameplate was still affixed to the wooden front gate. Lewis had planned to remove it and rename the house but Dorothy insisted that it should keep its name as it rolled on the tongue far better than Lewdot or Dollylew.

To the back of the far stretching garden there were numerous fruit bushes and behind them sprawling fields of corn and potatoes - many years later the couple's two sons Lewis Junior and Anthony, would take advantage of the proximity of these fields and earn 'pocket money' helping the farmer harvest his potatoes. The cornfields too proved of great fascination for the couple's youngest daughter Pauline, who as a young child with an active imagination, convinced herself that the cornfield was really a vast ocean because when the ears of corn grew high and the wind blew hard they ebbed and flowed like crashing waves. She remembers being bitterly disappointed when her parents finally took her for a day out at the seaside, for the North sea that day had been unseasonably calm and not in any way as enticing or as majestic as the cornfields she glimpsed through her bedroom window.

A train line ran to the side of the house. It was mainly used for transporting coal trucks but later on in the 1950s, when factories such as Winthrops and Rowntrees, with their massive chimneys emitting a rotten egg smell, started sprouting up alongside it, the trains were repurposed to distribute their wares instead. When Lewis and Dorothy's children were young there were only two trains a day and upon their sighting Lewis Junior and his friend Colin would run alongside the track and race the huffing puffing monster. One night, as a dare, the boys climbed the fence and changed the signal. Luckily Lewis Junior saw the error of his ways – as he knelt by his bed saying his nightly prayers – and he confessed to his mother who alerted the appropriate authorities and averted what would have been a pretty nasty accident. His reward for his confession was to be confined to his bedroom every afternoon for the following week, which he declared was very unfair, although to be honest he had been the one to make the dare.

Towards the bottom of the road lay the piggeries, and it was to be a constant niggle of Dorothy's that when the wind blew in a certain direction the smell was rancid because pigs – which are contradictory to popular opinion clean creatures who won't defacate near their living quarters – do nevertheless let off a very distinct odour. Lewis got into the habit of standing outside the back door every morning – just after rising – and licking his finger then raising it into the air to test the wind direction. That way if necessary he could advise Dorothy to keep the windows and doors tightly shut and stop the smell seeping into the house. But even this was not foolproof, for the weather is a fickle beast and would often change direction upon a whim. Many was the day it had done just this and Lewis would return from work and be met at the front door by his disgruntled wife cradling freshly laundered washing which she would thrust at him, stating it smelt so bad she would need to wash it all again. He knew even before he shrugged of his overcoat and trudged wearily into the kitchen that his tea that evening would be cold cuts. Likewise, he knew that to question how the changeable British weather was in anyway his fault would result in the same old row, so he kept his head down and made the appropriate appreciative sounds as he waded his way though his unappetising plate of leftovers.

The bungalow was very 'chocolate boxy' and indeed it was its appearance which had so endeared Lewis to it in the first place, as it reminded him of a Constable painting. Rose bushes clambered across the front porch and its meandering pathway was engulfed by tall privet hedges. These sometimes cast a shadow in the lounge but they did afford a degree of privacy from the front street so were allowed to grow unhindered. It was a different kettle of fish in the back garden because, rather too close to the kitchen window for Dorothy's peace of mind, there grew a rather large sycamore tree. Lewis was constantly at pains to reassure Dorothy that it was firmly rooted so not at all unsafe. He reminded her that he had after all been a lumberjack in Canada so was quite an expert in tree management. To which Dorothy would answer, "Yes Lewis that's all well and good but you were chopping them down not watching them fall and crush me as I stand cooking your blinking tea." Lewis Junior later repurposed the lower branch of the very same tree by tying a rope around it to form a tarzan-style swing. One day he was swinging to and fro while shouting the distinctive

Tarzan call when he slipped and let go of the rope. The heavily knotted end of the rope swung clean through the kitchen window, shattering it very effectively and covering the stove top with a fine layer of tiny glass shards into the bargain. Dorothy did not lose her temper, although she would have had the perfect right to. Instead she muttered under her breath, deliberately loud enough for her husband to hear, "I knew that daft tree would cause trouble one day. You would have done well to have listened to me in the first place." Which was her way of saying "I told you so". Lewis, who was sitting at the table reading the daily newspaper, did not utter a word in defence but instead shrunk lower into his chair and took a sip of his tepid tea. He knew when he was beaten. A short while later - after Dorothy had blustered out of the house on the pretext of shopping - Lewis calmly collected the axe from the shed and lopped off the offending branch. But even after that he could not go so far as to chop the entire tree down, so it carried on growing and remained a constant thorn in Dorothy's side until the day they moved out of the bungalow. A few weeks after they had settled into their new house in central Gosforth, word came through that during a particularly bad storm the tree had finally given up the ghost and keeled over. As my grandmother had predicted it had fallen into the kitchen and smashed the stove right through the floor and onto the foundations beneath. Thankfully the only casualty that fateful night had been the family dog – ironically named Lucky - who had been sniffing around the stove looking for scraps. Dorothy did not say a word on receiving the news. Nor indeed did Lewis but the accusing and knowing look she shot his way said it all.

My mother and her siblings appear on first inspection to have enjoyed an idyllic childhood reminiciscant of an Enid Blyton novel, but memories are strange things and have a tendancy to rewrite history. So for now their childhood was 'the stuff that dreams are made of' consisting of long sunny halcyon days. During the long summer holidays my mother, her siblings and the local neighbourhood kids would gather en-masse at the bottom of the road, each clutching a brown bag containing a picnic lunch of bread and jam – or just butter if there was often no jam – then ride their bikes up towards the red hills. At this time there was also a tiny stream, which was a subsidiary of the much larger river Ouseburn – long since gone, unfortunately, because it was filled with junk in the 1980s - and once they had crossed the little Brunton Bridge they would fish for tiddlers or collect frogspawn in empty jars. Then after feasting upon their makeshift picnics they would pick up their bikes and ride up and down and alongside the red hills. These 'red hills' were all that remained of a former pit which had closed in the 1880s. They were basically a slag heap pile of red ash, which was alarmingly prone to smoulder then self-combust. One incident – which my aunt remembers vividly - occurred when a young lad was riding his bike across the peak of the hills, showing off his wheelie skills to the girls. His front wheel struck a rock and as he lost his balance his trouser leg got caught up in the pedals. This resulted in him careering down the hill like a creature possessed, then crashing in an unwieldy heap at the foot of the hill. He would probably have suffered no more than a bruised ego if the impact had not created a rather substantial hole in the ash into which he tumbled. The unfortunate result of this was that the shin of his left leg and the palms of his hands were so severely burnt that he was hospitalised for a few weeks. Another time, my mother remembers her brother and his friend Colin daring each other – the same friend whom he had dared to change the railway signal and seemed to be his comrade in arms in most of these adventures – to walk barefoot over the smouldering ash. The boy, now a man of 80 years, still has problems with blistering to the soles of his feet to this day. Following these two accidents, parents began to forbid their children to play on the 'red hills' – which knowing the inquisitive nature of children made it even more of an attractive destination for the local youngsters. Colin and Lewis Junior would pinch potatoes from the field behind the bungalow then burrow deep holes in the hillside in an attempt to bake the potatoes. If they dug about a foot deep into the 'hill' the ash shone a deeper red and it was hot enought to scorch a potato, which was a real 'picnic treat.'

One other incident which stands out in my mother's memory is the time when Lewis Junior and Colin decided to play a deadly game of dare. It was the end of the summer holidays and the boys were bored. They had played a few half-hearted games of cowboys and Indians, then a rough and tumble game of Robin Hood and were now meandering down country lanes – looking for mischief – as they dragged their willow twigs along the hedgerows. They stopped for a while to tease the temperamental bull in the far field and it was then that Lewis spied a nearby bush heavy with brightly coloured berries. Leaving Colin to flick his red sweater in the direction of the bull he crossed towards the bush, stretched in and picking a large juicy berry from the top he tentatively licked it. Contorting his face at its bitter taste he hastily dropped it to the ground crying 'yuck!!! Sensing an opportunity for some mischief his friend quickly tired of teasing the bull and rose to the challenge.

"Cry baby!!! Cry baby!!" he mocked, "I dare you to eat one." Well versed in the game of his own making Lewis quickly retorted, "double dare you," Only for Colin to come straight back with, "treble dare scaredy cat and I dared first so I win." He followed this up by running alongside Lewis, frantically flapping his arms and clucking like a hen.

"I'm not chicken,"

"Are to,"

"Am not,"

"Are to, you're a baby. Run along and get your mummy to change your nappy Lewis Dowd cry baby."

Lewis could feel himself welling up. In the complex world of boyhood friends there was no greater insult than to be called a cry baby. There was only one way he could make his best friend stop and be nice again and that was to follow up on the dare. So he pushed his friend roughly away and ran back towards the bush. He then plucked off a dozen of the nasty tasting berries and quickly stuffed them into his mouth and swallowed without chewing. The 'dare' settled, the two boys carried companiably on their way until it started to get dark and their rumbling bellies reminded them it was time for tea. Lewis sat at the table and ate his meal with his usual boyish gusto, getting admonished twice by his mother Dorothy for speaking with his mouth full and resting his elbows on the table. It was later that night that Lewis began to feel queasy and it was not long after that the projectile vomit splattered and pebbledashed the rug beside his bed. At first, Dorothy was more annoyed than concerned, as she suspected her son had rushed his meal and not allowed it to properly settle before racing from the table. But seeing the look of agony upon his face and the way he rolled to the floor clutching his stomach, she soon changed her tune and called for Lewis Senior to quickly fetch the doctor. By chance the doctor was on a house visit at a neighbours house so raced straight to the bungalow. The doctor was quite brusque with the youngster, but by being so, he managed to get to the truth remarkably quickly and guessed what they were dealing with. He ushered Lewis and Dorothy into the hallway and spoke to them in whispers. "It is as I feared. We can only hope the infernal berries work their way out of his body themselves before the poison takes a hold."

"And if they don't? Dorothy asked, desperately trying to keep calm despite the tears streaming down her face. The doctor did not speak, he just shook his head and patted her arm. She had her answer. A deathly hush descended upon the hallway broken only when Lewis suggested he go to his mother's house and summon the priest. It was at this point that Dorothy suddenly regained her wits and snapped, "what good will the priest do you silly man? It's practical help our son needs not the last rites."

"I hadn't meant it like that," Lewis retorted, before fading out as he had meant exactly that and he knew it was useless trying to convince his wife otherwise.

"I tell you what you will do Lewis and that is you will get the other children up and dressed and take them all to your mothers. Dolly will help her see to them. I need to concentrate on getting our son through this and as your God is my witness I will." Then turning to address the doctor she demanded to know what might help. The doctor could see that she meant business and even though it would probably be of little effect she needed to be doing something constructive. "Well," he said hesitantly, "a drink of bicarb may help.... but I can't promise it will do any good, all I can say is it won't make the situation worse." No sooner had he uttered these words than Dorothy was out of the hallway and racing towards the kitchen. Warming the kettle on the stove she quickly mixed a paste of bicarbonate in the special pink rose-petalled teapot she had inherited from her parents. This 'magical' teapot was only brought into service when the children were sick and she needed its 'magic' now more than ever. Throughout the long dark night and the following day she would constantly be remaking a brew of bicarbonate of soda in the special little teapot. Lifting her son's head gently from the pillow she would encourage him to take just a little sip. "Just one". "Please my darling boy". "Just one for mummy". Her heart skipped a beat when Lewis complained at being made to drink such a vile concoction for his complaint was the first lucid sentence he had spoken since the doctor had visited. With tears once again coursing down her face she begged her son to drink just a little bit more. She promised him the world if he would just take a little more. That new bike he had been clamouring for would be his if only he would take a small sip. The brown leather football that he had been pestering his parents to buy for Christmas would be his, if only he could take one more little drink. Minute by minute, hour by hour it was as if her son recovered before her very eyes. Before long he was sitting up in bed and asking for a slice of bread and butter. Dorothy ran to the kitchen and sprinkled sugar on the bread watching in grateful wonderment when a few minutes later he wolfed it down almost in one mouthful. The doctor came again later that afternoon and examined Lewis' still tender stomach. He shook his head in amazement, proclaiming it a miracle and telling Dorothy that if it had not been for her tender care he would have been laying her son out. He had seen youngsters ingest much smaller quantities of berries than he and not survive. Lewis for his part loved the attention he received from his siblings and lorded it over the rest of the family for as long as they allowed. That evening Lewis senior had taken the axe to the bush. But I digress and have raced ahead in the story. I need now to return back to 1939 and a time when young Lewis was not even a twinkle in his father's eye.

SEPTEMBER 3RD 1939, HONEYMOON HIATUS

Lewis and Dorothy's newlywed happiness was unfortunately short-lived, for it was rudely interrupted by a contemptible and diminutive moustached man who would prove to be every bit as disruptive and destructive as 'the creature' had been to Dorothy's father Oshbert all those years ago. For this heinous creature had a wildly maurading army supporting his every mad scheme and as a result was rapidly spreading his evil throughout Western Europe. It was at 11.15am on September 3rd 1939 in a five minute broadcast that the Prime Minister Neville Chamberlain announced that England was in a state of War with Germany. Mothers and wives throughout England, who had witnessed the utter devastation of World War 1, wrung their hands in despair and wept for the dubious futures of their precious sons and husbands. This new war differed from the World War 1 from its outset because Parliament sidestepped the usual protocol of voluntary conscription and instead rushed through a law, named The National Service Act, and in doing so imposed a mandatory conscription of all able-bodied men between the ages of 18 and 40.

Because of his age - he was 33 by the time war was declared - Lewis was told that he would not be one of the first to be called up, but nevertheless he was still instructed to regularly check in the newspapers to see if his number was listed. He was allocated 7583313 so had to keep an eye out for the number 13. I suspect that now the number would be omitted due to its unlucky connotations but in 1939 the concerns of the soothsayers of doom were dismissed as poppycock. It was now a race against time in the hope that Lewis would be around for the birth of his and Dorothy's first child due in the December of that year.

Finding out about the prospective birth had been a blessed relief for Lewis's mother for she had been concerned about the state of her eldest son's marriage, especially when the announcement took so long to come. When an entire year had passed and no baby was on the horizon, Theresa had even been so indelicate, and dare I say interfering, as to enlist Lewis's best friend – her nephew Arthur Kinghorn – to have a quiet word with Lewis 'incase he was having problems in that area and doing it wrong.' This would seem incredulous today but in the thirties there were many tales of young inexperienced married couples who were trying to 'get pregnant' but were so inept in basic biology that the methods they were using were unlikely to ever result in a successful pregnancy. Arthur was much more a 'man of the world' although it was most likely partly bravado and wishful thinking on his part. Nevertheless, after taking Lewis for a pint he respectfully broached the subject to find his friend unsurprisingly reluctant to chat about such a private matter. Reading between the lines Arthur managed to ascertain all was well but Lewis was concerned about Dorothy's health so had been holding back on starting a family until 'he had built her up a bit.' Of course once Arthur relayed this to Theresa, she became a woman on a mission and from then on whenever the couple visited her at the presbytery they would be fed the most fattening calorie-packed meals and furthermore sent home with bulging 'doggy bags.' Dorothy - blissfully oblivious to the conversations which had been going on – declared to Lewis in a joking manner,"Do you think your dear mother is fattening us up for Christmas?" Her fluctuation in weight had long been a concern and although she joked about it she was convinced that was why the stray dog had mistaken her for a streetlight and peed up her leg all those years ago in Blackpool. Theresa's cooking seemed to do the trick and once Dorothy had gained a little weight she had reason to take her mother-in-law aside one day and divulge to her the joyous news that she was in the family way. I must now add that although Theresa did not say as much to Arthur - when she asked him to interfere -part of her earlier concern lay in the fact that she had heard through the grapevine that Jimmy Monroe had returned to England, and even more worrying, he had been discreetly enquiring about the state of Dorothy's marriage. As far as Theresa understood there had been no further contact - although her friend had hinted there might have been - since they met at his father's funeral, but still to be on the safe side it would be better if Dorothy was pregnant as she was less likely then to have her head turned if she was carrying her husband's child.

Jimmy Monroe had indeed returned home in the spring of 1939. He had not returned primarily for Dorothy – although he did have a rather vivid dream of a romanic reunion, in which he swept her from her feet and they fled from war torn Europe to the relative safety of Canada – but in the cool light of day, and once he had heard news of her marriage, he knew in his heart of hearts that 'that' particular ship had sailed. He did, however, hope for some closure should they meet as he felt he deserved an explanation as to why she had so cruelly rejected him and ignored his letters.

Jimmy Monroe, as the only son of the Grocer had been summoned from Canada by the Solicitor handling the 'estate' of his recently deceased father. It wasn't until he set foot upon British soil and the police suggested he '*visit the Station at his earliest convenience*' that he realised the police had instigated his return because they suspected him of having orchestrated the 'murder' for financial gain. This suspicion had come about because not long after his untimely demise the police had discovered that – despite appearances to the contrary – the Grocer had been a man of means. It appears that Clarence Monroe had been a canny businessman who had invested well, dabbling in shares after the 'Wall Street Crash' of 1929 and coming up trumps. Why he worked day in day out was subject to much speculation but the fact remained that Jimmy as his only son and heir was the sole benefactor of a very significant sum of money. So large was the sum involved, that if he chose to never work a day again he would still live a most comfortable life. This money was a double-edged sword for if it had been a pittance the Police may not have been so concerned to solve what should have been an open and shut case, but by its very presence the money threw up suspicion. The crime gained such notoriety with the 'war weary' population that the gutter press – who reported it with an unprecented gusto - even coined a phrase 'The mysterious case of the Grocer's dozen.' So named because the Grocer – a rather portly chap – had fallen on a dozen eggs as he tumbled down the back stairs on that fateful night. Every nuance in the life of the Grocer and his wife was carefully documented and every new clue gleefully reported, with the frenzy of publicity reaching a peak even before poor Jimmy arrived back in Britian. The Grocer's second wife Susie – who was Dorothy's mother's former housemaid – had been found collapsed in the shop, sitting perched behind the counter, the telephone receiver clasped to her bosom looking to all intents and purpose as if she was waiting to welcome her next customer. Initially the police believed that the Grocer had been pushed down the stairs by a burgler – employed at the behest of his son - and Susie upon hearing the commotion had raced into the shop to call for help before herself being attacked. The wound to her temple suggested she had been struck by a blunt object, and the police had combed the area searching for the probable weapon but to no avail. The blood specks on the pyramid cap of the banister newel post had been noted and duly recorded at the time the police had first attended the scene but their relevance was not made apparent until much later in the investigation. It actually took an amateur sleuth and famous crime fiction author Agatha Christie, to answer a plea from a low grade newspaper and finally solve the murder mystery. This, as you can imagine, proved of great embarrassment to the police who were compelled to issue a statement declaring that their lines of enquiry had closed as a result of further information becoming available, and then – in a quite unprecedented manner – they thanked Miss Christie for her invaluable insight. Agatha went on to use the 'mysterious case of the Grocers dozen' as a minor plot line in one of her most applauded novels - but that's by the by and I digress. Jimmy was understandably relieved that his father and stepmother had not fallen victim to foul play and, furthermore, relieved that the finger of suspicion no longer fell at his door. The facts of the case appear to have been that the Grocer had stumbled and fallen down the stairs, crashing as he fell into his wife, who had the misfortune to have been walking down in front of him. After pummelling into her back, he tumbled past her and landed on a dozen eggs stacked for delivery the next day. Severly winded Susie had tried to regain her balance then passed out and headbutted the newel post. Temporarily regaining her consciousness she then struggled to the shop to ring for an ambulance. As she slumped on the stool supported by potato sacks on the shelf behind, she began to bleed internally and unfortunately died before she made the call. Ironically the couple were found the next morning by the very customer who had placed an order for a dozen eggs.

Jimmy was grateful that he could at last set about organising a decent funeral for his 'parents'. He planned to return to Canada as soon as the legal stuff was cleared up. He knew he had no future in England because he would always be the 'suspected murderer'. The old adage rang true as 'mud sticks' and he was fully aware of the rumours already circulating around the neighbourhood, claiming that he had had a 'lucky escape', which by its very wording implied the gossips believed that he had been involved. Jimmy had hoped that Dorothy might have made an appearance in his hour of need and was extremely hurt and upset when she did not. But this is not to say she did not want to. She would have been there by his side in a heartbeat had Theresa not remarked how inappropriate it would have been. But Dorothy did insist on attending the 'media circus' of a funeral saying she needed to honour the memory of the family's former housemaid Susie. Jimmy's heart skipped the familiar beat when first he saw her, his darling Dorothy, and he had to remind himself of the impropriety of the setting and fight back the urge to race into her arms. Dorothy felt a similar rush of emotion as she spied his solitary bowed figure standing grieving by the graveside. During the internment she and Jimmy acted with all of the decorum society and the situation dictated and she answered his smile of greeting with a curt little nod. Later, when the time came for the mourners to file past Jimmy to pay their last respects, he politely shook her outstretched hand and after passing on his own condolences for the recent bereavement of her mother thanked her for attending. As this small exchange took place Jimmy deliberately averted his eyes addressing a spot above her left shoulder which felt most disconcerting to Dorothy. As she turned to leave, she inwardly congratulated herself on how well she had handled the rather awkward meeting but later that night she tossed and turned restlessly in her bed, as she could not get her former beau's haunted look out of her mind. She was so agitated that she eventually got up out of bed – for fear of disturbing Lewis – and she took herself into the kitchen where she sat a while nursing a mug of cocoa and staring at the night sky from the window. How long she sat there she did not know but sometime during the early hours Lewis must have awoken and missed her presence by his side. Dorothy was startled to see him illuminated at the kitchen doorway, his hair dishevelled, rubbing the sleep from his eyes. Crossing to her side he laid his hand on her shoulder, "Come on old girl," he said, "come back to bed. It's chilly in here you'll catch your death." Then taking her by the hand – rather like one would guide a young child - he led her back to their marital bed and then he lay holding her securely in his arms until he heard her steady breaths of sleep. Lewis never confessed to this and to the day she died she never knew but, he had been told 'by a concerned relative' that Dorothy had been seen speaking to Jimmy at the funeral. Theresa who had also been party to this 'news' even went so far as to ring him at work to reiterate that he needed to 'pull his socks up' and get Dorothy in the family way. It was, she declared, the only way he could ensure his wife would not have her head turned by her old flame. But Lewis did not want his wife to stay with him out of a sense of duty. For what kind of marriage would that be? If she constantly regretted her decision to marry him, what would that do to their relationship long-term? Lewis made the difficult decision to trust his darling Dorothy would honour the vows she had made in the presence of God. He knew her character well but still in the early hours after finding her so distressed sitting by the kitchen table he had been tempted to ask her for reassurance. He had fought to contain the words only because he was afraid of her answer and fearful that their carefully constructed life together would come tumbling down like a house of cards should Dorothy hesitate in her reply. So instead, he played the part of the blustering yet caring spouse and ushered his precious wife back to the marital bed, then feigned the steady breaths of sleep until he heard her do likewise.

Jimmy and Dorothy didn't cross paths again for quite a few weeks. Dorothy always believed the meeting to have been a chance encounter, but unbeknownst to her Jimmy had meticulously orchestrated the rendezvous so he could be at a particular place at a particular time and still give the illusion of it having been a coincidence. He had been monitoring her movements since the day of the funeral, rather like a latter day stalker or a burglar casing a joint. But, I must add that unlike the aforementioned characters Jimmy had the very best of intentions towards his intended prey. During the time he had been in Canada, Dorothy had never been far from his thoughts and he just wanted a chance to speak to her properly. To speak without an audience of nosy relations evesdropping upon their conversation and studying every nuance of their body language. He told himself that once he knew for certain that she was happy, he could finally move on with his life. He had had relationships in Canada - for he was after all a normal red-blooded man and a man had certain needs - but he had been guarded and not allowed any of his lady friends to chip away his carefully constructed veneer. He feared that after being so hurt and betrayed by his first love he would never entrust his heart to anyone again. He needed a kind of closure and he needed to know that he had not imagined the intimacy they shared all those years ago. Dorothy had moved on with her life – it broke his heart to think of this but she was married – and in getting some answers perhaps he too could move on with his.

On that Spring day, as she alighted from her pushbike to cross Salters Road, Dorothy glanced up the street and experienced a strange other-worldly sensation she had never felt before or indeed would ever feel again. It was as if the world stopped turning on its axis and time itself stood still. For in the distance strolling nonchantly towards her, seemingly without a care, was her first true love Jimmy Monroe. Jimmy of the future was as familiar to Dorothy as Jimmy of the past for he had not lost the confident swagger of his youth and as she stood transfixed - a rabbit in the headlights - he began to change pace and broke into a steady trot. Once he reached her side he did not acknowledge her or reach out to touch her. Instead he stood at a respectful distance, no doubt trying to regain his own composure. In the end it was Dorothy who made the first somewhat bold move. It was her fingers – which took on a will all of their own and outstretched towards his - and her fingers which tenderly curled around his. He greedily clasped her hand in such a swift clumsy way that her rings bruised the tender flesh of his palm. He promptly dropped her hand and settled his gaze upon the rings as if to acknowledge her married state. The rings glinted and mocked in the early morning sunshine. She saw a shadow of pain race across his features and they were once again ill at ease and difficult with one another. Casual acquaintences meeting by accident and both desperately searching for an excuse to make their leave. It was Dorothy who eventually made the decision to walk away and she would have done just that, if Jimmy had not suddenly come to his senses and grabbed her – somewhat roughly - by the elbow. She turned to face him, mesmerised by the pain which glazed his eyes. He started to speak. She started to speak. Their words tumbled and crashed and bumped into each other and as they did they both started to laugh. It was ridiculous that they had once been so close that they finished each other's sentences and now they both struggled to verbalise at all. Finally, Jimmy took the lead and asked her if she fancied taking a short stroll with him. When she seemed to hesitate upon her answer, he repeated his request. And then when she again did not answer he asked the question which had been playing upon both of their lips since they were first reunited.

"Why did you not write to me Dorothy? It felt as if you had ripped out my heart and thrown it away."

Jimmy had always been so eloquent with language unlike her husband Lewis who always experienced difficulty expressing his feelings. This realisation struck Dorothy like a thunderbolt and she spat out her reply,"how dare you accuse me of not writing," she cried, her voice overtaken with emotion, "I wrote to you every week Jimmy; every single sad and desolate week, for an entire year. It was you who took off without a care and forgot I existed. How do you think that made me feel Jimmy? I was so unhappy for so long and now I'm just angry..really really angry."

Witnessing this rare display of anger Jimmy felt his own hackles rise and replied haughtily, "do not lay the blame for this on my shoulders Dorothy. I wrote to you every week, more often twice a week and I never once received a reply, not once, not even one, nothing, not one word."

Dorothy could see the sincerity in Jimmy's eyes – it was what she had always loved about him, his inability to tell a lie. She replied but in a much more conciliatory tone than before, "but you must have received my letters. I wrote so many and my mother posted them to you herself..... so you must have..." Dorothy stopped mid-sentence for it was as she uttered these words that she suddenly knew the truth of what had happened. She turned once more to face Jimmy and she knew from his expression too that he had also reached a similar conclusion. For there was only one logical conclusion and it was that the letters had somehow been intercepted and destroyed. There could only have been one culprit. It pained Dorothy to think her mother had been so devious as to carry out such a terrible cruel act, but there really was no other explanation. They stood like that a while. Not saying anything just staring at each other trying to make sense of it all. Trying to come to terms with the betrayal and its consequences. Jimmy, her Jimmy looked so forlorn. A man adrift. Lost at sea. She yearned to step back to a less complicated time. A time when there was Dorothy and Jimmy, a couple in love with the future bright and shining in their grasp. For a moment she forgot she was no longer that Dorothy. That free spirit skipping through life. Jimmy, her Jimmy looked unchanged. Still the handsome boy who had stolen her heart. She made a movement to step closer to inhale the essence of her love, but the very movement brought her abruptly back to reality and her foot hovered mid-air before returning back in almost a hoplike gesture. Something, someone had caught her eye on the opposite side of the street. Suddenly she realised how vunerable they were standing there. How open to misinterpretation their accidental meeting could be.

"Can I suggest we take a short walk Jimmy. I think we need to talk this through without prying eyes spying on us." Dorothy was referring to her mother-in-law's best friend and former neighbour, Dora, who had just walked past on the other side of the road and made a point of stopping to stare in their direction in quite a rude and accusatory fashion.

They couple soon fell into step and started to stroll towards Gosforth High Street, the bicycle pushed between them as a makeshift barrier of respectability. They did not discuss their destination for it seemed irrelevant but as they walked and talked they automatically headed towards Jesmond Dene – their special place all those years ago when everything had seemed so hopeful and so uncomplicated. Once they reached the relative privacy of the Dene, Jimmy took Dorothy's bicycle from her and they walked arm in arm. There was nothing improper in this shift of position as it was a gentleman's perogative to take a lady's arm so, should she stumble on the uneven ground, he could help her regain balance. It was not until they reached the old water mill and the bridge overlooking it – and they stood gazing at the waterfall – that Jimmy turned and made the bold move of taking Dorothy into his arms. She fell into his embrace almost without thinking and it was not until he leant in to kiss her and his lips grazed her own that she suddenly remembered her married state and pulled abruptly away.

"Have you forgotton I'm a married woman now Jimmy?" Dorothy snapped. She was more angry at herself for so nearly kissing him back than at he for trying his luck.

"How could I forget when you wound me with your rings," Jimmy replied, holding aloft the damaged palm in an effort to regain the good humour and camaraderie the two had shared on their walk earlier. But Dorothy did not want to be swayed. She knew how easily she had fallen into step with Jimmy. She knew how right it had felt to be back in his arms. But just because it felt easy and felt right did not mean that it was. She would not and could not do this to Lewis. He was the man she had married and the man she had sworn chastity too. This was not the woman she was, nor the woman she wanted to be. This wasn't the movies. This was real life and she had joined her life with Lewis. Jimmy and she were the past. A past she could now remember fondly. But the past nonetheless. It was good to know she had not imagined his love but it was too late to go back.

"I should go. I shouldn't have come here with you Jimmy. Especially not here, especially not to our special bridge. Things have changed.... I've changed." She motioned to turn away and was swept once again back into his arms. He spoke very quietly and very determinedly.

"You have not changed a jot my love and nor have I. I've never stopped loving you Dorothy and after seeing you today I know I never will. I want you to come back with me. Come back with me to Canada."

I like to believe my grandmother did not hesitate long in her reply but I concede I will never know if she even seriously contemplated such a move. All I do know for certain is that she chose her marriage and chose my grandfather. One reason for her decision – although I hope it was not the overriding one – was that she suspected that she was with child. The signs were there and although it was too early to seek confirmation from the doctor her body felt changed, she felt different. She had yet to impart the joyful news to Lewis so I am at a loss at to why she saw fit to tell Jimmy, but perhaps as a way of explaining her decision and letting him down gently. Jimmy initially reacted as she had predicted and he briskly dropped his embrace. But to give him his due he quickly rallied around and declared, "If you come with me to Canada I promise to bring the child up as my own and, moreover, I will love it as if it were my own flesh and blood. Please Dorothy at least think it over. Don't dismiss me. Don't turn your back on us. The new us. The us we all three could be. You owe me. You owe us. You....." but before he could finish his argument Dorothy interrupted. Speaking in a calm and controlled voice which in no way reflected how she felt she interjected, "I can't come with you Jimmy and you must surely understand that there is no 'us' anymore nor can there ever be again."

"You can't come or you won't come? And there will always be an 'us' Dorothy. There will be an 'us' until the end of eternity, but if you tell me you no longer love me and no longer feel as I do I promise I will walk away now this instant and you will never hear from me again."

"I can't do that Jimmy and you know it. It is cruel of you to ask me to. Lewis is a good, kind man and he will be a good, kind father. I can't deprive a father of his child or a child of its father," then she added almost as a parting shot, "and I made a commitment before God."

"His God, not your God. I would never have asked you to convert for me. I would have understood you had your beliefs and I had mine. Tell me you believe in this precious God once this war takes hold and the blasted Germans start dropping their bombs. I can take you and the baby to safety. Please my darling Dorothy, I cannot bear to think of you both trapped here in England with this all bubbling away."

Jimmy believed he had talked her around to his way of thinking and relaxed a little when she moved back into his arms and upstretched her lips for a kiss. But as they kissed he could read her lips and he knew this was their last kiss. This was their final kiss. This was the kiss goodbye. After a while with her lips smarting from the pressure of his, Dorothy pulled away. Tears were streaming down her cheeks and she couldn't speak. She stumbled away picking up her bicycle as she crossed the bridge. Jimmy knew he had his answer. He had tried his best shot. He had even tried to goad her, but he knew Dorothy and he knew once she had made up her mind that was it. It was over. They were over. But despite knowing this he still spoke out through his own tears.

"Promise me you will at least think over my proposition. I sail from the Quayside on Friday at 3pm on the Empress of Britian. I will buy a passage for you and will be the last passenger to board. I promise I will wait on the dock for you until the ship sets sail. This is our chance to share the life we have always planned. The life we both deserve. Please I beg of you Dorothy, at least consider it."

Dorothy walked away not daring to turn around incase she were tempted to return to his arms, to his lips. She did not turn back until she had walked almost out of sight. Then and only then did she turn. He was watching her. Still watching her. And she knew he was willing her to return. It would have been so easy but she felt a twinge in her stomach and it brought her hurtling back to a reality. This child would know its true father. She could not do that to Lewis. Jimmy was strong. So much stronger in character than Lewis and besides that she loved Lewis. They could and would make their marriage work.

During the next few days she kept busy. Constantly alert for sightings of Jimmy, she confined herself to the house for she guessed he would not risk coming to the bungalow and running into Lewis. But she need not have worried because he kept his word and kept his distance. Friday morning came and went. That afternoon she ran a long deep bath. Steam filled the little bathroom as she gingerly climbed in. The water scolded the delicate flesh of her ankles but the slight burning sensation made her feel. She needed to feel. Just to feel anything to take her mind of the grief of knowing Jimmy was leaving for good and she would never hear from him again.

Once the water had cooled slightly, she lowered herself gently into the water and lay down letting the water rush over her face. But still she saw him in her mind's eye. She saw him standing on the dockside desperately searching the crowd for sight of her. She saw his expression of hope slowly change to one of acceptance and she saw him turn and slowly climb onto the gangway, his shoulders dipped and his spirit gone. After a while the water cooled and she shivered involuntarily. Something within her stirred. It was such a slight and fleeting sensation, almost as if it were a butterfly tickling her flesh with a gossamer wing. But she knew it was a sign. A sign from the child she had made with Lewis. A sign that she had made the right decision and a sign that time would heal her heart.

Dorothy didn't tell Lewis of the pregnancy that night. Nor the next night, nor the next. She kept it secret for as long as she was able. In a strange way the growing baby was her talisman. Whenever she was transported back to that day in the Dene she pressed a hand gently upon her now protruding belly and the baby seemed to press back in acknowledgement. When Lewis did make comment upon her expanding girth, she feigned confusion and made a big show of checking the dates on the calander then rushing back into the bedroom to tell him. He was thrilled and responded as she guessed he would – by swinging her into the air and expressing his great delight. That very evening they visited the Presbytery and relayed the joyful news to her mother-in-law. Who also responded as she guessed she would. But Dorothy noticed a fleeting glance cross between mother and son and in that moment she knew that Lewis knew. He had known all along and never said a word. He knew that she had met Jimmy that day on Salters Road and he knew that they had strolled off together. No doubt he and his mother would mentally be doing the sums and putting two and two together. There was nothing Dorothy could do or say. For is she addressed the suspicion she could incriminate herself further and plant more worrying thoughts into Lewis'mind. Her only hope was that the baby would arrive early and matters would be resolved that way. But as life often is and as life often pans out the baby, a girl, arrived late at 42 weeks. And she was a slight underweight newborn, most unlike a baby born so late in a pregnancy. Later that evening, as Lewis and his mother visited the hospital, Dorothy noted the self-same glance pass between them. Dorothy wanted to shout out her innocence, but instead she settled her gaze upon her tiny daughter wishing that the child had inherited Lewis's sea blue eyes, pale complexion and strawberry blonde hair. But wishes are just wishes and young Joan had deep dark brown eyes and sported a mop of dark hair. As Dorothy looked across at her baby cradled in her husband's arms her daughter's features began to mirror those of her long lost love Jimmy and she had to remind herself that Joan was not his and was Lewis's child and her memory was not playing tricks.

Jimmy had left England on the *Empress of Britian* that Friday but throughout the journey he constantly berated himself for not doing more to convince his precious Dorothy to come with him. If only he had not been such a gentleman that afternoon on the bridge. Perhaps if he had perservered and pestered more she would have eventually given in. He remembered that before her sensible head kicked in she had relaxed into his embrace, with an ease of their old courting days. Perhaps if he had told her more of the terrible atrocities the war would bring and spelt out more colourfully what a future of Nazi occupancy would entail she would have had a change of heart. As he set foot upon Canadian soil a few weeks later, he knew that he still had unfinished business back in England and it was not over. In his heart he knew it would never be over. Dorothy and he were meant to be together and if not for a cruel twist of fate the child she was carrying would have been his. His desperate need for closure had just reinforced his feelings. Nothing had changed. It never would change. His love for Dorothy had not diminished with the passage of time. If anything it had grown into an obsession.

Jimmy did indeed return to England in September of 1940. By that time the war had been rumbling on for a year and when Canada entered the fray on 10th September 1939, Jimmy was one of the first to enlist and join the Navy. In 1939 at the very start of the war the Canadian Navy had been described as *'pathetically tiny'*, but it grew rapidly as the war took hold and Jimmy as a new recruit quickly climbed the ranks. Jimmy was one of the first to raise his hand and volunteer for a - we now know misguided – mission to evacuate British children to the safer shores of Canada, Australia, New Zealand and South Africa. With the impending threat of a Nazi invasion a government organisation The Children's Overseas Reception Board 'CORB' had been quickly established and a scheme knicknamed 'sea evacuees' promptly established. The idea was that the children would be temporarily relocated for the duration of the war, and with the Navy stating confidently that the children would be quite safe sailing as part of a convoy of ships across the Atlantic, the scheme rapidly gained momentum. There was, afterall, the Navy assured the public - safety in numbers. Two ships the SS Volendam and the SS City of Benares were quickly earmarked for the rescue. As a member of the receiving Canadian envoy Jimmy was tasked to sail on the first ship to leave Britain but he pleaded with the Captain to be allowed to sail instead on the second stating he wanted to fetch his own child from Newcastle first. This was the argument he used as it allowed him to change ships. Indeed he had made this claim so frequently over the past few weeks that he almost came to believe that Dorothy's daughter was actually his own. The journey by sea would be perilous as the German presence was brooding but Jimmy reasoned that he could persuade Dorothy to trust him the care of her child. This way after the war had finally run its course, he reasoned, she would follow and hopefully remain with him as they had always planned.

So it was on a cold September day that Jimmy made his way towards Newcastle Central Station then on to Fawdon by foot. He had only been given two days leave to complete his mission so time was of the essence. He finally reached Dorothy's front door at the stroke of midnight, looking rather more damp and bedraggled than he had planned – due to the inclement weather. He had contemplated staying somewhere nearby overnight but he was so desperate to see her that he decided to throw caution to the wind and hope she would open the door to him. I must add at this stage that he had been canny enough to firstly ascertain that Lewis was safely out of the way at training camp in Tidworth, Hampshire. That said, I am certain he would have never attempted such a bold act had Britain not been in the throes of that dreadful war. I can only imagine Dorothy's reaction as she tentatively opened her door that dark, drizzly and gloomy night. Surely Jimmy must have been the last person on earth she expected to see standing there, indeed in the half light and glimpsing the uniform, she at first mistook him for her husband Lewis. As a result her cry of greeting was most inappropriate for a married woman alone in a house. Once she had recovered and realised that it was Jimmy and not Lewis, she had to caution herself to behave more appropriately. Seeing his sorry state she ushered him quickly in from the cold and wet. Once he had settled into a chair in the kitchen, she turned the oven on for some instant heat and filled the kettle to make him a hot drink. Seeing him shivering she then went to fetch him some clean dry clothes. Jimmy was taller than Lewis by almost a head so once he had discreetly changed in the hallway and stood before her dressed in Lewis' trousers and shirt the clothes gave him an almost comical appearance. It broke the ice and the couple fell into paroxysms of giggles when Dorothy remarked that Jimmy resembled Charlie Chaplin, whose silent movies they had so enjoyed in their courting years. They sat at the kitchen table - talking until the early hours of the next morning – Jimmy trying and trying to convince Dorothy to entrust her child into his care. But it was to no avail and eventually – after he had almost drifted off mid-speech and toppled from the chair – she convinced him to try and get some much needed sleep before his long laborious journey back to Liverpool the next day. Dorothy collected him a blanket from her own bed and he settled down upon the couch in the lounge falling into a deep slumber almost as soon as his head hit the cushions. She was sure she sensed him standing by her bed in the early hours of the morning, but was so sleep deprived herself that she smiled in his direction then fell back to sleep. She only fully awoke as Joan stirred in her cot much much later that morning. As Dorothy reached down to lift Joan into her arms, her gaze fell upon a shiny silver locket lying on the bedside drawers. She knew even before opening the locket that it would contain a lock of Jimmy's hair and she further knew that her precious Jimmy was gone forever. He had left as he had arrived, like a thief in the night. He must have gone from the house in the very early hours and was probably now on his way back to his ship. Dorothy felt a deep sadness along with a strange sense of relief and she knew in her heart that it would be the very last time she would ever set eyes upon him. This proved to be true for during the next few days the dreadful heartbreaking news filtered through the radiowaves to homes worldwide. Both ships carrying the children to safety had been targeted and torpedoed. The first ship the SS Volenham which had 320 children on board had thankfully limped away intact with no souls lost but the second ship – which Jimmy had boarded – did not have such a lucky outcome. On the 18th September in the cold cruel seas, 250 miles west of the Hebrides, the SS City of Benares had been spotted by Heinrich Bleichrodt the Captain of the German submarine U-48. Heinrich gave the fatal order to attack and a torpedo was immediately fired. It penetrated the ships hull before exploding in a blast of acrid smoke. The order was given to abandon ship and board the lifeboats but it was too late and at 11pm the Canadian ships bow raised in a final surrender before slowly sinking into the Atlantic Ocean. A total of 121 crew members – including Jimmy – and 134 passengers drowned that night and, sadly, only 13 of the 90 evacuee children survived. The 'CORB' mission was immediately abandonded with recriminations from both sides. The Germans even had the audacity to blame the British for making their children 'victims of war'. Dorothy knew the second she heard the news that Jimmy was gone for good and she blamed herself for his death. For if he had not travelled to Newcastle to try and persuade her to allow him to take Joan he would have sailed in the first boat and most likely survived. I wonder now if she was ever tempted to allow him to take her precious child, for what mother in those terrible frightening times would not have considered such a sacrifice to save her baby. I still have in my possession the locket that Jimmy left for my grandmother on that morning. She kept it hidden in the depths of her jewellery box until the day she died. A lock of her hair is placed opposite Jimmy's – she told me she put it there on the day she found out he had perished at sea – so in a bizarre way they are still joined and will remain an 'us' for all eternity just as Jimmy had predicted in the Dene that day in 1939.

LEWIS IS CALLED UP, APRIL 1940

Just a few short months after the couple welcomed their first born daughter Joan Marie into the world, Lewis was called up. Dorothy was stripping the walls in the lounge that Spring afternoon when she saw his call up number 7583313 printed in the newspaper and her first concern that day was of the purely practical nature. How, she wondered, could she possibly be expected to wallpaper a room alone, with a four-month-old baby constantly mithering in her cot? Of course once the realisation hit her that her husband was being called up to fight for his country and their freedom from oppression, she apologised and voiced how thoughtless and selfish her initial concerns were. Lewis had gone grey and ashen before slumping in shock into the nearest armchair, for he had been dreading this day for so long and now it was finally here and real, he knew he must address his greatest fears.

I will now step back in time, if I may, to a scene of a little boy walking through the streets of Jesmond clutching his mother's hand and asking her why the young girls were handing white feathers in such a condescending manner to the young boys strolling innocently past them. The year is 1915 and Britain is in the midst of World War 1 when a young Lewis – with the words why, who, when and where constantly playing upon his lips – asks his mother why. Theresa's words that day were so powerful that they resonated into his adulthood and played upon his mind all those years later. Namely, her reaction and branding of the recipients of the white feathers as cowards followed by her declaration that there 'was no greater shame for a man than to be branded a coward.' To understand Lewis's inner dilemma regarding the prospect of being trained to kill another man, we first need to walk a while in his shoes and keep in mind that he had once trained to become a Catholic priest. Yes, he had turned his back on his religious vocation but he still held strong beliefs and the Ten Commandments clearly stated 'Thou shalt not kill'. This problem had preyed upon his mind ever since Neville Chamberlain had first declared a state of war the previous year, but in a typically ostrich-like manner Lewis had managed to relegate the overriding all-consuming fear to a distant recess of his mind. Now the fear came flooding back and in such a manner that he began to hyperventilate. He could not, nor did not, want to relay his deep-seated fear to his wife Dorothy, as he was afraid it would emasculate him in her eyes, so instead he sought counsel from Theresa his mother. To her credit, she did not dismiss his trepidation out of hand but instead set about to seek a practical solution. I like to presume her reaction was based upon the knowledge that her son was unduly upset, but I must not be blind to the fact that she was also fearful that Lewis would declare himself a conscientious objector and bring untold shame upon the family name. Whatever the true reason, I can only speculate, but I do know that she called upon her own sister Agnes – whose son Arthur Kinghorn had been Lewis' best man – and Agnes in turn called upon her daughter-in-law's brother who as luck would have it was an Army Recruiter. Thankfully, a solution was cobbled together whereupon Lewis would join the Royal Army Service Corps *RASC*, which was the unit responsible for keeping the British Army supplied with provisions. Lewis would still need to complete his basic training and become proficient in the art of combat but, hopefully, this way there was a chance he would not be called upon to put this 'particular talent' into practice. Lewis was initially sent to Tidmouth in Hampshire for basic training before being sent to France late November 1941. I have a copy of a letter of reference he received from a Major in the First Tank Bde. O.M.W praising his skills as a chauffeur valet and commenting that his appearance and manner are above the average.

This next paragraph is difficult to write and, I confess, I considered leaving it out all together but it is important to recognise the plight of Lewis and indeed the other men who would have become 'conscientious objectors' but were afraid of the label and forced instead to become reluctant soldiers. These men were not treated with compassion regarding their strong beliefs, but instead belittled and bullied, so taking such a stance would bode badly upon future employment prospects and ruin a good family name. This is a deathbed confession, so I believe it to be the absolute truth, and I will therefore give it the reverence I believe it deserves. My grandfather lived a long and happy life but unfortunately 'death' comes to us all and the *grim reaper* called upon Lewis in the July of 1986. His passing was mercifully peaceful and he was surrounded by his loving family, but he nevertheless felt compelled to make this final confession before meeting his maker. Knowing of his deep distrust of priests and their ability to hold a confidence – a distrust based almost totally on Father Bradley and his wanton disregard for Lewis' confession all those years ago on Vancouver Island – he instead chose to confide in his eldest daughter Joan, my mother. She handled it with understanding and kindness, so he passed away hopefully feeling completely absolved. I will not record here the full and particular details of where and when this event took place as I don't deem them relevant but I will state that this happened in France during the latter part of the war. As I understand it, my grandfather and another soldier were called upon to keep watch as their comrades slept. The idea was that they would alert the rest of the camp to any potential danger lurking in the darkness and, if necessary, the orders were that they *shoot first ask questions later.* Lewis desperately tried to get himself excused from this task but his commanding officer – a man who had grown up in an army environment and constantly stated that the army ran like blood through his veins – had no time for 'namby pamby excuses' and threatened a potential court martial should Lewis choose to disobey a direct order. Lewis was in a moral quandary, his conscience working overtime. He knew he could not kill in cold blood another young man – most probably an ordinary chap like himself - who had been dragged into this dreadful war by a deranged dictator. He had, in fact, at the start of the war decided that if he was coerced into taking a life – and forced to break one of the Ten Commandments - he would turn the gun upon himself beforehand and so commit a mortal sin. It was a classic 'catch 22' situation and he felt it to be the lesser of the sins. He realised his darling wife, Dorothy, would be widowed as a result – and his children face a fatherless future – but this was the strength of his belief and conviction for he knew that he could not envisage staring at the face of a murderer in the mirror as he shaved, morning after morning until the end of his days. There really was no other solution. I know this is what he planned for I have in my possession the letter he wrote my grandmother that night – but never sent. Why he kept it I really don't know, but perhaps he thought if his actions that night ever came to light it would act somehow in his favour. I presume that it was as he sat, cold and scared, in the lookout tower that he had the sudden idea that if he emptied the barrel of his gun of bullets – and put them safely in his tunic to reload later – he could not physically commit either deadly sin. I don't for one moment think he thought the problem through, or realised that the natural conclusion of his impetuous act was that he could not properly protect his sleeping comrades. He had basically rendered them sitting ducks for any '*Hun* who came a' knocking'. This single act of 'mutiny' obviously weighed heavily upon his conscience until the day he died, for reflecting in retrospect, he never spoke of his time in France or regailed us children with tales of bravado as some other grandfathers did. Perhaps it was because in the intervening years he had time to reflect upon his decision that night and maybe even regret it. But again we will never know.

Nothing in life is ever clearly black or white and I think his deep-rooted belief in basic Catholicism coupled with the theological lectures he attended at Ushaw College whilst training to become a Catholic priest, played a major part in his decision that night. I've spoken to Catholic priests of my acquaintance – members of the Ushaw College Alumni - about this very dilemma and they have pointed me towards documents relating to the ethics of the 'Just War' theory. These ethics have now in more enlightened times been questioned and on the most part revised by the Catholic Church. The theory is a Christian philosophy that attempts to reconcile two fundamental things. The idea that taking human life is morally wrong, and the opposing view that protecting innocent human life and defending important moral values sometimes requires a willingness to use force and violence. The purpose of this 'Just War' theory is that it provides a guide to the right way to decide if it is morally acceptable to act in a certain way. A 'Just War' is therefore morally permissible because it is classed as a lesser evil despite its depiction of still being evil. The origins of 'Just War' originated with classical Greek and Roman philosophers like Plato and Cicero and were added to by Christian Theologians including Augustine and Thomas Aquinas. The Catholic Church has now – in the past decade – distanced itself from the theory of 'Just War' and is in the process of developing a vision of nonviolence and 'Just Peace'. The reasons the modern Church give are varied, but are based upon a renewed appreciation of the way the early Church practiced Jesus' teachings on peace, and the 'Just Peace' theory argues that modern wars have made the old theory obsolete as it is truncated and minimalist, focusing as it does on war, not on the prospect of peace. They further argue that it is the indiscriminate violence of modern warfare which renders the old theory null and void because in our era there is no such thing as a justified war. Pope John XXIII, who was Pope between 1958 and 1963, stated that 'peace was like a cathedral and must be built – as positive peace had many layers and facets.' Lewis would have fared well with his opinions in these more modern days as his strong beliefs, much like Pope John XXIII's, also had their roots in the Old Testament. It was the indiscriminate murder of a fellow man; a man who most probably had a wife and child at home to mourn his death which so turned Lewis's stomach; his argument being that, but for a simple twist of fate and geographical location, the unknown enemy would not be on an opposing side at all or wish him any ill. Both men were no more than pawns in a colossal game of Chess. Although I suspect that, if he had been faced with a situation where he had to kill to protect his own family, his actions that night may have differed. I honestly think whether religious or not, we all probably have that 'killer' capability built into our characters. My grandfather's decision that day – which thankfully, I hasten to add did not have any dire consequences – still haunted him until his dying day and I am eternally grateful that my mother, as his sole confidante, had the kindness of spirit to react as she did to his 'deathbed confession.'

Lewis returned from the war with an all consuming sense of guilt that he had survived when so many of his comrades in arms had not. Men, many of them just boys barely into puberty, whom he had trained with, exchanged confidences with, forged long-time friendships with. He never spoke of the war – bar his deathbed confession – so I know little of the atrocities he witnessed. Although from his very silence on the subject I surmise he bore witness to many. I do, however, know that something in him changed upon his return. In a similar way to how I expect it changed every young man who made it safely back to home and hearth. For how could they not have changed? After being forced to face their own mortality in such a brutal and unforgiving way. Often the change was so subtle and so minuscule that only those closest to the men were aware of its existance. But the change was always there. Lurking. Hiding. Waiting for an opportunity to rear its ugly head. The difference for Lewis to so many of his fellow comrades was that he returned to a seriously ill hospitalised wife and two young children who needed an emotionally strong and capable father figure. His mother and sister Dolly were doing sterling work 'child-minding' - and indeed Dolly had formed such a strong bond with Joan that the toddler often called her Mummy – which reinforced in Lewis the need to mend his fractured family. To the casual observer he fell back into his old life with apparent ease, picking up his 'books' and pounding the pavements to collect the 'payments' from his regular customers - much in the way he always had – with a ready smile and a reassuring dip of the head. It was so nice – they remarked – to have Mr Dowd back from the war unharmed and unchanged; still the same old Mr Dowd politely counting out their proffered coins and signing their account books carefully and precisely in his beautiful handwriting. Still the same old Mr Dowd gratefully taking a cup of tea and a slice of cake nodding at appropriate intervals as they regailed him with tales of their own problems.

It was the long and lonely nights which Lewis most dreaded. After his children had been dropped off. For once they were bathed and tucked up in their beds - their golden hair forming halos upon their pillows - he was alone and victim to his own terrifying thoughts. It was then - as the unforgiving darkness fell - that he flinched and instinctively ducked his head in response to any sudden noise from the street. It was then – when he finally gave in and drifted to sleep - that he was sucked backwards into the horrific part reality of his own nightmares. And it was then when he awoke, drenched in a salty film of sweat that he missed the physical presence of his precious Dorothy most.

Further evidence of my grandfathers 'compassionate' nature can be found in the anecdote of Snowy the goose. Snowy had been bought when the children were quite small and 'fattened' up for a Christmas dinner. When the day finally came for Snowy to be 'dispensed' of, Lewis procrastinated and procrastinated to such an extent that Dorothy eventually declared that she would do the deed instead. But, of course, as it had been she who had fed and cared for Snowy there was no way she could do such a thing either, so that year the family Christmas feast consisted of a string of cheap sausages. Snowy went on to live to a ripe old age but it was as if he knew his days had once been numbered, because from that day on he became very bad-tempered and prone to chasing the children around the garden for the slightest provocation. A constant complaint from the children would be "Snowy chased me and tried to peck my bum," and my grandmother would just shrug her shoulders and say, "well chase him back, he's more afraid of you than you of him."

DOLLY AND THE WRIGHT TWINS, 1940

During the war, Dolly Dowd, Lewis's younger sister, did her bit for the war effort by working at a church-run canteen for service staff. The canteen, which was based in a building owned by the church -

still stands on the corner of Claremont Road, opposite the Hancock Natural History Museum - was a haven of calm for soldiers based nearby. Run by a Catholic charity it provided a morale- boosting friendly face, hot meal and a cup of tea. For soldiers many miles from home and missing their loved ones it proved a godsend in many a way. Not least because it afforded them the opportunity to chat and flirt with the younger female volunteers. Dolly and her best friend Mary Hall – who had met while volunteering - had made a pact between themselves that they would not be tempted to date any of their customers. They both knew how easily a young girl of marriageable age could gain a bad reputation and also neither wished to incur the wrath of the formidable Mrs Potts who oversaw the canteen comings and goings discreetly behind the scenes. But, one young RAF chap in particular was most persistant. He would visit frequently and always try and engage Dolly in conversation, consistantly hinting that he would very much like to walk out with her. Lawrence Wright was a well-spoken young man, obviously well-bred – which bode well for his eligibility – and he seemed to possess a strong sense of family values as he constantly referenced his dear parents. He was based in Boulmer – a little Northumberland coastal hamlet near Alnwick - so the journey to Newcastle on his days off was not an obvious one, but he was so enamoured of Dolly that he made the tedious hour and a half long trip week after week. In the end he wore her down and she conceded that they could go out one night, but only if he brought a pal from the RAF Base for her good friend Mary. That way the girls could double date and be each other's chaperone at the same time. Lawrence raced back to the airfield that very afternoon and hastily offered a pack of 'Woodbines' to any chap who would agree to an impromtu blind date. His twin brother Dominic was first to volunteer and joked that they could both then be the young lasses' Mr Right. He had made this joke so often the rest of the lads on the Base rolled around on the ground mock groaning, but Lawrence was so eager for his brother to carry through his promise and so desperate to date Dolly that he laughed as if it was the first time he had heard this particular pun. The next question was where to take the girls? He could tell that Dolly in particular had her pick of chaps. She was a real 'looker' with her sparkling eyes and mane of dark hair so to bag her for his own would be no easy task. He really needed to pull out all the stops and show her he was serious about her, and not just some cliche RAF chap with a love-em and leave-em attitude. Dolly was the type of girl any fellow would be proud to introduce to his parents as a potential daughter-in-law, and even from the unexeptional conversations they had so far shared, he had an inkling she may have become the 'one.'

After much deliberation, Lawrence and Dominic ended up taking the two girls to a dance at the Oxford Ballrooms that night. Both Dolly and Mary agreed the two lads looks quite splendid – they were identical twins and had both inherited their dashing good looks from their father's side of the family - in their RAF uniforms with their glinting brass buttons and jauntily placed caps. The two couples danced the night away to the popular favourite tunes of the time. When the band started playing a 'jitterbug,' the two boys grinned at each other for they were both excellent dancers and this was their turn to shine. Lawrence swung Dolly into the air, whilst his brother swung Mary the opposite way in a simultaneous movement, while the rest of the dancers on the dance floor parted to form a semi-circle around the two couples. Mary was modest of nature so she did not enjoy being part of the limelight, but by contrast Dolly took to it like a duck to water, even performing a half bow to her impromptu audience as the band stopped playing. The only awkward part of the evening occured when Mary asked Dominic where exactly the two were based, and both lads shot each other a shifty look before splurting out 'Acklington'. This reaction gave Dolly in particular a few sleepless nights, for it was obvious the boys were 'fibbing' and she distinctly remembered Lawrence once telling her that he awoke to the sounds of the waves crashing around the point. Even with her sketchy knowledge of that area of Northumberland - she had once had a beau named Henry who lived in a tiny hamlet called Glanton - she knew that Acklington was not close enough to the coast to hear the sea. Later on that week in the canteen – after they had managed to escape the watchful eye of Mrs Potts the supervisor – the two pals talked at depth about the obvious lie the boys had told. The girls quickly came to the same conclusion, that the boys were probably spies which, if nothing else, elevated them instantly to being even more interesting and even more exciting. Mary declared that they must have been recruited by the War Office, due to being twins, as it would make it easier that way to fool the enemy. Dolly went one stage further and posed the question, "what if they were not even identical twins at all and had undergone plastic surgery to look alike?" No doubt their flights of fancy would have become even more fanciful if Mrs Potts had not caught them chatting and launched into a lengthy tirade which ended in her stating that, "furthermore if either of you are looking for a job to do there are plenty of tables to be cleared." The truth of the boy's 'white lie' was much less glamorous and much less exciting. Yes, whilst it was true the twins were both airmen, the airfield where they were stationed was actually a 'fake airfield' which had been designed to fool the German planes and distract attention from the 'real airfield' of RAF Acklington. This decoy airfield or 'K site' to give it its official designation had been hastily set up in 1940 and its very existence was on a strictly 'need to know' basis. War Posters of the time were very much along the lines of 'careless talk costs lives so zipp it and keep mum, she's not so dumb' and there was already much speculation of a planned German occupation with rumours abounding that the enemy had installed sleepers to make the transition easier. The 'K site' had three fake runways with wooden carcasses of Hurricane and Spitfire fighters as well as the empty aircraft hangers . The small army of personnel – which included the twins - stationed there were tasked to constantly move the aircraft around to give the impression from the air that the airfield was in constant use. But it was by night that the eerie ghost airfield underwent the most remarkable transformation as green and red lights traced the path of the runways and bright navigation searchlights scoured the sky above. Yet despite it being classified a dummy airfield it did, however, have real anti-aircraft defences in the shape of four Lewis machine guns relegated from World War 1. These guns were mounted on tripods around the site but in reality were of precious little practical use due to their age and limited range. The fake airfield was deemed a success when on the night of 16th September 1940 German planes missed their intended target and dropped two large bombs into a nearby field. It was susequently reported in the newspapers that 30 lives were lost that night but what was not reported was that the lives lost had been sheep grazing in the fields. Whilst the rest of the country mourned the loss of these tragic victims of war, those in the know apparently rushed to the site to collect the spoils of war, as meat was rationed at the time and a most valuable commodity. Later in 1943, when the risk of air attacks had somewhat abated, the dummy airfield was used as a relief landing ground before going on to be repurposed once again into an advanced training ground for Spitfire pilots. At the end of the war the land reverted back to farmland. These self same fields now form part of a caravan park called Seaton Park and the old runway is repurposed into the access road and car park. In a twist of fate my partner and I recently purchased a static caravan on this very site, not knowing at the time of the relevance it held to my family history.

Both of the Wright twins were the very epitome of gentlemen that night, escorting the ladies safely home and not even pestering for a kiss. This behaviour bode well for Lawrence, in particular, as Theresa had been watching the couple approach from the upstairs window of her rooms in Rothwell Road, taking the necessary precaution of turning the bedroom light off first. Upon seeing how

Lawrence respectfully shook her daughter's hand - rather than dive in uninvited for a kiss - she decided there and then that he would indeed be a suitable suitor for her daughter. At this stage, I should add, that Theresa and Dolly had moved out of the Presbytery mid-way through the war and Theresa was now taking care of Father Adam Wilkinson - the blind priest - in a house on nearby Rothwell Road. As a postscript, Dorothy and Joan also relocated to this house at the turn of 1942 on the advice of Lewis who said he would be happier if they stayed with his mother and sister whilst the bombs were dropping with such frequency upon residential areas. The Luftwaffe at that time were working from old maps and early arial photography which explains in part why they bombed Keyes Gardens in Jesmond in December of 1941 - in the process killing five civilians and injuring many more. Apparently they had mistaken the Ouseburn running through Jesmond Dene for being a much larger river and assumed the adjoining plant nursery to be a shipyard. Whilst civilian housing was never a real target, it has been reported that Goering had advised Hitler to make a more concentrated effort to bomb Britain in the hope we would surrender and make a much more risky German invasion unnecessary. The British military were so worried about bombs dropping on Vickers Armstrong Factory on the banks of the Tyne – where the all important Chieftan tanks were being manufactured – that they took to lighting up the Coast Road in the evenings because in the moonlight, especially after a rainfall, from the air it took on the appearance of the river itself. The bungalow in King George's Road did not stay empty for long and it was very quickly snapped up as a rental property. When Lewis and Dorothy eventually moved back into it at the end of the war they were shocked to discover that the tenants had been storing coal in the bath, and Dorothy was further irked to find that they had carelessly scratched the enamel in the process.

It was a surprisingly short while after that first date that both Lawrence and Dominic declared their undying love to their girlfriends and the twins, by way of confirming how serious their intentions, took their new sweethearts home to 'meet the parents'. Both girls gasped in awe as the car the boys had borrowed made its way up the long and winding tree-lined drive towards the 'family pile' in nearby Howick. By this time, both couples had seriously discussed marriage. It may seem surprisingly early on in their relationships by todays standards, but wartime had the effect of fast-forwarding courtships along at a breakneck speed due in no small way to the constant fear and uncertainity of the future. Lawrence declared to Dolly that he thought they should wait until after the war before officially announcing their engagement which would have been fine and dandy, if his twin brother Dominic had not presented Mary with a diamond the size of a knuckle. Dolly tried her best to put on a brave face and be happy for her best friend but behind the scenes she and Lawrence argued bitterly and for a short while they even broke off their 'almost' engagement. Eventually, Lawrence managed to win her around, but still he stuck to his guns insisting it would be better in the long-run if they were to wait until the end of hostilities before properly formalising their relationship. Lawrence knew that as both he and his brother were training to be fighter pilots the odds were stacked against either of them surviving the war, and he reasoned that Dolly would find it easier to recover from his 'inevitable' death if they were not actually engaged. I will add that I do not doubt that Dominic was also fully versed on the risks, but from my observations of his character, he appears to have been much more optimistic in nature than his brother. Dominic was given to grand gestures and constantly teased his much more pragmatic brother for being over cautious and thinking ' stuff' through too much. From my investigations, I can confirm that Lawrence had not in anyway underestimated the risks he and his twin faced, for the 'life expectancy' of a Spitfire pilot was shockingly only four weeks. This was in part because the German Luftwaffe were so much better equipped for air warfare than the British, they had 2,600 aircraft at their disposal while the RAF had a mere 640. It was due to the brave spirit and tenacity of the British pilots that we went on the win the Battle of Britain. The British RAF lost a total of 544 pilots in the process and unfortunately one of the twins was part of these sad statistics, but more of that later in the story.

DOROTHY AND JOAN TRAVEL TO LONDON DURING THE BLITZ, OCTOBER 1941

Dorothy was adamant she would go to London to say a 'proper goodbye' to her husband Lewis before he was posted overseas to France. No amount of reasoning from either her mother-in-law Theresa, or sister-in-law Dolly would make her change her mind. Dorothy was equally adamant that she would take baby Joan with her on the journey. In her mind, Lewis needed to see how well his little girl was growing up and, if nothing else it would provide him with a focus throughout the long hard months which lay ahead. Eventually, albeit reluctantly, Theresa came around to Dorothy's way of thinking and even helped her to pack a few special treats so Lewis would know how much his family loved him and were praying for him to return home safe and sound.

Dorothy had read many newspaper articles about the devastations of London from the Blitz, but she was so determined to carry through her planned visit she had blinkered them out. It was only as she alighted from the train at Kings Cross that she conceded that perhaps her trip with a young toddler in tow had been romantic and foolhardy, and Theresa and Dolly had been right afterall to voice their concern. Photographs did not properly depict the full extent of the constant German bombardment upon the capital. The London of 1941 – even from where she stood at the entrance to Kings Cross

Station - was a far, far different place to the London she remembered from previous visits. Indeed, if it had not been for the familiar landmarks, such as Covent Garden and Trafalgar Square, which she passed on her way towards the boarding house she would be unsure of which city she was scurrying through. During the early part of the war, London was a favourite target of the Luftwaffe with the heaviest bombing period being between September 1940 and May 1941. The result of this 'Blitz' was that by the end of the war 30,000 Londoners had lost their lives and many many more were seriously injured. From May 1941 onwards, the Luftwaffe concentrated their efforts upon the Port areas of Liverpool, Hull and Clydebank but that wasn't to say that London was left alone to rebuilt itself, and often - mostly during the hours of darkness - a random bomb would be dropped as if to keep them on their toes. The Londoners Dorothy passed that late afternoon had a haunted resigned look about them, as if they were worn down and rapidly losing what little spirit they had left. More than once as she hurried through the suddenly unfamiliar streets, she wished that she had agreed to Lewis's suggestion that he meet them at the station and hadn't been so darned independent. She paused at a street corner to regain her bearings and to remind herself of the address of the boarding house - she had written it on a slip of paper pinned safely into the breast pocket of her blouse - for she was afraid of losing it. All of a sudden and without prior warning an all to familiar wail started in the distance and as it became louder and gained momentum she was swept back - the way she had just came - by a surging throng of people who seemed to emerge from the very depths of the ruined buildings near where she stood. Making the decision to stay where she was as the crowd seemed to have a destination in mind, she decided to follow in the wake of a young woman who was dragging a child by the arm and carrying a youngster of a similar age to Joan in her arms. It was as she hurried along that Dorothy misjudged her footing and stumbled on some debris - leftover from a previous bomb - and both she and Joan fell heavily to the ground. They were unceremonously plucked from the pavement by a young lad dressed in overalls but there were no time for social niceties - bar a brief thankyou - as Dorothy shouldered her way back once again into the centre of the crowd. It was not until they began descending steps that Dorothy remembered reading somewhere that the underground train stations had been repurposed into air-raid shelters. Once her eyes became accustomed to the half-light she could just about make out figures lying, squatting and sitting everywhere for as far as her eye could see. The stench of human life at its most basic, invaded her senses as she made her way tentatively along the damp, dank platform all the while searching desperately for a spare section of station wall to lean against so she could feed Joan. Noticing her plight a middle-aged woman shoved her husband in the ribs and he shuffled along to make room for Dorothy to squeeze in alongside them. Turning her body away from the couple, Dorothy popped open a few buttons of her blouse so she could discreetly nurse Joan. It was as she sat there alone in a crowd that she realised that somehow – most likely when she stumbled – she had parted company with the suitcase that she and Lewis's mother had so carefully packed the previous day. All of a sudden, emotions got the better of her, and despite her previous best intentions to be brave, she started to sob uncontrollably. The man - who had earlier shuffled along the wall so she could sit down - turned towards her and with his hand outstretched offered Dorothy a sandwich from a tin box. This one simple act of kindness and basic humanity was all it took to encourage Dorothy to wipe away her tears and pull herself together. She twisted around to thank the couple and before long she and the chap's wife were gossiping away like old friends. Somewhere on the opposite platform an old man struggled to his feet and started to play a ukulele – much in the style of George Formby – and it felt as if the mood of entire crowd changed as they raised their voice in song to the familiar tunes. If it had not been for the circumstances in which she found herself Dorothy would probably have joined in, but she was too worried about Lewis to enjoy such frivolity. Had he also found his way to a place of safety? Or had he been searching for her and got caught up in the whole thing?

In what seemed like no time at all but was in all probability a few hours, the 'all clear' sounded and a cheer went up all around as people started gathering their belongings together and making their way ponderously towards the exit. Dorothy struggled to her feet before saying a heartfelt goodbye to her new-found friends. The couple and she exchanged addresses so that they could write to each other and perhaps one day – after they had 'blown Hitler to smithereens' - even meet up. As Joan and she started to ascend from their underground sanctuary, Dorothy suddenly let out a cry of recognition. She had spotted Lewis leaning over the wall which separated the pavement from the station steps. He was desperately searching the departing crowd, an anxious expression playing upon his features. He already feared the worst and was so afraid that he would ever see his wife and child alive again. Dorothy and Lewis raced into each other's arms in the way that only lovers do. Dorothy would later tell her sister-in-law Dolly that Lewis had held her so firmly and for so long that she believed he would squeeze the very breath from her body.

Lewis never forgave himself for putting his wife and child through such an ordeal. He blamed himself for agreeing that she could come and stay with him. He had been so desperate to see his young family - for what he feared would be the final time - that what he perceived as his own selfish needs had overtaken his normal cautious protective nature. He knew he should have gone with his gut instinct and not allowed Dorothy to persuade him that it would be fine. His mother had written to express her concern and he should have put his foot down and forbade his wife to make the perilous journey. Although in retrospect, knowing of my grandmother's determined character, I doubt she would have adhered to his wishes anyway.

That night as they lay chatting - on the rather uncomfortable and inexplicably bumpy mattress of the boarding house bed – they reaffirmed their love for each other. I can now add that this was the very night that my grandmother conceived her second child Lewis junior. I suspect that this had been her plan from the outset, because she had always suspected that my grandfather did not believe that Joan was really his – a thought planted by his mother and left there to fester and brew. The quintessential elephant in the room. I assume that this was Dorothy's way of assuring that Lewis knew this child was without a doubt his actual flesh and blood.

JUNE 17TH 1942, LEWIS JUNIOR IS BORN

It was nine months later – almost to the day - on Wednesday June 17th 1942 that Dorothy and Lewis's second child made his rather loud appearance into the world. His anxious grandmother, Theresa, sat drinking endless cups of tea by the kitchen stove, whilst his aunty Dolly was tasked with taking Fr Adam Wilkinson and Joan out for the afternoon – both women deemed that the act of childbirth was not an event that either a man of the cloth or toddler should be party to. I must now tell you dear reader, that from the moment she had returned back pregnant from her trip to London Dorothy had been in poor health – such poor health that she had, indeed, on more than one occasion coughed up blood. Initially it had been blamed upon her pregnant state – for she had frequent bouts of morning sickness and was quite violently vomiting - but when she did not get any better and sputum tests were conducted, the doctors realised that the problem lay in her lungs. They could not do the usual indepth x-rays – mass miniature radiotherapy was introduced in the 1940s with the hope it would increase the efficiency of screening - due to her being in confinement but she was scheduled for a short stay in a Sanitorium once the child was safely delivered. It was during this stay in hospital that Dorothy – very soon after giving birth to her second child Lewis Junior - was X-Rayed and finally diagnosed with Tuberculosis. She was told that it had probably lain dormant since her mother Mary had died of the very same terrible disease in 1937 and it may have been brought upon by the stress of her journey to London.

Upon his wife's diagnosis, Lewis was allowed home on compassionate leave for a few weeks so that he could sort out suitable childcare. There followed a brief altercation when Theresa - his mother - expressed her concern at taking over the care of baby Lewis and suggested that perhaps she and Dolly could care for Joan, while the new baby be put into the local Catholic Children's Home, Nazareth House. In Theresa's defence Joan was now nearly three, so much easier to pacify than a newborn baby whose constant crying might disturb the elderly priest she was paid to housekeep for. Despite her exhausted and emaciated state Dorothy put her foot firmly down and declared to Lewis that he must tell his mother that she either cared for both siblings or neither, for under no circumstances would she entertain the idea that her two precious children be separated. At this stage, Dolly thankfully intervened declaring that she and her friend Mary Hall would ensure that both children were well cared for and Dorothy reluctantly packed her case and returned to the Sanitorium.

Dolly kept her promise to her sister-in-law and took her niece Joan firmly under her wing, thereby enabling Theresa to concentrate on caring for the young baby. She started to take Joan to work with her in the canteen and Mary and she would take it in turns to entertain her, while the other did the lion's share of the work. Even the formidable Mrs Potts – after initially claiming to be aghast at the prospect of a young child running about the place getting under peoples feet - seemed to grow a soft spot for Joan, to such an extent that she would bring her sweet treats and chocolate from her very own rations. This rationing of sweets and chocolates had only properly begun in July 1942, so for one with such a sweet tooth this was a big sacrifice for

Mrs Potts, and one which I must add altered her equilibrium in such a negative way that her husband Mr Potts insisted she instead commandeered his. So poor Mr Potts was reduced to sitting in the parlour sucking on the licorice root which he had purchased from the local Chemist, and which was basically - despite its vivid description - little more than a flavoured twig. He confessed that it was not quite the same as his favourite boiled barley sugar, but for the peace and tranquility it brought to the household, that little twig was worth its weight in gold. That was until his constant sucking and slurping started to irritate Mrs Potts and, under her watchful glare he retired to his garden shed to pore over the racing results. Although even this small pleasure had been curtailed by the war with horseracing and betting being at an all time low. Poor browbeaten Mr Potts. Bizzarly the sweet rationing continued long after the end of the war – until 5th February 1953 to be exact – and on the memorable day it was finally announced that it was over, youngsters nationwide broke open their piggybanks and formed excited queues outside sweet shops. Mr Potts - by then quite an old man with precious few teeth left – took his place patiently at the back of the queue, waiting for the chance to once again purchase a quarter of his favourite boiled sweet, the barley sugar.

Lawrence had had some initial reservations about the prospect of having to share his precious time with Dolly but Joan was such a sweet-natured and biddable child that she soon wormed her way into his heart too. His brother Dominic – no doubt in part due to his own childlike outlook on life -adapted straight away. He took his role as surrogate uncle very seriously indeed. "My mission in life," he would declare rather grandly, "is to ensure that this little girl's life is smack bang full of joy and happy memories." As a result, young Joan would squeal with excited anticipation whenever the twins entered the canteen for she knew that their very appearance spelt fun with a capital F. I must now add that the brothers despite their 'joie de vivre' were still haunted by the spectre of their future, for they had made great strides in their training and would soon be capable of flying their own planes. Lawrence viewed this development as a 'ticking time bomb' but, as usual, Dominic was much more 'gung ho' and constantly prattling on about finally having his chance to 'blow the blasted Luftwaffe to Kingdom come.'

THE SANATORIUM

Once she returned to the sanatorium – after saying a tearful goodbye to Lewis and her two precious babies - Dorothy was subjected to yet another XRay, whereupon the Consultant confirmed that, as he had suspected, it was her left lung which was worst affected. Treatment was discussed but it was decided before undertaking invasive treatment – such as collapsing the infected lung under local anesthetic, then slowly refilling it once it had had a chance to heal itself - they would first see how she fared after a few months of complete bed rest. This bed rest entailed no movement at all with the exception of going to the toilet once a day. She would not even be allowed to sit up in bed, unless lying in a semi-reclining state propped up by pillows. She was also instructed to only take shallow gasps of air and to attempt to speak only if unavoidable and even then in a whisper. This way, by not taking a deep breath and straining, she would give her damaged lung the best chance of healing. The next stage of her treatment - if this was successful - was described as a 'baby step'. This essentially consisted of a short period out of bed, sitting in a chair, or perhaps taking a relaxing bath. Eventually, after a while, if she showed no adverse effects from this extra exertion, she would be permitted to take a small stroll around the grounds. Just a few yards at a time and it was drummed into her that if she felt at all tired, she had to give in and not fight it, for it was essential that she did not exert herself in anyway. This consultation frightened the life out of Dorothy. She had witnessed this dreadful disease take her 'nephew Alun' followed in quick succession by her mother, so she did not take the advice lightly. At this stage, I must add, that I have been unable to ascertain if the Sanatorium charged its patients for care. I have seen reports of charges being levied, but I have also read conflicting reports that the Government employed special Tuberculosis Medical Officers at this time in an attempt to curtail the spread, so as a consequence treatment was often free. Whilst staying in the Sanatorium, and once she had recovered slightly, Dorothy would be allowed visitors. While she was on bed rest she was told that they could visit between the times of 3.30 to 5.15 then later on, once she was up and about, they could visit every Thursday and Sunday from 2 to 6. But, and this was a big but, all this depended upon if she recovered as hoped and would be dictated by the result of her next X-Ray and sputum test.

Dorothy's main concern during this time was not unsurprisingly for her two small children. In a way it was not so much baby Lewis she worried about, because he was too young to notice his mother's absence, but Joan was a toddler and clingy at the best of times. For so long – the entire time that Lewis had been away training in Tidmouth – it had been just the two of them so the bond they shared was very close. She had tried to take Joan aside before she went to the Sanatorium to explain what was happening but at such a tender age she doubted whether Joan understood the abandonment. Many years later, when Dorothy was finally allowed back home, it broke her heart, as Joan was noticeably shy in her presence and visibly shirked from the hugs she tried to shower upon her. This was understandable in hindsight, because during the formative years, when she had not been able to visit her mother, Joan had come to look upon Lewis' sister Dolly as a mother figure. Bearing in mind Dolly had taken on the role when Joan was still a toddler, she was the only maternal figure she knew. This broke Dorothy's heart and was yet another reminder of the cruel consequences of the disease she had recently battled through, but in typical Dorothy style, she pulled herself together and told herself that in time - with gentle love and persuasion Joan would come around and remember her. Nevertheless, it broke her heart when night fell and the time came around for Dolly to return home. Joan was inconsolable to such a degree that Dolly had to promise to stay the night and be there as she awoke the next morning before she would settle. The next morning dawned and Dolly remained, but deliberately kept a low profile, allowing Dorothy to do the mundane 'mother' tasks and later that afternoon while Joan helped Dorothy to ice the cupcakes, Dolly quietly took her leave. As she was tucked up in bed that night young Joan reached up and kissed Dorothy's cheek, then asked why her mother was cryng. Dorothy's reply – through streams of tears – was that Joan had made her the happiest mummy alive.

The Sanatorium proved to be a deceptively pleasant place despite the constant presence of the medical staff. It was situated in the middle of a wooded area with towering pine trees, well away from city smoke and with grounds that seemed to go on forever. Her initial thought had been how much Lewis would love the tranquil surroundings. It reminded her of his many descriptions of the time he had lived on Vancouver Island. The rules were, nevertheless, very strict and she was warned that if she did not adhere to them there were plenty of others who were desperate to take her place. There was no alcohol allowed on the premises – whatever its guise - and it was strictly forbidden to speak to the opposite sex. Even saying a polite good morning was not allowed. This irked Dorothy's sense of politeness and, when she was eventually allowed to take short strolls through the grounds, she was constantly ducking and diving behind trees so she would not be put in the position of having to be so obviously rude. The food though was plentiful and packed with goodness. Dorothy was encouraged to eat regularily and build her strength up that way. It always amused her that the cutlery was marked with her 'number' then engraved with the word 'stolen' to avoid it going missing. She questioned who would stoop so low as to steal from the very place which was saving your life. But she supposed there were all sorts of people there, from every walk of life, for that was the indiscriminatory nature of the disease.

During this long nine months of her incarceration, Dorothy implored Theresa not to bring the children in to see her, however much she missed them, or even in her weaker moments begged her. She was so afraid of spreading this dreadful and most contagious disease. Dorothy instead resigned herself to receiving regular written updates about her children's progress, along with a few precious photographs which she would carefully pin on the wall nearest her bed. Of her siblings, only her youngest brother Rhys John - with the bravado of youth - visited his sister and I suspect this may have been how he caught the disease, which ultimately robbed him of his own life many years later in 1950. Meanwhile, outside the calm sanctuary of the Sanatorium walls the war rumbled ever on and on. Dorothy fretted constantly for Lewis abroad fighting in France, and for her poor motherless children, and she wondered whether things would ever be normal again.

I confess that I do not know the full details of the treatment she received, although knowing how rapidly her state of health deteriorated, I surmise that it is probable that she did undergo the invasive lung collapsing treatment at some stage to save her life. The usual ritual was that the beds of the seriously ill patients were moved nearest the door each night - so if they did succumb to the deadly disease in the early hours - their removal would be less traumatic for the rest of the ladies. My grandmother vividly remembered one young girl named Poppy who had been about her age. They had been chatting quite happily - in whispers - the previous afternoon and then the next morning Poppy's bed was empty - stripped of its sheets and stripped of all visable reminders of her ever having lain in it. This so traumatised my grandmother that it led her to a complete relapse, and resulted in her own bed being moved nearer the door the very next day. I have been told that Dorothy received the Last Sacraments a total of three times, so they must have seriously feared for her life on numerous occassions. One such time her brother-in-law John - a

Catholic priest serving at the time as an Army Chaplain in India – was on leave so he was called upon to administer the Sacraments and in her delirious state she was confused and thought it was her husband Lewis saying goodbye. So convincing was she that one of the nurses standing around the bed went so far as to question the Matron later on as to the actual true relationship between the two. Dorothy survived against all odds, more from strength of character than rude health. She went on to give birth to two more children, Pauline in 1948 and Anthony in 1950 who joined Joan and Lewis Junior and completed her family – although much later in the mid 60s she and Lewis went on to adopt a baby called Martin. But the trauma of childbirth had a detrimental effect upon her health and throughout their childhood, Dorothy would be hospitalised on an almost annual basis. My mother Joan, who was only eleven when Anthony, was born remembers that she missed so much school during this time that when she did actually manage to attend, the new Headteacher queried who she was and asked if she was a new pupil. My mother Joan also remembers that when her mum was first discharged from the Sanitarium, she would be confined to bed so my mother would drag the baby bath into her parent's bedroom to allow Dorothy to supervise the bathtime. Once they were bathed, Joan lifted her siblings from the bath and placed their wet and wriggling little bodies onto her mother's lap so she could cuddle them dry. During this time, Joan basically took on the role of 'mother' – for Lewis had to go out to earn a living and his own mother and his sister, the children's grandmother and aunty had long since moved away. By the time she was ten, my mother could prepare an entire meal from scratch, whilst simultaneously juggling a load of laundry. Dorothy at this time did herself no favours – she knew she must rest – but to watch one's child having to do the household chores you should yourself be doing must have been so demoralising. One bug bear Dorothy had was the desperate state of the garden, for before she had become so ill – and when Lewis was posted in France - she had toiled day and night to make it presentable and productive. She had constructed a makeshift raised bed for vegetables, and now, it was overgrown and overtaken by weeds. Being of a determined nature, Dorothy devised her own plan to 'trick her dreadful disease' whereby she would go into the garden and dig a patch of soi,l then scurry back inside and lie on the sofabed in the lounge, count slowly to a hundred, then race back outside and start the whole process again. For a while this system worked, but she was susceptible to the slightest germ and when one day Pauline came in from school sniffling with a summer cold, Dorothy wished she had followed doctor's orders and not overstrained her damaged lungs. The very next week as the children sat eating their tea Dorothy began to cough. She coughed and coughed uncontrollably before dramatically hemorrhaging so much blood that poor Joan – who had raced to her mothers side – was very soon covered head to toe in bright red splatters. Pauline ran screaming from the house to alert the neighbours and an ambulance was swiftly called. When the ambulance crew arrived at the 'bloody scene' and found Joan sitting on the kitchen floor shaking and covered in blood they were at first unsure who was the patient. Lewis arrived home soon after and managed to calm his traumatised children before settling them down with the neighbour so he could travel to the hospital in the ambulance with Dorothy. Ironically a few weeks later, the first green shoots appeared in the vegetable patch Dorothy had been so determined to cultivate. During this time, my mother remembers a new medicine being prescribed to Dorothy which came in the form of an injection into her thigh and was a combination of streptomycin and PAS. The district nurse would come out and administer this to my bedridden grandmother at regular intervals. Steptomycin had first been discovered in 1943 and was the first antibiotic to prove effective in the fight against TB, but in 1948 there was a growing awareness that patients could develop a resistance to it and a strain of TB resistant to Steptomycin could be transmitted between patients. I am happy to say that my grandmother did eventually 'beat the disease' but, as a result of the trauma her lungs had gone through, would be prone to constant chest infections and phneumonia for the remainder of her life.

17TH SEPTEMBER 1944, ARNHEM, NETHERLANDS

Dolly and Mary had not seen the twins properly since the last week in August, when the two couples had made the trip to the boys' parents home in Howick, and had spent a jolly afternoon learning the rules of croquet. The boys had blamed the high pressure of work for their frequent unexplained absences - as they were sworn to secrecy about the Operation Market Garden mission they were about to embark on – but both Dolly and Mary were well enough atuned to their moods by then to realise it was more serious than that, and something was most definitely afoot. How right the girls were, for the twins had been undergoing intensive training for their most life-changing assignment to date. This dangerous operation was code named 'market' for the airborne assault and 'garden' for the simultaeous ground attack and had been carefully orchestrated by Field Marshall Montgomery, Winston Churchill and Franklin Roosevelt. It was hoped it would be the ultimate attack to bring about the end of hostilities. The idea was that troops would be airdropped in the Netherlands, near the town of Arnhem, and they would go on to build a bridgehead across the Rheine thereby creating an invasion route into Northern Germany for the landforces which followed. This was the single biggest airborne operation in military history and ultimately one of the most flawed for, despite the training the twins received, the majority of the other troops involved were woefully ill-prepared. Montgomery himself later coined the phrase a 'bridge too far' -which went on to be the title of the award winning movie in the late 1970s starring amongst others Sean Connery and Anthony Hopkins - but paratroopers fighting the battle changed it to 'three bridges too far', as a reference to how ambitious and complicated the planned attack was.

Lawrence and Dominic were only two of the many pilots tasked with dropping the paratroopers near the town. The initial problem came about because, as the 17th September that year was a 'dark moon', the planes couldn't risk operating with no light so it was decided that the drops would be carried out in the full glare of daylight. Lawrence was part of the first squadron of planes to reach the designated drop zone, and as soon as he had ascertained his coordinated position, he signalled for the order to be given for the paratroopers to start their descent. What Lawrence had not realised was that high above them, shrouded by cloud cover, the Luftwaffe were lying in wait. It was a mere few seconds after he had signalled that he heard the whirr of the engines and made out the telltale insignia of a Messerschmitt warplane. Thinking quickly and without a thought for his own safety Lawrence dropped altitude to ensure the safety of his human cargo. To a man they managed to drop safely from the aircraft, but in the process this had made Lawrence's plane a sitting target and it took the full barrage of bullets. They pierced his fuel tank and his plane rapidly sank into a nose dive, crashing in a blaze of flames just a few yards from the paratroppers, who had just landed. Lawrence did not stand a chance of survival but mercifully his death was instantinous, as he passed out seconds before crashing to the ground. A similar fate awaited poor Dominic when he reached the same designated spot. Dominic survived only because he managed to leap from his plane a few minutes before it exploded in a fiery ball of flames. Once on dry land, Dominic swiftly found his bearings and belly crawled across the scorched grass towards the plethora of deflated parachutes. Dominic was one of the 2400 paratroopers that day, who successfully crossed the Rhine in rubber bottomed boats and survived that most bloody of battles. Wel,l I write that Dominic survived, and technically speaking he did for he was physically unscathed and to all intents and purposes he looked to the casual observer very much as he did before his dreadful ordeal. But appearances can be deceiving, because poor

Dominic was severely shell-shocked, and upon coming home and finding out about his twin's untimely death, he seemed to give up the ghost. He never again uttered a word; it was as if the effort of forming the sounds became a pointless excercise. One had only to look into his eyes to realise the desolation that lay within his soul. His spirit was crushed. Dominic was gone and only an empty shell remained. He sat on the garden chair in the grounds of his parents' house staring, just staring, at some point far far away. The nights were the worst. For even a lifeless corpse craved sleep and when he could not hold his eyelids open any longer and his head dipped into his chest, it was as if the 'hounds of Hell were released. To bear witness to his tortured expression and his crazed yet petrified cries broke his parents' hearts. His mother's reaction - indeed the reaction of any mother - would be to comfort her son and make him safe but as his arms flayed and the madness took a hold she could only stand by, helpless, and watch her son descend further and further into the depths of Hell. If purgatory was as horrific a place as the artists of old imagined then Dominic was stranded there, engulfed in its very flames. Such was his mental state that his parents decided that it was kinder to imply to his fiancee Mary that he was still 'missing in action.' They reasoned that by saying this she could at least retain a kind of normality and perhaps start to forge a new life for herself. Of course, telling her that created a bizarre kind of limbo, because Mary could not grieve while there was still the slim chance her beloved Dominic was alive. Although once Mary found out the truth - in the cruellest of circumstances - she wished that they had at least given her the chance to nurse her precious love back to a semblance of normality. For surely, if he had realised the full extent of her love, it would have given him hope and in life there is always hope. It grieves me to write this but a few months after his discharge, in the frosty winter of 1945, Dominic determinedly got up from his chair and made his away across the meticulously manicured lawns towards the Hunting Lodge. When he reached the doorway, he elbowed his way through the door and crossed towards the unlocked gun cabinet. Retrieving a small pistol that his father used daily to scare the crows and which he knew was always loaded, Dominic with no preamble aimed the muzzle at his own head and pulled the trigger.

Dominic's father would never divulge the full truth of his movements that morning because after watching his son stride so purposefully across the icy grass that morning he had deliberately turned his back and returned to bed. For to see his own son in such pain was unbearable and if this one final act gave his son some blessed relief well so be it. The sound of the shot ringing out into the dawn was all the confirmation his father needed that his assumptions had been correct.

And what of poor Dolly and Mary, the twin brothers intended brides? Well as often happens in life, there was a terrible and painful mix up in reporting which twin had died and who had survived. It came to light later that this was because the twins had accidently switched dog tags a few days before they flew out on that ill-fated mission. Apparently the twins had been visiting their parents for Sunday lunch, and their father had asked if they could change into civvies before dining, because the sight of her two boys in full uniform had so upset their mother the last time she had seen them. The two boys nipped into the Hunting Lodge to change into the civvies which their father had left in a pile upon the bench. They also took the precaution of removing their dog tags when they realised that they could be seen quite clearly glinting and shining beneath their open necked shirts. It must have been whilst they were tucking into the Sunday roast that one of the hounds slipped its lead and made its way into the Lodge to search for treats. Leaping clumsly upon the bench it knocked the two neat piles of uniforms clear to the ground. In the following commotion the 'dog tags' rolled across the uneven wooden floor and wedged themselves against the gun cabinet. The boys fell about laughing later on. And as they scrambled around for their clothes, Lawrence remarked wryly that old Winston had never been the most agile hound of the pack. Somehow in the ensuing confusion, the brothers had accidently picked up each other's 'dog tag', a small mistake which otherwise - were it not for the mission they were embarking upon – would not have been that much of a problem. But this small mistake magnified into momentous proportions because it was the actual 'dog tag' which was later used to identify the remains of poor Lawrence. The resulting confusion led to a mistaken report that Dominic had died and Lawrence survived. I can only imagine poor Dolly's emotional turmoil, when after being told her 'fiance' had survived, she was informed a few days later that a grevious error had taken place and it was now firmly believed that he had in fact perished. Mary meanwhile was going through opposite emotions, first to be told her 'fiance' had died – and going through the grieving process – then at the next juncture to be told that he had survived but was still 'missing in action.' Mary did her very best to console Dolly but all the while she hung desperately on to the hope that Dominic would eventually be found. She prayed and prayed that he would soon return to her loving arms. Each night she would kiss his photograph, then crouched by the flickering light she would delicately stitch even more elaborate detail onto her lace wedding frock. It was a cruelty of fate that she was to find out a few month later about her precious Dominic's suspected suicide from a local newspaper article reporting on the inquest into his untimely death. Her first reaction was overwhelming anger towards his parents, who she believed had prevented her from even the slimmest chance of 'healing and nursing' her soulmate back to health. But this was soon followed by a deep sadness that her poor love had reached such a low point in his life, that he believed this to be the only solution. It pains me to write this as it seems such a waste of a young life, but Mary could never love another man in the same way she had loved Dominic and as a consequence she never married. It was not long after her precious Dominic took his own life, that Mary suffered a terrible life changing accident herself. She had been walking home after a shift at the canteen when all of a sudden and without prior warning a lorry swerved to avoid a cat and mounted the pavement. Mary didn't stand a chance for, even if she had seen the lorry speeding towards her there was nowhere to run. She was squashed between the side of the lorry and a brick wall. So severe were her injuries that for a long while it was doubtful she would survive, but her best friend Dolly never lost faith in her recovery and would sit day after day by her hospital bed encouraging her to keep fighting. Slowly Mary's external injuries began to heal, but she was soon to be dealt another cruel blow when the doctor who had operated on her poor broken body took her aside and explained that due to the damage inflicted upon her internal organs it was doubtful she would ever bear her own child.

As a postscript I will add that dear Mary remained a firm friend of the Dowd family for the rest of her days. There is barely a family photograph without her in it. Dolly went on to name her first born daughter Mary after her good friend and she was also godmother to Dolly's son Peter. A role which she wore with pride and took very seriously indeed.

Dolly later married a local lad called Dennis Smyth in the May of 1946. She had met Dennis not long after Lawrence died and had constantly pushed him away stating she did not want another relationship. But Dennis was persistant. Eventually he wore Dolly down and she agreed to one date, then another and before long they were engaged then married. The couple relocated to Derby when their daughter was still quite young and after Peter they went on to have another son called Martin before returning back to the North East. Theresa – Dolly and Lewis's mother – also moved to Derby after the end of the war when Adam Wilkinson the priest she had been housekeeping for died. Her youngest son, Father John Dowd had recently taken over a parish there and the Presbytery which came with the job was vast. John was rattling around the empty rooms so having his mother there would be great company. Hopefully, she would use her prowess in the kitchen to bake some nice cakes too for John had inherited a sweet tooth from his father.

LAST CHAPTER..

When I started to write this novel I always planned to end it in 1950 for I didn't want to 'stand on any toes' or reveal any deep seated 'family secrets'. I was desperate not to cause offence or harm but I've now realised that I must jump to the future to tie up loose ends, and in doing so I will have the opportunity to fully acknowledge the many cousins, first, second and removed, who have been so helpful and supportive in collating this book. The anecdotes they have shared have brought this journey alive and in doing so I hope I have done their memories justice and brought our joint *ancestors* alive in a plausible three dimensional way. I will now, if I may, skip through the decades so you dear reader have a sense of how Dorothy's and Lewis's lives panned out. My grandparents – if they had been asked to describe their lives – would in all probability have stated that they had lived remarkably 'ordinary' lives but upon writing this novel I have discovered that no life is just 'ordinary' and the most ordinary events dramatically change the course of one's future. Dorothy, despite her complicated health issues went on to live a full and relatively long life reaching the grand old age of 78. Although I feel compelled to make mention of the fact that in her mind she had celebrated her 80th year. So convinced was she that her birthday in the April of 1989 would be her 80th that we all never thought to question her despite her advanced dementia. The whole family gathered together on that spring afternoon, and what a memorable afternoon it was. It was not until she passed away eleven months later, and the Undertaker asked us to confirm her date of birth for the headstone that it dawned upon the family that Dorothy was actually just shy of her 79th birthday. But in retrospect, what a tremendous blessing it was that we had all been there to celebrate what was her last birthday. What a joy it had been to see her sitting there – every inch the matriarch - beaming with happiness, in her high backed rather regal looking chair, surrounded by her precious extended family. Because for Dorothy it had always been about the family. Her family was her greatest achievement and to know that her legacy lived on in them made her life struggles fade into insignificance.

In the early 1960s, not long after they became grandparents to my sister Leonie and myself, Dorothy and Lewis made the decision to become foster parents. When I reflect upon the reasoning behind it now, it was probably because Dorothy had missed out on so much of her own children's growing up and still had an abundance of love left to share. She and my grandad were excellent foster parents, treating the children in their care with exactly the same love and affection they had shown their own. I have a page from the Family Bible and beneath the recorded births of her own four children my grandmother has carefully listed the children she cared for alongside their date of births, so this, if nothing else, proves that she viewed each child as part of her extended family. It was unfortunate that bad health still plagued her days for whenever she was bedbound - following a nasty dose of pheumonia or even just a chest infection - the children would be removed from her care. These unfortunate breaks in continuity of care and the constant 'toing and froing' must have caused much confusion for the poor, already vunerable, children. But being children they seemed to take it in their stride and trotted off quite happily back for a holiday in the orphanage secure in the knowledge that once their 'mum' was up and about again they would return. Dorothy and Lewis looked after two sets of siblings at this time – one family of a brother and two sisters and another of two brothers - and they also cared for a young baby boy called Martin who they later tried to formally adopt. It was so upsetting when they were told that they were too old to adopt but they got around it by changing his name by deed poll once he reached maturity. Martin has such fond memories of his mum and dad. Perhaps different memories to the rest of his siblings because he was in their lives at a different time, a time when they were slowing down physically, but still had an abundance of love to shower upon him. He recalls being constantly told that he had been chosen to be their son and he remembers - as I do too - that the house was always a melting pot of chaos and laughter.

My memories of this tumultous household are many but I especially remember the long summer holidays when Dorothy and Lewis would rent a farmhouse in Unthank, a remote little hamlet in Cumbria. We children – for including my sister and I there would normally be seven of us – dubbed ourselves the 'secret seven' – after the characters in the Enid Blyton novels we all so loved - and would have some amazing adventures exploring the farmyard, the barns and the wider countryside beyond. A favourite game was in the hayloft where we would take turns to clamber up the rickety wooden ladder to the balcony above, then dare each other to jump down into the haybales below. We would pester the farmer to allow us to ride on the back of the tractor as he tilled the fields then pester my grandparents to take us out to the nearby Lazonby for ice creams. Lewis would make a big song and dance about being too tired to drive – a part of the game he played – so we children would plead and plead until he finally got up grinning widely from his chair and collected his wallet. Then we would all pile into his ancient bottle-green Riley car – no thoughts of safety or seatbelts at this time!- and chug off through winding country roads, up the hill. The Riley was ponderously slow and prone to frequent breakdowns – this was probably more a result of the dodgy fuel guage than the actual reliability of its engine – and if, or should I say when, it broke down my grandfather would heave a large sigh before calmly collecting the empty fuel caddy from the boot of the car and trundle off to find the nearest petrol station. Dorothy in the meantime would stretch her arms under the front passenger seat and gather up the shopping bag she had prepacked earlier in anticipation of just such an event. Then, whilst we children searched in the hedgerows by the side of the road for blackberries, my grandmother would extract a breadboard and butter knife and start spreading margarine upon a cheap white sliced loaf of bread. We children would queue at the open car door and issue our orders – normally the options were jam or golden syrup – we would then stand and gorge ourselves on the folded over slice of bread sandwich before taking our place once again at the back of the queue to wait for our next sandwich. Then, when my grandfather eventually returned with a caddy of petrol, we would continue on our quest for ice creams. My grandfather would frequently stop the car on the the country lanes so we could stretch our legs and ride along. This entailed us children standing on the footplates with one hand clasping the car door handle and the other waving in a helicopter motion whilst squealing at the top of our voices. Reflecting upon this now – although he was driving at a speed of only a few miles per hour - it was a very dangerous exercise but the seventies were a whole world away, and it was long before 'seatbelts' and car safety adverts. My mother vividy remembers once - when she and my father had made the trip across to Cumbria midweek to drop off clean clothes and underwear - they stopped the car so a group of local muddy 'urchins' could cross the narrow lane - little realising until they reached the farmhouse that the motley crew had actually included their own children. My mother still remarks upon this memory, especially on the occasions we watch the Sound of Music and we reach the scene where Captain Von Trapp's children are playing in the trees, dressed in such outlandish curtain material that he does not recognise his own offspring. To wash off the ingrained mud and muck Dorothy would set up the hosepipe in the farmyard and we would run through it screaming with glee as the cold water rained down upon us. These are such special blue remembered halcyon days of fun, frivolity and innocence.

As long as we still have these memories and we fondly recollect them, Dorothy and Lewis will live on forever. The lasting memorial they have left their devoted family is a sense of fun and enjoyment in the simpler things of life, and an acceptance of diversity in all its forms. I believe the world would be a much better place if it were populated with more Lewises and Dorothys. I dearly hope they are up there in the wild blue yonder looking fondly down upon the dynasty they created *just another century* ago.

THE END

EPILOGUE

LE BRITTON FAMILY

Oshbert Junior married a woman named Kitty and, after losing their first child Dennis in such tragic circumstances, the couple went on to have three more three children named Oshbert (known in family circles as Sonny) Olive and Anita.

Anita married Jimmy Young and they had one son named Derek.

Arthur married Ada Barker and had two children Annette and Peter.

Rhys John married Nora Meddes and had two children David and Vera Dorothy.

DOWD FAMILY

John became a Catholic Priest.

Dolly married Dennis Smyth and had three children Peter, Mary and Martin

Lewis married Dorothy and they had five children, Joan, Lewis, Pauline, Anthony and Martin. Numerous grandchildren followed, then great-grandchildren, great-great-grandchildren, and so the story goes on and on. I am their first born granddaughter, and it has been both a privilege and pleasure to write this novel.

BIBLIOGRAPHY

- West Jesmond Book, by Christine Jeans 2002

- Wikepedia. For info on Rudyard Kipling, World War I, Omar Sharif, Kitchener, Morpeth Olympics

- *broughttolife.sciencemuseum.org.uk* – women in medicine

- *TheWhiteReview.org* for Rudyard Kipling information.

- Pale Rider: The Spanish Flu of 1918 and How it Changed the World, by Laura Spinney, Johnathon Cape Publishers 2018

- Ushaw Magazine Artice – Monsigneour L L McGreavy 1977

- *BBC.CO.UK* – Ethics – War; Just War

- *NCRONLINE.ORG* – Why is the Catholic Church moving away from Just War theory

- *www.ncbi.nlm.nih.gov* – Tuberculolosis sanitarium regimen in the 1940s; a patient's personal diary.

- *www.history.com* battle of Arnhem

- *www.chroniclelive.co.uk* – phantom airfield fooled incoming bomber crews.

ACKNOWLEDGEMENTS

I have been helped enormously in writing this novel by my many relations, many of whom as a result of this endeavour I have only recently made contact with;

Joan Creigh,Pauline Morgan, June Dowd, Vivienne Dowd, Martin Dowd, Mary O'Dowd, Peter Smyth, Mike Bundock, Vince Lauzon, Emil Le Britton, Dave Lebritton, Paula Westwell, Judy Le-Britton,

Friends; Charlotte Hardman – editing and proof reading, Melanie Byers – editing advice, Amanda Lipman – legal advice.

My daughters Katie Harland-Edminson, Claire Harland, Ami Curley and my wife Liz Webb for their enduring support and plot suggestions.

Andrew Lobb singer/songwriter whose Millennial song *Just Another Century* inspired the title of the book.

People who grew up in Jesmond facebook page; Gerard Anthony Donnelly, June Tracey, Simon Donald, Jan Gifford, David younger Spinks, Claire Stephenson, Judith Smith, Thea Lyst, Claire Louis, Wendy Simmons, Paul Noble, Pat Robson, Anne Tait, Vici Bennett, Rob 'Bertie' Collins, Pazza Harris, Trudi Jackson, Sacha Dodds, Angus Gifford, Steve Gunter, Gary Andrew Carlisle.

Cochrane Past and Present Facebook page; Susan MacMillan, Theresa Dunn, Mel Robbins, Kate Moore, Sue Hotte, Dan Girard, Kendra Brisson Robin, Maria Fasano-Krahn, Brent Irvine, Don Ross, Ardis Proulx-Chedore, Chiquita Anderson, Ryan Lebel, Bob McIntyre, Candace Prior, Agnes Salvalaggio.

Whatever Happened to Port Alberni Facebook page; Daphne Dobie, Drew Waveryn, Bob McLaughin, Vince Lauzon, Charlie Thompson, Bob Vandermolen, Lynne Roth, June Hills, Eric Sirka, Johanna Claire McMenemy, Christine Ansell, Claude Jean, Cheryl Hoegweide.

Usher College Alumini Facebook page; Sid Cumberland, Alex Walker, Paul Sanderson, James Duffy, Dennis Jackson, Davie Woodier-day, Anthony Keefe, Sean Toner, Faz Faraday, Lawrence Emm.

Printed in Great Britain
by Amazon